MW01058728

# KATRINA'S WINGS

"I laughed and cried as I read about Katrina's endearing, dysfunctional family and discovered all the lovely facets of Katrina herself—courage, faithfulness, compassion, strength of character, self-sacrifice, obedience, loyalty (and a great sense of humor). Through her tremendous capacity to love as Christ loves us, Katrina is the glue that holds the family together—without being a 'co-dependent.' Patricia Hickman has found her strong, lyrical, literary voice. Once you enter the world of *Katrina's Wings*, you'll find yourself thinking about it again and again."

—Francine Rivers, author

"I was captivated by *Katrina's Wings*, an irresistible novel with unique charm and depth. This is Ms. Hickman's absolute best!"

—Robin Lee Hatcher, author

"The pain of growing up is dramatized skillfully by Hickman, and by the time Katrina reaches her goal, the reader has identified with her. A fine treatment of the growth of an artist—and of a human being!"

—Gilbert Morris, author

"Patricia Hickman is a bright light among southern writers. *Katrina's Wings* was written with the skill and insight seen in some of America's classics, without the dark hopelessness that pervades so many of them. This is a keeper you'll want to read again and again."

—Terri Blackstock, author

"*Katrina's Wings* takes the reader on a journey through the introspective places of the soul to a place where love is launched and faith begins."

—Karen Kingsbury, author

DISCARD

"I can think of few greater indulgences than a quiet place to prop up one's feet, a glass of iced tea in one hand and Patricia Hickman's *Katrina's Wings* in the other. Keep some tissues handy, and be prepared to laugh as well. Beautiful language, fascinating characters moving about the pages, and a richly woven story make this a delightful read!"

—Lawana Blackwell, author

"Patricia Hickman's lyrical and evocative prose draws the reader into the mysteries of the human heart. Her characters stand up and cast their own unique shadows. It is a novel salted with humor and pathos, despair and redemption. Had Eudora Welty grown up in Arkansas, she would have written *Katrina's Wings*."

—Robert Funderburk, author

"I stepped into the world of *Katrina's Wings* with a shock of recognition, for it was my world! I grew up in a small Arkansas town, and for page after page, I relived a time that is now gone. It's all there—the southern world with its smells and music and small town pettiness and hospitality. From the jarring noise of the high school hallways to the gentle whisperings of the river, a world has been resurrected in *Katrina's Wings*."

—Lynn Morris, author

"A haunting, lyrical story of a young woman who faces some of the toughest things life can offer . . . and finds the strength to fly through simple faith. Amazing."

—Angela Elwell Hunt, author

MIRACLES HAPPEN
*in the* MOST UNEXPECTED PLACES

# Katrina's Wings

PATRICIA HICKMAN

WATERBROOK
PRESS
CPL

KATRINA'S WINGS
PUBLISHED BY WATERBROOK PRESS
2375 Telstar Drive, Suite 160
Colorado Springs, Colorado 80920
*A division of Random House, Inc.*

The characters and events in this book are fictional, and any resemblance
to actual persons or events is coincidental.

ISBN 1-57856-293-7

Copyright © 2000 by Patricia Hickman

Published in association with the literary agency of
Alive Communications, Inc.
7680 Goddard Street, Suite 200
Colorado Springs, CO 80920

All rights reserved. No part of this book may be reproduced or transmitted
in any form or by any means, electronic or mechanical, including photocopying
and recording, or by any information storage and retrieval system, without
permission in writing from the publisher.

WATERBROOK and its deer design logo are registered trademarks of WaterBrook
Press, a division of Random House, Inc.

Library of Congress Cataloging-in-Publication Data
Hickman, Patricia.
   Katrina's wings : miracles happen in the most unexpected places / Patricia
Hickman.—1st ed.
      p. cm.
   ISBN 1-57856-293-7
      1. Sisters—Fiction. I. Title.
PS3558.I2296 K38 2000
813'.54—dc21

                                                             00-022429

Printed in the United States of America
2000

10 9 8 7 6 5 4 3

## TO JUDY

*Sisters are the oddest creatures,*
*sniping at one another in one moment*
*and yet, when faced with criticism, standing back to back,*
*fangs bared and claws exposed,*
*challenging any dissenter to traverse the loyal circle of sisterhood.*
*To you, my dearest and only sister, and to all sisters*
*this book is lovingly dedicated.*

*M*y best childhood memories loom large in my mind, with the royal colors of the sky a parallel parade to our small one below. In a shine, I conjure up the most delicious smells of the park where we played and chased after dogs and butterflies and dreams. Folks who saw the barefoot, ragged band of Hurley girls and cousins—dragging their homemade kites over the daffodil hills and running wild through Galla Creek—never thought we'd grow up to amount to much. We grew up, and pretty well at that, in spite of those who wagered it would never happen. Most people never thought of Mockingbird Valley as much of a runway either, but if you stood out on the northernmost precipice of Skyline Drive and closed your eyes, you might believe that you could fly.

I tell my babies now that success is life's greatest revenge. When you grow up having names like "hick" and "hillbilly" hurled at you, you're apt to daydream about a day of revenge. Not in an evil way so as to get arrested. Simply in a manner that justifies the suffering.

Memories of early days usually taste the sweetest for most people, like the flavor of watermelon split open and eaten in the field. But my early memories are clouded now. They offer only black-and-white snapshots of an old white frame house running over with sniggering cousins, all of us surrounding the gray vinyl throne of my grandfather, Papaw Hurley. It was in his house, under his watchful gaze, that I found protection.

I attribute most of my happy childhood memories to this man who adored me, called me his gleaming princess, and granted me wishes such as spur-of-the moment excursions into the county's peach orchards. He bought me whole pecks that I sat on, my only way of defending my rightful endowment. I was the runt among the oversized pack of mongrel Hurley children. But Papaw must have had a special place in his heart for runts, for he and I had a secret language, one that sent a jealous twang through all twelve of my cousins and one that forever dubbed me "your highness" among my honky-tonking aunts. But he did not live long enough to aid in my continued reign. The day he died in May of '63 was the day I turned back into an ordinary, skinny waif. So I hid his adoration in my heart and kept it to myself, praying that someday it would sprout wings and carry me far away to some little coronation that had awaited me all along.

I did not sit next to Momma or Daddy at Papaw Hurley's funeral and was relegated with my younger sister, Eden, to the care of my Aunt Pippa. To women like my momma, Aunt Velda, or the other aunts who wrinkled the Hurley archives with their brittle, grizzled lives, death was like a gaping vortex with a razorback's teeth. I imagined death tying them to the church pews, forcing them to watch the finishing chapter of someone they knew while they cringed and shivered and blanched. Momma looked particularly waxy that day. When the preacher ascended to the platform, Momma's head reeled back and her body lifted upward, undulating. Falling against the pew, she slumped as if gutted. I thought she had died. My Aunt Pippa tried to hold me back, but I was moved by Momma's despair. "Momma!" I shouted. I was forever worried that my mother might do as she threatened and pack up and leave us, one way or another.

Several adults hushed me, shamed me into silence as, confounded, I watched Momma succumb to grief. Death has always been such a hopeless thing to us Hurleys. I knew other families that could sit through funerals in a civilized manner, saving their grief for private moments. But for the Hurleys, when faced with death, there was nothing left to do but faint.

I have my own ideas about death. Somewhere I've heard it said that the darkest part of a shadow is called an umbra. Some tout that black is black and white is white, but when it comes to suffering, I believe certain elements of it are gray while others deepen to a fierce black pitch, the umbra of a journey. Just before you die, I think you taste the umbra. But beyond the dark valleys is where the most radiant part of light is found.

Most Hurleys didn't give much consideration to journeys, or if they did, seldom did it spill out into their speech. Almost none considered the consequences of today, how it joined hands with tomorrow and such. The notion of all that came to me at an early age, and when I voiced it, I was probably labeled as odd—the child that should be kept on a short leash. I thought about it a good lot of the time. That must have accounted for my childhood insomnia and imagining how things might turn around if I were adopted.

Momma sat next to my Aunt Bernice and Uncle Willy at my grandfather's funeral. She had personally driven them all the way from Phoenix the year prior. Their hopping brood had added four extra Hurley children to the already overfilled cousin cauldron in my grandparents' home. When Momma left for Phoenix, she left Eden and me with my grandparents, two anxious girls waiting through a miserable month. Daddy recuperated in the hospital from a fall he had taken at work before Momma's excursion to Phoenix. He never got better, just more alive than dead.

Granny's lap was the dropping-off place for the offspring of all of her children who had gone out into the world to seek their fortune but then returned dirt broke. Some returned to Mockingbird Valley to work and have a place to keep their kids while others who I never really knew just dropped off their kids and disappeared altogether. By the time Momma returned later that month, I felt as though I had died numerous times over. The older cousins could be a vicious lot. One girl cousin in particular, Freda, had sport with Eden and me. She invented games like "tie up the babies," where she would chase one of us down into Galla Creek and back while she left the other sister tied under the bed. All of this happened while Granny and my aunts went gallivanting off on day trips without mentioning where they were going. I've never been inside an asylum. But having Freda as our keeper left me with no feeling of security. I was a moth in her weird little jar.

Daddy had been a milkman, a job that didn't bring home much money, but it was a job he'd seemed happy doing. On the day he fell from a platform inside the creamery's warehouse, it landed him his month-long stint in a Little Rock hospital. It also left him disabled. So when Momma was called upon by the Hurleys to fetch Uncle Willy's clan, she did so dutifully, although she cursed them all later for it.

Daddy remained in the hospital for a month. I heard later that he almost died. But I didn't know anything back then. Nobody talked to us children about adult matters or told us nary a thing.

"You okay, Kat?" Aunt Pippa held my hand while Daddy joined Momma. I liked Aunt Pippa. She made me feel as though she liked me. Most of my aunts were an assortment of raw, unrefined females who acted like men. Maybe that's why Pippa stood out so much. When she walked into a room, all the spinning and havoc ceased. Her calm demeanor set the tide of my family's emotions upon a steady ebb and flow. She moved with grace and wore that same elegance on her face. Pippa was the swan among a soiled band of renegade crows. It was obvious to any observer that she had married into the Hurley clan. No one would have ever believed a woman of her natural beauty and calm demeanor could come forth from a Hurley's loins.

I still remember her white lace gloves that day as her fingers made a comforting curve around mine. I noticed for the first time that her hands trembled, a condition that worsened as time passed.

"Kat?"

"I'm okay," I said.

"Everything's going to be all right."

Tears welled in my eyes, overran the rims, and spilled onto my starched print dress. I stared at Papaw's coffin and willed it to set free the man held captive inside its satin-lined prison. I played out the entire scenario in my mind. God would reach down, touch my grandfather on the forehead, and press his God magic into the lifeless shell. Then Papaw would sit up, causing a great stir among the unbelievers. I would be the only one expecting it. So I would run to him and say something like, "See, he's not dead! Jesus brought him back to me." Then he would take my hand, the hand of his favored grandchild, and we would walk away from the lunatics and live happily ever after...

The words on the hymnal's page looked foreign to me on that day. We seldom graced the inside of a church with our presence except on Easter. Momma always said we'd not miss an Easter service even if it rained. But I had attended services enough times to recognize the melodies of the songs we sang directly after the opening prayer, besides hearing Momma singing out choruses she had heard in her own past. I still remember the song we sang about heaven. Unrehearsed voices lifted, with no sense of harmonization, every mean lyric puncturing my stomach and wrenching my sorrow from me. I am uncertain as to why we only cried during the singing. I say "we," but I mean everyone except Aunt Velda. Velda was what all Papaw's brood called the baby sister. She did not stop crying when the singing ceased, but instead, threw back her head and bawled as though someone was sticking her with a red-hot coal. I cannot explain her cry in words, except to try and describe it as something from the devil himself—a wounded bobcat from hell. I did not believe other people could act like the Hurleys did at funerals. If they did, all the preachers would have had to pad the walls.

"Katrina, hold my hand." Aunt Pippa's right arm made a tent around my small shoulders while she slid her long, feminine fingers around mine. When she touched me, it sent a pleasant wave of comfort through me. My own momma had not touched me very often. Human touch can be a marvelous thing. I sometimes wonder now if those who are touched on a regular basis take it for granted.

I sat, wordless, and settled myself against the hard pew. But I did keep one eye carefully trained on my mother in the event that she called out for me.

When the preacher concluded with the benediction, I watched my father take his slow, steady approach toward my grandfather's casket, aided by a cane. Daddy never cried. From time to time his head dropped forward. He buried his face in his hands. But nary a tear did he shed. He hesitated in front of the casket with Momma next to him. Next came Daddy's sister Nola followed by Lillibelle, each woman flanked by a silent, submissive husband. They fell upon each other, two sisters dependent upon a patriarch now dead. Then Aunt Ruby led Velda, thirty-year-old Velda, by the hand, just as she would a three-year-old child. Velda fell upon Papaw's body and let out another squall.

"My daddy, my daddy, don't leave me," she begged my dead grandfather. Her voice sounded kind of falsetto and childlike. It reminded me of Bette Davis in that movie *Whatever Happened to Baby Jane?* Velda reminded me of her in lots of ways.

Ruby blushed and commenced to whisper all kinds of things in Velda's ear.

It took three ushers to peel her off the casket, then three more to carry her writhing body from the chapel.

"I like it when Velda faints," I whispered to Eden, "'cause it's the only thing that hushes her up." I ran my finger back and forth along the slivery curve of the pew until a loose piece fell into the hymnal holder.

Standing in front of my grandfather for the last time would usher me into a world I did not want to enter. So I did not hurry the matter. Aunt Pippa nudged me along. I allowed my eyes to caress his face—artificially rosy from the paint of the undertaker. He had never dressed in the manner in which they dressed him on that day. Instead of the faded olive coveralls that smelled of tobacco and motor oil, he was laid out in a dark blue suit, his silky white hair parted on the side and combed neatly. He looked like a king instead of the retired grease monkey we all knew.

"Time to say good-bye, Katrina," I heard Aunt Pippa whisper.

Something sour churned inside of me. No one had bothered to tell me of my grandfather's illness. In those days, little children could not go to the hospital. So my final reunion with him was full of bitter resentment at those who had kept us apart for what seemed like months to my six-year-old mind. I could no longer climb into his lap and stare back in defiance at anyone who tried to rule me. I was tossed in with the other Hurley children and looked upon as ordinary and in the way. My precious Papaw flew away from me without saying good-bye. I ran from the church, wordless, in my own way reciprocating what I thought had been done to me.

Those days before Papaw's illness and death had been quiet calms
before the Hurley storm. The blithe memories of Saturday afternoons spent on Mount Nebo with picnic lunches, men drinking beer
out on the car hoods, and telling ghost stories by flashlight and
campfire, descended into hollow echoes trampled underfoot.

Daddy was home from the hospital for good then. Every morning I
found him in the same place, seated at the small metal kitchen table
in the alcove of our kitchen. He fired up a cigarette first thing, then
sat drinking coffee while the morning passed him by. He poured the
remaining black coffee into a tin pot that boiled until the coffee
turned to tar.

"Bring me another pack of Salems, Kat." I was his errand boy,
and I often wondered if Momma had disappointed him when she
presented him with a daughter.

Eden never fetched anything, nor did she do much in the way of
chores. She had a gift for fouling up anything that got handed to her.
Quite a wonderful gift, I soon decided, since it got her out of doing
anything.

Momma had gone to work at the only factory in town, a Poll
Parrot shoe factory, but managed to stay home on weekends. It was
on those weekends that most of their wars erupted. But on one particular Saturday, instead of their ritual battle of the checkbook, I
heard rumors of a different brand.

"You can't be sayin' that's true, Ho," Momma said. "That farm
belongs to all you kids. I heard your daddy say so a million times." I
always remember her short frame standing in the open doorway of
our kitchen. Daddy forbade us from spending money on air condi-

tioning, so during the warm days of late spring, the doors and windows invited in the sounds and scents from Momma's garden. On this day it smelled hot and airless.

"Velda's put my momma up to it. I'm gettin' a lawyer." Daddy sat in his undershirt and a pair of worn khaki pants neatly creased at the knee. The smoky haze in the alcove was thicker than usual.

"Who's goin' to pay fer it, Ho? You've got other brothers and sisters. They should pay too."

I could tell by the look on Momma's face something bad had seeped into our world. She had looks for everything, and this one reeked of ruin. I stood with my back to the wall and peered into the kitchen from our small living room, knowing that if I walked into their midst, the flow of information would become skewed and not nearly as colorful.

"My family don't have any money, Donelle. Not two nickels to rub together. You know none of them will stand up to Velda."

"Velda's crazy as a March hare!"

I knew Momma was right about that. Aunt Velda had been locked up in the sanatorium more times than I could count.

"I'm goin' to see Momma right this instant." Daddy stood. I inched farther away from the doorway.

"Call Ruby and Lillibelle first. See if they know what Velda's up to." Daddy fell silent.

"What are you doin'?" Eden's voice whispered right into my ear.

"Nothin', now shoo, why don't you?" I said.

"You listenin' in on Momma and Daddy?"

"No, interrupting is rude, don't you know? I'm *not* interrupting them. That's what."

"Come and play with me." Her eyes, so large and blue they caused me great jealousy, sparkled up at me and, in an Eden sort of way, baited me.

"Eden, let me be."

"Katrina, what are you two doin' standin' outside the kitchen like that?" Daddy towered over us. In spite of his recent hospitalization, he was a bull of a man, quiet spoken until his ire was kindled.

"Playin'," I lied.

"Go play outside."

Eden headed for the door. She turned as though she expected me.

"Momma, what's wrong?" I looked past my father.

But instead of answering me, Momma lifted one brow, bared her teeth.

"Is this about Papaw Hurley's farm?" I asked.

"Katrina Louise, your daddy done told you to git outside. Git now 'fore I take a broom to your hind end!"

My shoulders lifted, stiff bones fashioned by dread. Our unending jaunts to the Hurley farm had left me believing the hundred-acre spread was all my own: the shabby barn, the little white anemic cows stippled with russet patches that stared downfield at me with brown marbles for eyes. Papaw had not farmed on the place in years. He and my grandmother lived instead in the white frame house, number twenty-three Clementine Avenue.

Clementine was the longest street in Mockingbird Valley that cut through the center of downtown before curving the head of its arrow out to the lake. According to what Daddy had always said, the farm meant more to him than any member of the Hurley family. He had fought in the Korean conflict, and every paycheck he earned was sent home to pay for the farm. The land meant everything to him and made him somebody. To be *somebody* in Mockingbird Valley had many meanings, but to Daddy, it meant that you owned land and that nobody could snub you or call you poor. I believe he hated being called poor more than anything else in life. Nobody likes to be looked down on, but to Daddy, it was apparently soul crushing.

"Eden," I said. She followed me. I led the way out into the yard and deposited myself beneath a peach tree. Eden joined me, cross-legged. Perhaps she anticipated some cue from all I could gather. We waited until Daddy took his leave.

"Looky, there's a rose on the mailbox, Katrina."

"Don't talk like Aunt Velda, or they'll put you away."

"It's not crazy talk. See? Stuck between the flag and the box—it's a rose. A red one."

I saw it, blood red petals lilting, gasping for water. We bolted, two fools running for some poor man's treasure. Crickets chummed together inside the mossy bed of portulaca when our sneakers pummeled the frazzled driveway-side edge. Our race to the mailbox sent us spilling, leaping pell-mell over a large ceramic urn overfilled with more portulaca. I snatched the rose first, not because I ran faster but simply because, as the eldest, I could exert my will. "The sun's opened it up full, and it smells like one of Momma's."

"Reckon someone picked it from Momma's rose garden and stuck it there for meanness?" she asked. Both of us knew the penalty for picking roses.

"I don't know. But I don't want her blaming me for picking it."

"She best not blame me neither, Katrina."

"Let's keep it with our dolls and not tell Momma or else she'll switch us for it," I said.

"But if she finds out we're keeping secrets—"

"If you tell, I'll not play dolls with you, Eden. Ever."

"I'll not tell it, Katrina," Eden whispered. She slunk back toward the peach tree, guilt painted fully across her innocuous face.

"What's wrong with Daddy?" Eden always asked me the hard-to-answer questions.

"Don't know." I settled us both beneath the peach tree. "You be the mommy and I'll be the daddy," I said to her.

The blush of morning matched the pale flush upon her cheeks. Eden always looked like a little doll herself, squatted among our baby dolls. She immediately turned her baby doll across her lap and spanked its naked backside. "Bad baby! Mind Mommy!"

When she hit her babies like that it made me hurt inside. "Don't, Eden. Love the baby." I showed her how to cradle it with the head in one hand and its bottom in the other.

"You be the mommy," she said.

"I don't know if I ever want to be a mommy," I said. "I want to be an artist. I want to see Paris." I liked to interject that statement whenever possible. It made me feel less common.

"I want to be an artist too."

Eden always made me sigh. If I had been a more dependent sort of person, I might have appreciated her perpetual mimicking of my every action. I've observed twins that answer in unison, agreeing on every matter. But I would have made a horrid twin. Instead, I saw myself as an individual explorer determined to unearth the answer to every question that popped in my head. When I wanted to find out what catastrophe had my daddy so undone, I did not desire an audience.

"Here, Eden, you dress the dolls and I'll go fetch the teacups." I stood in the middle of all of my children and observed the perfect circle I had made with them.

If we had a dozen baby dolls at that age, by the time we were grown we had three times as many. Momma saw to it because of something bad that happened to her as a girl.

"I'll go get the teacups with you," Eden said.

"No, hardhead. Let me get the teacups and you dress the dolls." Whenever I called her a name like that, it had the same effect on me as twisting a knife into my own heart. But before I could think, out would fly the worst of names from the acrid tongue I had inherited from my momma. It was the worst part of myself and the part that I hated most.

I brushed the anger at myself away with the freshly cut Bermuda grass from my gingham yellow pedal pushers. I had business to attend to with Momma and didn't want my conversation riddled with the nonsense interjected by a younger sister.

"I'll go with you, Katrina."

"Fine. Then you go get the teacups." I tried a new strategy.

Eden sat down upon the cotton pillowcase spread beneath the sprawling shade of the tree. "No, you go get them, Katrina. I'm the mommy."

Eden always took the bait. I escaped and ran up the rear porch that led into our kitchen. The collection of empty pop bottles chimed like a dime-store register as I pressed back the screen door against them to enter. For that reason, we always referred to the back landing as the pop-bottle porch.

"Momma, where are you?"

"Back here brushing my old ratty hair."

Seated in front of a weathered walnut vanity, Momma was dressed in a floral print blouse and matching walking shorts. She could be counted upon for running down the way she looked, as though God had cursed her with hopeless flaws. Keeping a list of reasons to be mad at God was the only part of her world she had fully organized. She often said that when she got to heaven, she would show him the list and then sit down and listen to his explanation. For his sake, I always hoped it would be a good one.

Because of her obsessive gardening habits, I seldom found her wearing anything that matched, let alone something from her own closet. More often than not, she could be seen by our entire neighborhood stooped over a bed of dahlias clothed in one of Daddy's old shirts.

"Are you going somewhere, Momma?"

"We're going to your granny's, so call in Eden and put on some shoes."

I always felt a quiver of excitement when hearing that we were going for a visit to my grandmother's home. It had felt so much more like home to me that I had run away over and over again, trying to find the place that beckoned me back to its braided rugs and crocheted dolls. Even under threat of a switching, I never ceased to try and return.

Momma lifted a lipstick tube and applied the cosmetic to her bottom lip, then pressed her lips together to color the top lip. She always used an orange-red color, bright like the petals of the evening sun.

"I want to wear some lipstick."

"No, you're too young."

"When will I be old enough?" I stood in the doorway of her bedroom, watching her ritual as she sprayed her hair and teased the top layer into a tangled bouffant.

"I said, call in your sister, Katrina. You lost your hearing?"

"No, but I—"

When Momma swore, it always had the same effect on my insides as acid. It ate clear through me and tarnished my image of her.

"Is Daddy still mad?"

"He's been done dirty by his family." She swore again. When Momma cursed about Daddy's family, it was always in ways that lumped them into the same seething ball of profanity.

"It's about Aunt Velda, ain't it?"

"Ain't none of them doin' right by him. I don't want to talk about it right now. He'll be back any minute. Went to get some gas in the Chevy."

I stood with my face against the varnished wood frame and watched her continue to transform herself.

"You talked in your sleep last night, Katrina. Did you have a bad dream or somethin'?"

"I had a dream about you, Momma."

"What was it?"

"The dream scared me. I saw you riding in a parade going down Main Street in front of all the town stores. You stood on top of a parade float just like the town homecoming queen, all decked out in a tight-fitting dress with a full skirt and laced petticoat." It was true. When I had seen her in my dream, I felt the most powerful awe, as though I beheld a goddess. She had looked just like Loretta Young.

"Sounds like a silly dream to me." She pressed the lipstick against each cheek and rubbed the edges of color into her skin. Growing up in hard times had taught her to employ the most practical means of achieving beauty on a shoestring.

"But just as you passed me by, your float collapsed and you fell to the street. Your ankle was broken—"

"Go get Eden before I box your ears!"

"I'm here. Where you goin', Momma?"

Eden had walked up behind me, no doubt after undressing and dressing the baby dolls beyond the bounds of her limited attention span.

"Get your shoes on, Eden. We're going to Granny's." Momma fingered a pair of matching earbobs, then pushed them aside. She hadn't worn them since Easter Sunday. She always saved her best things for days that never came.

"We better bring in our dolls." I left to fetch the babies in the yard, then my shoes. I quickly slipped my feet into the worn-out canvas flats, a faded grasshopper green with pink rose print. My big toe peeked out between the raveled fringes of string that strained to contain my ever-expanding feet.

I had just rounded the corner when I heard Eden yelp. My eye caught the sight of Momma striking her across her face.

Eden shrieked and I saw blood splattered across her lip. She turned and looked at me. Her face was contorted in pain and her blue eyes brimmed with tears.

"Momma, Eden's nose is bleeding!" I shrieked.

"Katrina, run fetch a cold washrag!" Momma yelled at me as though I had hit Eden myself. But I saw the guilt etched in her face. Eden could sneeze and get a nosebleed. But this one wasn't caused by a sneeze. Momma had struck her good.

When I returned with the wet terry-cloth rag, Momma yanked it from my hand. By now Eden stood with her head back, large tears streaking down her face in accusation.

"Stop your cryin'!" Momma's voice trembled. "I didn't mean to hurt you."

"What did she do?" I asked.

"I'm just tired of her mouth is all." Momma took Eden's hand and pressed it against the cloth. "Keep your hand here." She walked into the kitchen, and I heard the screen door slam.

"It's just a nosebleed, Eden." I struggled to find assuring words. "You get them all the time."

"Momma hit me on my nose." She continued to sob. "I didn't do nothin', Katrina. Not nothin' at all."

"Sit in this chair and quit your crying. I'll get another clean rag." The one I had given her was saturated in blood.

I ran into the kitchen to fetch a clean one from a pile of fresh laundry. But before I stooped to paw through the laundry basket, I saw Momma sitting on the rear porch steps. She held her face in her hands, and her body shook. "Momma, are you crying?"

"Get out of here! Can't I have a moment's peace from you kids?"

I backed away, feeling a sickening pain inside as though I had witnessed something unspeakable. I felt sorry for Momma and for Eden. One sat in the bedroom, her spirit crushed and her body wounded, while the other sat crushed and wounded of heart and hating herself. But try as I might, I failed them both miserably as a healing bridge.

Such was my lot in life.

The car trip to my grandmother's house was more silent than usual. Momma had cleaned Eden's face and changed her clothes, even combed and styled her hair into two curly ponytails. But Eden sat next to me on the rear car seat, and her eyes were still red from crying. She stared straight ahead, emitting soft, weepy hiccups.

Daddy said little at all, and I still failed to understand the details of what had happened between him and Aunt Velda.

Mustering the courage to speak, I finally asked, "Are you mad at Aunt Velda or Granny?"

Momma glanced across the seat at my father. She let out a ponderous sigh. "Your Aunt Velda and Uncle Ned have sold your Papaw's farm. But it wasn't theirs to sell. It belonged to all the kids."

"Why did they do it?" I asked.

"They traded it for a small house for themselves."

"I'm not goin' to allow it!" Daddy started muttering again. When he disagreed with something or was mad at someone, he often had conversations with himself. Instead of working out the problem face to face, he would work it out by himself. I suppose his way of problem solving was less confrontational, but it solved nary a dilemma.

"But they can't just take Granny's land without asking, can they?"

I sat forward, trying to understand the matter in the simple manner of a child.

"They're movin' your grandmother in with them."

"But—"

"Katrina, that's enough! Your Daddy's already bitin' bullets. Don't add no more fuel to the fire!"

Momma's tone had a finality to it that I didn't dare cross.

When we arrived at Granny's, I could see Uncle Hank's old car parked out front. He was Daddy's brother and the husband of my Aunt Pippa. They had a daughter, Roxanne, who was several years older than me and prettier even than her own mother. While the rest of the cousins would always scatter down into the creek, shrieking like wild natives, Roxanne sat primly at her mother's side, a trait that left me awestruck. Poise and gentility had never been my companions. I could only admire them from afar, coveting what did not belong to me.

Eden and I spilled into the house in hot pursuit of a cold drink and hopeful that my cousins had not completely devoured Granny's morning allotment of chocolate gravy. Even cold bacon became a delicacy to us, as we slid it between the fluffy planes of Granny's homemade biscuits and stovetop jam.

Without glancing up, I knew exactly where my grandmother sat: on the old brown sofa near the picture window of her living room. Sitting near the large multipaned glass offered her the best light for her needlework. But I always had to take care rounding the sofa, for near the frayed corner next to a cheap veneer table sat a coffee can she used for spitting out her snuff. To misstep would mean catastrophe for any unwary pedestrian.

"Hi, Granny!" I called out, with Eden fast on my heels. "Can I have a Coke?"

After my grandfather's death, I realized soon enough that the hospitality dished out so freely beforehand was due almost entirely to his unfettered generosity.

"Don't have any Cokes," she said.

I peered into the refrigerator anyway. Behind the metal pots of leftovers and milk cartons sat a silver tin can. "I see a pop, Granny. Can I have it?"

"Kat, I done told you I don't have no sody pop." It makes sense to me now that a widow woman whose house continually spilled over with grandchildren and unemployed daughters and sons might become somewhat protective of her pantry. But I wasn't just anyone.

"Look, see what I have here?" I held up the can and kind of shook it at her.

"Katrina Louise, you put that back!" Momma used her acid voice on me. She hated for us kids to ask for anything. Imposing was intolerable, and to make a request of anyone, in her estimation, was imposing.

"She don't know what it is, Donelle." Granny muttered it low.

Momma and Daddy had left us with such a fright of beer and whiskey and such that it never occurred to me that my dear sweet Granny nipped from time to time. So I held the can close and pulled back the tab. Momma and Granny never looked up from their morning soaps. The smell was overripe to me. I sipped it and mulled over the taste. It was bitter and tasted toxic. As I held my first taste of beer in my mouth, a fire threshed around my mouth and trickled down my throat. But I did not know to call it beer or any such thing. I only feared it would eat out my insides and leave me dead on the linoleum like a rat that's eaten poison.

"Put it back and go play with your cousins." Momma never knew that I had already opened the can. Granny probably later wondered about an open can with but a sip of liquid gone. I shoved it to the rear of the refrigerator next to the burned-out bulb. My whole life, I never acquired a taste for liquor.

Until my grandfather's death, I had enjoyed the run of this house. Perhaps Momma didn't realize it since she worked such long hours. I was welcome in this place, but knew that to press the issue might land me a switching or, even worse, a tongue lashing.

Seated in a corner chair beneath the hanging cage of Granny's neurotic parakeet was Aunt Velda. She smiled sweetly at Eden and me. "Hello, little Kat. Eden." Her raspy voice reflected the tar and nicotine coating of her smoking habit.

"Hi, Aunt Velda." Eden spoke woodenly, not because of the circumstances but because she spoke that way to everyone.

I took a seat on the sofa next to my grandmother while Eden seated herself cross-legged in front of the television.

"You kids can stay in here and watch TV," said my mother, turning the channel. I watched as she and my father crossed through the kitchen, followed by my grandmother.

Aunt Velda fidgeted for a few moments. She used one cigarette to light another and bolted for the rear bedroom.

"I'm going home, girls. Tell your parents I said good-bye." Aunt Pippa gathered up her handbag and walked out the front door, followed closely by Roxanne. Uncle Hank left with them.

"How's your nose, Eden?" Seeing that we were all alone, I decided to ask.

"It's kind of sore."

"What did you say to Momma to make her so mad?"

"I don't know." She shrugged, her gaze fixed on a telecast of *The Cisco Kid*.

I could hear Velda's kids outside, giggling and playing with the water hose. I was considering joining them when I heard a shriek from the rear bedroom. An icy chill shot through me.

Eden glanced up but then returned her attention to Cisco. She could tune out the most amazing things.

Anxiety crept up inside of me, and I half stood to peer over the bar in the kitchen.

"Oh, Velda!" I heard my grandmother cry out.

The door flew open and my mother marched through, red-faced. Her eyes wide, she nodded at me. "We're leaving! Head for the car."

"But, Momma—"

"*Now,* girls!"

Daddy ambled behind her, leaning on his cane and shaking his head.

Behind him I could see Aunt Velda lying coiled up on the floor, motionless. My grandmother administered a damp cloth to her forehead.

I feared the worst. "Daddy, is she all right?"

"Katrina!" Momma gestured with her head.

I hadn't realized that my Uncle Leland had been stretched out asleep in the middle bedroom. We called him Uncle Lee. He was Freda's daddy. He emerged at once, rubbing his eyes and stretching his limbs.

"Hobart? What's going on?" He asked my father.

"It's Velda, Lee. She's fainted—again!"

I was rushed out of the door and toward our Chevy. No one noticed that Eden had remained inside.

Velda could faint in a blizzard. Perhaps the sight of our skinny aunt collapsed on the floor is what drew Eden to stay behind. Or maybe just the thought of a fight in general lured her to dawdle. I do remember how as fights would break out on our high school campus, Eden would be among the hecklers. Her thirst for seeing a freshman's blood spilled onto the sparse Bermuda grass of Mockingbird High proved a temptation she could not resist. Where I took flight from the heat of redneck combat, Eden would dive right into the fray just so she could get a front-row seat.

I glanced across the sprawling rear seat of Daddy's Chevy, then leaned casually over the front seat between the pained faces of my two parents.

"Sit back, Katrina," Momma said.

"Momma, Eden's not back here."

"She didn't come out with you?"

"Nope." I peered toward the window of my grandmother's home. I could see Velda's wiry frame just beyond the stained chiffon sheers. The ember glow indicated she had revived herself and found immediate comfort in her nicotine addiction.

"Run back and fetch her, Katrina." I could see Momma staring at Velda, but did not yet understand the glint of bitter hatred that caused the human eye to shimmer.

"Can't you just honk the horn, Daddy?"

"Katrina Louise, git!" Daddy seldom did the hollering because Momma always beat him to it. But when he did snap at me, I knew better than to talk back.

I scrambled from the backseat and kicked at pebbles all the way up to the small front landing. "Eden!" I hollered out her name several times and then waited for her response. Just as I pulled open the screen door, I heard a screech from inside. My fingers froze on the latch, and it was the first time I recall recognizing my own cowardly nature. Momma would preach at me my whole life about the importance of finishing a fight, of landing the first blow, and of teaching the villains in my life a lesson they would never forget. But I never got the hang of it.

When I glanced back at the Chevy, I saw Momma's head bobbing at me, her thin cord of patience stretched beyond its limit. I pressed the palms of my hands against the weathered front door. More screaming from inside sent a chill through me. Momma hung her head out the window and fell into a tirade. Velda and Uncle Lee could be heard going at it, but I heard nary a sound from my sister.

The door hinges groaned as I pressed against them. Tobacco smoke wafted past, escaping the room as I opened the door and peered inside.

"You ought not do it, Velda! Not to your own family. Not to blood!" Uncle Lee towered over his younger sister.

"Don't you be tellin' me what I ought or ought not do!" Velda stood glaring up at him. She took a long drag on her cigarette, then tossed it into a cereal bowl on the kitchen bar.

"I'm tellin' you 'cause no one else will do it, Velda!"

"You stay out of it, Lee!"

Finally, I saw the small towhead of Eden. She had planted herself right below my aunt and uncle. Neither of them acknowledged her. My grandmother had retired to her bedroom to avoid "taking sides," her customary ritual in sibling rows.

"Eden!" I whispered. I crouched low, hoping to draw her attention without drawing fire from my cantankerous Aunt Velda.

Her soft lashes lifted and waved at me flirtatiously as her primrose lips formed an innocent smile. She then gestured with her thin finger and pointed up at her quarreling aunt and uncle.

"We're leaving!" I said it between bared teeth, but I could see that Eden assessed the matter before her in the same manner she assessed *The Cisco Kid*. Nothing was real, and every scene was a new episode created to entertain her, to make her happy. And then, just like a summer cloud that covers the sun for a brief instant, her recognition of me faded. Her eyes lifted and fell upon my aunt and uncle. She had turned me off and switched channels to seek the adventure of a greater conspiracy.

By now Daddy had commenced to blow the car horn, and I knew that if I didn't succeed soon in bringing back the straggler from our litter, my legs would be switched. I inched toward her but kept my eye on my unpredictable aunt, who continued to scream into my uncle's face.

"Momma's going to whip us both, Eden!"

"Lee, you back away from me now!" Velda's persona now reflected the wild bobcat that dwelled inside the cave of her dark, confused soul.

"Not till you swear to make that husband of yours tear up that fake will and—"

"Shut up! Shut up!" Velda's arms flailed against him, and her knees buckled. I thought for certain she was headed for one of her fainting spells again.

"*Eden!*" I stooped over and slapped both hands against my knees as I pleaded.

Velda's hand fell back against the bar. As with any of her decisions, they were seldom premeditated and always impulsive. I saw her bony fingers curl around a butcher knife that my grandmother had used that morning to slice slab bacon.

"Uncle Lee!" I screamed.

Velda, driven by her insane sense of justification, swung the knife over her head and down toward my uncle's chest.

A curious light came into Eden's face. I recalled seeing that same expression during *The Wizard of Oz* when the witch wrote in smoke across the sky, *Surrender Dorothy.*

"No, Aunt Velda!" My hands flew to cover my eyes.

I hated being a Hurley. In that instant I knew that my placement within the gnarled twigs of their wretched nest had been a mistake. God had sent me to the wrong place, and somehow I had to get a message to him about it. I did not belong here, but some yet-unseen hand forced me to assume the role that I despised.

A clatter that sounded like metal against cheap linoleum caused me to look up. I could see Eden's body shaking uncontrollably. I ran toward her as Uncle Lee shoved Velda out of the kitchen.

Eden bent over and picked up the knife and held it out to me.

"What happened?" I asked.

"It bended. Bended right against Uncle Lee's old fat belly." Eden laughed so hard that it ignited my strong sense of right and wrong.

"Eden, Aunt Velda tried to kill him! It ain't funny, girl!"

My sister always described that incident in a manner that likened it to an episode of *The Three Stooges*. Even after she was fully grown, she would recall the day Aunt Velda rammed the dull kitchen knife against my uncle's belly and it bent in her grasp. The fact that Eden could never sense danger must have given rise to her life being surrounded by a battalion of heavenly guardians. The Good Lord knew she would need them.


I never saw my grandmother again after that day. Not alive, at any rate. Aunt Velda and her husband paid a snake-in-the-grass lawyer to weave a will that left the farm solely to my weak-willed grandmother. Then they coerced Granny into selling the farm and buying a small house in a cheap HUD subdivision, with the promise that they would care for her. The house reverted into their greedy grasp when she died. Since the farm had been worth ten times what the house had cost, the mystery would always remain about what happened to the profit and why none of the other six brothers and sisters shared in it.

It was things like that—the loss of the farm, the Great Depression—that always affected Daddy. I often wondered if he could have overcome his disability if he hadn't allowed the past to so overtake him. But he never allowed himself the luxury of dreaming of the future. Moreover, he had a list of people for whom he held no respect. Dreamers topped the list, with preachers and gypsies taking a close second. So he settled into the sedentary world of partial disability payments. He always believed that beyond the boundaries of Mockingbird Valley lay the gaping jaws of fear. Satisfaction for Daddy came dressed in a pair of overalls that surrounded itself with cronies down at the local spit-and-whittle club.

But dissatisfaction stirred the bland mash of my own brooding ideas. It called out as I slept that catastrophe did not lie beyond Mockingbird Valley. I imagined what waited outside the valley's brim was something much sweeter, like the embryo of desire. I could not help myself as I listened in silent awe to the siren's call and wondered if it was my name in the indecipherable whisper.

With Daddy home, our house became a place of longing. I longed to be set free from his fearful, overprotective grip, longed to see my mother return home for good from her toil at the factory, and pined for the grandfather I could never hope to see until heaven.

Where Momma viewed Eden as a troublesome waif whose only purpose was to shadow her days with worry, Daddy saw her as a victim whose life he must shield from all the catastrophes that befell her. Thus, the remaining shreds of my guileless kingdom fell into the dust. My reign as Papaw's little autocrat ended with the soundless drumroll of my own frustration as I watched Eden shaped into the next mindless recipient of the American welfare system.

But life took a drastic about-face the day Daddy began receiving full disability pay. Momma came home, established herself as the new despot, and sent Daddy off with more time on his hands than he could manage. That's when the real trouble started, I suppose.

In November, I awoke to the most glorious sight. While some travelers drove for miles to view the splendor of fall in the Ozarks, I coveted those rare mornings when we would awaken to snow. So seldom had I seen it blanketing our own yard that I threw open the front door and stepped out. The hoary powder that had blown onto the wooden porch nipped at my bare feet, but I ventured further, hoping to discover that no trace of the ground peeked through. When every flower bed, every border brick was hidden from view, I knew that we had been snowed on but good.

That's when I spotted the tracks. I had remembered seeing footprints in the snow the previous winter when Momma walked to the shoe factory. When the roads were treacherous, the factory would offer extra pay to those who would show up. So Momma would slide a pair of plastic rain boots over her shoes and walk to work before the sun had begun to trickle across the frozen crust. But on this morning, the footprints were twice the size of my mother's tiny feet. I could hear the splendid crunch of boots against snow. My eyes followed the tracks. I tiptoed to the western edge of the porch where I spied Daddy stealing away.

"Daddy, where you goin'?" I hollered.

He lifted a stubby finger to his lips and waved me away with his other hand.

"I want to go!" He often heard that phrase spill from my own lips as well as Eden's. It meant that we had sickened of staying around the house and begged for diversion of any kind. But Daddy had tired of playing nursemaid.

"Wait for me, Daddy."

By now he had a frenzied mien and gestured wildly for me to go back inside.

"Why can't she go, Hobart?" I had not heard my mother slip up behind me.

The color drained from Daddy's face. This would not be the first time I witnessed their odd game. Until the day I stepped into adulthood, I never realized my unwitting role as eyes and ears for my mother's suspicions.

"She ain't got her shoes on, Donelle. She'll catch her death."

"Katrina, go get dressed. Daddy can wait for you."

Life had given her no reason to trust him. She had been married twice before, and not a one of them had proven faithful. I sensed the strange tension between them but knew when to seize opportunity. I scrambled inside and threw on my usual assortment of last year's rags, layering them in slovenly fashion for the sake of warmth.

"I'm comin', Daddy." I slid off the porch and scrambled to keep up with him. I had no need to query about our destination. Mockingbird Valley had little in the way of commerce. Not once do I recollect sitting down as a family to restaurant food. But a small processing plant had moved in behind our home. To serve the laborers, a café had been erected. The aroma of hot coffee, biscuits, and greasy fare assaulted my senses even before we entered the dive's austere portals.

I had but one agenda. The glass counter was daily filled with the choicest of chocolate bars. No matter that my rumbling stomach groaned for lack of breakfast. Laying all other techniques aside, I went for the throat—the assumption close. "Daddy, I want that one." I tapped upon the top glass directly over the most delectable of chocolate bars—the Krunch.

I always loved the sound of jingling coins in my father's pockets. It meant that I had struck pay dirt.

"Mornin', Ho." The waitress poured hot coffee into a cup and shoved it in front of Daddy. She had a teased hair job with a color that looked accidental, a shade similar to the color of one of our tomcats.

"Mornin', Evelene." He tipped back his felt hat and took his seat on a swivel barstool.

I seated myself next to him, engrossed in peeling back the soft aluminum candy wrapper.

"Have you ever seen it so cold?" Daddy asked.

"Not in years." She wiped an invisible stain from the countertop. "Reckon Faubus'll ruin the state?"

"Now, Ho, you know I don't know nothin' about politics." She giggled in a manner that caused her bony shoulders to lift up and down like a mechanical monkey's. Her mascara-laden lashes fluttered while she rested her chin in the palm of one hand. "Besides, I thought you was a Democrat."

"Not no more. I changed parties. I was a Democrat, but they's a lot of difference between that and a yellow-dog Democrat."

"What's that mean?"

"I vote for the man. A yellow-dog Democrat'll vote for any old mongrel long's it's a Democrat."

She laughed hard, and I felt uncomfortable with the way she spoke to Daddy, like they had known one another their whole lives.

"Are you a Democrat?" I finally asked her.

"What's that?" She righted herself and looked at me as though she had noticed me for the first time.

"'Cause if you're a Democrat, my Daddy won't have no use for you."

"Katrina Louise!" Daddy could say my name in a way that made hairs stand up on the back of my neck. When Momma came after me, I knew that pain was about to connect with my posterior. But with Daddy, I always felt the poorest sort of shame, like he didn't want to claim me as his kin.

After that day, when he was forced to take me with him, Daddy devised ways to place as much space between him and me as possible. At times I wouldn't even know where I was, but only knew we'd driven far out into the country and I'd been left on the doorstep of one whose name I wasn't given. So when Momma would ask where we'd been, I could only answer, "I don't know."

# Chapter 1

I was never fully awake in Mockingbird Valley. It was better that way, God's sedative to see me through. But I'm awake now. I can look beyond the blue and green hills in my mind, see down into the fertile dogwood-embroidered valley, and know that the past cannot contain me. I am now a child of the present. Living in the present makes me feel omniscient, a cloak I wear when I must return to the land of my ancestors.

It was a not-so-lovely year. Plain ugly, if you ask me. We lived somewhere between Watergate and *Gunsmoke,* depending upon your tastes. Puberty forced itself upon me. My legs were so long and thin they threatened to entangle themselves in one another. At sixteen, I towered over all the boys and hated the acne-faced stranger who stared back at me from the mirror.

To me, this was my time of passover. I felt as though everything that was good and beautiful passed over me without so much as a blink. The girls my age blossomed into shapely women. They teemed through the hallowed halls of Mockingbird High, their as-yet-developing feet shoved into imported platform shoes. I watched from the onlooker's gallery, still clad in my practical homemade garments and discount-store loafers, amorphous, grasping, and socially illiterate.

I do not believe that my mother wanted to make me stay a child or spent her days thinking of ways to keep my growing extremities from sticking so far out of the sleeves and hems of my clothing. But childhood had left me long before she noticed. So a good pair of bell-bottom Levi's, in addition to a store-bought dress, became my heart's longing.

I awoke every morning to Momma's usual ranting.

"Katrina Louise, if you don't get up, you'll miss the school bus!" She defined the mornings in such a way as to make me believe that if I missed the bus, the world might come to an end, or the sun might neglect to appear. But I plotted to try it at least once to see if she were as much a prophetess as she believed.

"I'm up already." Voices drifted beneath the door to my room. My father's Aunt Mosie jawed with him in the kitchen. Great Aunt Mosie lived on whatever food her retarded son, Elvin, could club, skin, and cut up. Since urban renewal had encroached on her little kerosene-lit haven, the pickings had slimmed: raccoon, opossum, and squirrel were commodities to Aunt Mosie. That was all that she admitted to eating anyway—and beer; she loved her beer. Momma's irritability climaxed with Aunt Mosie underfoot.

The voices integrated with the whisk of Momma's broom as she swept the floors in her bedroom and Daddy's room. Momma had funny ideas about sleeping arrangements. She backed them up by saying, "Lucy and Ricky don't sleep in the same bed, and that's good enough for me." The first time I noticed my folks were different from other families was at a friend's house. When she pointed to the main bedroom and called it her parents' room, I felt stricken. It mortified me. I thought that poor girl lived under the roof with a couple that had succumbed to mortal sin.

I combed my hair out long and straight, cursing the remainders of the Toni permanent that clung to the curly ends of my hair. When my younger sister Eden and I were small, Momma gave us identical Toni perms, a yearly occurrence. She sewed matching outfits for us so that people mistook us for twins. Then she lied further by telling everyone at Sterling's dime store that our blond hair was naturally curly. It was one of the many lies I learned to endure. After so many declarations, a lie begins to sound just like the truth anyway. But our lies were so big they became our walls and the roof over our head.

I applied blue shadow to my lids—glittering aqua, it was called. My eyes were pinto bean shaped, with little blond insect legs for lashes that encircled them, lending even less definition. That was made worse by the new eyeglasses I was forced to wear. I had inherited my mother's hazel irises, a color that was neither brown nor blue nor green. All of the nondefining that went into my features made it difficult for me to remember my own face. The smell of Faultless spray starch rose from two freshly ironed articles that lay atop my dresser. Momma deposited a home-sewn blouse and skirt, a swift sewing project put together over two evenings.

I held up the lavender blouse. Peasant style, it was sewn for me the night before with fabric bunched around the elastic. All of that formed the circular neck. I pulled it over my head, first allowing it to drape loosely around my hips. But that only magnified my lack of definition. The drooping sleeves pinched my elbows. "Momma, will you look at this?"

"I'm fixin' coffee, Katrina. What you need?" she called from the kitchen, using the hallway that led to my room as a conduit for sound.

"You can see straight through this blouse."

"It's a little sheer, but you'll look pretty." She stepped into my room, and I noticed for the first time that I looked down at her. We were all aware of her hatred of having to cut five inches from every new pair of slacks she bought. She complained about clothes being piled up on store shelves that were sewn for people who did not exist.

All that I knew about her was summed up best in the way that she complained. She had a bureau drawer full of photos that revealed as much about her as a footprint reveals a passerby. Some of the photographs were of people who looked shabby and beaten down, like the Hurleys, while a few looked like they had fixed themselves up for the picture. Her single infant picture fascinated me. She had a wide-eyed stare, like little children have when they haven't been looked at enough.

I tried to imagine Momma as a child and couldn't. The old sepia photographs offered the only glimpse into her wounded soul. Some people lived through the Depression while others were devoured by it. I have known people who shared stories about how it taught them to do with less and how it brought families closer together. But Momma's stories left me with a barren image of her childhood.

The worst one was about a baby doll. She had asked Santa for one for Christmas. But being the oldest of nine children, she had been told the facts of life about the old elf. When a neighbor boy ran into their sharecropper's shack one winter, saying how the women from the WPA were coming all loaded down with sacks of toys, it sent my mother and all her siblings into a frenzy.

Momma pulled on her ragged shoes, awkward hand-me-downs from her own mother, and ran out into the chill of the morning. Full of anticipation, she and all the impoverished children from the valley were made to line up on the cold side of a shallow berm, their toes numbed by the frost. The WPA women handed out their toys in Nazi fashion. Momma said that the only place worse to stand was at the very back of the line, where the coloreds were forced to stand.

I could tell when Momma relayed her story that—more than anything—she hated the way the do-gooders looked down their noses at them in pity. I believe that folks who help others in such a way, getting a charge out of tossing a crumb to the derelicts, lose their prize in heaven. If they don't, I shall lobby for it.

When she threw down the cracked-face doll handed to her, she was dealt a harsh switching. Meemaw scolded her for her ungrateful behavior and sent her home without a doll. All of that accounted for the baby doll given to my sister and me every Christmas and well into our adolescence. Between the two of us, we had around thirty or more in our collection.

"The bus won't stop if you're not out by the curb."

"You'll not see *me* in this. It's no different than, than cheap lingerie."

"I paid good money for that fabric. You'll put it on or I'll not make you another thing."

I wanted her to swear on that promise. But sympathy defeated me. I knew that Momma warred with Daddy over our clothes and over anything a girl might consider pretty. The lavender-colored fabric was a hard-come-by good. I had not noticed that it was so utterly sheer when she brought it home, all folded up with a new spool of purple thread. She hadn't, either.

"Momma, you can see my bra." I stood in front of the mirror, gawking at the blue bra that she had insisted on buying for me from Fred's. Fred's was a department store that displayed all of its goods inside Depression-green dump bins. All of the bins lined the linoleum aisles flea-market style. You could buy a bra for a dollar right next to a soup kettle. The kettle cost a little more. Colored bras you could buy by the gross if you had the income.

"No use in buying a colored brassiere if you can't see it," she said.

She stared at the blue cups through my blouse. I felt naked, as if she had invited the whole town to drop by and have a look.

"You don't expect me to wear this to school."

"The bus is coming. Don't forget your sweater. It's still nippy out of a mornin'."

"Sure enough. I'll wear it over my head."

"You miss that bus, and you'll walk to school."

"I'll stay home."

"You'll do no such thing." She swatted my backside. Big girls still got whippings for sassing except in the better parts of town. Momma had backed off the whippings but gave us a firm smack from time to time. It proved, she believed, that she was still in charge.

The bus motored toward our house, now two blocks away, and made faint thunderous rumbles as it battered our street. When I heard the screech of the air brakes, I slipped into the purple skirt, threw on my good pair of socks and shoes, and stumbled down the hall.

"You remember about my home economics class today?" I asked. "We're cooking for our moms."

"I remember. I got myself a hair appointment with Evelyn down at the beauty college," she said. Evelyn was the goddess of hair among the ladies who lived on fixed incomes. My mother visited her perhaps less than a dozen times her whole life.

She smiled at me, and I smiled back. I knew that she hated how, in her estimation, the teachers snookered our mothers into parental involvement. I wondered if she would truly make an appearance. "It's at noon, and it's for a final grade. Don't you forget—"

"I'll not forget; now git on out of h'yere before you're late."

"Bye, Daddy. Aunt Mosie." I met Eden at the end of the drive. My younger sister appeared tired and more sad than usual. She had stopped wearing Momma's homemade clothes altogether and put on the same T-shirt and discount-store jeans every morning, her loathing for school evident in her slouched posture. I never knew of a schoolteacher who could teach Eden a blessed thing.

I understood her better than anyone else. The one thing that she taught me is that if you resist education, it will not force itself upon you. Nothing created a bigger racket in our house than when Daddy got bent on trying to teach Eden her arithmetic. In the first place, our teachers did not call it arithmetic. So half the time I felt like Eden just never could grasp Daddy's Little Red School House language. He wanted her to use noughts and to cipher. Eden did not grasp ciphering at all. But even if she did grasp the rudimentary gist of it, it would not have interested her the least little bit.

"You want to borrow a little eye shadow?" I asked.

"No, and quit tryin' to fix me up."

She had grown belligerent over the last few months. The more I tried to do for her, the more agitated she grew.

"Momma's coming to the school today," I said. "Mrs. Crawford wants us to cook a whole meal and serve our mothers. I'm a might nervous over it."

Eden shrugged. Entering into a conversation with me threatened to open the doors to her tightly clenched heart. So we stood in silence and took our places inside the bus—Eden in the very rear seat with me perched up front. Somehow, I felt our chasm was caused by me. I had said to her once, "Why don't you quit copying me and find out what you like and don't like? Be an individual." But Eden never fully shaped her likes or dislikes. So from then on she observed me from her solitary roost. If I went left, she went right. If I chose blue, she chose red. So when she chose the bad, I felt the blame.

I sat down holding my books over my bright blue bosom.

Out of all of my teachers, Mrs. Crawford paid me the least attention. I could not sew, nor did I see a future in it. I hailed from a long line of bean burners and casserole sloppers. Hurley women could not cook, and I saw no need for defaming the lineage. But she had grouped me with some girls who felt as at home in the kitchen as my gardening daddy felt in composted manure. When I was forced to stand close to the popular girls, I felt overly thin and inelegant.

Mrs. Crawford favored those girls so much that they were often called out of a class to help her with grading papers and such. They were the same bunch that had given me a C on my apron project. Now I had to work beside them and pretend to like it.

"Katrina, you and Carol Anne will make a homemade chocolate cake," Mrs. Crawford said.

I smiled woodenly at Carol Anne and her perfect teeth.

"Sure, Mrs. Crawford," said Carol Anne. She snapped up the recipe card and headed for the kitchen. I joined her and ignored the stares. I had just measured a perfect cup of flour when Carol Anne tipped her head, her eyes hot with cynicism. She ran her gaze up and down me like a new zipper. "Your bra is showing, Katrina. And it's ba-lue."

"Shut up, Carol Anne." I turned my face away from her. The sun bled in through the café curtains on our faux kitchen window. My feet moved away. I wanted to become one with the shadows.

Without so much talking now, we managed to create something that resembled a chocolate cake. When we pulled our creation out of the oven, the mothers were arriving. I watched for Momma and knew how the day would make her nervous. She never liked milling around people much. Hauling her into a cackling group of socialites was like sending her on an errand to hell.

Mrs. Crawford asked us to invite the mothers into the room, like so many little Stepford wives.

Carol Anne greeted her mother, one of the loveliest ladies I had ever set eyes on, next to my Aunt Pippa. She wore a yellow dress with matching pumps. She chewed gum in time with her graceful, sway-ing hips and donned a minidress when all other mothers swathed their plumpish selves in polyester.

"Well, it looks as though everyone has arrived," said Mrs. Crawford. "Almost everyone."

She gave me just enough of a look to cause the other girls to toss me a flippant stare. Three other friends of mine knew their mothers were not coming. I seated myself at their table, made a great show of arranging a cheap white hobnailed vase of flowers, and handed each girl a sad little folded napkin.

In the event the cake was a dismal failure, I covered my backside. "Don't eat the chocolate cake," I whispered. "Carol Anne can't cook worth a flip."

I forced myself to stop glancing back at the door, in hopes my mother would appear. We finally finished with the meal. Mrs. Crawford called Carol Anne and me up to the front to serve our cake. She cut the slices while I supplied the paper plates. I sampled the cake and hoped Mrs. Crawford would cancel the dessert altogether.

"Tasty, dear," Carol Anne's mother said. I could see the dry mixture wadding up inside of her mouth. She was too polite to spit it into her napkin. Mrs. Crawford placed a waste container beside the tables. Most of the mothers made haste to dispose of the evidence.

"Hello?" The greeting was voiced as a question. I detected it above the chatter and recognized it as Momma's voice.

Most of the mothers collected near the doorway and made their farewells to Mrs. Crawford and to their daughters. Each woman stared at my mother—slicing her open with their eyes—and then turned their backs on her.

The beautician at the beauty college had teased her hair up in an unnatural way. When she moved just in front of the sunny window, light spiked through the mound, illuminating her crown. She stood, shoulders slumped, her arms making a V as she clasped her ten-year-old oversize handbag. The large pink exotic flowers on her blue dress swirled around her hips, making her look older than her years.

"Your mother is here," one friend whispered.

"I see her." I approached Momma and hoped she did not detect the heat upon my cheeks.

"Evelyn took longer than usual, Katrina," Momma said, breathless. The whole time she spoke, her gaze traced the faces around the room, but finding none friendly, fastened on me.

"The meal's over, Momma."

"If I had rushed Evelyn, she wouldn't have done a good job and—" Her voice trailed off. Her eyes connected with Mrs. Crawford. Crawford's wordless assessment of my mother needed no explanation. We were the Hurleys, the end-all definitive for white trash in Mockingbird Valley.

"It doesn't matter. I got my grade anyway." I wanted to run around the room and shake every critical, silly head until it softened and invited her in.

"I guess I'll go," Momma said.

Mrs. Crawford watched her go but never said a word to her.

I always wondered if a woman who had to work for her kind of pay felt better about herself when someone like my momma showed up. I guess people like her believe that is why God put white trash in the world—to make them grateful for their station. But they never do ponder why he would choose to dine with us lesser beings. That is when the question about who is more pathetic is brushed aside for nobler causes.

Imagining all of the fears my mother had faced that morning just to show up and prove to Mockingbird Valley that we were just another average family tortured me for the rest of the day. My imagination flashed images of her nervously selecting what she would wear, mentally rehearsing what she should say, and digging costume jewelry from the cracks in her vanity drawer. I determined that she had not purposed in her heart to arrive so late, but rather delayed her arrival in hopes that a miracle would arise. If she sat in Evelyn's chair long enough and wished—no, *willed* it to happen—she would emerge an acceptable person.

Although no one ever admitted it, that became the secret desire of every Hurley woman.


I had taken art classes until I could almost teach them. But I had also taken to teenage tantrums and hated the results that appeared on my canvas. Seldom did the finished work take on the form of the vision in my clouded head. Each night I sketched with pencil or ink. But before bed, I tossed the hideous draft into the trash can. I broke in two the pencils that resisted my coaxing hand. I despised myself for not bending my craft into perfection.

Our art teacher, Mrs. Riley, stood out from the rest of the crows who tortured us throughout the day. Her long hair gleamed about her shoulders, shimmering black tendrils over elegant Cleopatra shoulders. But it was her first name that fit her—Lillith. I never saw her sitting with the other teachers during breaks or lunch, and she dressed herself in clothing as bright and colorful as her paintings. Some of the kids called her odd, but I followed her around, hoping her distinctions would rub off on me.

"What is that?" I stood over my friend Carla, who sat at the potter's wheel jabbing her thumbs into a wobbling orb of wet clay and making a mess of things.

"It's a vase for my grandmother. Don't make fun of me, Katrina. I know I don't have your talent."

"Use a more delicate touch, Carla. Like this." I allowed my fingers to glide up the wet form until it took on a perfect shape.

"You make it and I'll glaze it," Carla said.

"No. Keep trying. You'll get the hang of it." I could not cheat, not for any amount of money.

"Katrina?" I heard Mrs. Riley's voice behind me.

"Ma'am?"

"If you don't mind, I want to enter your *Woman with Child* oil painting in a contest."

"Mine?"

"Unless you don't want me to."

"What kind of contest?"

"It's for high school students. First place is a scholarship."

"As in art?"

"I think you have what it takes, don't you?"

I did not answer Mrs. Riley. I never believed that I had the power to make myself fly. I only hoped that it would happen. Hoping and believing roomed in separate quarters on Erie Lane, just like Momma and Daddy.

"Here's the application. You'll need to get a parent's signature."

The bell rang, and I stood holding the application as though it would break.


Momma read in some book that girls should make their own decisions about boys and such. So it should have come as no surprise when Eden's first boyfriend crawled up on our doorstep. She was a mere fourteen, but I did not know this man's age. He stood peering through our screen door from the pop-bottle porch. He gave me a fright. I thought a homeless man had wandered up from the creek.

"Who's there?" I dropped my pencil.

"Eden here?"

"She's in her room. What do you want?"

He grunted. His eyes shifted left, and he would not look at me. I have seen children who have the same look, dirty-faced waifs left to fend for themselves in the toy aisle of Magic Mart, but who would never get any of the toys they coveted. I've felt the worst of sorrow for them, but never would have matched one of them up with my baby sister.

"Momma, someone's at the door." I crept into my mother's room and found her reading a tabloid story about a woman who birthed an alien's child.

"What's wrong, Katrina?"

"Some man's at the door asking for Eden. He's got a beard to his waist and his hair's longer than mine." I stepped back as Momma headed for the kitchen. "Don't let her go, Momma."

"May I help ye?" Momma marched right up to the screen door. But then she stepped back and fell more silent than I had known her to be.

"I'm here to pick up yer youngest girl, Eden." He mumbled his words instead of saying them outright. He stood with his hands shoved into the pockets of his ill-fitting trousers. He reminded me of a bridge troll in one of my old picture books. He had a habit of covering his mouth when he spoke and nudging an old pair of horn-rimmed glasses.

Momma and I both looked him up and down. His pants were coated in dirt, and his fingernails were black. We did not want to let him in the house.

"Daddy," I whispered. "This man says he's here to date Eden."

"Howdy, Mister." Daddy sat at the table, stirred his coffee, but scarcely glanced up. He could not see the bearded troll from where he sat.

"Invite him in, Donelle," Daddy mouthed the words and scowled at us. He often accused us of being too ignorant to extend hospitality to a visitor.

But Momma could not muster a single word. She stood staring at the man while he stared down at his feet.

"For crying out loud, Donelle!" Daddy came to his feet and we stepped aside to let him deal with the man.

"Katrina, is someone here for me?" Eden hollered from our room.

Daddy lifted his left arm to brace himself against the doorframe. The linoleum dented where he pressed his cane against the floor. He gave the man a once-over. I could only see the back of his head, so I could only imagine how the color drained from his face. "Sir, what is yer business here?"

From the driveway, the sound of giggling was carried on the night air to our threshold.

"I'm here to pick up Eden and—" He turned, impatient with the carload of people who now made catcalls and honked the car horn.

I ran to the window and looked out. The sunset cast a rosy light upon the old Chevy and its occupants. In the front seat, a young woman who wore a halter top lit a cigarette and blew the smoke into the face of the hoodlum seated next to her. The backseat must have been reserved for my sister.

Eden ran into the kitchen, breathless. She had changed into a clean pair of jeans and wore a pullover top. Her fresh appearance bore evidence to the fact that she had exercised a great deal more decorum than the man on the porch. She bolted past Momma and offered no introductions. Nor did she explain this gentleman's origin or tell us from under what rock he had crawled.

Relief glinted from the troll man's face, as though his tedious obligation would soon be finished.

"Eden, you want to tell us your friend's name?" Momma glared at Daddy.

"Momma, Daddy, this is Dub." That was all she said before letting herself out and disappearing into the night with her troll.

"I cannot believe you let her go!" I stormed into the living room and slumped onto the couch.

"You should have talked to the girl, Donelle," Daddy said.

"You're her daddy, Ho! Why didn't you stop her?" Momma opened the screen door and watched until the red taillights disappeared toward the bad side of town.

"What if something terrible happens to Eden?" I asked. "She's too young to date, Momma. And from the looks of him, that man was too old for her."

"You don't talk to these girls enough, Donelle." Daddy took his place again in front of his coffee cup.

"Eden's out of control, Ho!"

"Don't I know?"

"I've been saying for the longest time how you need to help me with her. I couldn't have stopped her no more than I could stop the evening train."

"But you should tell her she just can't go, Momma. Why can't you tell Eden no? You tell me no all the time," I said.

Standing between Daddy's blame-laying and my badgering sent Momma off her course. "Shut up, all of you!" she shrieked. "Leave me be!" Through the tattered screen, a neighbor's porch light all of a sudden illuminated Daddy's garden patch.

Momma hid herself in her room.

Daddy fell silent and sat in the semidark cubicle of our kitchen. I left him to comfort himself with tobacco and combat his silent adversaries.

I lay awake for hours and stared at the moonlight making its dry puddles on my bedroom floor. More than once, I went for water. Through his doorway, I saw the amber glow of Daddy's bad habit and the haze that stood sentry outside his room. But his wakefulness was habitual. Therefore, I did not know if he worried over my sister or simply lay fretting at some courthouse crony who raised his ire that day. When he tired of playing cards with the veterans, he often roamed in the marble halls of the town courthouse, talking politics with the tax collector.

"Katrina, git in the bed!" Momma hollered. "Your pacin's driving me nuts."

I sighed and trekked back to my room. Eden's rumpled bed was still void of her presence.

Atop my textbooks lay the papers given to me by Mrs. Riley. I filled them out but knew better than to ask Momma or Daddy to sign it in their volcanic state. Daddy had his own ideas about a girl's vocation. Artists could find no market for their work in the valley, he assumed. He never imagined me living elsewhere. I would approach them both in the morning, when the new day had its chance to clear away the sting of trouble.

But our troubles always became our mountains. And I stood alone, the only Hurley who desired to make their ascent.

The best thing about the valley was the way she dipped down in the middle of town and then lifted her skirt up all around us with green tree petticoats rustling almost to the clouds. Mockingbird Valley was a comely, freckled square dancer who knew nothing about the places beyond her bounds. So she danced her jig to the strains of the past, while she turned a deaf ear to any modern ditty.

My daddy loved her more than he loved my own mother. He loved her even more than the women he courted the nights he said he was gone to the baseball park. So it displeased him to know that I pined to glimpse beyond the rim of our own small cup.

"You can't make no livin' that way, Katrina. *Artist,* my hind leg!"

"This ain't the Depression. These are the seventies, Daddy," I said. Salome, our speckled mongrel dog, scratched and dug at an imaginary bone around my feet.

"Hand me that wranch." Daddy fiddled under the car hood on days he stayed home. "If I take it down to that shop on Fourth, that colored man'll charge me twice what it cost me to fix it myself. Got to watch the coloreds."

"Now, Daddy, I'm sure Mr. Robinson has to charge the same as every other mechanic in town." He did not respond. While one hand twirled the wing nut that centered the distributor cap on his Pontiac, the other steadied him against the car. What he did under the hood of his car held the same mystery for me as his frequent visits to the downtown haunts did. Seldom did he invite me into the places that welcomed him and his male ways. I soon surmised the places that made him comfortable were those clearly off-limits to females. That very thing is what caused my trouble—the way I walked into the men's territory, wearing trousers and forgetting my place, or examining the Pontiac's entrails and pretending to know about wing nuts and politics.

"I'm not like you," I said.

"Say, you're not listenin' to me, Sis. Are ye?" His voice took on a hard edge. Cigarette smoke burst from his lips like steam.

"Just sign it, Daddy, please."

"Go on out of here and let me work."

"It's just a little contest. What's the harm of it?"

"Not gon' let you waste your education, that's what."

"Mrs. Riley says I have what it takes to be good. Besides, I got fifty dollars saved from working at the Pizza Delight. I can pay my own entry fee."

"Silly-headed fool, that's what she is."

"Daddy, she's not, she's—"

"Are you callin' me a lar?"

"I never said that."

Momma spied us out talking in the yard sometimes and thought we had good talks between us. She told me, from time to time, how Daddy always bragged on how he could always get through to me but not Eden. Although Daddy appeared to hear me, he never listened; his mind was not set on me but on what he knew about the past. That's what got him so riled, I felt. He only heard the voices from a time I never knew, the ones that made him feel so wholly insignificant, and they were hateful to him. So when he slapped me, he wasn't slapping me—just the ghosts from his boyhood in Sunny Point. He muttered about them when he lay stretched out on the couch, those hateful men who made fun of his bare feet down at the general store when his momma sent him for lard. So I don't fault him for taking a shot at them after all those years. He was finally being heard. I just lived too much in the present to hear them speaking through me.

"Daddy, things is different now—"

"You're callin' me a lar, Katrina!" He whirled around too fast for me to step away. The first blow sent me to the ground. My tears made him even angrier because I took on the face of a powerless girl. He hated bullies and that made him loathe himself. He never confronted self-loathing because of his simple ways. Understand, self-loathing is complicated.

"Daddy, what's wrong?" I pulled myself up into a sitting position and swept the hair from my face. He grabbed my arm and wrenched it enough to pull me up onto my knees.

"Ain't no kid of mine gon' call me a lar!"

"I didn't! Don't, Daddy!"

He struggled to pull his belt from his loop with one hand while wrenching my arm with the other. I yanked free, but he grabbed me again and brought the belt down across my backside. My legs kicked and I flailed so that when Momma stepped out onto the porch, she laughed.

"Make him stop!" I yelled.

"For heaven's sake, Ho!" Momma laughed again.

"She called me a lar!"

"You know better, Katrina." Momma's face drew up pensive, like a hare's. I had never known her to be afraid of him, but her stretched

smile said otherwise. She dusted flour from her hands and left powdery wings upon her pockets.

Daddy tried to land another blow with his belt, but he could not
hold me still.

A car slowed in front of the house. Momma told Daddy he'd best
quit, folks was noticing. That helped the most. Daddy's reputation
was a medal he polished to a high sheen, even more cherished than
the Purple Heart tucked away in his undershirt drawer. His arm fell
at his side, and he shambled away without looking at me.

I rose and approached my mother. "Why didn't you stop him,
Momma? I thought you would help me."

Momma's awkward smile sickened me, since it neither offered
me comfort nor promised me better days.


Aunt Pippa and Uncle Hank dropped by to see us. Uncle Hank
hefted a quart of apricots canned by Pippa. She had taken a job at
Gordon's Foods factory, if for nothing else, to keep her days busy. In
her arms, she carried a sack of frozen pies and TV dinners. Her hands
shook as she gripped them close to her. "Anyone about?"

"Aunt Pippa," I said.

Uncle Hank joined Daddy in the hall. He jawed at Daddy. His
chin lifted whenever he asserted his opinion. I could see my father in
his eyes as clearly as if some precise button maker had popped out the
same eye prototype for them both. Although twins did not crop up
in the Hurley stock, Hank and my daddy lifted their stark aggressive
stare, their bony noses, and cleft chins from the same designer and
then placed it on loan to Kirk Douglas.

"Roxanne sent over some record albums. Thought you might
want them." Aunt Pippa pulled the albums from the sack of frozen
dinners.

"The Beatles. Vintage." Loretta Lynn albums and records by Conway Twitty littered the area beneath the ironing board. The first time I heard a syncopated rhythm it was like being given the right to breathe again. I could no more imagine a world without rock-'n'-roll any more than I could conceive of a garden without marigolds. Not everyone favors marigolds, but they have their place. Just like some people remember the day that JFK died, I remember the night that rock-'n'-roll music came to Mockingbird Valley. Four lovely boys with silky hair and electric dreams had strummed their way into our town via the *Ed Sullivan Show.* We gathered around the TV on Sunday night as faithfully as the Pentecostals in town gathered around their wooden altars.

The Beatles mesmerized me. When they let loose, I wanted to move. I wanted to fall in love. And then they were gone. "You sure she wants to give these up?"

"She said you might like to have them." Her right hand trembled.

"You should see the doctor about that hand, Aunt Pippa."

"What good would it do me? My daddy's hands shook and his before him. We all just got us the shaky hands, that's what. Your momma and daddy about?"

"Daddy went for milk. Momma's watching the news. Go on in, Aunt Pippa."

"You'll put up these dinners for your Momma?"

"Glad to."

"You know your eyes are red?"

"Must be something I'm allergic to," I said.

"Oh. Thought for a moment maybe you'd been cryin'. But you'd tell me that, wouldn't you?"

I looked away and just nodded.

The high school steps warmed the backs of my legs. The last day of the school year had sent all the students running for the large old buses or to take a smoke behind the coaches' equipment shed. I wanted to tell Mrs. Riley myself that I could not apply for the art scholarship contest, so I sat upon the hot concrete landing and waited for her lithe frame to appear. Hers was the only class I did not have to visit for finals, but she was the only teacher I wanted to see.

Arkansas summer had already seized the valley in a headlock. Those who came in from out of state would visit the only lake for twenty miles—our lake—hoping to flush out a breeze. But even the muddy waters of the Dardanelle could not break free from the hot doldrums of the dog days of summer. I found a shaded place beneath the overhang of the school office. I parked myself as close as possible to the air conditioning that seeped beneath the door, with my legs lifted off the pavement.

"Katrina, you'd better come or you'll miss the bus." Eden stood at the end of the walk. A cigarette butt smoldered in the grass next to her. I never witnessed her taking a smoke, but once I spied a pack in her open purse.

"They're not leaving for ten minutes," I said. "I'm waiting to see Mrs. Riley."

"She isn't here, Katrina." I turned to find Betty Semples standing on the landing behind me. She was the only girl my age named Betty. Most of us were named after the late fifties starlets like Patty Duke or Judy Garland. But Betty's momma named her old just like she dressed her. Old.

"Mrs. Riley left town night before last. It's all over town," Betty said. Eden turned away and headed for the bus.

"Walk with me, Betty. What do you mean?"

"I thought you might have heard by now, what with you being her favorite," Betty said.

"I'm nobody's favorite. What's all over town?"

"Amy Tyler told me. Her parents said Mrs. Riley's husband got the phone call late last night."

"She left him?"

"She was at a party. That's how they met, her and this big shot."

"Who? What big shot?"

"He's some big New York writer. Anyway, they up and ran off together. Flew plumb out of the country."

"It's a lie."

"Ain't no lie, Katrina."

"What about her kids? She's a momma, ain't she?"

"They're with their daddy. But I don't know the particulars. Call me." Betty spied her bus and headed for it.

"I still say it's a lie." I stood in front of bus 052 and saw the faces that stared straight ahead, all of them as glazed over as Eden's. The news twisted and churned through me until it rang of some truth. Mrs. Riley flew away without so much as a fine nice-to-know-you. When the door was left open for too long, she spread her elegant feathers and took flight, while the rest of us gasped and stared up from our primitive nests.

The inside of the bus smelled of sweat and encumbered dreams. The driver packed us three to a seat, and we sat like gherkins. My anger at Mrs. Riley caused me some guilt. I could not determine my true feelings until the bus finally stopped at the corner of Erie to spit out the remaining few of us. I stood at the mouth of our driveway and finally realized that I hated being left behind. My world did not take me to parties that honored writers or politicians. When Mrs. Riley had stood next to me, I did not realize that her sweet perfume was the closest I had stood to the scent of renown.

Daddy sat on the pop-bottle porch, whittling. I could see Momma talking to him through the screen door.

I walked around him, and he nodded at me as though the lull of early summer had deadened his senses.

"Katrina, you best be glad we didn't let you get mixed up with that Riley woman," Momma said.

Daddy slid his knife against the small gray whetstone but said nothing. I joined him in his silence. Before they could disparage her any further, I sidled past and opened the screen door.

"She up and ran off with another man." Momma pulled on the screen door until it snapped closed behind me.

"He was a writer," I said. My fingers gripped a pot lid and I looked inside a simmering pot of beets. "Not that I'm excusing any of it."

"Left her husband and her kids."

"I'm going to my room."

"From now on, you'll listen to your ol' man, that's what."

It was the last thing she yelled before I closed the door to my bedroom.

In the corner next to a pair of roller skates, my tattered portfolio lay pressed against the corner. I pulled out a charcoal of Bobby Kennedy. He was alive when I sketched it, but now he was gone. I held it up to the light. The amateur strokes around his mouth and eyes mocked me, and I hated the whole thing more than I hated Mrs. Riley right then. I tore the portrait into long shreds and left them to lie in a curled heap at my feet. I pulled out another picture, a pencil sketch, and tore it up as I wiped tears and left dirty charcoal smudges in their place.

The late afternoon sun hit me in the face. I yanked down the window shade.

"Katrina, come eat," Momma said. She pushed open the door as though to find it closed made her irate.

"Don't set a place for me."

"You git yourself in that kitchen and eat."

"I'm not hungry."

"Katrina Louise, what have you done?" Momma stood partially in the doorway. The sight of the shredded sketches kindled her primal ire.

"I've given up art." I said it as though I would say "I'm going to town," or "I'm fixing myself a glass of Coke."

We glared at one another for the time it would take one dove to call to another. Her anger turned to a look of sickened horror, and she stared through me as though I had dismembered a family pet.

"What does it matter, Momma?"

"Your purty pitchers." She held her hand over her mouth and finally stood fixated over the shredded drawings. Her eyes misted, but only enough to shame me. With her fingers still stained by beet juice, she knelt and sifted through the papers until she recognized the portrait. "This was the pitcher of Robert Kennedy. I loved that one. He had such a queer look, as though he knew he was going to die."

"Shut up, Momma!"

"Every pitcher is tore up. You didn't leave nary a one! Not even one, Katrina!"

"They're worthless, Momma."

"You did this to punish me, didn't you—"

There was a pause.

"You might could have sold 'em. Anything but to tear 'em up."

"You never said you liked them."

"Something's not right in your head, Katrina, that's what!"

"Don't you say that about me! You don't even know me!"

"I know a crazy when I see 'em. You're crazy, that's what!" Momma righted herself, and as she stood, she allowed the shredded remains of my plans to slip through her fingers and back to the floor.

"Why can't you just leave me alone?" I crawled onto my bed and drew the covers up around my face. The door slammed closed. Momma left me alone to nurse my wounded soul. I spent much of the month of June there, wrapped in cotton sheets and self-doubt.

The talk about Mrs. Riley and her New York writer beau drifted about town for the summer, then floated on down the river as did everything else that passed through the warm brown waters of the valley's lock and dam.

Summer rolled through the valley like a fat woman gathering food into her pockets. The A-1 Market resorted to selling fertilizer and extra large cuts of beef in the summer because the produce demand had fizzled. Everyone that had a garden shared it with the rest of the town. Daddy's garden grew the biggest cabbages in the county, a fact that caused the occasional motorist to pull off the road and gawk at the monstrous green heads. He would not give away his secret, but I knew and remembered the smell of chicken litter so rank it made me retch.

Summertime breathed life back into our household. It made up for the lean Christmas. Nobody hated Christmas worse than Daddy did. He and my mother tangled through the whole month of December like two alley cats tied up together in a bag. But this particular winter left a void almost as deep as when I had lost my grandfather. Granny died, and with her ebbed any hope for healing within the Hurley clan. As with Papaw, I had not been allowed to say goodbye to her. Even when Daddy's siblings had begged him to come to her bedside, he refused to go. He wore his bitterness like a red badge to her funeral and refused to cry. So I welcomed the summer, happy to find that it washed away the memories and left only the smallest of stains on my heart.

A few aunts and uncles hoped that bridges had not been totally burned away. When all of them had stood back and allowed Aunt Velda to steal the family farm, Daddy had vowed to never speak to the lot of them. They turned up on our doorstep from time to time, as did the drunken men who came to my father for help. Just before dawn I remember the stench of tobacco so strong that it clouded the hallway outside our bedroom. I tiptoed to the kitchen and found Momma pouring hot black coffee for a man I did not know. Daddy sat beside him, and the two of them talked of relatives and the Depression like they knew one another.

"Say, Sis, look who we've got here this morning."

"Hi," I answered Daddy in a whispered, sleepy stupor. I rubbed my eyes and stepped back, not wanting a stranger to see me in my baby doll pajamas.

I followed Momma from the kitchen. "Who is he?"

"A cousin of your daddy's, Marlon Trent. The man showed up drunk at our door this morning, and we didn't want him to drive home in sech a way."

"It's so early. He drinks in the morning?" I asked Momma.

"He showed up at three-thirty."

"Is that who called?" I remembered out of my haze how the telephone rang in the middle of the night.

"No, that was Aunt Velda."

"She's back?"

"Her husband's left her. They had a big fight and he left her. Aunt Ruby had to put her in the sanatorium again."

"Uncle Ned left her?"

"Packed up and left her with the kids. Ruby's got her kids right now."

"What will she do?"

"She's not squeezin' a dime from us, I'll tell you that!"

"Why can't she get a job?" I should have known the answer.

Seldom did any of Daddy's family work except for Uncle Hank, Pippa's husband.

"She don't have no skills, and she can't get along with a soul, Katrina."

"I feel sorry for her kids, Momma."

"Women like her ought to be neutered. Go under the house and fetch me some taters."

"You're cooking early." Momma never made breakfast and said that eating lunch made her fat.

"Your Meemaw is comin' over. I told her I'd fix us some lunch. Just some cornbread and ham and sech for her and Daddy and us."

My other grandmother, Momma's mother, made us all feel awkward. We only called her by the affectionate term *Meemaw* because her favorite grandchild, who lived in Oregon, had dubbed her that early on. She never had a kind thing to say to any of us and wore religion on the outside of her, dressing it up in floral polyester and layers of Adorn hair spray. You could tell whom the holiest of women were who went to her church because they competed for the highest stacks of hair and the longest of faces.

I dressed at once and crawled under the house to gather potatoes into the hem of my shirt. In the fall, Daddy spread the potatoes under the floor of our house and sprinkled them with sulfur to keep them through the winter. As much as I loved hiding beneath the cherry trees and grapevines that traversed our two-acre lot, the dank crawlspace under our home was once a favorite getaway in years past. I knew every inch of it. My fondest memory was when I found the litter of kittens that our old mother cat had birthed in hiding.

I dumped the potatoes into a tub and hosed them down good before taking them into the kitchen. Daddy walked his cousin to the car. Even though he could not work, he made a great show of the fact that he had much to do.

Marlon Trent had no sooner chugged down Erie Lane than my grandmother appeared, driven by my grandfather. They peered over Grandpa's dash, two bent and feeble European nesting dolls.

I greeted them both and then rinsed the dirt from my knees and brushed sulfur from my cotton shorts.

"What's that on your face?" Meemaw asked.

"Is it sulfur?" I wiped my cheek. "I've been under the house."

"I'm talking about all that paint."

I sighed. She pointed out the mascara and shadow applied to my eyelids and pale lashes. She never used modern words, so in that sense she could characterize every little thing as sin. Makeup was harlot's paint.

"You look like Jezebel—"

"She ain't no Jezebel!" Momma stepped out of the house, riled to the gills.

"The Bible says Jezebel painted her face." Meemaw's jowls shook when her righteous ilk took over.

"Katrina's a good girl, Momma! Don't you be talking about her like that, not at my house. I won't have it!"

"Want to come inside?" I asked.

I peeled potatoes while Momma stirred up the cornbread batter. With as much courtesy as I could muster, I made small talk with my mother's folks.

"How was church, Meemaw?" I asked.

"Good. You all ought to go."

"I want to go. Why don't we?" I addressed Momma.

"You go if you want, Katrina." At the time, I did not understand her agitation. She and Daddy had changed churches several times but had quit them all, except for the Easter visits. My father stopped going altogether, and if my mother attended, it was short-lived. Each time the change occurred, it followed a house call from the church visitation committee. I never knew the particulars. But I knew that Momma would cuss about it for days, calling the pastor all kinds of names and saying how he must be in the back pocket of every Democrat in town. I did not know until then that Democrats went to church.

"We can pick you up," Meemaw said.

We set the table and my grandmother prayed over the food. It always made my mother cry.

Eden observed a swarm of bees, little bodies hovering around Daddy's honey boxes. Momma griped a good deal about the bees, saying that she couldn't eat watermelon on the back porch now without assault. Daddy kept pushing the boxes closer to the wildflower field in hopes of appeasing Momma.

Momma hung the wash out on the line. "Eden, you'd best keep your distance. Those bees'll swarm you before you know it."

"I'm not botherin' nothin', Momma." The bees had taken to swarming the house all of a sudden, like the whole thing was a big watermelon. But Eden couldn't shake the feeling that Momma just wanted to get rid of her.

"Why don't you go on inside? Hep your sister with the dirty dishes."

Katrina's good deeds caused Eden considerable bother. "In a minute." After their grandparents pulled out from the drive, Katrina set to raking out the dishes. It grated on Eden, the way she could launch into chores and win favor. And now she had Meemaw in her pocket with all that church talk.

"Hey, Eden!" Deedee Wallace sidled up the yard toward her. She was a heavy girl with bad teeth and hair that frizzed around her round face. She had dyed her hair black. It had no sheen and lay like frayed wool upon her crown.

"What you up to, Deedee?" Eden knew that Katrina would have nothing to do with Deedee. That made her like her.

"I want to tell you about my new boyfriend." Her voice lilted in a way that made Eden nervous, but she did not show it.

"What boyfriend?"

"Johnny Mace."

Momma glanced up at them and slowed her pace at pinning shirts to the line. She had her own opinions about Deedee and her reputation among boys.

"He's goin' to make me rich. I thought you'd like to be in our deal."

"What deal?"

"Turn this way, so your momma don't hear."

Eden turned rigidly but kept her gaze on her mother.

"Johnny's goin' to be my pimp and make me his madam. He's goin' to let all the girls around here in on it, whoever's smart enough to come along. Stop lookin' at your momma, girl. The way we're doin' it, she'll never know. We'll use Johnny's old house up the road."

"You're scarin' me, Deedee. You pullin' my leg?"

"Wait till you see me drivin' down Erie in my sports car, and we'll see who is pullin' legs."

"Nobody around here's goin' to go along, Deedee."

"Are too. Those two Tucker girls say they'll do it."

"Be prostitutes? You're lyin', Deedee. Yolanda and Brenda Tucker are younger than me."

"You in or not, Eden?"

"Not."

"You afraid your sister will find out?"

"This don't have nothin' to do with her. I make up my own mind."

"You'll have a whole new group of friends, all the money you need."

"I can't."

"You just remember Deedee Wallace asked you first," she said.

Eden watched Deedee walk toward the road. She was funning her, she decided. A honeybee buzzed past Eden's head. She swatted at it and then picked up a stone and hurled it at the box. Momma complained too much about beehives and girls with reputations. Eden could handle herself around the tough crowd. She wouldn't follow after no Deedee Wallace. Katrina acted like it was so easy to get sucked in, sayin' how if you took too many little steps into the world, you got yourself there eventually. But Eden liked Deedee and her kind, too. She could have her friends, if she wanted, but keep them at a distance. She was counting her steps, whether Katrina knew it or not.

A honeybee swarmed Eden's head. She swung at it. Another appeared.

"Eden, you'd best run!" Momma hollered.

Eden tore off for the house and ran in through the back door to her bedroom. She peered out her window and saw the bees swarming the porch below. It was a little thing, she realized. The bees could go on about their business and leave her to hers. That is all she wanted, she realized. To be left to her own devices. No harm in that.

Sunday arrived. I embraced it with a great amount of preparation. Having slept in Momma's thorny hair rollers, I smoothed the curls at the ends of my hair. "Momma, you want to loan me a pair of your hose?"

"I've got a pair if you think you can pull them over those long legs."

When I stepped into her room, I noticed cardboard color wheels and other pamphlets scattered over her doily. "What's all that stuff all over your dresser top? Brochures and such."

"Paint swatches. I believe I'll paint the kitchen. Look at this color, won't you? It's called *daffodil.* I like it," she said.

"It's certainly yellow." She placed the stockings in my hand.

I had tried to go to Meemaw's church once before. But they put me in a room with little girls all dressed up in silly turquoise skirts with hems nearly to the floor. Momma refused to make the hideous skirt or pay for the tedious workbook, so I could not attend the children's club. I had hated how all the girls eyed me up and down when I walked in, anyway. But I was older now and could sit with the adults in the church service and wear my own things.

Momma sewed me a miniskirt. My long, thin legs hung out of it like wet leggings on a clothesline. It was the shortest thing she ever made for me, and I kept tugging at the hem. "You think I should just stay home? Last time I visited, all the girls at Meemaw's church wore their skirts quite long."

"No, you go on, and if anyone says a word, you tell me, Katrina."

She sent me out to Grandpa's car as though she had shot an arrow in the direction of Mockingbird First Community Church.

The church was as old and filled with traditions as the families who filled its pews every Sunday and Wednesday. People would come and go from around the valley, but the families who had endured its fifty-year heritage stayed like hot wax on onion paper.

The McClintocks took up a whole pew with their brood, while right behind them sat the Cornwallis clan. The more spiritual families sat toward the front and hollered at the preacher when they liked what he said. But the family that caught my eye had a passel of boys—six to be exact. Led by a proud momma and daddy, the Houstons marched down the center aisle as though they parted the Red Sea.

Grandpa dropped us off—I never saw him in church until his funeral—and Meemaw led me to her place, in the middlest of the middle pews. It surprised me the way every person had a kind of catalogue system about those pews. I reckon if someone new walked in that did not know the system, they might be educated about it right fast and put in their place. I stood in the aisle as Meemaw lumbered past the hoary heads to take her self-designated seat. She surrounded herself with women who had not succeeded in extracting their men from the Herculon sofas that they had labored so hard to pay off.

"Mornin' to you, Flora," Meemaw said.

"Weather's been nice, ain't it, Winifred?" Neither of them smiled. Such severity was built into their piety, stacked like bricks against their hearts.

I smiled at the woman and squeezed past two plump matrons in order to help Meemaw, otherwise known as Winifred O'Neal, settle herself and her oversize handbag.

"This is the old folks' class, Katrina. You go on and join the youngsters in the Sparrows class."

"Where is that, Meemaw?"

"Down that hall. Then you youngsters come back here after Sunday school and join the adults."

"Meemaw, I'm sixteen."

"Go, then, over to that man in the red coat. See him yonder passin' out ballpoint pens? He'll tell you where to go."

I did as I was told, but my sights remained on the families engaged in conversation all around the sanctuary. I had been in church no less than five minutes and had already broken the commandment about coveting. I wanted to belong to one of those families.

After church, I started for the front door. The Houstons gathered in the lobby. The oldest boy herded the youngest ones back to their momma. Next to a large potted plant lay a small blue Bible. I looked inside. It belonged to a Houston.

"Excuse me." I approached the oldest Houston boy, who had dark curls that framed his face and set off his blue eyes.

"Pardon me?" He looked at me, and I felt my cheeks redden.

"I found this on the floor." I handed him the Bible.

"Oh, thanks. My little brothers leave these all over the church."

"How many brothers do you have?" I knew the answer, but felt the urge to detain him.

"Five." He grabbed one of the youngest boys by his head and held him under his arm. "Five monsters in all."

"I don't have any brothers at all."

His brother wriggled free and ran squealing after the others.

"You can have them all."

"Thanks. By the way, I'm Katrina."

"Oh, I'm Sol. Sol Houston."

"I've seen you at school."

"Thanks for returning this." He held out the blue Bible.

Grandpa sat out front beeping his horn.

"I'll see you around," I said.

"Sure." Sol marched out into the sunshine, loosened his tie, and stuffed his coat into his mother's arms.

I watched them all leave and wondered if they would like to adopt a skinny girl who wanted to fly.

CHAPTER 3

*M*omma liked for me to drive her places. Thursday evening she had a list of extras she needed from the grocer's, so we climbed into Daddy's old car. When Momma sat down on her side, Daddy's cigarette ashes lifted into the air and swirled around her. "I wish your Daddy would stop that smokin' of his."

"I do too. You think maybe first you all might come back to church?"

"I'll go when I'm ready."

I looked behind us before pulling out into the street. "Look, Momma. There's a rose stuck in the mailbox flag. You think Daddy picks them to get you riled? Or is he being sweet?" She didn't answer. When we drove past the mailbox, she looked away. "They're having a singing Sunday at church. Some group from Tennessee is coming in. Maybe you could go with me."

"This Sunday?"

I nodded.

"I like a good singin'. Maybe I'll come. If I take a notion."

"Which store, Momma?"

"Safeway. I got coupons for them this week. You stay awfully late down at that church. What kind of goings-on would keep folks at such a late hour?"

"Sometimes the kids go out afterwards for pizza and such. I've caught rides out with a couple of the older ones on occasion."

"So you're not actually at the church?"

"Other times, Preacher Sweeney lets us stay late for prayer."

"You can pray in bed."

"I know."

"If I didn't know better, I'd say you're out runnin' around town with some gang of kids."

"I'm at church."

"Your daddy feels you go too far with it."

"With God?"

"And religion."

"I need God, Momma. Now that I found him, I wouldn't like my life any other way. One night I just felt him close. I was praying. It was as though he came down and met up with me."

"You ain't hearing voices like your daddy, are you?"

"No voices. Just the one he uses without words. It's more like when you're watering your violets. You know how careful you are to let the water flow softly beneath the leaves and the petals?"

"Violets are hard to grow."

"His voice is like the soft water soaking inside of me. I need it every day."

Momma directed her gaze to the passing trees and the rose trellises in full bloom along the neighbors' fence lines. I believe she might have preferred to hear I was out running around with a gang of my classmates.

Sensing she was ill at ease, I switched the conversation to other things besides church. "We're here."

"Katrina, you take the bottom half of this list, will you? We'll meet up front. How's that sound?"

I took the list. A-1 Grocers had gone out of business. Two blocks down, a new Safeway capped the end of the only minimall in town. Momma pushed her cart down the breakfast-cereal aisle. I headed for the canned tuna and beyond.

When we met up again, I placed the items I had collected into her cart while she took her place in the checkout line. She nodded over my shoulder, and I turned to see a pale, nervous boy from my tenth-grade class behind me. He wore a red apron, gripped a broom, and appeared ill. I never made fun of boys like him or said anything that would lead them to believe that I found interest in them either. His black frame eyeglasses formed thick tunnels and made his eyes look insectlike as he stared at me. Finally, he made his move.

"Hello, Katrina." His name was Douglas Witherspoon. He stood with one foot braced against the other. Several people walked around him. That made him nervous too. His words seemed to fall into his thick bottom lip. It hung like a hammock.

"Hi to you, Douglas."

I looked away, trying to end the conversation, but his presence had sparked Momma's interest. She smiled at him. Her taste in boys assumed an opposite pole from my own. I believe this is true of mothers in general. But her predilection swarmed somewhere at the bottom of the food chain. She smiled at Douglas and then at me as though she intended to connect our gazes with the thin thread of her approval.

"Want to go out?" he blurted. I wondered how many times he had rehearsed the line in his head before he circled me and then made his final approach. He made no attempt to warm me up with pleasant conversation, but just spilled it at my feet. Down aisle seven near the closeout ice pops and frozen corn stood two pock-faced cronies, hidden behind a floor display of canned deviled ham. I was certain that Douglas was pressured into the invitation.

"I'm busy."

"Okay, then." He walked away. I wrapped my arms about myself, chilled.

Momma's eyes bored through me.

"What's gotten into you?" I asked.

"Why, you turned down that handsome feller's nice invitation. I don't understand you. Not at all, girl."

"Douglas is not handsome, Momma. He's as ugly as one of Salome's speckled pups." But even our mongrel dog had its endearing qualities. As disgusting as I found the boy, though, I could not carry on about his pathetic flaws. She watched him as he walked away. Her gaze lingered over him. Perhaps Douglas might have been a catch in her day.

Momma stayed peeved about it longer than I imagined—long enough to seek out a fix. She had her own ways of teaching a head-strong daughter about the ways of the world, passing up perfectly good men, and knowing what was best for one's own welfare. To a Hurley, slander is the favored parental restraint. The only reason I knew that she had slandered me was because of a visit to Aunt Velda's place. It surprised me to know that Daddy continued to renew his acquaintance with my Aunt Velda. I never knew Momma to ever pay her any mind since she had wound her way into the entire family land inheritance.

Daddy parked himself out on Velda's lawn in a webbed chair to talk politics with her husband, a man I never thought would return to Velda. I gathered with the cousins in Haley's room. We all sat cross-legged in a circle, gawking at one another, surprised to see how much we all had grown. Eden even joined us.

"I brought some cards," I said. I pulled out a deck and shuffled it for a game of pitch.

Haley whispered to her brother, Dale. But I could not understand them.

"You playing, Dale?" I asked.

He did not answer but turned to whisper to his older brother, George.

They all sat like three pigeons, staring at me.

"What's up?" I dealt a hand to each of them.

Haley moved away from me.

"You all act as though I have the plague. What is it?"

Dale piped up, his round cheeks shiny and taut from too many trips to Burger Bob's. "We all heered you was a lesbo," he said.

A woozy feeling swarmed through me. *Momma.*

When we returned home, I lit into Momma with all the rage she had passed on to me. "What are you trying to do to me?" I asked.

She straightened up in her brown rocker and scowled at me. "I don't know what you're talking about, Katrina."

"You told Aunt Velda—of all people—that I am a lesbian. Me— a lesbian."

Her countenance weakened. "I just meant that—"

"Did you say that about me?"

"I just mentioned to Velda that I don't know why you won't date boys."

"You said that, too? I thought you and Velda weren't on speaking terms. "

"Why don't you date boys?"

"All of this is about the fact that I won't date Douglas. Is that right, Momma?"

"Nothin' wrong with that young man."

"Can't I dream of something better?"

"Why, he's handsome as they come. Had his shirttail tucked in and that hair cut razor short to the scalp. Not all nappy like those hippie boys." When she felt right as rain, she had a habit of pursing her mouth and lifting her face, full of herself, bloated with indignation.

"I won't let you toss me to the dogs like you do Eden."

"I can't control Eden."

"You won't control me either."

"You go to your room. I'll not have you talkin' to me that way."

"I'll go, but don't you be tellin' another person that I'm a lesbian."

She crawled out of her chair and left me standing alone.

"I'll burn in Hades before I'll date the likes of that sleazy Douglas Witherspoon!"

Momma and I did not speak again until the next day.

Sunday.


A soft drizzle dampened the church roof, the brick bordered walks, and those church members running inside with nothing over their heads but the Sunday *Courier*. Where a heavy drencher might pare down the Sunday school rosters by a good third, a light mist only clouded the faces in attendance. I dropped Momma off beneath the overhang. "Go on in, Momma. I'll be right there if ever I find a parking place."

Her hesitation was palpable in the way that she sat with only one foot out in the rain and the other one leeched to the car mat.

"Meemaw comes early. Find her and sit with her. She'll be glad to see you." I left her on the sidewalk. Her knuckles appeared white, gripping the large green Bible I had given her for her birthday. The oversize *Living Bible* seemed to be the only entity anchoring her lackluster russet and ivory pumps to the walk. A gust of wind and rain drove her inside. I imagined God bending over her damp head, his little dandelion, nudging her to step inside and see what revelations might be whispered if she would sit still and lift her ear to things bigger than herself. I wondered if all those years spent hunkered down in a rose garden on Sunday mornings, she had expected God to shout his ways onto her. But he's always been a whisperer, best I can recollect.

I wedged the Chevy into a curbed, street-side parking space only a few feet from the neighbor who loathed Pentecostals and swore she would have our cars towed if so much as one bumper crossed her property line.

A gaggle of ushers stood just inside the door, grinning and wielding their handshakes in such a manner so as to haul the little old ladies in from the soggy weather.

I found Momma. She stood in the crowded lobby outside the sanctuary doors. Even shrouded by her drab rain parka, her drawn shoulders colored her whole body angst ridden. "Is Meemaw here?" I asked.

"I'm sure she's inside. First of the month, she comes early to fill the communion cups, her and that pack of beehive hairdos she runs with. A blizzard couldn't stop them."

"Inside is a place on the back row that no one's taken. You see anybody you know?"

She peeked through the door glass, keeping her distance, as though pressing her face too close might spoil her own reflection.

"I usually sit up front, but I can sit with you today," I said.

"There's Evelyn from the beauty shop. When did she start comin'?"

"About a year ago." I saw Evelyn's tower of hair, stiff and platinum and as keenly formed as cast iron.

"I'll sit with Evelyn. You go on and join the young people."

"I'll meet you here in the lobby afterwards, then?"

She nodded. I watched her pad down to the second pew from the back and take her place next to the beautician.

The percussionist, Charley Fritters, was in fine form and started up the small church band with a loud volley of beats most likely gleaned from his high school marching days. The choir commenced its swaying. When outside talent came in, the enthusiasm swelled. I took my place on the front row. Vowing not to venture glances at Momma, I joined the congregation in hand clapping and singing. I prayed it was not too much zeal for one inured to quiet Easter Sundays.

The family quartet came to their feet. Preacher Sweeney gestured, and the entire congregation stood.

*On that great getting' up mornin', fare thee well, fare thee well.*

*On that great getting' up morning, fare thee well, fare thee well...*

Next to me stood a young girl I had met in Sunday school, Brenda Miller. "Was that your momma I saw you with this morning?" she asked.

"Yes. She's seated in the back. If she doesn't like it, I may have to leave early." I recalled the evening our junior high choir had performed a Christmas concert for the public. Mrs. Crumpton, our director, had divided us into several groups based on our grade, including a superior group of singers who would most likely take their talents with them on into adulthood. I was with the youngest group, which meant that we would be seated in the auditorium after our performance to listen while the other groups performed. The ninth graders had just begun the first bar of "Kyrie Eleison" when I heard a flurry of whispers all around. Finally, Beth said, "Katrina, it's your mother."

Momma was at the end of our row, arms akimbo. She wanted to leave and waved her arms at me to make me understand her impatience with the entire affair. After I clambered over the students to meet her and usher her out as quickly as possible, she muttered all the way to the car about the boring mess I had just put her through and would I please warn her in the future if Mrs. Crumpton got the idea again to torture folks with foreign lyrics like "*Carrie Alayson*— Lord have mercy, Katrina!"

"I'm glad she came with you, Katrina." Brenda said, bringing me back to the present. She wiped her eyes from time to time, stirred by the quartet singing. When the music slowed, the pastor took his seat and so did the rest of us. Brenda turned to borrow gum from the boys seated behind us.

"Katrina, your mother…" she whispered.

I sighed, certain to find Momma marching up the aisle to fetch me. Slowly, I turned my head. With the congregation now seated, I saw her at once. She stood in the rear, oblivious to those around her. With her eyes closed, she was unaware that all those around her had taken their seats. She swayed slowly, her lips moving, but out of sync with the lyrics we sang. She bowed her head, and I was certain I saw her wipe a tear.

The ride home was silent, in a peaceful way.

A quiet restlessness settled upon the house on Sunday morning. Eden stirred. The valley itself sat in somber quietude. The honky-tonkers who drove out of town to drink on Saturday night slipped into their trailers to sleep off the effects of Jim Beam and Red Ripple long before dawn. The sun rose silent on the valley and made her look pristine and holy for one day.

On Sundays past, Momma's whistling rose up from the thorny patch of tea roses just outside the girls' bedroom window, interrupted only when she hollered out for one of them to fetch her a glass of iced tea. But the rhythmic clip of pruning shears did not invade Eden's sleep this time. She pulled a lavender T-shirt over her head and stood out in the hallway in nothing but that and her underwear. Katrina's nightshirt lay heaped on the floor next to a lone sandal. Her hairbrush, poised at the edge of her dresser, had a long blond strand hanging from it. Eden was annoyed whenever Momma and Katrina hurried off again to *that church*.

Eden had nothing against church in general and readily recalled the night she was baptized in the small Baptist church right after the Easter just before her ninth birthday. Momma took them on Easter for appearances. But when Katrina had asked the preacher to baptize her, Eden refused to be left out of anything. A retarded man got baptized on the same night and squealed liked Ziffel's pig when his feet hit the unheated baptismal water. Eden got poked in the ribs for laughing, and then it was her turn. Momma had dressed her in white. The lacy skirt spread out around her legs, undulating like the petals of a water lily. She felt like a water nymph and received her initiation into the fairy kingdom with the greatest of wonder.

But she envied the way the preacher took extra care with Katrina. He smiled when she went under and wept when she came out. Everyone wept. And why wouldn't they? The sight of a little girl with her hands lifted in tender surrender crushed the hardest of hearts.

When Momma stopped taking them, it pleased Eden.

In April, Katrina had given their mother a Bible and told her she had need of it. Eden found Momma reading it in the afternoon while a pile of romance novels lay neglected at her feet. Now the only noise on Sunday morning was the distant roar of Daddy's mower as it ate up the unpedigreed grass from the Erie-side ditch.

Eden blamed Katrina for Momma getting religion. The change in Katrina already grated against Eden. But she lacked the words to describe the mixture of envy and resentment that coiled around her heart. Her sister shot up six inches taller at the same time she shoved her dolls to the back of the closet. But worse than that, Katrina had found God. Eden enjoyed the strife and the arguing—any old diversion as long as Katrina paid her some heed. But she no longer argued. On occasion, Eden raised a ruckus on purpose to draw her into a good brawl. But she always failed.

Everything had changed. Eden's best school chum, Pam Haney, got herself pregnant. She never tried to hide the fact and acted like a queen about it, her pride swelling along with her pregnant belly. By her second trimester, Pam developed into a full-fledged woman. Even waved a welfare voucher around to prove it. Eden knew she was pulling away the day she found their usual territory on the junior high campus vacant. Pam stood next to some of the older and tougher girls who dated the high school seniors for reasons less than virtuous.

Eden could not bring herself to tell Katrina of her pain. She wanted to. But Katrina had moved away from her, just like Pam.

It angered Eden whenever Katrina spouted off scriptures as an answer to her problems, a habit that drove her near to lunacy. She had not wanted her, or their tight little world, to change. And Katrina's behavior baffled her. Daddy and Momma were good people but never shoved religion down her throat. So why her older sister had chosen to sop it up like gravy made no sense.

She noticed few changes in Momma, thankfully, and felt a swell of relief when Momma's profanity continued to puncture the air, leaving nail holes in Katrina's soul. Eden read it on her face every time Momma fell into one of her usual tirades. She recalled how Katrina stood outside Momma's bedroom door with her head bowed. Eden vowed to curse her to her face if she ever found her praying outside her own door. Eden stood in the doorway and stared at the rumpled sheets on Katrina's vacant bed and wondered why God had come into their house.

The necessity to date at the age of fourteen had caused me great pain, a pain compounded by the unavailability of bright young men who lived within my station. So when age sixteen wedged me into a more blatant time of courtship, I found the need to obtain a steady boy, one who would cause me little trouble, pay my way into the Ritz Theater on occasion, and keep my mother out of my business. When I finally began dating, her tormenting ceased, and any unfounded notions about me that may have lingered in the minds of my aunts or cousins were settled. Daddy never commented one way or another, until a fellow from across the Dardanelle in Riverton asked me to go steady. He was a couple of years my senior. He had a tank full of gas and just enough ambition to aim him toward the Arkansas State Highway Patrol. He talked of it often to my daddy.

Security was everything to Daddy.

The first time I laid eyes on Leon, he was standing out in our yard, wearing a brindled shirt that made him almost invisible against the pile of chicken litter. Jenny McAbee, my latest run-around-town pal, had invited him only because he hung out with her boyfriend, looking hound eyed and pitiable. His first sentence summed up all that he knew of culture and ethos in Arkansas: "Want to go get a Slurpee?"

Leon's tall, hefty frame filled the doorway of our kitchen quite often after that, especially during the summer months. The more I observed his mannerisms, the more I realized why Momma and Daddy liked him. As Momma often said of his kind, he was a good eater. His shoulders were wide but not athletic. Just wide and round because of his voracious appetite. Leon loved to park his feet under Momma's table and brag on her cooking. Seldom regaled with compliments in regard to her kitchen prowess, she cottoned to Leon at once. Naturally aloof, his amiable ways elevated him in Daddy's sight. He agreed with everything said by my father.

Leon was by no means a looker, but I was not ashamed to be seen with him. That satisfied me for the time being. His coloring was not too memorable and leaned more toward pasty and far left of ruddy. He had a curly mass of dark hair, a nondescript brown that looked violated if it was cut too short or pathetically unshorn if he allowed it to grow out. He had no sense of style, but folks who lived on the other side of the river seldom cared about such things. Matter of fact, if anyone leaned too far to the trendy side of fashion, the Riverton circle had a tendency to poke fun at their outlandish garments.

Leon had a plaid shirt for every day of the week, a clean pair of white socks to accompany each shirt, and several pairs of practical blue jeans. He was an orderly sort who was good to his mother and worked hard to keep his daddy's boat-and-bait shop in the black.

Best of all, he drove.

Leon was not big on religion. But if I badgered him enough, he drove across the river and picked me up for church. His kind looked comfortable in a tractor seat cutting hay or parked in front of the television as he watched Saturday afternoon football while he chugged down a cold one with his buddies. But he looked so odd seated in church. I do not believe churchgoers all fit within one guise, but they ought to at least appear easeful. Or maybe the church folks ought to pay more heed to make them feel easeful. But I do not meddle in such things. Leon's countenance at church mirrored my daddy's on occasion, when Momma managed to drag him down the church aisle.

Although the Bible offers lots of examples of how the men once led the women to God, a few men—quite a lot, actually—strayed from their churchly duty. So, in that sense, I guess Leon fit in after all. A good dozen men like him warmed our church pews tugging at their collars and scowling. Some disappeared but then a few months later reappeared right next to their wives, though I never knew the reason. Maybe they were like my daddy. He looked for reasons to be mad at the church people or the preacher, just so he could point a finger and disappear too. It never takes long to find a flaw in a bolt of fabric, if you've a mind to locate the flaws.

Leon took me to church only a handful of times during the first six months he courted me. Decent and mannerly in every way, he was hard to find fault with otherwise. But he never said a word to disagree with me. He just smiled and often told me he thought I was pretty.

"Leon, do you like it here in the valley?" I asked on one of those rare occasions I got him inside the sanctuary of Mockingbird Community Church. We took a seat three pews from the front, fifteen minutes early.

"No, Katrina."

"I don't either."

"It's too big. That's why I like Riverton. Nice, quiet little place.

I'm going to get me a place next to my momma and daddy someday and have me a garden, plant some tomaters and such. You like gardening too, don't you?"

"You think the valley is a *big* place?"

"Yeah. I don't like all these city people." He glanced around the sanctuary, letting his eyes linger at the back where other young people sat gabbing and popping gum. He had a natural dislike for the self-assured and the ones most likely to pay him no heed.

"You want to stay in Riverton?" I asked.

He allowed his eyes to settle back on me, and they softened. "You don't like it here?"

"The valley is too…confining."

Leon just stared at me like I was speaking in an unknown tongue.

"My daddy believes Mockingbird Valley is paradise. But it isn't to me. What would I do here? There's nothing for me here."

"Your daddy says you'll make a fine teacher someday, Katrina."

"He told you that?"

"I thought you—"

"I never said that," I whispered.

I must have sounded harsh. His face reflected a whipped demeanor. "What else is there?"

"For girls, you mean?" I asked.

"Don't tell me you're a libber."

I hated that term. Men hurled it at women back then in the same way they asked an angry woman if she had her period. Instead of taking time to find out what anomaly pounded on a woman's heart, they attacked the very God-instilled things that made those women feminine. I eyed Leon closely. "Girls can think bigger than themselves, Leon, and not go to jail for it."

Leon studied the faces of the choir members. "You know all these people?" he asked. "You can't know them all. They's too many of them and only one of you. Now you take Riverton—that's a place where folks all know one another." I followed his gaze to the choir. "No, Leon. I don't know everyone."

I still had not found my way into the sacred inner circle at Mockingbird First Community. Every town had its beautiful crowd of young people. Entry into ours was sealed at birth. Most of them had taken to sitting together upon the back pew. That accounted for the bad poetry pencil-scrawled inside the hymnals. *"If you want to see me giggle, then just keep an eye on Brother Wiggle."* They all had the most raucous time making light of the aging choir director, Brother Earl Wigglesworth. Round and tall, he lumbered across the platform and then assumed the most dainty posture to direct the choir. As much as I longed to make a friend among the rank and file at Mockingbird First Community, I could not bring myself to demean a preacher. Momma would have slapped me for less. Having Leon at my side eased my feelings of aloneness. "But I'd like to try and get to know them. It's not a mortal sin to know more than a handful of people in your lifetime."

After the tension between us eased a bit, I asked, "Do you like it here, Leon? Do you like church, I mean?"

"I like it fine, Katrina."

"Your folks go to church? If you told me, I can't remember."

"They're Baptists."

"But do they go? My folks once told people they were Baptists just to get them off the subject." I saw Momma enter from the rear and take her place next to Evelyn. Two pews ahead, Meemaw scowled.

"Momma goes, usually. You think you're the only one that goes to church?"

"Of course not."

"You don't have to go to church to believe in God."

"Is that what you believe, Leon?"

"It's the truth."

"You're right about it. The devil doesn't go and he believes in God."

Leon shifted in his seat, pressed a thumb against his cowboy belt buckle, and fidgeted with his collar.

"But, then again, I guess the devil does go to church. How else would he run off so many from inside it?"

"I don't know, Katrina. I'm not a preacher."

That was the sum total of any spiritual discussion I tried to flush from Leon's philosophical bunker. The fact that he paid heed to all that surrounded him, but neglected the only part of himself that lived forever mystified me.

Preacher Sweeney called the congregation to stand and sing.

For curiosity's sake, I positioned my handbag in such a way that forced me to turn and adjust it before I could take my seat. But the chorus went round and round getting lengthier in its customary fashion. I turned to dig through my handbag and pretended to search for chewing gum. From my perch, I lifted my eyes in a casual way and glanced back at the Houston brothers. The sight was candy to my sweet-starved soul. Sol Houston did not just sing, he moved and swayed, his eyes alight with every bar of the chorus.

Sol and his brother, a year younger, moved away from their momma and daddy's pew. They now hobnobbed fully with the other young people who all sat at the very rear of the church. I wound myself away from my grandmother's side months ago and toward the front. But it seemed the closer I got to God, the lonelier I felt. Sitting next to Leon was better than sitting alone.

No church in town touted girls as pretty as Mockingbird First Community. They looked nothing like their mommas. The old ways had been cast aside to allow for shorter hemlines and the painted faces my grandmother so despised.

My fingers continued the search for Juicy Fruit a moment longer. Sol wore a knit shirt that fit his sinewy form well. He allowed his hair to grow, much against custom in the valley, and it fell across his brow in black, silken defiance. The tallest of the Houstons, Sol had a physique that looked like it belonged on a "Be Proud! Be a Marine!" poster. He had a sensible manner, a shimmering charm that drew people to him, especially the girls from the pillar families—those who had attended the church since their conception.

"Need some gum?" Leon held out a piece to me.

My face felt flushed, so I kept my head down while I slid the powdered stick from his fingers. Then I closed my eyes in hopes that Leon took my cue to leave me to my thoughts in prayer. It was not completely deceitful to believe that I was praying. It resembled a prayer in the same sense that beggars beseech the heavens for a scrap of bread. That's how I first came to God—as a beggar. Now I was simply begging him for Sol Houston.

The choir burst forth in a final strain of "I'll Fly Away."


Jenny McAbee and her boyfriend, Albert, often double-dated with Leon and me—a great relief, since I seldom wanted to be alone with him.

Jenny had likeable ways, but not a serious thought in her head. She sprayed her hair with Sun-In so many times it turned copper first and then a sort of brownish straw. Everything but the dazzling blond shade she so desired. Although we shared a civics class, Jenny and I did not link up until we found ourselves alone one night at the Pope County fair. She walked right up to me as I stood in line at the Tilt-A-Whirl and said straight out, "Want to hang out?"

She never said much about Albert, but I always knew she stayed with him only until a better choice floated her way.

Our foursome spent most Saturday afternoons at Long Pool, a placid lake that formed a raging river in the spring. Even the best of canoeists stayed away from the roiling waters in March and April. But by July, the sun bore down so fiercely it drove us to the tranquil banks to loll in the shade by day and roast marshmallows at sundown. A string of massive oaks lined the entire length of Long Pool, except for the clearing where the state dumped brown river sand and called it a beach.

For years, yards of rope hung from the strongest tree limbs and provided us with the best Tarzan swings around. A flat-topped boulder, festooned with crisp, dried algae, rose up out of the lake, a good fifteen feet from the water's surface. Erosion had dug out handholds in just the right places. We called it Long Pool Rock, for lack of a better name. Once we swam out to the slick green ledge that rose out of the water, we all fought to be the first to dive from it.

Leon leaped from the edge, grabbed his thick white thighs, and shrieked, "Cannonball!" just seconds before he hit the surface and nearly emptied out the lake.

"So cliché, Leon." I yawned and stretched the edges of my towel out beneath my tanned legs.

"Why is that cliché?" Jenny asked.

"Everyone does a cannonball off Long Pool Rock."

"Nothin' wrong with that," Albert said. He hollered and let out a whoop before dropping his own misshapen frame into the cool green waters.

"Do you think anyone in Mockingbird Valley has imagination?" I asked Jenny.

"You have one. Got to have one to see something in Leon."

I grabbed her calf with my toes and pinched.

"You're feelin' mighty brave, girl."

Before she could retaliate, I stood and took two steps toward the boulder's precipice, then lunged straight out. My arms came around and then forward to form a perfect V. With nothing but air between myself and the water, I drew in my knees while my form turned one and a half times before stretching out into the vertical arrow that launched me straight toward the bottom of the lake. I slid in, leaving hardly a wake. I opened my eyes and saw nothing but the cerulean depth as I glided downward to a stop. With serene mermaid strokes, I moved forward, not wanting it to end. As I paused, feeling the lake effervesce around me and a school of fins flutter past my ankles, time stood still for a moment. I basked in not belonging to anyone for the few sacred seconds it took to rise to the surface When my head bobbed up, I saw three forms looking from high upon the boulder.

Jenny clapped, my lone fan, while Leon and Albert stared dumbly.

"What was that, Katrina?" Albert said.

"Imagination, Albert. Imagination."

CHAPTER 4

$S$unday afternoon the wind picked up. Lightning intruded upon our quiet June trance, surprising us with things known, just like Uncle Ned leaving Aunt Velda again. Clouds, appearing blue and bruised, cluttered the hilly horizons. Momma closed up all the windows and pulled the box fan in from the sill in the living room. "Hear that, Ho? It's goin' to storm." She had a quiver in her tone.

"Don't get yourself all twisted in a knot," Daddy said.

When Momma was a girl, her mother, my Meemaw, feared twisters. She imagined she saw one every time lightning licked the sky or thunder slammed its belly against the firmament. She would grab my mother by the hand and run screaming across the yard to her sister's place.

On many a turbulent night, Momma woke Eden and me and herded us out to the car, rain pounding our little blond heads. With her eyes so wild, she looked the little child herself. She would scream at Daddy, saying, "Just stay here, then, and get killed!" Each time Daddy waved at us from the rear kitchen door. Momma would drive us out to the ballpark. We would sit quietly until she felt the threshing storm had passed. We went along with it until we got old enough to lose our belief in Santa and demon-possessed storms.

"Daddy, Aunt Velda's here," I said.

"Ho, don't you let her in. We both know what that woman's about—to manipulate you out of some money. Pippa told us we'd be hearin' from her, and here she comes."

"Why does Velda think Daddy's got money?" I asked.

Daddy gave Momma a foul look.

"Ho, your baby sister is here." Velda pressed her face against the screen.

"Why, come in, Velda, before you get yourself wet," said Daddy.

Velda wore a green polyester summer suit, tattered at the hem. Momma called it her "beggar's suit."

Momma turned her back on Velda. She stirred her tea and cut herself a piece of cherry pie.

"Fix us all a hunk of that pie, Donelle." Daddy waited as Velda crossed the threshold into the kitchen.

Momma dug out two little slabs and dropped each onto a plate. "Have your pie, then," she said.

"Ho, Ned left me and the kids again."

"I heard, Velda."

"How we goin' to make it?"

"Now, Velda, Ned's got his flaws, but he'll see you and those kids get supper on the table. I'll call him."

"He's left town, Ho. Ain't none of us can call him." Her voice took on a high, tinny pitch. It unnerved Momma when she carried on so.

I turned on the iron. "I'll finish the ironing," I said to Momma.

"Velda, you took all our family's land. What happened to that money?" Momma asked.

"That was Ned's doin', don't you see? I ain't got nothin' now."

"You've got that house." Momma cut her eyes at Daddy.

"But what will I do, Ho? Tell Donelle to listen to me. Who else can I go to?" Velda wiped tears, wrung fists, and toyed with my daddy's sensitivities. She stumbled into the living room and curled up in Momma's chair. Her shriveled frame, abused by years of night-clubbing and chain smoking, curled into a fetal slump in the curve of the chair.

"Don't talk like I'm not in the room, Velda!" Momma said.

"You goin' to let her scream at me, Ho, your baby sister?"

"She's destitute, Donelle. What am I supposed to do?" Daddy paced. Agitation consumed him.

"Give her *one dime* and I'm takin' the girls and leaving, Ho!"

I turned off the iron.

"What if we just write her a check for a few hundred, Donelle? What's the harm?"

"I'll take it," Velda said.

"Hobart Hurley, you make me and these girls run around in rags, but let this sot squeeze out a few tears—"

"She's callin' me names, Ho!"

"You shut up and listen to me, Velda!" Momma trembled. I hated to see her like that and felt sick about it.

"You just listen to me! I know about your shenanigans, Donelle, and I've kept it to myself." Velda jerked the cigarette from her thin red lips. "But I'll not protect you anymore!"

"What is she talking about, Donelle?"

"She's manipulating you, Ho! Can't you see that?"

"My poor brother was laid up in the hospital and you were out romancin' behind his back." Velda threw back her head and blew out a stream of smoke.

"You lyin' witch!"

"Velda, why do you say that?" Daddy slumped onto the sofa.

"Everyone knew but you, Ho! While you lay helpless, Donelle took advantage."

"I'll tear your hair out!" Momma shrieked.

"Just like that congressman you had an affair with back when it was in all the papers, Donelle! Was it him, Donelle? You still hold a torch for the honorable J. B. Holderman?" Velda asked. Her eyes glinted with a sick sense of power.

"Velda, that's enough!" Daddy stood and tossed his cigarette into a sandbag ashtray.

"Momma, Daddy?" I lifted my denim purse from the sofa.

"Go to your room, Katrina!" Momma said.

"What did I do?"

"Nothin', honey. You just got a whore for a mother." Velda smiled like a child ready to spend her copper penny.

Momma lunged for Velda. "I'll kill you dead!"

"Donelle!" Daddy grabbed Momma's arms and pulled them back like butterfly wings.

"Aunt Velda, don't you call my mother that!" Hot tears stung my eyes.

"I'm leaving, Ho! And I'll just tell the whole town you turned your back on blood!"

"Leave and don't come back!" Momma shrieked.

"Go on, Velda. Give Donelle some time." Daddy stood poised with his bad leg against the sofa while he held on to my mother.

"I'll not leave until you say you'll help me."

"Here, Velda." I dug fifty dollars from my purse. "Take it. And go on."

"You're a sweet one, little Kat. Ho, you've raised yourself a good child—now don't let anyone say any different." Velda took the money.

"Don't you take my baby's money!" Momma shrieked.

Velda waltzed out the back door, waving one hand with my wad of bills cavalierly clipped between two fingers. She ran out to her car just as rain started pelting the glass bottles on our back porch.

She had slapped, scratched, stabbed, or blessed out every member of Daddy's family at least once. The saccharine words she poured out on my father had only one motive—her desire for my daddy's pocketbook. At the time, even I did not know that the reason we lived so dirt poor was because my father hoarded every penny, fearful that another Depression would take us all away. Velda's knack for sniffing out hidden lucre baffles me to this day.

"Katrina, you ought not to have given Velda your money," Daddy said.

"What about you, Ho?" Momma asked. "You ought not give her any, either."

Daddy wanted Momma to come into the kitchen, but she would not go. Eden peeked in from the hallway, curious, and buttoning up her blouse. I thought I saw a trace of mascara on her lashes.

"You know Velda's a liar, Ho!" Momma said.

"Let's don't air family problems in front of the girls." Daddy lit another cigarette.

"I worked and cared for our two babies, Ho, the whole time you was in the hospital. You know I was faithful."

"Come in the kitchen."

"I'll not go with you in there until you say you believe me. Say it, Ho!"

"I believe you, Donelle."

Momma ran from the room. "Families is turnin' against families.

The world must be comin' to an end! She hid herself in the bathroom for the rest of that Sunday. I thought I heard her crying. She did not mind yelling in front of us but she would take a beating before she would let us see her cry.

"Who is J. B. Holderman?" I knew better than to ask Momma, so I asked my grandmother instead.

"Who told you that name?" Meemaw kept her eyes forward while my grandfather drove us to church again that night. The wiper blades squeaked back and forth, slinging rain against the side windows. The car smelled mustier than usual in the rain, like cellar dust.

I memorized the Holderman name in hopes of unearthing the man's identity on my own.

"I just heard him talked about. He's a politician or something, right?" I asked.

"Somethin' like that."

Grandpa never said a word. He pursed his lips and sighed.

"He's a congressman, right, Meemaw?"

"Why do you want to know, Katrina?"

Her voice sounded funny to me. I did not heed well the warning. "I like politics, that's all."

"God knows if you're lyin', girl."

"Why would I lie?"

"Don't bring up that name ever again."

"All right, then." I paused for just a moment. "Do you know the Houstons?"

Saturday brought clear weather and ushered in a mountain festival attended by most of the valley dwellers. But Eden never attended public events for the same reason Momma seldom left the house. A crowd made her feel embarrassed.

The summer sunset kissed a trail of scarlet along the Chevy's back window behind Eden. It was rare for Eden to recognize the image in the rearview mirror at all. She thought it silly the way Katrina and her friends all but twisted the car mirror off the front windshield to examine their mascara every ten minutes. She never checked herself in the car mirror. Mirrors reflected none of the good and all of the bad. Besides, the boy she dated never took the time to notice things like mascara or sunsets.

The drive-in speakers next to the driver's side of the car cackled out the attendant's request for their food order. Her date, Darrell Lunsford, responded in a nasally tone, "Hold on a minute." He reminded Eden of the dud card in Katrina's Dating Game box. Darrell always smelled of engine oil and allowed the black grease to meld with his fingertips.

Momma and Katrina had quibbled over the meaning of *dud* the first time the two sisters sat down to play the game. Momma contended that the grease monkey–looking character was just a hard-working man who earned his keep and kept food on the table. Katrina shot back that even a two-fifty-an-hour grease monkey should have a decent respect for a bar of Lava soap.

The fact that they argued over it at all confirmed the gorge that widened between Katrina and her parents.

Somehow, Momma's argument had soothed Eden.

"What you want, Eden? Tater tots with a corn dog?" Darrell's words annoyed Eden, although she could not determine why. He watched her drop a candy wrapper to the floor and then scooped it up. Things like that annoyed her too.

"Get me a hamburger and a Coke. That's all."

"Want mustard on that?" Darrell ground his teeth together. When he asked her a question he always looked as though he had been slapped as a child for asking too many questions. Eden never met his folks, so she did not know exactly how he got along with them. For that matter, she never recalled meeting any boy's folks. It was not the custom in her circle of friends. But she was certain some persuasive relative had cut his hair at home and that they disagreed about the length. It was cropped short around his face with a longer shank of hair hanging down the back. Katrina would call it "faux shag."

"No," Eden said.

"No, what?"

"I don't want mustard."

"Something wrong with you?"

Eden drew back her shoulders, then jutted her head forward as though she examined a cockroach she was about to crush.

"Baby, if I've done something to make you mad, I'm sorry."

"Just order me the burger, Darrell. If I want to sit and think sometime, ain't nothin' wrong with that. Is there?"

"Well, tell me what you're thinkin' about. We'll think together."

"Shut up, Darrell! Some thangs is private."

The boy placed the order, but Eden saw how mad she made him.

"I saw Leon out at the bowlin' alley. Is Katrina marryin' that jerk?"

"Did he say that?"

"Not in so many words. No."

The sun performed a disappearing act behind the crest of Skyline Drive. Before the drive-in parking lot darkened, the fluorescent bulbs snapped, flickered, and then illuminated the cars with a cheap purple haze.

Their food arrived and they ate in silence. Eden took her time and carefully peeled back the wrapper around the burger. Darrell finished his foot-long Coney right away and then started up the engine on his sixty-nine Chevy. A small fuzzy Dalmatian vibrated from the mirror. Eden thought about how she was only ten years old the year Darrell's car was manufactured. Only five years later, fate placed her in the front seat of it. She surprised herself that she even thought of it. It was a thought that Katrina might toss around.

"What's the hurry?" Eden asked.

"Tonight's the night, baby."

"Darrell, I said I don't want you pressuring me."

"Move over here next to me." He patted the seat without looking at her. Then his right arm slid up to grasp the back of the seat while he turned to check for any other wet-behind-the-ears motorist that might cruise past in the quest to find an empty slot at Al's on a Saturday night. "Look there. Bobby Peters put new glass packs on his Ford truck. I'd die for those. Die." He revved the engine.

"Let me finish eating, Darrell, will you?"

"I drive. You eat."

Eden disappeared inside herself, an art she had practiced since age three. Her first remembrance of this skill focused around a particular Easter day in the park.

Katrina had walked her across the street to her first egg hunt. Momma dressed them both in cotton dresses with puffy sleeves. Eden's frock was a passive yellow with tiny white buttons shaped like rabbits with orange smocking across the bodice. Katrina had always been more mindful of color than Eden, so she habitually chose the more assertive color for herself; in this case, a royal blue. Eden didn't care. She always wound up with Katrina's wardrobe by default anyway.

Families from all over the valley gathered in the park to join in the annual citywide egg hunt. Eden did not remember collecting eggs. But the basket filled with green cellophane straw and three large candy eggs had appeared miraculously in her lap. Five-year-old Katrina sat next to her and assisted her with the clear wrapper of a lovely purple egg, calling it "the grape one," as opposed to the neglected "lemon or orange one." Daddy kept paper bags filled with citrus-flavored candy in the house year-round, so the girls might have neglected orange or lemon, but never the grape. The purple egg tasted nothing like grape, but it was delicious and sweet, more a marriage of cotton candy and marshmallows. The two of them might have sat in the sun, basking in their quiet sisterhood, Easter egg communion all day had the stranger not appeared.

Eden sensed the change in her sister and noticed the way her shoulders tightened while a short gasp shot from her tender lips. Katrina scooted away, crablike. Her feet and the palms of her hands became her swiftest escape.

Eden followed her sister's timorous stare. A large black lens gaped at her. She froze and sat limply, like one of her old dolls.

The man said, "Smile, honey," and she did as she was told. Then she disappeared inside herself. That was just the first time, though.

The next day, Momma made Daddy go out and buy extra copies of the evening paper. She called Katrina a coward for running from the newspaper photographer and declared Eden a natural-born model. The curly-haired Hurley child graced the front cover of the *Mockingbird Daily,* and for one brief moment, she reveled in the glory of her fame. Momma phoned every aunt, and they all oozed over Eden's photogenic qualities.

It would have sat well with Eden, but Momma always made certain that Katrina was within earshot, so she could feel the certain sting of defeat. Momma often concocted traits like that for Eden in front of Katrina. She said things like, "Eden's really the girl with the brains," or "Katrina's got book smarts, but Eden's the child with the most common sense." It was her way of keeping Katrina down and trying her best to elevate Eden to a thinking-man's level, although Momma had never tasted of that cup herself. Momma's own brand of social order had a sense of balance, and she spent most of her energy trying to make the girls equal. But it only made Eden feel like less. It only made her feel like disappearing again.

"Have you ever been to Twinkle Land?"

Eden had forgotten that there was somebody else in the car. She lifted her gaze to meet Darrell's and struggled to remember why she was with him in the first place. "Twinkle Land. Ain't that where all the bad girls go?"

Leon never fully understood my gratitude to him for falling from grace. The longstanding nature of our relationship had little to do with my interest in him and a lot to do with the fact that it never migrated from a colorless neutral.

Momma had taken to baking whole cherry pies for him, and although she reserved her references to him as the "future son-in-law" for my ears only, the fact that she did so only served to increase my anxiety. Hill people speckled her ancestry, and despite the fact that arranged marriages no longer forced custom over a girl's will, the taint of it still colored her words.

Small festivals drew large crowds in the valley. So the annual Mount Nebo Chicken Fry drew families from three counties to see who would take the top prize for the Little Mr. Pullet and Little Miss Drumstick crowns. Fried chicken sputtered in oily vats, along with Texas fries and hush puppies, while hundreds of locals filed into line, eager to satiate their hunger.

Teenage girls took turns parading off and on to a little platform, graced by three-foot letters that twinkled with shake-on silver glitter and Elmer's glue, announcing the 1974 Miss Poultry Pageant. If a Chicken-Fry spectator had a mind to do so, he could pull up his best lawn chair and be regaled all afternoon by the pomp and splendor of the best little talents in the region. The winner dripped with appreciation and called herself a "pageant personality" for the entire year, racking up a portfolio full of grocery store appearances. The losers spat nails and plotted how they might take away the title next summer. Each girl vied with the zeal of a presidential candidate, topping out her daddy's budget in upwards of five figures for some of those showy gowns—all for a one-thousand-dollar scholarship and an infinitesimal moment in the sun. But mostly for the latter.

My remembrance of the 1974 Miss Poultry Pageant is clear for only one particular reason. Leon took his place in line behind those nonessential elements that remain a part of my past.

Jenny and I had planned a trip to the shopping center that morning to pick out a new blouse each and matching sandals. Although wearing identical outfits with my sister conjured up the worst of taboos, dressing like a best girlfriend still had its merits.

We arrived atop Mount Nebo earlier than intended. Leon and Albert arrived at dawn, young initiates of the fry-cook brigade. Jenny and I tooled around the swimming pool for a while in her Daddy's Jeep, then decided to surprise the boys and see if they could slip us a plate of food behind the chow line.

Upon our arrival at the cooks' pavilion, we circled twice before we finally spotted Albert bent over and flipping chicken parts. He was coated in flour and ready for the frying vat himself.

"Oh, hi, Albert." Jenny liked making up different voices. If she hid behind a curtain, you would swear you stood inches from Edith

Bunker. So when Albert looked up, startled, it did not strike me as odd. Not right away.

"Jenny, Katrina. You're here."

"Of course we're here, silly," I said.

"Leon went for another sack of flour." Albert stared into the vat and shoved around several pieces, lending too much attention to the task. The fact that Leon went for flour did not surprise me. But Albert's shaky tone and the way his eyes raced from the front of the line to the rear, told me Albert knew more than he confessed.

I leaned forward. "Did I ask where Leon was?"

"No, I guess you didn't. But I knew you were about to ask, Katrina. I'm fast like that."

"Jenny, you see Leon?" I asked.

"Both of you, just wait. That boy'll be back in two shakes," Albert tried.

"I'll go look for Leon myself." I turned away and enjoyed the sputtering sound that Albert made, kind of like a little toy lawn engine in need of an overhaul.

It did not take long to find Leon. I only had to follow Albert's tortured gaze. He led me smack into the furtive tryst with one of the less fortunate contestants in the Miss Poultry pageant. The poor girl, Lela Starbuck and her dancing poodles, had not even made it through the first round, and so I found her in Leon's arms, desperate for consolation.

While she cried, he stroked her hair, and it took several minutes of my standing only inches from them with my arms folded before Leon finally looked up and saw me.

"Katrina? You're here."

"I'm here, Leon."

"Baby, I can explain."

"No need."

"Who is this girl, Leon?" the poodle contestant said.

"She's—Katrina is my girlfriend, Lela."

"You're the girl from the valley," she said to me, and I could tell my presence affected her in no manner. "I heard around school how Leon took up with a girl from the valley. What's the sense of that, I ask you?"

"Jenny can take me home," I said to Leon.

"Don't leave, girl. This is nothin'. Lela's just a—she's nothin' to me."

Lela swore at him then stepped away to readjust the sweaty straps on her pink chiffon gown. A ring of moisture formed around her thick girth.

Jenny appeared and stared at all three of us.

"I'm leaving, Leon. Don't call me again," I said.

"Katrina, please don't go."

I so appreciated Jenny for following me all the way to the Jeep without so much as a word. We took the longest winding road down the mountain into the hollow that led to the river's bridge. I reflected on the few good times with Leon and then realized how long it had been since I felt so relaxed.

"I'm sorry, Katrina. Leon's going to regret this and then he'll come around beggin', sorry dog that he is."

"Jenny, that's not what I want."

"But I always thought you two would be the first to marry."

"I never said that."

We drove a little farther in silence. I heard Jenny heave a sigh. "You're not sad."

The mountain and its jamboree loomed behind us. I watched over my shoulder until the trees absorbed the mountain music and the cheap lights and the rude clatter of the loud public-address system. In minutes the festival grew distant, while roving car lights moved like giant fireflies caught in a jar.

My hand quivered against my stomach and I laughed out loud and let out a strange kind of ritualistic whoop.

"You're crazy, girl. Have you lost it?"

"I'm free, Jenny. I don't care what Momma and Daddy say anymore. I'd rather die a spinster."

"You're right, you know. When I can't sleep at night, I think the worst thing in the world is bein' alone. But then when I've listened to Albert droning on about rebuilding a car engine, I can't help but wonder if this is all there is."

"Your daddy rebuilds car engines too, Jenny."

"It's heaven to him."

"What about you?"

"I'm not like you. I don't know what I want."

"All I know is that I won't find it here in the valley. I have to leave, Jenny. I'm dying here, real slowlike."

"Don't be morbid."

"I'm serious. Just dig a hole for me if I have to stay."

"I want to see you do it—leave, that is. You'll call me before it happens, won't you, Katrina?"

We slapped fives and headed for Al's to split a Cherry Coke, giddy from the tough talk. I added that if we spotted Eden, we could invite her to join two sophisticates for a girls' night out. We felt invincible and empowered all at once. What folly to believe such a thing endured in Mockingbird Valley.

A sixty-nine Chevy rolled up the gravel path to the hill some adolescent dreamer had long ago dubbed Twinkle Land. A developer once bought the property for the purpose of subdividing it into an upper-crust neighborhood. It included a twenty-acre hillside that lifted up above the river and at night seemed to kiss the sky. The financing for the subdivision never met with the bank's approval, and so Twinkle Land became renowned as the best make-out spot in the valley.

Eden sat even closer to the door, and when Darrell ground the gears and brought the Chevy to a halt, she stared straight ahead and said nothing.

"Don't be like that, baby. Slide on over here, and let's do a little nuzzling."

The chrome of the door latch felt cold against Eden's knuckles. She lifted her hand and shoved it down with a force. Before Darrell could say a word, she slipped out of the car and left the door standing open. The walk to the crest of the hill invigorated her. A barge floated down the river, while the horns blasted from the lock. Eden had never seen this part of the valley and wondered why Momma stayed so holed up all the time, worried that the world might come to an end. If it did, she would stand on this crest to watch the last star fall into the river. Beauty could certainly be found even in the throes of nature's final moments.

"Girl, what are you doing?"

"Hey," she greeted Darrell, glad she made him leave his Chevy. He looked more vulnerable in the moonlight when he wasn't clutching the gearshift and shouting obscenities out the window to his friends.

"We goin' to stand out here in the middle of nothin' all night?" he asked.

"Who drove us out here?" She pulled a cigarette from his shirt pocket and held it up for him to light.

"It wasn't my idea to stand out here on this ledge like two crows." He lit her cigarette with a disposable lighter. It flickered just enough to fire up the tobacco. Then he hurled it off the crest, and it disappeared into the dark.

"You think lookin' at this river is doing nothin'?"

"You're talkin' nonsense, Eden."

"Don't say that. I'm sick to death of hearin' how stupid everyone thinks I am."

"I ain't heard nobody say you're stupid."

The wind turned and lifted Eden's hair off her shoulders. She blew out a hard breath of smoke and watched it swirl in the wind and around her face. It surprised her that the barge moved so fast and shrunk so small in such a short amount of time.

"Let's go back to the truck, Eden. You look kind of chilly."

"I'm goin' to build me a house out here someday."

"Ain't nobody can afford it. That's why it's still sittin' here vacant."

"I like it."

"I like you." Darrell tried to pull her close, but she stepped away again. It caused him to swear and throw down his cap with the razorback hog emblazoned above the bill.

"You don't love me, Darrell."

"Don't put words in my mouth. You know that makes me mad."

"Look at me and say you love me." Eden pressed her elbow into her hip. She jutted out the two fingers that held the cigarette.

Darrell pretended to have a sudden interest in the valley. "You can see Mount Nebo from here."

"Not that I care, Darrell. I don't love you, either."

"What's it supposed to feel like, anyway? Girls are always talkin' about love. It's just a way to get what they want from guys."

"I've not asked you for a blessed thing, Darrell."

"We can give one another somethin' tonight."

"Say it, Darrell! Why don't you just go ahead and say it?"

"Let's fall in love tonight, baby. I'm game."

"It can wait, can't it? My sister is doin' everything the right way. I can do that too."

"Someone's pulled the wool over your eyes, girl. Your sister lost her virginity weeks ago."

"You're a liar, Darrell!"

"Leon told me all about it. Guys talk. She's happy about it. You act like lightning's going to strike or hell's going to open up and swallow you. You have to learn about love sooner or later. Katrina's a woman now. When will you grow up, Eden?"

"She didn't tell me."

"Maybe she's afraid Little Sister will tattle to Momma. It's her business."

Darrell slid his hands up Eden's shoulders. He said gently, "You got chill bumps. Let me warm you up."

Eden didn't fight him anymore. She buried her face in his chest. The news about Katrina had the same effect on her as if she had been told she had died. Living up to her high-and-mighty standards angered her at times. But hearing that Katrina had given up the one thing she flashed around like sophomores flashed their driver's licenses saddened Eden. Never would Eden admit that she had placed her sister upon the highest pedestal, a pedestal that she never dared ascend. But she knew the truth in her heart. She hated herself for believing that Katrina flew with the angels. Maybe Momma and Daddy weren't far from wrong. Maybe the world had come to an end.

"I'm scared, Darrell."

"We'll take time, so much time, baby. You like the stars? Let's do it right here beneath the stars, right where we'll build that house."

She smiled and he kissed her face. Twinkle Land was such a lovely place to dream.

CHAPTER 5

*I* remember the pain of being the child on the side of the road, waving good-bye when a best friend moved away. Like the time Rebecca, who had lived with her mother in the rent house that Momma hated, moved. Rebecca had played with Eden and me that summer along Galla Creek. She learned the fine art of crawdad catching faster than most girls and was not squeamish in the least, while others found us beyond primitive.

One night, using stolen matches and stealing away ourselves, we roasted marshmallows over a camp grill in the park. It was then that she told me the most hideous secret about her mother' s boyfriend. Right away, I broke my promise to her and told Momma about the lecher who slipped into her room at night. Momma tore over to Rebecca's house without hesitation but left me at home. Rebecca and her momma moved the next week. Such was life in the rental district.

I lived the despair of the lone molecule trapped within its own membrane while it watched the other cells grow and divide and progress into something else or journey onward. Momma and Daddy never moved or changed or traveled beyond the misty veils of the Ozark ridge.

That, I believe, is why outsiders called us "green." Our exposure to society's changes was fed to us over the airwaves: reruns of *I Love Lucy* and *The Real McCoys*. I hated the assertion by some that we were simpletons let loose upon the earth, no eyes with which to see, no ears with which to listen. But I knew it to be true. I was green to any kind of shift away from the axis of ordinariness. So when we faced our summer of change, I was caught unaware. It was not anything as pleasant as a transformation or even as hopeful as a metamorphosis. Our change always tasted bitter.

Eden drifted so far from me that I scarcely recognized her. When our eyes met, she looked away. The prettiest thing about her was her hair. It hung like auburn silk around her shoulders. But even that had lost its sheen. She had vaunted such a flirtatious femininity as a young child. When Momma dressed her in lace, she always made a big show of rustling about and reminding us of her girlishness. But now she hurried past us with shoulders stooped and arms crossed unnaturally at her bosom, as though she wanted to hide from our sight.

Our days of communing as sisters along the banks of Galla Creek dissipated along with any qualities we once held in common. So it surprised me the morning she crawled into my bed and wrapped her arms around me.

"Are you awake, Katrina?"

"I am now."

"I'm sick. When I stand up, everything spins, and when I lay down, I feel worse. I think I'm dyin'. Is this what it feels like?"

Eden's theatrics were not unknown to me. Once when she had a headache, she made an appointment with the school counselor and told her that she had a brain tumor and that her parents neglected such things.

"Go tell Momma you're sick. Good grief, Eden, it's only six in the morning. Don't you know I took that job at the pizza place? I got off work this morning at two!"

"Can't tell Momma I'm sick."

Before I could reply, Eden bolted from the bed and stumbled into our shared bathroom. I knew her retching might draw our mother, so I slipped from the bed and closed the door behind us. She looked pathetic and colorless, curled in a heap with her face in the john.

"Quick, Katrina, wet me a washrag for my face."

"Did you drink last night, Eden?" I ran cold water over a cloth. She swore at me.

"Fine. I'll go get Momma. Let her deal with this."

"No, Katrina, close that door!"

"Momma and Daddy know about your drinking, anyway."

"I didn't get drunk." She sat back on her feet while I wiped her face.

"I'm not asking you again."

"I may have gotten myself into a mess." Her face contorted while the tears flowed.

"What happened?"

"I just want to know one thing before I tell you, Katrina."

"Okay."

"Why did you give in to Leon?"

"You're not making sense, girl."

"You lost your virginity, Katrina. How could I stand up to Darrell after that?"

Her words startled me. I felt cold inside.

"Darrell told me all about it. Leon has a big mouth."

"Eden, if Leon said that, he lied."

"It's okay. I did it too. I'm not about to tell Momma."

"You're not listening to me, Eden. I didn't lose anything. Especially that."

Eden sat in silence, stunned and unable to breathe.

"You gave in to that scum Darrell because he lied to you about me?"

She nodded and her body shook while she sobbed. I held her hair back from her face and let her cry for a moment or two. "Eden, I broke up with Leon. But you think I'm about to tell Momma?"

"When did you break up with him?"

"The night of the Chicken Fry."

She threw herself on me and cried some more. "I should have known Darrell was a liar. You're too pure to do such a thing. I swear, one day, Katrina, they'll make you a saint."

"They don't make Protestants saints, Eden."

"They should start. Leastways when you die, you'll be an angel."

"They don't make humans angels, either."

Eden toppled forward and buried her face in a large terry towel. "Get me Momma's sleepin' pills. I want to sleep and not wake up."

"You hush that talk! Now you tell me straight what's going on. Did Darrell get you in trouble?"

Eden nodded and when she opened her eyes, I felt as though I looked into the soul of a five-year-old. I warned our folks about Darrell, of his crude ways, and his reputation for deflowering young girls who hailed from the unlucky side of town. Every night Eden flew out the door with him, Momma and I had fought.

"I haven't had a period in two months. How can I know for sure, Katrina?"

"I don't know. Momma says you get pregnant every time."

"She's done it at least twice then. Maybe I've just got the flu."

"Maybe you do. You know your cycle's never been perfect. But if I drive you over to old Doc Miller's all his nurses will make a beeline to the phones."

"Tell me what to do, Katrina. I'll do whatever you say."

"We could drive down to the county health clinic. But we have to be careful. Daddy's card-playing buddies hang out on the steps of the clinic when they're giving out that free commodity cheese."

"I'll go get dressed." Eden shambled back to her room and closed the door.

I used powdered cleanser on the fixtures and mopped the bathroom floor. It surprised Momma to find me cleaning the floor just beyond the hours of dawn. But it pleased her too, so she hurried back down the hall to the kitchen to start the coffee and eat a bowl of Special K before the sun came out too hot and ruined her chances for digging potatoes.

I walked to the kitchen and stood by the rear door. I still wore the same smiley-face T-shirt and faded cutoffs I had fallen asleep in the night before. Momma and Daddy sat opposite one another in the kitchen alcove as they shared the newspaper, neither saying a word to the other. Momma had painted everything daffodil—the walls, the sideboards, and the cabinets. Modern décor confounded her. So she simply chose one color and allowed it to dominate a whole room. The sunlight spilled into the yellow kitchen, melded together the walls, the cabinets, and the floors—a butter-colored cube. I stared at them, two bronze beings, for once appearing dignified, and otherworldly. No foolish soul dared break that spell, I decided.

I could not bring myself to confess Eden's plight anyway. If the clinic nurse confirmed her pregnancy, Eden's task of breaking our vow of silence would be carried on without me.

"I haven't seen much of Leon lately." Momma sipped her black coffee and finished off a piece of dark toast. Braided yarn lay across her lap. Every night for a week, we braided yarn until our cuticles were frayed and fuzzy. Momma wanted a homemade rug. Her latest project consumed her, like the yellow cabinet that turned into a brilliant sun of a kitchen. This morning I was glad for her consumption.

"His daddy's had him working long hours at the Boat and Bait." I stood erect and walked over to look out the window.

"You found a hard workin' young man," Daddy said, then stubbed out his cigarette. "You hold on to that one, Katrina."

"You digging potatoes today?" I asked. The long handles of Daddy's gardening tools were left leaning against the peach tree. I knew that if I said Leon's name, the resentment and the truth would spill out soon thereafter. But the longer I stared out the window, not confessing what I wanted them to know, the more cowardly I felt.

"Yes, and we could sure use your help, Katrina. We got two rows of Red Pontiac, and we've got to get them rolled around in the wheel barra and shoved under the house."

"I'm working later on at the Pizza Delight. Barry's got me on that late shift. I hate it. Sometimes we don't get out of that place until three in the morning."

"Nothin' wrong with long hours. You keep it up and they'll be promotin' you." I heard the click of Daddy's lighter again but did not look at him. The most wonderful string of sarcastic remarks passed through my mind, but I held my tongue. My pity for the mire that lay ahead for Eden helped me keep my wits about me.

"I heard you girls up early," Momma said. She stood to brush the toast crumbs from her bosom.

Daddy ran his thumb beneath the thin white strap of his undershirt and stared out the window. A small flock of martins moved into his birdhouse and seemed to transfix him. "Eden wants me to take her shopping for some back-to-school things." I pretended sudden interest in the scorched ironing board cover and rearranged the straight pins stuck into the end of it.

When Momma lifted her face and cocked it to one side, regret told me I had blurted out what was implausible. Eden had not shopped for herself in years and only wore the simplest and most boyish pieces from her wardrobe, all of them brought home and hung in her closet by our mother.

"You got that girl to go shopping?" Momma asked.

"Say, you take her on, then. Get her some trousers," said Daddy.

"Good night, Ho, she ain't no boy. Here, Katrina. Let me give you some money." Momma rushed right past and went for the brown patchwork handbag she kept on a nail in her closet. She had no reason to doubt me. I was her honest child. But the fact that she trusted me released a cage full of guilt inside. When she handed me a crisp twenty, I thought lightning would strike. "And while you're out, pick me up some cake flavorin'."

I stared at the twenty for a moment, then Eden bristled in.

"Katrina's taking me over to Belinda Moorefield's house. I'll be gone most of the day." Eden walked between Momma and me as she snapped the strap of her shoulder bag over her right shoulder. Then she opened the door and left me standing with my hand out, mouth agape.

"Belinda Moorefield's? I thought you two were going shoppin'."

"*First,* we're going shopping. *Then,* that's when we're—I'm—dropping Eden off at Belinda's." I felt the twenty slipped into my hand in a gingerly fashion. A thin bead of sweat traveled down my spine.

If Momma detected my lie, she did not articulate it. My feet could not carry me fast enough out to the old cocoa brown Chevy Daddy gave us to drive.

Before I slammed the car door, Momma stuck her head out and hollered, "Katrina, Leon's on the phone."

"Tell him I'm gone."

"He said he's on his way over here. Want me to have him meet you two?"

"No!" Eden and I yelled in unison. Our eyes locked, and we waited while Momma stared at us.

"What does *he* want?" I hissed.

"He misses you, Katrina. He must have really made you mad." Eden studied me in a kind of imperious fashion.

"He says tell you he'll be over later." Momma slammed the door shut.

Gravel skittered behind us as I peeled out of the drive.

I brooded in silence until we were a block away. "Why did you make up that story about going to Belinda Moorefield's? I told Momma I was taking you shopping."

"Shoppin'? At least I told her somethin' believable."

"You're making me crazy, Eden."

"Don't blame me!"

"If I'm the driver, let me come up with the excuse."

Eden said little for most of the drive into town.

"I can't believe I lied for you, Eden."

She fidgeted around in her purse and then, after a nervous glance my way, drew out nothing. "Stop spewin'. You sound like an old cat."

"I know what you're looking for. You can't smoke in my car, anyway. Besides, if you're pregnant, you need to quit."

"I'm lookin' for a tissue and don't say it all out in the open like that." She sniffed at me, but I couldn't tell if real tears were welling up again or not. "Remember, I'm fifteen. Just seems like we put away our dolls yesterday and—do you still have that little tea set, the one with the baby roses?" She let out a ragged breath. "Let's talk about those good times and nothin' else. Okay?"

From that moment on, Eden always referred to our past as the "good times." I could tell when she spoke about it, her mind had perfected our past into an assortment of bright and wonderful colors while she dulled the present to a colorless sepia ink. As for her future, she gave no thought to it at all.

"After this is all over, want to go to Al's for a burger? We haven't done that in a long time. Momma gave us a twenty." I drummed the steering wheel as we approached the road that led to the county health office.

Eden did not speak again until she had to answer questions for the nurse at the clinic.

A big fierce looking woman took down Eden's information but kept shifting her eyes to me as though I had placed this burden myself on my sister. At least she made me feel that way.

"Don't I know you? Who's your daddy?" She flicked the pen head up and down.

"Eden, why don't you answer the questions for the lady and I'll go and get us a Coke?"

"No, Katrina, don't go." Eden curled her arm through mine and held me tightly. Her eyes glistened, and I could see the dam just beginning to break.

"All right, I'll stay, but just talk to this woman, will you?" I nudged her toward the woman.

The door swung open and a real nurse appeared, one with a more appealing countenance. "Elvira, why don't I take care of this one and you take your break?"

"She's not answered any of the questions. I haven't given her a number. She can't go back without a number."

"We'll take care of it in back. I've got a few minutes till I go on break." She must have noticed my pensive face.

The room was already crowded with an assortment of mostly

women, laps and arms filled with children. The ages of the tykes varied, I supposed, according to the length of the relationship with their man. My gratefulness to the second woman for her swift rescue of Eden spilled over into whispered appreciation while Eden buried her face in my shirt. Another minute in that waiting room would have sent her emotions over the brink.

Eden looked so small as she looked over her shoulder at me from the clinic doorway and let them lead her from my sight. The look in her eye remained with me long after the swinging doors closed rudely behind her.

I might have wept, but fear barred any feelings other than the paralysis that accompanies dread. It was more numbness than feeling. I tried to do as Eden had suggested and remember the good times, but I could not strew flowers along that path. I do believe that goodness and bitterness can reside in the same house, but they are at war.

The hard plastic clinic chair irritated me, so I paced in front of the dingy plate glass and then planted myself in a corner that gave me a view of West Main. Being the hub of Mockingbird Valley, little change had come to the two-mile stretch in fifty years, other than the occasional new blacktop. But all the talk drifting around town spoke of nothing but change. The city authorities sweetened the pot with the promise of a lower tax base to seal the bid for a nuclear plant. Its construction along the lake soon began, along with the revenues that benefited the town with a new high school. Before long, West Main would reflect change just as Eden's once-small waistline would soon reveal her secret.

I pressed my forehead against the cold glass and questioned God's hand in all of it. I feared God too much to blame him for Eden's plight, but I had to ask him why. When I did, he touched me on the inside and I could smell the breath of him, right there in that sterile waiting room as my sister was poked and prodded and questioned on the other side of two swinging doors. Right there.

It gave me comfort when I realized he could handle any of my queries with grace, while at the same time pouring that grace out all over my life as though it hadn't cost him a thing. If Daddy had his say, I would have to believe that our lives were hapless and only a few lovely and serendipitous individuals could claim the right to share in the bounty of life. The rest of us, born under unlucky stars, were forced to work like slaves, then hide ourselves away and hope the whip did not find our backs. I refused to buy into a hopeless philosophy. Daddy reminded me more of an ant in an ant farm, tunneling and digging and scurrying as fast as he could to flee from an Unseen Power, all the while not realizing he was in plain sight of him.

A tear slipped across my cheek, and it relieved me. I closed my eyes and prayed for Eden, although I did not know how I should pray. But the Spirit knew all and was kind enough to take up where I left off.

"Miss Hurley?" The nurse who had walked Eden to the examination room looked at me, her reflection poorly clouding the melancholy that settled over her.

"Is Eden all right?"

"I'll take you back, Miss Hurley. She could use your support."

Times like that push you past the weeping. You stand more at the precipice of aching. It is a drier place. And stony.

"Eden?" I rapped at the flimsy door that separated us. The nurse nodded, urged me to go on in.

Eden sat slumped on the table in a clinic gown. Her toes looked white and shriveled as her bare feet dangled over the table's edge. The room was icy. "They still have to get back that test they're runnin' on me. But she says, that nurse says they's somethin' already growin' inside of me, Katrina. I want to run away from it." She strangled on

her words. "Get it away from me, Katrina. I…It don't belong in me."
She was slumped against the wall. Her trunk shook and she could
not stop crying.

"Dab your eyes. Here, take this tissue," I said.

"I don't want it. Dear God, I don't want it."

"How long until they know for sure?"

"An hour or two at least."

"Let's go for a drive and then come back. Momma's not expecting us for a while."

"You know what Daddy will do, don't you?"

"We won't let him do a thing. He'll just have to—to listen. For
once. Is it all right if you dress now?"

"They said I could."

"Let me help. You pull yourself together. If this is a baby, it's not
some alien life form growing inside you. It's a little child. You start
thinking of it like that, Eden—a baby with pretty little eyes, all its
fingers and toes."

"A baby."

She whispered it all the way out to the car.

CHAPTER 6

*E*den and I sat in the car, two stones. Instead of fully driving into the Hurley driveway, I hesitated near the mailbox. But reality told me it was too late to retreat. Leon and Darrell stood out on the lawn and talked with Momma and Daddy like members of the family instead of the interlopers I knew them to be. They all stopped and looked at us, and it appeared that some sort of verdict had been handed down, but in our absence. No fairness about it.

"Oh, this is just swell. Darrell's here, Katrina." Eden smoothed her hair. "Leon's with him and I just feel this is goin' to be awful. I just don't know what I'm goin' to say to him. What if he says he hates me and starts actin' like I'm just a slut and this baby ain't his? Daddy might believe him, and what will he do to me, then? I think I'll just want to die all over again."

"We can leave, Eden. But what would it accomplish to leave them standing out in the yard? It's not likely they'll go away until we've had our say and they've had theirs."

"What are you goin' to say?"

The envelope that bore the news of Eden's pregnancy lay in my lap. I drove her all the way around the lake and back up to Al's, all in hopes she could pull herself together. Eden never cried so hard, and the longer she wept the more I fumed. She cried and then smoked, and it would have taken a Mack truck to stop either one.

"I guess I'll just have to open my mouth and see what happens. But why don't you stay in the car, Eden? I don't want Darrell upsetting you."

"No, I can face him. I want to tell him myself." Her fingers gripped my sleeve and I sensed her ardor. "It's somethin' he has to face, and if he doesn't like it, well that's just the tough breaks, mister. But tellin' Daddy—when he finds out, he'll light into me. I know. I can sense this business."

"Eden, you shouldn't expect Darrell to do the right thing. He would make a horrible daddy, so don't expect that of him."

"You don't know that about him."

"And maybe it's better you tell Daddy with all of us here together."

"Do you always think so far ahead, Katrina? Can't I just sit here and figger it all out for myself?"

We looked at each other while the rain sprinkled around us, pinging off the glass and stirring up puffs of dust in the driveway. I knew where she needed to go, but I could not take her there myself. It was too wearying to try and live two lives when the other one made choices I could not control. "Figure it out, then." I stepped out of the car and left her fuming inside.

Leon and Darrell swaggered toward me, and their smug grins vexed me just enough to cause me to throw open the door.

Daddy limped up onto the porch and seated himself on the top step.

Rain clouds continued their move in from the west and continued to spit small droplets at me, just enough to make my skin feel sticky and uncomfortable. "Leon, I need to ask you something."

Leon leaned against my car, staring down at me in a haughty

way, his fingers shoved so tightly into his front pockets they turned white. "You didn't tell your folks about us breakin' up, did you?"

"There's a lot more we need to talk about, Leon, than our breakup."

"Your daddy's not too pleased, Katrina. But I told him I knew how to handle you."

"Shut up and listen to me, Leon."

Eden slid into the driver's seat and rolled down the window. The wind blew across her gauzy top. It sent cigarette ashes whispering over the ragged upholstery, just like our father's before us.

"Darrell, you need to hear this too." I prayed my confident shell would not crumble and reveal my neurosis.

Darrell joined Leon. They stood over me like two bulls, while Leon gave the occasional glance back at Daddy, just so he could mop up the machismo he lacked in his obsequious nature.

"Darrell, you said that Leon told you that I gave in to him. True or not?"

I watched his feet shift. He bit his lip and shot an oblique gaze at Eden.

"Gave in to what?" Leon asked. There was no honor among the lowlifes; I could see it in Leon's expression and the way he regarded Darrell.

"You know, Leon," Darrell said. He lowered his head and spoke, somehow scarcely moving his lips. But I could still hear him. "All that trash you told about Katrina that night at the bowling alley."

"Just get it out, right now, Leon. You may as well." I looked back at Eden. She gripped the clinic papers in her hand and sat coiled and tight, prepared to have her say, for once.

"Baby, you know guys get together and talk. It don't mean nothin'."

"Liar!" I slapped him hard, but it wasn't pain enough. My hand stung. It felt as though it moved on its own accord. Another slice through the air and a second wincing blow against his cheek stunned both of us. He stepped back and almost lost his balance. I gasped and hated myself all the more but hated him worse for the misery he had caused.

Daddy adjusted his glasses and glared. The last ounce of control ebbed from me. Leon righted himself, stood like a wall, and heaved a breath. I had forced his hand. Rage consumed me, and I wondered later if God withdrew or stood beside me trying to coax me away from my troubled self. I tried to slap him again, but his hand prevented it. If a small voice did try to stop me, obsessive ire and any available word stones drowned it out.

Darrell yelled and Eden screamed.

Leon pinned me against the car, but it did not prevent me from slapping him again.

"Katrina!" Daddy moved off the porch and toward us, his trunk outrunning his hobbling feet. The loose change and keys in his pocket echoed each step. "You lost your mind, girl?"

"You're the cause of this, Eden. You been spreadin' your lies?" Darrell said. But he cowered when Daddy tossed him a look.

Eden threw open the door. She lunged at Darrell and yanked his hair. "I hate you!" She clawed at him until Daddy grabbed her arms and held her close.

Momma stepped out on the porch. She wiped the remainders of her kitchen project from her hands with a frayed terry towel but looked up in enough time to see me slap Leon again. Only this time he drew his fist back. He would have brought it down on me, but a stronger arm gripped it.

"I can't let you do that, Leon." Daddy let go of Eden to shove Leon off of me, and then staggered to find his balance against his cane.

"You're all crazy!" Momma swore from the porch. "Leon, don't you hit my girl!"

I felt as though I couldn't breathe. Eden fell against me and sobbed.

Leon pressed his hand against his cheek. "I'm sorry, Mr. Hurley, but I just couldn't stand there and let her hit me like that."

Momma approached us but kept her distance.

"Somebody better start talking in a way an average man can understand," Daddy said and wiped his face with a rag. There was a pause, and then he turned to Leon.

"Katrina's all bent over some foolishness I said to Darrell." Leon raked over me with his eyes, his tone more disparaging than apologetic.

"Tell him what you said, Leon." Eden's face was matted with hair, so I brushed it back and doted over her.

"It was nothing but talk. Ignorant talk is all."

"I'll tell him if you won't. Leon told Darrell that I slept with him, Daddy."

"I don't want to hear that kind of trash talk, Katrina." Daddy said. He appeared to withdraw, like he could not look at me. So I moved in front of him and made him look.

"You're going to hear what I have to say, Daddy. He lied about me." I turned back to the boys. "You lied about me, Leon, and your lies spread. Now you've brought shame on us all, on Eden. You never had sense. You don't have any now."

Darrell turned, headed toward his car.

"You may as well stay, Darrell," I said. "I'm not letting you out of the driveway until you've listened to what Eden has to say."

He lit a cigarette and tossed the match on the ground next to a pile of smoldering cigarette butts. "I don't have to listen to anything."

He walked toward his car, propelling himself further from Eden's inquisition.

"Eden, what is Katrina talking about?" Momma's words were taut.

"You come back here and listen to me, Darrell!" Eden cried. She ran toward him. "You said you'd build me that house up on Twinkle Land, you liar!"

"Eden!" I couldn't bear to see her run after him the way she once ran after me in the park. Her whole life had been nothing but chasing after another's life, trying to claim a part of it for herself. At some early age, failing at autonomy or an identity, she settled for close imitation. But her life merely mirrored shadows of my own choices and that grieved me to no end. Grieved me.

"Stop her, Donelle!" Daddy leaned against his cane. "What's got into that girl?"

"Katrina, what is happenin'?" Momma wept now.

Before she could reach him, Darrell locked himself inside the classic Chevy and revved the engine. Eden stood in front of it.

"Darrell, get out of the car!" Leon finally spoke up.

The Chevy inched forward. Eden stood her ground.

Darrell popped the clutch and ground the gears. The Chevy reversed while spinning sideways. He tore off across the backyard, paying no heed to a small bed of strawberry plants. That ignited my mother more than anything else.

"I'll shoot you and kill you dead!" Momma made a run for the house, but my father managed to stop her. All Momma ever waved around was a pellet rifle when she was bent on waylaying an enemy. But it scared the blazes out of whoever stood looking into the barrel, like boys who threatened her strawberry plants or her daughters' virtue.

Eden chased Darrell until his car attempted to clear the ditch on the Erie side. It did not make it.

"Darrell, no!" Eden stopped behind the apple tree and clung to it. I had never seen her cling to anything. I believed she'd always wanted to, though.

"Momma, call an ambulance!" I pulled my mother away from Daddy and aimed her back toward the house. The look on her face revealed her inability to think at that moment.

Darrell's rear tire rolled on its axle, but slowly. We could see nothing of Darrell because the Chevy rested nose first in the ditch. It lay with the headlights and grill crushed against the hard rock of the incline and the taillights red and blazing, up in the air.

"He's killed himself, Katrina! My baby won't have a daddy." Eden wept uncontrollably and could not help herself. Her talk of a baby spilled out through unfettered sobs and coughing, as though that were the only way she could share it without getting slapped. I suddenly understood Aunt Velda.

Daddy stared at her for a while as she clung to the apple tree and babbled on about a baby. He seated himself beneath another tree until the county ambulance skidded into our drive.

People who lack decorum and are unable to command their words may appear colorful and wild in emergency rooms. But I can attest that from my own experience, we also feel small and insignificant and out of control.

All of the Hurleys piled into the emergency room, along with Leon and a couple of neighbors who had nothing else to do. Momma looked awkward and stood with her hands clasped and her chin lifted while her eyes traveled over every face.

I sat on a plaid sofa and waited next to Eden. We promised

Momma we would wait in the ER until Darrell's daddy showed up. So Momma and the neighbors drove home while my father sat in the lounge drinking coffee and nursing the blow Eden had just landed atop his heart.

Leon stood over us. He spoke very little, and when he did, guiltiness colored his words. "Eden, you know for sure you're pregnant?"

Eden nodded.

"Darrell used my words to manipulate you?"

"He did."

"I'm sorry as I can be. Darrell should have known it was just a bunch of ignorant bucks sittin' around the bowling alley. Just jawin' is all we were doin'."

"I guess I'll never understand." I turned away from him and hoped it would be the last time I would see him.

"Katrina, I never told you why I came by."

"It's not important now," I said.

"I was lonesome for you."

"I want you to listen to me, Leon. Lonesome has a lot of faces and each one can fool you. You're not lonesome for me."

"What do you mean?"

"You're just lonesome in general. Another girl will come along and latch on to you and keep you company. That's all you really want—a girl in a parked car so you can talk about her and tell lies with your sick buddies."

He could not look at me.

"I think it would be best if you just left us now, Leon. Whatever we hear about Darrell, we'll call your mother and tell her."

Eden and I sat alone, the sole lobby dwellers, except for an anxious young husband whose wife had gone into labor too soon. He mostly paced and twisted the top out of a wilted pothos plant. I dug some change out of my purse and split a candy bar with Eden, something we had not done in many years. Eden said that she had never met Darrell's father. When we saw a man enter the waiting room with dread on his face, we assumed it was Mr. Lunsford.

"What's happened to my boy? His name's Darrell, Darrell Lunsford." He wore a red apron adorned with the Tyco poultry plant emblem. His rubber boots squeaked against the fake marble-looking linoleum as he marched toward the receptionist's window.

"Should I go talk to him?" Eden eased forward on the lounge sofa.

"Are you girls the family of Darrell Lunsford?" A nurse entered the lobby and addressed Eden and me.

Darrell's father looked at us and then answered, "I'm Darrell's daddy. Is my boy going to be all right?"

"We're moving him into surgery, Mr. Lunsford. I can take you there."

"Mr. Lunsford?" Eden stood, moved toward him, looking aberrantly fragile.

Lunsford blinked and only gave her a glance.

"Has Darrell ever mentioned me to you? I'm Eden Hurley."

"Can't say he has, but Darrell never tells me nothin'."

"I'd like to stay with you through the surgery. I'll tell you all you want to know."

Eden had never handled herself in such a way as to endear herself to anyone. But Lunsford's hard gaze softened when she spoke, and that impressed me. But I worried that she would say too much too soon. "Eden, are you sure you don't want me to take you home?"

"No, Katrina. I want to be here when Darrell wakes up."

"All right, but call me when he comes out of surgery."

"I will."

Before I could turn to leave, she said something that surprised me even more.

"Katrina?"

"Yeah?"

"I love you." She padded down the long green corridor, following Lunsford, aging in plain sight as she made her way behind him. *I love you too, Eden.* But she had not stayed to hear it, which was good because it was stuck in my throat.

The ER waiting room was beginning to fill up, and I figured I should relinquish my parking slot. Besides, I hated the smell of rubbing alcohol that pervaded the lobby and felt as though it permeated my clothes. The slow rain subsided enough to allow me to make a run for my old jalopy. A young man opened the emergency-room door for me, and I attempted to swish past, but it seemed he fixed his eyes on me. I stopped, one foot across the threshold.

"I know you," he said and continued to hold open the door.

"Sol Houston." I hated myself for blurting it out.

"You were at Joy Hillerman's party last Friday, weren't you?"

It surprised me to know that a church boy, especially a Bible-thumping Houston, would be found at such a place. Hillerman parties included the wealthier set from the west side of town but also implied a fusion of drugs and drinking. "I've seen you at church."

"Church? That's right." He blushed, but it only gave him a more vulnerable air.

I stopped just short of telling him his brothers' names and what he wore to church last Sunday.

"Is everything all right?" He still held to the door.

"Sure."

"I mean, well, you're coming out of an emergency room."

I realized that I had been wrong about his eyes. They were not a dark blue at all, but a blue flecked with green.

"Are you all right?"

The feeling of standing so close to him might normally have left me feeling inept, but instead I felt comfortable. But not in the way Leon made me comfortable. I also felt completely safe with Leon, just as I felt safe with my dog, Salome. Sol left me feeling unguarded. But I liked it, if that makes any sense. My quiet reverie popped and I came fully awake. "My sister's boyfriend was hurt in an accident."

"I'm sorry. Is it serious?"

"He's gone into surgery, but we don't know how serious. Say a prayer for him. His name is Darrell." I looked down and saw he carried a large handbag. He must have noticed that I saw it.

"It's for my mother. She forgot it when we brought in my brother Ronny."

"He had an accident or something?"

"Ronny snitched my minibike and ran it into a ditch."

"Seems to be goin' around. Is everything all right?"

"He totaled it."

"I mean, is your brother all right?"

"Oh, yes, he is. Just needs some stitches above his eye. The doctor's office was already closed, so I drove them here."

"Sorry about your minibike."

"I was about to trade it for a Honda, anyway. Something bigger. Besides, I still have my car to drive. I better go. She needs her bag."

"Nice to see you, Sol." My eyes lingered after him and then I turned to go.

It was raining again.

CHAPTER 7

Life is only the diving board. As your feet leave it behind, your hands reach for the same place they reached for in life. The afterlife comes in two flavors: dark or light.

Darrell Lunsford reached a little too far into the dark, slipped beyond human grasp, then fell through the gray veil. The doctors could not save him or his mangled insides. He only lasted three quiet days.

We met Mr. Lunsford as soon as he called us. Once we arrived, he ran with a pocket full of change to the pay phone in the hall, while Eden and I stood vigil over his still body. I kept to myself the grief that eddied through me, a little river of pain and guilt I had not ventured to share with a single soul.

Eden mourned at the foot of his hospital bed. She had kept a sober mien for the days she waited, hoping for a call that Darrell had awakened from his coma. She was in the shower when Darrell's daddy phoned to tell us he had slipped away. Her freshly shampooed hair hung loose and damp around her shoulders with the ends bleached from the sun. She wore a blue halter top tied at the back and a pair of cutoff shorts.

The entire predicament delivered more attention to her around our house than when her appendix had burst. She rambled on about her own part in his life more than his death, letting us know how much importance this sudden tragedy had, in her own eyes, lent to her stature.

Darrell's daddy could be heard down the hall swearing into a pay phone. His ex-sister-in-law had helped him track down his estranged wife in a bar. She must not have offered the kind of support he wanted.

I stood with my shoulders pinned against the wall and watched my sister cry. "Want me to call Momma and Daddy?" I glanced down the hall again. Nervous, I ran my fingers back and forth behind my back, making star shapes and nervous Morse-code-like taps against the concrete wall.

"He never woke up, never knew about his baby, and nobody, especially me, thought it would come to this with him so young and all. I never noticed before, did you, that he's so beautiful? Look at what a perfect nose he has. I hope my baby has that nose and not one all wide and spread out like Daddy's side of the family." Eden eased around the bed to the bedstand and read one of the cards from the menagerie of auto shop buddies who never came to see him. Those kind of boys ripped up and down Fourth Street in homemade T-buckets and fired-up Mustangs because it tasted like immortality. But when one of their kind fell, they turned away as though witnessing it might hurt them, too. Somehow their mommas made them send cards to Darrell, but we never saw peep of them personally.

Eden pushed a strand of hair from his forehead. "He's still warm." She stepped away, as if poised for a resurrection.

"Darrell's gone, Eden. Sometimes it takes awhile for the skin to turn cold."

"Blamed if I don't even know these people." Eden shuffled the get-well cards poker style into a stack. "Worse than that, I don't know you, Darrell Lunsford. I gave my virginity to a stranger." Crystalline tears dripped from her eyes and fell from her chin as though weighted. "Guess that makes me a tramp. Momma always knew that about me, but I'd never tell her. I hate it when she's right."

"That nurse said to wait here until the doctor shows up with the death certificate. But I'd rather not stay. Don't you feel eerie, Eden? Now I know what they mean when people say the dead have gone on to another place. Look at Darrell's face. You can tell he's not there anymore, kind of deflated, but I can't explain it, really. Like there's nothing behind his eyes, if that makes any sense. It's as though God pulled him right out of that body as easily as you or I would slip out of a pair of pajamas."

Eden leaned over his body, offered a tender observation to the bruised eyes and swollen lips, then sort of effused all the breath out of her lungs. Her trunk slumped against her palms. "You're right, Katrina. I never thought of such a thing as that. Not even when Papaw Hurley died. Darrell's gone. Really, really gone."

"Here's a tissue. They got boxes of these all over so you may as well use them. St. Mary's charges three dollars and fifty cents apiece, but you don't know it until the bill comes. If it's stuffed in this little green pan, you can bet Mr. Lunsford has already been charged for it."

"My stomach's roaring like nobody's business. We can go to Al's, I guess. They don't need me here to sign. I mean, it's not like I'm his wife or anything."

"We should wait, though, make sure Mr. Lunsford doesn't need anything. He probably won't," I said.

"You wait, then. I've got to have a cigarette. I'll be in the stairwell just down the hall. You know where it is?"

Fine, I thought. *You and your baby go and have a Pall Mall.*

Every now and then I checked to see if Mr. Lunsford had made any headway with Darrell's mother. I could only see the back of his head, how he slumped into a black leather armchair and sobbed quietly with the telephone cord coiled around his forearm. He cradled the receiver between his shoulder and ear. Somehow he and the former Mrs. Lunsford had found common ground in the midst of their loss.

I believed it a profane disrespect to stare at Mr. Lunsford's dead son. But I had to think through some things myself, reflections that Eden would never allow because it might disrupt the course of her pixilated journey. I remembered how Darrell tore off across the grass in his Chevy because I trapped him. Sure, Eden had stood in front of the car. But it had been me that caused him to run. Cornered he was, the little fox, by my diatribe. If Darrell's nemesis dictated that he kill himself anyway, it mattered not beans whether he did it in our ditch or driving off the ridge at Twinkle Land. But I did not put too much stock in fate. Although Momma would say that this was his time, I couldn't see it. I killed Darrell.

Now I felt cornered. God had not set me up as this boy's judge and jury. Darrell could not change from the outside in, and I could no more make him do so than Job's friends.

*I am a wretched girl.*

God was the Big Man, but I could not fathom him placing his fingers in his mouth and whistling while he called for the angel boys to come cart Darrell Lunsford away, kicking and screaming.

*I murdered you, Darrell, the same as if I came to your house and killed you in your bed.*

The ache of self-hatred is like bone cancer. It dances up and down your limbs and spine until it drives a satisfactory hole. Then it seeps inside and becomes your intrinsic foe. I imagined Darrell floating between the ceiling and the second floor of St. Mary's, watching me and waiting for me to meet with cognizance.

*Laugh at me, Darrell. I'm the clown that got you your front row seat to the Big Pearlies or wherever you went.* My vision blurred, and I could not see straight. I fell onto the bed. My fingers hit the blue curve of his right hand. I laid my hands on him and prayed like a faith healer for God to bring him back. It was done in other places, I knew, where missionaries had nothing but God.

"It's me that caused this. Take me instead, God. I can't live with the suffering."

"It's all right, Katrina."

I felt warm fingers cup the crown of my head as a stratum of tobacco scent rose like overripe apples. It was Darrell's daddy. "Mr. Lunsford, I'm sorry you had to find me in such a state."

He spoke like he had been talking to me for a while and was in the middle of his story. "Once, Darrell's momma and I took him to that big mall up in Little Rock. It was his first time out away from the trailer park. I told him to stay next to one of us, but he never was one to mind real good. We turned around and, sure as dickens, found he'd run off from us. My wife had one of her hysteria fits while I ran around the store asking those clerks if they had seen my boy."

"Eden used to get lost like that too."

"I finally found him running up the down escalator. I grabbed him quick before he could get his foot stuck in it or some such. But I've not been the best one at keepin' up with him. His momma left a few months after that day in Little Rock. I been raising him best I could. That boy of mine, he always defied rules. You didn't kill him, Katrina. I didn't kill him. We can't blame the good Lord, neither. Darrell drove himself into that ditch. I'm just glad he didn't take your little sister with him."

"You know about the baby, Mr. Lunsford?"

"Here, wipe your eyes, girl. Your poor little sister's too young for this kind of mess. I always wondered who he'd drag with him into trouble. I'm just sorry as I can be it had to be little Eden."

"You ever been a granddaddy?"

He stared for a while at nothing with his hat in his hands.

"Darrell's your only son, though. I guess you haven't."

"No, never."

"Eden's too young to be a momma and she's never had good sense. But I'll help her with that baby, and if you ever want to see it, well, you've every right."

"You'd do that for me?"

"I would, sir, and you know this baby needs family around it."

"You're a good girl. I hope your momma and daddy know that about you."

"It's time for me to go now, Mr. Lunsford. You got any errands you want Eden and me to run for you? We'll help out, bring you some food, and such. Funerals can be taxing, especially your kind of funeral." I touched the hand that had pulled little Darrell Lunsford off the Little Rock escalator.

"I got a sister who's on her way from California. Thank you, anyway. You girls get on with your business." He handed me a ten dollar bill. "You take this and buy that baby somethin' purty. Kind of hope it's a little girl. Boys is too much heartache." He turned and hovered over the body of his son. A small whimper rose out of him, the kind made by a kicked pup.

The ICU door opened a crack. Eden fixed her eyes on me and drew her mouth up sort of poutylike. She clutched the Pall Mall pack in her right hand. "Katrina, I've smoked half a pack waiting for you. You comin' or not? Al's will be covered up."

"Eden, I'm not hungry after all. Mind if we just go home?" Instead of waiting for her answer, I sauntered past her and squeezed into a group of older couples who waited for the elevator. I had to show Eden the right way about things. One more time.

❧

Life fell into a smooth, saucy kind of simmer. Momma commenced to taking Eden shopping for maternity clothes. It satisfied her longing to dress Eden in better goods, even if it was in the shape of a tent.

Darrell Lunsford's short hospital stint had given Eden a reason to get up in the morning, but now that was behind her. Her proclivity to sleep all day returned. When evening battered the rest of us into our beds, Eden watched old movies, while our house became the last firefly on Erie Street to extinguish its purple haze.

Neither my mother nor my father ever mentioned Leon's name again, and that issued me a new life. Oldness crept into a girl's heart at a young age in the valley, but I realized that somehow I had escaped it when I escaped from Leon. The long strands of my hair grew to my waist and turned blond and silky in the sun. If I pulled it away from my face, a bit of sophistication appeared, although most people might have been remiss to notice any lovely contours behind the thick lenses of my glasses. Every time the preacher asked us to come forward for prayer, I always asked God to fix my bad eyesight. I wondered if the other folks in the prayer line got their grocery cart list filled better than mine. But I never said a word to Preacher Haggard about it because he might have thought I questioned his methods.

When I dated Leon, we spent a lot of Sundays on the lake. He taught me to water-ski, but I never managed to teach him squat about God. It suited me fine to not have him dragging me away from church and spying on me if ever I wanted to steal a glance in the direction of the Houston pew.

My first Sunday school teacher, Sister Evelyn Trueblood, did not like me much, I guess because I did not dress like her or her three girls. She wore the most cumbersome dresses, which enclosed her pear-shaped body like a coffin. Her sleeves never revealed her arms or wrists but could not hide their sausage shape. As was common among those in her circle, you could often see her downtown on Saturday with her church cronies, their hair in rollers and covered with a scarf, which said, "I'm going to church tomorrow. Are you?" Once when I was waiting tables at the Pizza Delight, a whole passel of those ladies came in, calling one another sister like they were nuns, only they weren't. The leader of the pack had braided bright red and yellow gladiolas through the front of her bun—at least a twelve-inch stack—and it looked pretty spectacular. I believe their rules, like my Meemaw's against makeup, allowed a few loopholes in female adornment.

But my Sunday school teacher, Sister Evelyn Trueblood, never put flowers in her hair, and she never could get anyone to do exactly as she wanted. That caused her considerable grief.

Time passed, necessitating that I move ahead into the older youth class. Even though she will never remember, I kissed Sister Trueblood's cheek and told her good-bye because I always learned a little something from everyone. I felt I owed her at least one kiss.

We were shuffled into a smaller room that had been used for other things like storing books and janitorial supplies. But our new teacher fixed it up with a new piece of blue carpet. Even though I could tell she had tucked the frayed edges beneath the baseboard, I appreciated her efforts.

We called her Sister Bickle. Her hair reminded me so much of my Grandmother Hurley before she died. Some women are blessed with hair that never grays. Because they never dye it or do anything to it except a once-a-week practical shampoo, it shines and never thins. God had blessed Sister Bickle with such hair. She wound it into a smooth French knot and pinned it around the crown of her head. Even though she had a class of young men and women, she was partial to us girls and had stay-over parties at her house on occasion. Gertrude Bickle called us her girls and always took pains to make us each feel like we were her favorite.

Time for me stood still after I met Gertrude, because of her way with me, resulting in my refusal to move on, on my first occasion to do so. If you would have asked her about me, she might have said that I never asked a stupid question. She made me feel like that, anyway. Although I had once dreamed of a Houston adoption, I now yearned to go home with Gertrude Bickle.

She was a widow, a retired schoolteacher, and a poet by hobby. Two of her poems were published in a pale green, hardcover book. All of her writings were about God, and she fashioned them with antiquated expressions as a dressmaker fashions a skirt with lace. Her face belonged in a history book as well—a somber, high, intelligent face that displayed eyes that flashed with life behind copper-colored wire spectacles. Mockingbird Valley put us square in the middle of the country so that we never saw an ocean. But I imagined Gertrude's eyes foaming like frothy waves around the pupils and undulating out to the iris edges in a deep blue Pacific shimmer. I floated in their approval quite often.

She lived a life free of extraneous obligations, and so we girls became the disciples of Gertrude Bickle—I being the most devoted of her disciples.

Our favorite meeting place was a small natural foods café that opened for a short time on West Main. We sipped on banana flips while Gertrude talked about the Lord. While the other girls grew up and away, I kept up our monthly ritual throughout my high school years and found that confiding in her made me feel whole. Two other girls joined us, Beth Hoover and Jane Beasley.

Jane, prone to emotional highs and lows, leaned opposite of Beth, who had a steady way about her that we all envied. Their differences drew them into a fist-tight friendship. Jane complained about her weight while Beth moved about on lithe beanpole legs. According to Jane, her greatest enemy was her mirror. She fought with it every morning—straightening the brown cursed curls that made an un-seventies wreath around her face—and plucking the two thick brows that reefed her forehead until there was nothing left except two thin apostrophes. Although she was the most curvaceous among us, we knew that any compliment we tossed her way fell on deaf ears.

In contrast, everything about Beth was pale: her blond hair that moved in silken furrows when she walked, her pink cheeks, her kittenish blue eyes, and her homemade, soft cotton dresses. She looked as sweet and fragile as cotton candy.

"I love this little avocado-y sandwich thing," I said.

"Mine's got bacon bits and cheese." Beth lifted the dark bread and examined it.

"What are these little stringy weeds?" Jane slid a long green stem out of her sandwich and then let it dangle from her fingertips.

"Alfalfa sprouts. Very good for you." Sister Bickle explained the food because we saw so little of anything besides the run-of-the mill meat and potatoes fare of the Southern palate. "More vitamins than lettuce."

"Beats Burger Al's all to squat," I said.

"Katrina, did you bring a picture for me?" Sister Bickle asked.

"I did. It's a still. Charcoal." The portfolio lay next to me on the floor.

"I'm glad you're drawing again. You should keep it up. Can I see it?" she asked.

"It only took a week or so, so it may be a bit rough."

"Let me be the judge." Sister Bickle moved her spectacles forward.

The still was of a long-necked bottle I found under the house.

The cloth that draped behind it was from Momma's quilt-scrap trunk. The rest was just fruit from the refrigerator. "It's nothing special."

"Is this one mine?" she asked.

"If you want it."

"That bare spot right over my piano needs such a picture. I'll frame it myself."

Jane kept chewing away at her California-imported sandwich and barely mustered a glance at my picture. As often as I complimented her on her lovely singing voice and how I really thought she should leave the curl in her hair, she never volleyed back a sprinkling of a compliment. But Beth sat forward with interest.

"You should take art class in school," Beth said.

"I did once, but I quit."

"Beth won an art scholarship," Jane finally said. "No one can touch her, really."

"Don't be so sure. Katrina oozes with talent. Such a pretty bottle. You still have the bottle?" Sister Bickle ran her fingertips across the charcoal without causing a smudge.

"You want that, too?" I asked.

"Unless you need it for something. I'm collecting bottles for a project."

"I'll bring it Sunday."

"I'm so glad to see you coming to our Bible study on Thursday nights now, Katrina."

"I need it, Sister Bickle. Been in a dry desert lately."

She set her freshly poured glass of water square in front of me. "Have a drink, then." And then she opened her tattered Bible and fed us some more.

Chapter 8

*E*den called out to me in the night. The moonlight washed the bedroom floor with its blue wax. I stumbled around in a haze, not remembering my name or how to find the door. My feet managed to aim me across the hall just as she yelped again. The doctor said that with her young age, she might go into labor early. Her cry made me shudder.

"Was I dreaming, Eden, or did you call me?" From her doorway, I found her sprawled out, clutching her green veneer headboard. Her elfin hands moved to the pillow and then to her hair and she gripped both with the ferocity of a hungry newborn. She was a spider pinned beneath the weight of her large egg sac.

"I'm hurtin', Katrina. Is this it? Labor, I mean?"

"Girl, I wouldn't know the difference, but it's too soon."

"I want you to hold my hand, Katrina. I'm scared. Like, what if I die from this? Momma said she almost died havin' me."

"Hush up, now. You'll not die from it, and Momma tells too many of her stories."

"My stomach, Katrina, it's hurtin' again. Oh, it feels like I'm comin' apart! Hold my hand, I said."

"I'm here, Eden. Do your breathing thing. Blow, girl. That's it."

"Breathin's not helping. Get me to the doctor and have him knock me out with a hammer. I can't do this."

"Momma! Eden's in labor!" I shouted. I turned back to Eden. "I believe that woman could sleep through the Second Coming."

Eden cried in a guttural way. Between her sobs, the sound of Momma's feet marching up the hall caused a vibration in the door hinges.

"It's four in the morning," Momma said. "You two got good reason for waking the dead?"

"Eden's having pains, Momma, and I believe they're bad."

"Probably false labor. Go back to sleep, Eden."

Eden shoved a pillow between her knees and turned onto her side. "I'll get dressed," I said. "I'll take her to the hospital."

"Don't wake your daddy. He's got too much to worry about as it is. Besides, you'll bring her back. It's too soon to be havin' that baby."

"Get my pack of Pall Malls, Katrina. I need a cigarette," Eden said.

"See? She's not in labor. Theatrics, that's all this is and just another way to draw attention. I'm headed back to bed," Momma said.

"You shouldn't smoke, Eden. It might hurt the baby. You got to think about that baby now and not just yourself." A pair of pink maternity pants lay on the floor. I handed them to her. "Dress yourself now. I'll be back to fetch you."

The wooden hall floor creaked as I headed past Momma's bedroom for the telephone. I whispered into it so as not to evoke one of her tirades. I told the night nurse that Eden was not due for another month but she was hurting something fierce. The nurse from the emergency room said to bring her in.

Before we pulled out of the driveway, I saw an ember glow through the stained white window sheers in Daddy's bedroom. He watched us leave but said nothing to either of us.

"Fix your eyes on the moon, Eden." A white halo encircled the moon, a powdery nimbus that whispered in farmers' dreams of rain. I listened to the crunch of the gravel beneath the car wheels as I turned them away from the house. The sound was intrusive at such an hour. "If you think real hard about something else, like a fixed object, that baby book says you'll be better off for it."

"Momma hates me, Katrina. I can see how she is with you, that she loves you."

"Don't say that about her, Eden. You know Momma loves you."

"She don't even want to be around when my baby's born. She's actin' like it's not happenin'." She made ragged breathing sounds. "How I wish to God it wasn't."

"Why, that's not true. She bought you all those maternity clothes."

"Only 'cause she was ashamed of how I looked."

"Momma just thinks you're having false labor. Maybe she's right."

"She's never had labor, Katrina. They took you and me both."

I laughed. "She thinks Cesareans are the new wave of child birthing. Doc Lingle liked it that way, I guess. Like he was the god of her body."

"You're talkin' over my head again, and I'm not in the mood for it. Where did you hide my Pall Malls?"

"Blow, Eden. And breathe."


The midnight shift at St. Mary's was having an awful time treating a burn victim. Seems a car-wash hose had come loose and scalded him. Only one other person sat in the corner, a man who folded his hat brim in and out until it flattened altogether.

"I'll get you checked in, Eden. Have a seat by the window. I reckon someone will tell us what we're to do next."

"Would it cause trouble if I went outside for some air? The smells in here are givin' me fits like—what is that stuff they use in mortuaries on dead people? This place reeks like a mortuary. I don't want my baby born next to the dead."

Eden's skin had an ashen cast under the flickering fluorescent lights. Her hair wound around her neck like a wet towel left in the sun and she looked uncomfortable all over. She wiped her palms repeatedly against the pink knit slacks.

"Stand outside the door under the lights, but don't wander." The front desk nurse drew up like a barricade of nerves, frowning at me through the smudged glass. "What do you need?" She had a bony face and oversize plastic eyeglasses.

"My sister's pregnant. She woke up hurting and someone here said we should bring her in." Momma kept Eden's Medicaid card thumbtacked to a corkboard in the kitchen, so I had grabbed it on the way out. I drew it from my pocket and slid it into the indention beneath the glass.

"She looks like a minor. Is the baby's father with her?"

"Just me. I'm her sister."

"We have to have an adult to sign for her."

"My folks are coming later," I lied.

"When is she due?"

"Not until next month."

"I seen lots of girls her age come in here all walleyed and scared, thinking they're in labor. It's usually false labor first time out." She looked walleyed herself.

"Her pains are fifteen minutes apart. Don't that count for something?"

"If she's in premature labor, she shouldn't smoke like that."

I turned and found Eden with one hand pressed against the glass, the other hand poised at her lips with a cigarette. Next to her stood the car-wash burn victim who had apparently signed himself out of the ER. They passed one cigarette back and forth between them, taking long, purposeful drags like the kids with bad haircuts who stood behind the junior high gym each morning.

"Excuse me, ma'am. I'll be right back." Eden never turned to look at me when I passed through the automatic doors and stood behind her.

"You got any beer? I'm thirsty as a fish, and I know they won't let me have diddly to drink once they stick me in delivery. I'm weak as all get out." She spoke to the man whose arms and one side of his face had been wrapped in white gauze. "Did they really let you come out here without a wheelchair?"

He did not answer. Before I could say a word to her, her hand trembled at her mouth. Suddenly Eden leaned against the glass, then slid downward to the ground. The cigarette fell to the sidewalk as she cried out and clutched her stomach. The burn victim backed up, wide-eyed and bristling at the sight of a pregnant girl sprawled at his feet.

"Katrina, don't let me birth this kid out here like this!" Eden moaned and looked up at me. Her mouth bled. "Something's happening. This ain't right at all. God, please help me, I can't bear this! Take me home and put me to bed, Katrina, so I'll just sleep through it."

"Eden, you've bit your lip." I knelt and dabbed the blood with my T-shirt hem. "Mister, go fetch someone. Drag one of those orderlies out here or just anyone big enough to put her in a wheelchair. We got to get my sister inside."

The car-wash burn victim took two steps away from Eden. Then he hotfooted his way across the black parking lot, climbed into an old Ford pickup, and drove away.

I pounded the plate glass with my fists. "Hey! We need help out here!"

"Once I saw a birthing on a soap opera. Gayle Starling had her baby with her hair done up and her lips pretty and red. If that was true, then I'm the first lady. This baby's pounding its way out with a mallet, and it cares nothin' about the shape I'm in."

"Take my hand, Eden. I think your water just broke."

"Find someone who knows something. I need to know more about this child-birthing business, like if it's supposed to hurt this bad and all. Oh, me, I'm just a kid. How could this be? Bring me my dolls, will you, Katrina? Bring me Baby Peggy, the doll with the pink gown."

"Hold my hand, I said, girl. No tears, now. That won't help matters. You have to be grown-up about this." The sky lightened in the shape of an acre-long thumbnail. Daddy would be boiling his coffee soon.

"Momma will have to come now," I whispered.


Outside of labor and delivery, anxious faces looked up from the green vinyl, padded chairs. Doc Lingle had funny ideas about the birthing moms. He wanted full control of the matter and would not even allow the fathers inside the delivery area. So every time the swinging doors flew open, the waiting parties fell silent, each hoping to be presented with the news that they could now cross the threshold of Lingle's inner sanctum and view their wriggling, squalling, new family member. Eden's pleas to allow me to stay beside her just fell upon the deafness of Doc Lingle's old ways. I stood closest to the labor area entry and pressed my face against the small glass in the door. The nurses streamed back and forth between labor rooms in their white dresses, looking like photo negatives of the black gowned sisters who milled around St. Mary's.

"Katrina Louise?" Momma's voice had a queer shakiness. She looked odd, like she longed to make herself invisible.

"Eden's fine, Momma. Is Daddy with you?"

"He's parking out back. This place is full. This always happens with a full moon. Probably the reason Eden went too soon."

"They got some coffee over on that table with all the fixings. Pour yourself a cup, if you want," I said.

"Has Dr. Lingle said anything about this baby coming too soon?"

"It's premature, all right. But his nurse told me the baby's vitals look good. They said we still have lots of time, though. Want to go downstairs for some breakfast?"

"I can't eat right now. My stomach's all wadded in a knot. Is Eden all right?"

"She's scared, Momma. They ought to at least let one of us in."

"That's against hospital rules."

"No, that's against Doc Lingle's rules."

"I hope she's good and scared. Maybe it'll teach her a lesson."

Daddy peered above the heads of two other men. He stood back from the waiting room, shifted his feet, and stared down at them.

"Daddy looks nervous."

"He hates hospitals. Spent so much time down at the VA in Booneville, I reckon, when you and Eden were young."

Momma had a hasty, dime-store checkout way of measuring the thoughts and feelings of others. Even if her assessment failed to hit the target, she swore by it. I knew Daddy and how awkward he felt outside of his little tent of possession. As long as he wandered inside the bounds of his crony hangouts or the comfort of his family domain, he strutted like a rooster, telling us all how to live. But outside of his paper walls, he turned into a big, fat hen.

"Eden was such a sickly baby. I was sick too, you know. Both of us nearly died."

"I know, Momma."

"I couldn't be Momma to her and you both. She just came at the worst time, and how could I be expected to tend to her, being so sick and you being so pretty and perfect? You were so different from all the rest of the babies on my side of the family, not homely and big eyed."

"I hate it when you talk like that."

"It's the truth. Eden's always been hard to love."

"If you didn't love her, you wouldn't be here."

"Worrisome, that's what she is—what she always will be."

"I wish they would let me in to see her," I said.

"You know now that I'll be the one taking care of this baby, too. Here I am too old to be, well, your momma, for that matter, and having to care for a child I never asked for."

"I told you I'd help with the baby."

"You watch how this all pans out after this baby's born. She won't even pay it any mind. That's just when I'm going to hit her up with something I've been saving."

"What have you saved?"

"I been talking to an adoption agency. This baby needs to be given to a good home, one that will offer it proper care."

"Eden's not having a puppy, Momma."

"This whole matter should be up to me, seeings how I'm the workhorse that has to tend to everything, even to Eden and all her messes she gets herself into."

"You don't mean a word of what you're saying."

"They got this couple from down around Sunny Point who can't even have kids. They'll pay the whole hospital bill and fix this baby up with everything that Eden could never afford."

"Lower your voice, Momma."

"If I don't step in, your daddy's going to get strapped with this medical bill, and now with it being premature and all, they'll ask triple the money, and just see if he won't pay it—he will and then give me grief for three months and not let me have nary a stitch of clothes to wear. It's not right, that's all."

"Maybe the baby will die and you won't have to deal with anything." My angry comment did little to mitigate her denunciation of her younger daughter. I walked away and left her to babble to a stranger who agreed with all she said.


I paid for coffee down in the cafeteria, although I could get it free in the waiting room. The indulgence offered me time to stew, and then I prayed and asked the Lord to forgive my hotheadedness and my sharp tongue and most of all not to hold the innocent responsible for my acrid pronouncements.

"Katrina, is that you?" I looked up to find Gertrude Bickle standing in the lobby with the morning sun waltzing in behind her. Tucked beneath her arm, she held an old weathered devotional filled with bookmarks and ragged pages that dropped worn particles from the edges onto her hips. She wore a dress made of brown, comfortable cotton and her brown flat shoes made no noise when she walked across the waxed linoleum.

I returned her smile.

"I've a sick friend here, but I heard a rumor about your little sister. Is she having her baby?"

"She's in labor. I brought her in early this morning."

"*You* brought her in? I can see your eyes are a little droopy. I live close by. Want to go to my place and take a nap?"

"I should stay. Eden might curdle if she had a kid and I wasn't around to look at it."

"You'll make a good aunt. We should give her a baby shower."

"She could use some baby clothes. We've not bought a lot for the baby yet. Momma said to wait and find out what it's going to be."

"I'll see about it at the church. How are your mother and father?"

"Fine."

"You need to talk, Katrina?"

"I should go. That's a new dress, isn't it?"

"Old as Moses. Join me for some tea. I'll get you a handkerchief for those tears."

We sat in the cafeteria, drinking tea, and Sister Bickle talked until she saw I looked more peaceful. "Are you worried about Eden?"

"I'm worried about this kid she's having. Eden's never been right herself, and what if this baby's got her ways and all and can't learn or gets made fun of by the other kids?" I felt Gertrude's large hands clasp my right hand and dared to look at her. "It makes no sense that God would allow someone like Eden to have a baby."

"Everyone has a measure of pain to suffer. Even with good parents, every child endures pain."

"I just wonder if God knows a baby is sliding down the rainbow from heaven and landing in the lap of a girl who can't count back pocket change, let alone change a diaper."

"Look out the window. It's starting to rain. I'm glad I brought my umbrella."

"I thought I heard thunder," I said.

"God's son was born in an imperfect world. Look at you, Katrina. You have the same parents as your sister. But you've chosen a different road. This world is not spinning on the axis of perfect families. It's all about the choices we make as individuals. Look at pain as a fire. Either it refines you, or it consumes you."

"I feel consumed."

She laughed.

"This world's eating me alive."

"It's not. When all's been said and done, Katrina Hurley will stride forward on her own two feet and then stand. Maybe you'll stagger around for a while. But then you'll stand."

"I'd rather fly, Sister Bickle."

"First you stand. Flying, my young friend, comes much later."

CHAPTER 9

*M*omma never looked so old as she did crouched next to the wheels of a hospital incubator. A grizzled sky spilled rain on the valley the morning that Eden delivered her baby. I watched while another kind of rain darkened the inside of my mother. I heard not a word from her about adoption agencies or barren families from Sunny Point.

She did not see me watch her from the corner of the nursery. But I heard her plainly when she prayed. The words trickled out of her just like when Meemaw prayed over dinner. Her right hand held to the incubator leg while the left one quivered above the clear bubble that made the lid. The only occasion that I recalled hearing a prayer spilling out of her in such a way was when I had been stricken with flu.

"Where's Eden, Momma? I saw you through the window, and a nurse's aide let me slip in." I read the nametag on the foot of the incubator. "Baby Girl Hurley. 5 pounds. Date of birth: February 3, 1975."

"Eden's sedated. They had to take the baby just like they did with me. Doctor Lingle says she'll be up and around soon. But your sister's built just like me, small boned, with no room for a kitten, let alone a baby. When they told us that baby was breech, I just knew they'd have to take it. Your daddy's sitting in the waiting room with a cup of coffee, if you want to go see him. And while you're out there, look in on Eden."

"It's a little girl," I said. "Won't Eden be happy to hear that? Has she named her?"

"She doesn't know a thing. But she'll wake up soon." Momma stood.

I looked in on the child. "Oh, they've taped tubes all over the poor little thing. Next to all the other babies, Eden's looks like a doll. Tell me straight, Momma—is this little girl baby going to live?"

"This baby's a fighter, just like her own momma was when she was newborn."

"Five pounds and look at all that dark hair. What with her premature, I never would have thought she would have such a thick head of hair. She looks like Eden. Maybe she has blue eyes," I said.

"Maybe so."

"I want to hold her."

"Can't do that, Katrina. Besides, it wouldn't be right. Eden should be the one to hold her first."

The nurse's aide inspected the reed-thin tubes that ran in and out of Baby Girl Hurley. The newborn skin was pink and creased at the joints of her limbs, as though her wrinkled hide had been sewn too large for her infinitesimal bones. If I held her, I imagined I could almost cup her in one hand. She lay on her flat little stomach and occasionally jerked her arms or wiggled her feet, making them quiver like doorstop springs. Momma never took her gaze from inside the incubator, but stood over it with both hands clasped at her breast and her large macaroni-colored handbag swinging from the crook in her arm.

Another nurse, a portly woman with a dark shadow above her

lip, stood with the door opened partially. "Someone's awake," she said.

An orderly wheeled Eden into the nursery. Her pallor startled me at first. "Congratulations, little momma!" I said to her.

She acted like she hadn't heard me and weakly groused at the nurse, "Does this chair lay back? Get me a gurney, why don't you?" But then her face lifted, as if she had noticed where she was for the first time, and she saw Momma and me flanking the incubator. "I had a little girl, Katrina. Is she pretty like you?"

"Pretty like you, Eden. Thick, dark hair. It almost touches her shoulders in the back. Just look at her all laid out like a little queen on her tummy."

I stepped away from the incubator while Eden was wheeled up beside it. She sat forward, being careful with the IV pole that connected a tube to her wrist. When she stood over the frail baby, she covered her mouth with one hand and let out a whimper. The infant girl flinched, and Eden recoiled. Like an awkward little sister, she stared at the miniature rump and the spindly legs until a dam broke loose inside of her. A single tear fell and wet the top of her hand, and she whispered, "I have a baby, Katrina, and she's beautiful. And mine. I've never owned a thing in my life, and now I do. I can't for the life of me figure out what I'm feeling, but it's the finest kind of pain. Like my heart's so full it's bustin' wide open." She implored the heavier nurse. "Can I hold her?"

"I'll get you a mask, Miss Hurley." The nurse had a faint smile, as though she had anticipated the arrival of this moment. "But I'm afraid the rest of you will have to leave."

"We'll wait in the hall with your daddy, Eden," Momma said. "Lee and Pippa have shown up too."

All five of us watched her through the glass. Baby Girl Hurley opened her eyes slightly, and the light flickered against them, dark granite moons in search of a safe orbit. She held us all under the spell of her gaze. Her lids closed again to snatch another second of blissful sleep and then took another peek when her mother moved her around in too clumsy a fashion. Eden swayed gently while the nurse kept cupping the baby's head and speaking into a child's ear about how babies should be handled.

"My stomach's in knots," I said. "Eden looks so lost, like she's been set adrift."

Daddy stood next to his brother, my Uncle Lee, while Momma stood next to Pippa. We all stood, each of us, in front of a glass panel, speechless at the gate and wanting to run in and cradle Baby Girl Hurley in our arms and protect her. But we hid behind our resolve to hold back and watch Eden wade into strange waters, not a lesson to her credit.

I watched mother and child touching fingers, communing. "Momma, have you ever wondered about things like—has Baby Girl seen the face of God yet?" I asked.

"Katrina, not now," Momma said.

"Tell me what you mean," Pippa said to me.

"I sometimes wonder if a few souls are allowed a glimpse of heaven. You know, like before they enter the birth canal or maybe sooner. Then they spend their lives trying to paint or sing the last thing they saw before they hit land."

"Maybe that's where artists come from, Katrina." Pippa touched my hair, stroked it, and then pressed a strand behind my ear.

"That's not in the Bible," I said. "Not exactly like that, anyway. Sister Bickle says that eternity is written across the heart of every man. I was just wondering."

To my mind, God must've left his notes on our baby souls instead of on a refrigerator.

I sat at the foot of Eden's bed and watched her doze. She had slept in the same twisted S position since I could remember. My gaze followed the curve of her hand, which lay palm up with two fingers bent outward like the Christ child in an icon painting. When she slept, she looked wise and comely and ten years old again. But when she was awake and chattering, it spoiled her looks.

She whimpered in her sleep. The night nurse had given her pain pills. But only time would restore the lost feeling that so entangled her. I lifted myself by the bedrail and pulled her sheet down over her ankles once more before leaving her for the night.

"Is she asleep? I don't want to wake her."

Aunt Edith, Momma's sister, surprised me with her presence. "Aunt Edith, I hoped you would drop by."

"Sorry I'm comin' so late. I took a job cleaning the floors at the bank. I get through about this hour every weeknight. Maybe I should come back tomorrow. Would that be best?" She saw Eden. "Look at that little thing asleep. Poor girl. Did she have a hard time of it?"

"They had to take the baby. It's a little preemie. But she's a pretty little girl. Want to see her?"

"I don't want to be a bother, what with it so late."

"Come take a look. Eden's so out of it, she wouldn't be good company, anyway. Did Momma call?" I led her from the room.

"She called home and got Charley Ray. He dropped by with my dinner and told me Eden had her baby. I ain't spoke with Donelle myself. How's she takin' all this?"

"I think the baby's got her wound around her little pinkie. I don't think Momma ever knew a grandbaby would affect her in such a way. To hear her talk, this baby's the prettiest ever born."

"She said that about you, I recall."

We walked down the hallway and stopped in front of the nursery window. "Look at that little incubator back there with the pink sign on the end. That's Baby Girl Hurley."

"Eden's goin' to give it a name, ain't she? I've heard of babies that weren't expected to live, so the mommas never named them. I believe every baby ought to have a name. I named mine before they was ever born. God named his babies early. Don't ask me which scripture, though. I ain't good at that kind of thing."

"Eden has a big baby book. I brought it home from the library. She made a list of boy names and girl names a couple of times. But she didn't expect to be having her so soon. After she's had a few days to heal up, she'll come up with something. But Eden's baby's going to be fine. You worry as much as Momma, Aunt Edith."

"No one worries as much as my sister. That woman could put a hole clean through a worry stone. Momma says Donelle's been goin' to church. Is that right?"

"I think she likes comin'. She seems peaceful after service. I've never known her to get involved in much of anything, so I'm not expecting to see her heading up any committees or teaching Sunday school. But I'm glad to see her sitting back there."

"Has she committed to the Lord? That's the most important thing."

"I saw her crying in church and praying. When I asked her about it, she said she had a bad dream that made her think about a lot of things."

"Dream?"

"She dreamed that she was tied in chains and couldn't get free. It was dark, and she was afraid and felt like evil was all around her. The only part of herself she could move was her right foot. She kept trying to kick herself free, but nothing could free her. Then she woke up." We watched as a young nurse peered into Baby Girl's incubator and wrote things on her chart. "Momma says that when she woke up, her face was drenched in her own tears and she felt lost and separated from God. It was the first time she ever realized such despair. So she prayed and asked the Lord to forgive her of her sins. And wouldn't you know, she fell back to sleep and slept all peaceful. The chains were gone."

"I been prayin' so long, Katrina, for your momma to find Christ."

"Now don't expect any big revelations to come out of her mouth. This is all so new to her. But she's been reading the Bible. At times she does really well. Other times she gets all full of herself again. Some people grow by leaps and bounds. Others by the inches."

"I reckon I'm just an old inchworm myself," said Aunt Edith.

"Would you join me in prayer before I leave? Eden needs prayers in the worst way."

"I'd be glad to, Katrina. Long's you don't mind holdin' to these old chlorine-bleached hands."

We went back to Eden's room. Edith prayed with me for Eden's well-being and for Baby Girl to be whole and well. Edith said, "And God, please keep holdin' Donelle in your lovin' hands. And deliver Katrina into the future you have for her."

When I opened my eyes, Aunt Edith was smiling.


For six weeks, I drove Eden back and forth to St. Mary's because she was not old enough to drive, but just old enough to have a kid.

Daddy broke down and let Momma and me buy Eden a new pair of denims (the faded kind), a hair-grooming collection mottled with glitter on the brush and mirror handles, and a pair of blue sneakers. Her old clothes still would not fit, and her shoes had worn thin from the summer nights she drifted up and down the hallway to hover in front of the new window air conditioner that Momma made Daddy buy. The glitter-handled brush set was meant to encourage good grooming.

Eden named her baby girl Lolita Dream, but it was shortened in a blink to Little Dreamy, and then just plain old Dreamy. Dreamy finally gained enough weight to leave behind her grasping incubator at St. Mary's and come home. Eden's hair had grown longer. While we waited outside the nursery, she twirled the ends of it in a repetitious fashion until Lolita Dream was placed once and for all in her thin, rigid arms.

"Reckon this baby's going to look like her daddy, Katrina? Or act like him?" Eden stared straight ahead as I drove them home from the hospital. "How do I tell Lolita Dream about her rascal of a daddy without rupturin' her little soul?"

"No need to worry about it today. Does Mr. Lunsford know about her yet, or did you wait?"

"Momma got all red in the face when I talked about calling Darrell's daddy and acted like it wasn't none of his affair. But I ought to call him, I believe."

"Mr. Lunsford is Dreamy's grandparent just like Momma. When she gets all odd acting, it's best not to say a word to her about anything. You'd think we did something like put cayenne in her tea the way she takes to spouting off."

"I can't talk to either Momma or Daddy, can't say hi-de-ho to Daddy 'cause he sits in the corner talking to people from the Depression, and most of the time he gets riled at one of them and takes it out on me."

"Are you going back to school, Eden?"

"Can't see it. Maybe I'll get one of those BBDs and call it quits."

"GED? Don't drop out now, Eden. You know you want to buy

better things for yourself and this baby. How you going to get out of here if you have to live off Daddy like some welfare freak?"

"Not every person wants to leave the valley like you, Katrina."

Lolita Dream fussed and twisted her face up all red like a pomegranate.

"Nothing wrong with seeing what's waiting beyond the hills of Arkansas," I said.

"Dogged if this baby can't keep still!"

"Maybe she's wet."

"Will you just drive, Katrina?"

"Don't get mad at me, Eden. You act like it's some big red sin if I offer you a piece of advice."

"I'm not going into all that with you."

"Not so loud. You're scaring her." The baby wailed with a newborn mewl. Not earsplitting, just angry.

"She won't stop cryin'! What am I supposed to do now?"

"Hold her close and love her. Don't smack her, Eden, she's too small! *Eden!* I'm pulling over!"

As soon as I stopped, Eden threw Dreamy down on the seat next to me like she was her old doll, Baby Peggy. She tugged at her black vinyl miniskirt with one hand, fished out a cigarette from her purse with the other, and galloped down the creek bank.

Dreamy wailed. It was the first time I held her, and she smelled so sweet—the faint hint of daffodil and grape hyacinth after a rain.

"Don't be mad at your momma, little girl. She's not right, never has been." I tried to think of a song, but what popped in my head was not a lullaby. I sang it anyway.

> *Jesus is calling the weary to rest,*
> *Calling today, calling today*

*Bring Him your burden and you shall be blest;*
*He will not turn you away.*

Dreamy must have had a fondness for it because she nestled right in the curve of my neck and sucked her knuckles. I held her close and then got out of the car to see what had happened to her mother.

I watched Eden from the bridge. Galla Creek serpentined in small algae-caked rivulets throughout the valley so we could throw a stone and hit a bridge in any direction. To the best of my recollection, Galla Creek was never aggraded or treated, just left on its own to wind throughout the county with sewage pumping through it. But no threat of blood poisoning or snakebite could keep out the young rogues bent on tormenting crawdads and snapping turtles.

Eden walked up to the water's edge, sliding along the length of the green unctuous loam, and planted herself on an encrusted rock. The clay that stuck to the heels of her black vinyl knee boots she had paid six bucks for at Fred's obviously annoyed her. She spent endless minutes scraping the mud from the boots. Finally, she unzipped them and pulled them off altogether.

"Want to go talk to Momma? Let's go drag her by the hair and make her apologize, sweet Lolita child," I said.

By the time Dreamy and I joined Eden down on the bank, she was scooping up tadpoles with a discarded paper cup. She groaned, still sore from the surgery six weeks prior.

"You ready to go home, Eden?"

"Just a little while longer, please, Katrina." A rather large tadpole had sprouted back legs. It held her fascination. She stared into the cup while a vapor of white tobacco smoke escaped between her lips, made a ledge above her upper lip, then dissipated.

"You've had yourself a fine child here, Eden; pretty little thing.

I've never held anything so soft and she's light as a feather. Dreamy needs her momma to love on her and make her feel wanted. What if this baby grows up to be a singer like Tina Turner, but she won't have anything to do with you because you were so mean to her and all?"

Eden poured the tadpole back into the stream.

"If you don't want her, then give her to me."

"That sounds just like somethin' you'd say, Katrina!" Eden stood and paraded back and forth in front of me still barefoot and waving her cigarette around. "But this is my kid. I had her and nobody's takin' her from me. See? You think you can do better than me at everythin', that I'm not worth a Mexican peso to anybody. But I'll see that baby dead before I let someone take her from me."

"Momma was right, Eden. Lolita Dream should have been adopted out to a good family. I can't stand you doing this to her, making her feel all abandoned. A momma shouldn't talk that way about her child!"

"Can I help that my head's not on straight right now? It's not right, you makin' me feel guilty and all like this baby's goin' to remember a bit of this. You and your religious ways make me sick."

"I haven't said a word about religion, Eden. I'm talking about loving this baby, and if it takes God to help you do that right, well then, it's high time you found God."

"I knew this was comin'. You're bound to find a way to squeeze God into the conversation."

"And you exaggerate because what little I do talk of God must hang around in your thoughts so long. You can't blame me because God is talking to you, trying to bring you to him. God is real, Jesus is real, and he's going to talk to you if he wants."

Eden had a way of reversing everything she had just said when she realized the conversation was not going her way. "Jesus is not talking in my head. I know what I'm thinkin' even if I am all muddled up about it. You can't make me believe those thoughts are the words of God."

"He loves you, Eden. God can help you through this mess. I know how you feel. I've been through it too. I hurt inside and know that tomorrow may not be better than today. But I'm not alone."

"Give me that baby and take me home."

"Take her then. I'm sorry if I've made you feel guilty. I'm not try-ing to play God, Eden. But please let me help you with this baby girl. You'll always be her momma. But I'll always be your sister. Let me help."

She stubbornly refused to look at me. "You're not going to make me cry, Katrina," she said, then turned to take the baby and strode up the hill barefoot, her elbows alternating side to side as she clutched the tiny pink bundle. She rocked Dreamy back and forth as though she were a Christmas ham. I sighed and picked up her muddy boots, following her up the hill and tossing them onto the floor of the Chevy. She cried all the way back home.

When we careened onto the clay-and-pebble drive, I saw a single red rose stuck between the mailbox and the postal flag. I left it alone until the petals turned brown and brittle and then one day just blew away.

My coaxing compelled Eden to doll up Lolita Dream in a blue ruffled dress in order to pay a visit to Darrell Lunsford's daddy in July. She was six months old by the time we slipped away from Momma, who still feared that Eden might forget and leave Lolita Dream in a shopping cart when she went to the grocery store.

Mr. Lunsford had such high aspirations about us, he prepared the house with generous abandon, throwing himself into the job of making his place ready for the visit of his granddaughter. He phoned several times that morning to assure us the hounds had been put out, the drapes had been aired, and every item small enough to fit into an infant's mouth had been locked in the root cellar. He was so eager for the day to arrive that he invited half the Lunsford clan.

Eden stood in the middle of the trailer's living room, her sneakers leaving matted impressions in the green shag carpet, and held Dreamy up for all the admirers to regard and gush over. Seated on either side of him, Mr. Lunsford's two sisters prattled back and forth, oblivious to the brother between them.

"Eden, has the baby had colic?" Darrell's Aunt Nally sat with her knees slightly spread. Her long cotton skirt lapped between her legs and brushed against her faded red bobbysocks. Whenever she spoke, her sister, Foley, echoed an antiphony of protest.

"Don't let Nally near that baby with her remedies, Eden. It's all poison and witches' brew." Foley's gracile appearance and her sleek attire was diminished by her critical assessment of any Lunsford with an opinion. That would be every Lunsford.

"I've heard of colic. It's a stomach disease or something, ain't it?" Eden jiggled Dreamy and the infant made a new game of it, bubbling out baby mouth music to the pumping of her mother's hip.

"All those nights we passed Dreamy around like a hot potato, Eden—that's colic," I said.

"You mean all that time she had colic and I just thought she hated me?"

"I wish I'd have known," said Nally. "Buckthorn bark's a good purgative. I mix it with chamomile to ease colic."

"Just call her Granny Clampett," said Foley, flaunting the gold bangles on her wrist and flipping the dog-eared pages on a television guide. "It isn't every family that has its own snake-oil hawker and underground brewery."

"The wine I make is for stomach complaint and isn't filled with all those additives. And wine isn't brewed, it's distilled," said Nally.

"Like I said, 'Granny Clampett.' I don't see anything good on today and I suppose we all got our dance cards filled, what with wanting to hold this baby, anyway. Who wants hot cider besides me?"

"None for me, Foley. I'm still nursin' this here beer," said Mr. Lunsford.

Foley and Nally appeared to speak from a script they had rehearsed since their childhood. The Lunsford sisters tossed their words back and forth in not so much a baneful manner as it was like two bantam hens pecking over a single grain of corn.

While Eden passed Dreamy off to the Lunsford aunts, I decided to fade from all the attention. So I eased down a hallway and through a doorway, believing I had stumbled upon the bathroom. A stiff fabric raked across my face when I entered the room: a musty dark cubicle that had no window.

My fingers searched the uneven wall of wood veneer paneling until they found the light switch, sunken in a bare encasement. I flipped on the light. The sight of the room nearly took my breath from me. It gave me the same feeling as standing in my dead Papaw's toolshed. Once, I swore I felt him standing right there next to me. Still taped to Darrell's bedroom walls, old posters of barely clad girls riding Harley motorbikes and sitting atop the hoods of roadsters painted bright red and yellow littered the paneling. The yellow tape curled at the edges with dusty filaments of spider art rustling silent when the old central air unit blew dusty air into the room. I could tell that Darrell had been a grubber among grease monkeys by his collection of foreign hubcaps and RC Cola calendars and antique oil cans that brandished fifties slogans—all mottled with greasy sediment. Mr. Lunsford made certain the shrine remained just as Darrell had left it that last morning—full of boyish clutter, lacking in strategy, and with enough dirty laundry strewn about the place to make a casual observer believe a teenage boy had just left the building. Nothing like the pristine haven found inside Darrell's Chevy.

My hand curled around my denim handbag, and I remembered a gift that I had tucked away inside the zippered pouch. Lolita Dream had posed in a perfect little Buddha deportment for the Magic Mart photographer, her fingers cupped at her belly and a serene smile dimpling her round face. I had bought up all the three-by-fives and cut them up to tuck inside the Christmas cards that Momma never mailed. When Eden and I made plans to visit Mr. Lunsford, I found a small gilded frame with a tiny hook on the back and slid one of Dreamy's photographs inside. I now felt foolish for having wrapped it in pink paper and curling ribbon, so I tore off the paper and stuffed it back inside my purse.

"I should give this to you, Darrell," I said. The photograph fit squarely between a baseball cap and ratchet set left pointlessly atop the splintered bureau. "Name's Lolita Dream Hurley and even though she doesn't have your name, she has your eyes. They will always remind me of how you scammed my sister and left us all here to worry over a little girl with a child for a mother. So here's her picture to remind you of all you missed because of your reckless ways."

All the biker chicks pinned to the paneling stared down at me with their mindless gazes. I bet they all would have loved to hold Lolita Dream, had they had the chance.

CHAPTER 10

Another banal season of summer and then fall wound a meaningless thread around the days until they became a past without echoes or mile markers. Then, from out of the blue, time hurtled me straight into the path of demanding expectations. Hurleys never shaped their offspring into pliable instruments of learning and productivity. Instead, they set them out on the curb, hoping they would be carted off by the first individual who stopped to pick through their lives and take what pleased them. When you do not plan for such things, they will eat you alive.

Dreamy matured into a plump toddler with dark ringlets of hair. The coils always made a springy sort of crown around her head except for when the weight of bathwater pulled her tresses down into silken spirals around her shoulders. Each morning she sat in the path of the kitchen's open door. She wore only a diaper while she played with thread spools from Momma's splintered sewing basket. In my opinion, you could stick a pair of pumpkin-colored wings upon her shoulders and she would have flown for Raphael. After she quietly sat on the kitchen floor while the morning sun dried her hair, she came and stood by my chair in the alcove until I picked her up.

"Hey, little girl. It's your birthday. Aunt Kateen has something special. Come see." I buckled her in and filled her highchair tray with Froot Loops prior to heading off to my first period class. I pulled a soft terry doll from a Magic Mart bag. "Happy birthday from Aunt Kateen."

Dreamy squealed and held the doll against her chest. She gripped it in one hand while stuffing Froot Loops into her mouth with the other.

Eden shuffled past, her eyes not completely open. "I wish you'd stop givin' her stuff, Katrina. You'll have her more spoiled than she already is."

*"My doll!"* Dreamy squeezed it and tucked it beneath her chin.

"Brat!" Eden reached for her Pall Malls that lay beneath a kitchen towel on the countertop.

Dreamy practiced manipulation as skillfully as my Meemaw practiced her crocheting. Her habit of toddling toward me and throwing herself against me whenever her irascible mother was around sent Eden's temper soaring. But secretly I loved it. Eden's inquietude had swelled until the day she announced that she was going back to school at night. Aunt Pippa then volunteered to lend a hand with Dreamy the evenings that I worked.

"It's her birthday, Eden. Remember?"

"I know you think I forgot, Katrina. But I didn't. I'll pick her up a thang or two this afternoon."

"Mind if I buy her a little cake from Safeway? We could have a party for her after I'm finished with school today."

"I don't care."

I kissed Dreamy's forehead. "Aunt Kateen will bring you cake, then, little girl."

Eden took her smoke out to the back porch as though she had tired of looking at us.

After my last class, I ran into the kitchen and put together Dreamy's care package: a plastic sandwich bag of animal crackers, her terry-cloth dog, a rat-tail comb, her diapers, and her nightclothes. Before Aunt Pippa showed up, we celebrated Dreamy's birthday with cake and ice cream. Eden bought her Crayolas and a coloring book.

"She might eat them. Why don't I keep them up for her until she's a little older?" I asked.

Eden shoved aside her cake and left the room.

Aunt Pippa arrived with a wrapped gift in hand. "I brought somethin' nice for you, sweet little thang." She helped Dreamy tear open the pink-and-blue paper to reveal a chime ball inside.

Dreamy put it to her mouth.

"I guess I'll take her on to my place, then," said Aunt Pippa. She kept her until bedtime.

I usually picked up Dreamy after work, unless I got stuck on the late shift. On those nights, Daddy picked her up when he brought Eden home from the high school. We worked together like that, trying to ease Eden's jitters about her role as mother by helping. Truth be told, it made us more easeful too.

But Daddy's worries spread beyond the muck and mire of Eden's problems. He queried me often about my college plans, how I would spend my life, and would I fritter it away on something as injudicious as fine art. I could discuss the matter with anyone but him without hint of combat. But when he approached me about my future, I felt as though I was being gently splayed and left to dry out on some desert where women were reprocessed into little societal patties. *Take your number, Katrina, and sit quiet like a good little girl. We've only room for a few, so be grateful for your station and for the fact you're not standing in some bread line in Russia.*

I grew adept at avoiding him.

Strawberry season made our entire house smell like sugar and candy. The cloud of sweet steam blended with the faint trace of lacquer— Momma, bent on making the cabinets look new, had stripped away all of the yellow paint and recoated the wood in a glossy cedar.

Momma dragged me out of bed on Saturday to help her with Dreamy and to pick and slice the berries. My mother stood red-faced over a pot of syrupy fruit. First she ladled hot, soupy jam into jars. Then she sealed brass-colored lids onto the Mason jars, saved every year since before the passing of my father's mother. I cleaned and sliced strawberries until my cuticles turned pink.

Daddy watched us. "Women are made to teach, Katrina. It's the only job that makes any sense."

Caught in the jam work, I couldn't flee. "I'm going to have to make up my own mind, Daddy."

"I can't get anything through that thick head of yours. Why I try, I don't know."

"Here's the next batch, Momma," I said. "We need to sharpen this knife again."

"Just look around the valley and see who's who and what's what. The teachers run the town, have all the jobs, and live in the best houses." Daddy had picked up this fable somewhere between the courthouse and the Corner Café, where the girls from the legal pools and the courthouse clerks stood out on the sidewalks engaged in conceited jactation and goings-on around the county. Most of the talk had little to do with actual facts and a lot to do with each one trying to out-best the other on what they knew and who had told them.

"Momma, do you have a stamp?" The Cirrus Bible College registration forms lay in a neat stack, filled out and ready to mail; only the last paper still needed my signature.

"Stamps are in the junk drawer," she said. "Need an envelope, too?"

"I have an envelope. It came with the registration forms."

"Reece Caldwell's girl, she's smart about such matters. Got herself a scholarship right here in town to go out to Sumner Hill, and she'll have a job, too, as soon as she graduates. A *real* job. She'll be teaching down at the elementary school down by Parker Road. Clayford School, it's called."

"Crawford School, Daddy. Remember? I went to Crawford six years."

"Here, Katrina, dry your hands before you go groping around my stamp and envelope drawer." Momma draped a mildewed kitchen towel across my shoulder.

"I have to sign this paper, and the ink has run out of this pen. Daddy, pass me your pen," I said. He pulled the clip pen out of his shirt pocket and handed it to me. All the while he spouted the virtues of women who matriculated off to hometown Sumner Hill to study education while the boys majored in business or agriculture. I ignored him and signed the last paper for my Cirrus application.

"Knock, knock."

I heard the voice through the open kitchen door.

Dreamy waved at the visitor through the mesh in the aluminum screen door then returned to smashing Cheerios on her tray with her fist.

"Who's there?" Daddy took back his pen as I handed it to him.

"It's me, Mr. Hurley. Stanley Houston."

I threw off the apron.

"Mr. Houston, step on in," Daddy said, "and have some coffee. Donelle, put on a fresh pot, will you? And warm up those sticky buns while you're at it."

"Daddy, we're a mess." I turned my face from Mr. Houston, who stared in with an expectant grin. The house looked small and cluttered to me all at once.

"How do, Mr. Houston?" Momma had a tight smile with a trace of familiarity. She knew the Houstons sat two rows over from her pew on Sunday mornings.

"You called about some insurance, Mr. Hurley?" Stanley Houston wore a brown leisure suit opened in the front with a practical tan shirt. "Life insurance?"

Daddy pushed the door wide open. I almost slipped away to listen to Peter Frampton. But Stan Houston stepped back and invited his son to precede him through the doorway. "Mr. Hurley, I don't believe you've met my son, Sol. He'll be joining my brokerage after he graduates in the spring. I knew you wouldn't mind me bringing him along."

"Nice to meet you, young feller. This is my daughter, Katrina."

I felt plastered against the cedar-lacquered kitchen cabinets, a fly trapped in amber. Between "Hello, Sol" and "Yes, we've met," I crossed the chasm into old age. The shirt that I had tie-dyed in art class two Christmases ago was ragged at the sleeve. It had doubled as a nightgown until it shrunk up to the belt loop of my jeans. My hair was pulled back tight, a stringy ponytail with no bangs. I was a dead ringer for David Bowie.

"I've seen you at church, haven't I?" Sol studied my face. I felt shriveled and brown, an old apple. I never knew if the boys who ran in his circles really never noticed girls like me or simply did not admit it.

"And at school. Once at the hospital." I wish that I hadn't said that, as though I had marked off every meeting with a cool precision of thought.

"Katrina, why don't you take Sol to see the rabbits out back?" Momma stood with arms akimbo, and I could see the way she studied him. "I'll bet you'd like that, wouldn't you, Sol?"

"You don't have to go see the rabbits," I said.

"We can go." Sol looked away from his father.

"Sol, I was going to show you these A-2-40 forms while we filled out Mr. Hurley's contract." Stan Houston opened a briefcase and readied a pen. "These documents can be tricky."

"We won't be long," Sol said.

Behind the house, I led him to the garage built by my Papaw Hurley. "We keep the rabbit cages inside the garage. The big white female just had babies."

"You don't have to show me the rabbits."

The way he sort of laughed and looked away made me feel foolish. His hair was darker than before and nearly touched his shoulders with silky wisps that kissed his cheeks. He took on a complexity and buoyancy that sent me farther into his shadow. "I don't really like rabbits. They're just—rabbits."

"Over there, is that where that mechanic died?" He stood between the garage and the house.

"Darrell Lunsford died in the hospital. He crashed into that ditch by Erie, if that's what you want to know."

"I'm not prying. I was just standing here, and I remembered all the stories about him all of a sudden. Remember? We met at the hospital."

"I remember."

We both looked away.

Sol stared at the ditch for a while, his eyes soft and lambent, flickering under a tent of spring-blue sky. He shook some change in his pocket, stole a gander into the garage to glance at the rabbits, and then paced in front of me, taking two-foot strides before he stopped altogether. "Would you like to go for a Coke?"

"Inside the house? You thirsty?"

"Not like that. I'm not asking you to go and fetch me a Coke. That is, we could go somewhere. Maybe eat too."

"Eat?"

"Or—not eat. Just go for a Coke."

"With your daddy?"

"Sometime we could go for a Coke."

"Sure." He stared at me for a moment, a familiar warmth connecting our gazes. I realized that he had known me all along. Boys have their odd ways, and I was just catching on.

The Cirrus catalogue had a big fiery logo emblazoned at the top of the cover. Underneath it were the words "Pray for the Harvest." I kept it tucked beneath my pillow so that I could pull it out each morning and thumb through the pages. It was all Lillian Trasher's fault that I had ordered the Bible school catalogue in the first place. My paperback library now stood in stacks eight high, arranged in a single row, and pressed against the royal blue baseboards in my bedroom. Lillian Trasher's biography was tucked into the "great women whom I could never emulate" stack between Corrie ten Boom and Kathryn Kuhlman. Kathryn, I could do without. But next to Lillian, I was a burl on a tree.

Lillian threw away a perfectly good marriage proposal to run off to India and take care of orphans. She kept nothing for herself. When a group of women pitched in and bought her a dress, she cut it up and sewed little dresses for the children.

If I could not be like Jesus, perhaps I could be like Lillian.

"Katrina, take me over to Mr. Lunsford's, will you? He wants to see Dreamy, and I've put him off too long as it is."

I laid the open catalogue upon my chest and uncrossed my feet. "Eden, drive yourself."

"I can't drive with Dreamy in the car. You know how she

caterwauls when I buckle her in that child seat. I can't tolerate her squealin' at me when I'm fixin' to drive. She listens to you better. Besides, Mr. Lunsford likes you."

"Mr. Lunsford likes everyone."

"Katrina, are you going to take us or not?"

"I can't find my keys."

"They're here. Right next to the potted plant."


Mr. Lunsford stood out in the yard. His face grew flushed when our Chevy wheeled onto the sparse lawn in front of the trailer. His entire mien reflected expectancy. "Give me that baby. Pappy's been waitin' all mornin' to hold you, little girl." From his perch on the small front wooden landing, he made wide, invisible loops with his arms to coax us onto the porch. Clad only in worn trousers and a transparent white undershirt, it was evident he expected us to come in out of the brisk morning air.

Eden handed Dreamy off to Mr. Lunsford. She turned her back and tapped a cigarette out of the pack, while thin metal bracelets clinked together against her wrist. Motherhood evoked a certain bent for what she must have considered more womanly trappings. I found her quite often rummaging through the bargain jewelry bin at the Magic Mart.

"Little Eden, I'd appreciate it if you'd kindly smoke outside. My emphysema's been troublesome all winter, and I just can't tolerate tobacco smoke anymore."

Eden took a long, hard drag on her freshly lit smoke, then flicked it into a rusted watering can. "You got company besides us, Mr. Lunsford? I see a Mustang's parked next to that tree."

"My nephew, Carl, is visiting today. Probably wanting money, but I appreciate the company." He straddled Dreamy against his hip just so she could grip the straps of his shirt like a horse's rein. It delighted him to no end to hear her say, "Giddup, Pappy!"

The musty odor inside the trailer had vanished and smelled more like perfumed wax.

"You got a new rug, Mr. Lunsford?" I noticed the shag had disappeared altogether.

"I been datin' a gal down at the Corner Café, and she talked me into it. It's that wall-to-wall sculptured, high-low business. Feels kind of good to my old tired and callused dogs. Does it look good?"

"Right nice," said Eden. The young man who sat in the vinyl armchair nodded at her, and she returned the gesture. He wore boot-cut denims and a western-styled shirt with abalone snaps up the front, although he did not bother to snap the top four.

"Carl, say 'hi' to the girls. This here girl is Eden, the baby's momma. That un's her sister, Katrina."

Carl muttered something, but I could scarcely make it out.

"Can I fix you girls a bite to eat? I got some of that Petit Jean bacon." Mr. Lunsford handed Dreamy a soft peppermint stick.

"Nothing for me," I said.

Eden fixed her eyes on Carl's belt buckle, an oversize chrome disk adorned with a large bucking bull surrounded by little aqua stones. "Is that real turquoise, Carl?" She leaned forward with her hands on her knees and stared at his belt buckle.

"I believe it's real. As much as I paid for it, it better be the genuine McCoy."

"Are you a real cowboy, like the kind in the rodeo?" Eden had an odd glow about her that usually indicated how impressed she was with someone.

"I ride the circuit pretty often. Make a little money with it, but can't say that I can quit my regular job, just yet."

"What you do—ride bulls?"

"I ride bulls, broncos, do some ropin'."

"Let's go watch him, Katrina," Eden said. "Carl, can you get us tickets for the next rodeo?"

He cut his eyes toward Eden. One side of his mouth curved into a smile.

"Mr. Lunsford, I see you've made coffee. I believe I'll just pour myself a cup if it's all right with you. Eden, you want a cup too?" I asked.

"I'll bet you rode in the March rodeo at the Pope County Fairgrounds, didn't you, Carl? I knew I should have gone, but it's so hard to take a kid out on those bleachers. Dreamy wants to get into everything, and it would be just like her to slip right through the stands."

"Eden, you're sure you don't want coffee?" I said.

"If I look away for one second, she'll eat dropped candy right out of the dirt," Eden said and tossed Dreamy a scathing glance.

"My sister's got a kid. She does the same thing. I figger it's surprisin' they grow up at all." Carl conversed with Eden, the only other person in the room.

"I'll just fix myself some coffee, then," I said.

"Have some coffeecake, too, Katrina. Darlene brings that stuff over from the café, and I can't eat it all," Mr. Lunsford said. He seated Dreamy on the floor. "This baby's put on a pound or two since the last visit, or I'm getting' too old to lift her."

"May's coming up, Mr. Lunsford. If I mail you an invitation to my graduation, you'll come, won't you?" I asked.

"I don't know, Katrina. You know my social calendar's pretty full up this time of year." He winked from his sunken-down roost on the old plaid couch. "'Course I'll come, girlie."

After I stirred the third teaspoon of sugar into a mug that read "Go, Hogs, Go!" I heard the front door click. I only saw belt loops through the kitchen pass-through. "Are you going somewhere, Eden?"

She bent to make eye contact beneath the cabinet and said, "Carl's showin' me his Mustang. I'll not be but a minute." Then she was gone.

"You findin' ever little thing you need, Katrina?" Mr. Lunsford sat scrawling stick people onto a yellow pages book. He showed them to Dreamy while she traced them with her fingertips.

"Yes, and I sliced myself a piece of this coffeecake. Darlene made this, I'll bet."

"She makes all the pastries. I keep telling her she ought to open her own place, but she likes the security, I reckon."

"You think women feel secure here in Mockingbird Valley?" I joined him on the sofa.

"I believe they look for security here same's they do anyplace else."

"The valley's a nice, quiet place, I suppose." I wanted to make him feel that I did not find fault with everything in the valley. "But security here is for the kids whose daddies have been in business here for years. They inherit their security. I don't see many options for me." I liked his sympathetic face. I felt I could trust him. "Daddy wants me to be a teacher."

"I reckon you have to make your own options, Katrina. When I started up my own shop, I didn't have two nickels to rub together. Took me five years to turn a profit, and I worked the night shift at the poultry plant quite often until the business had a chance to take off. But they's a lot of satisfaction in that for me. Always had it in mind to leave the shop to Darrell, but fate changed all that. Don't reckon my only granddaughter here will have much use for it."

"You selling the shop?"

"I'm considering it. When Darrell died all of sudden, it took the wind out of me. I been trainin' my nephew, Carl, here to take it over. But he don't have much of a business intellect. Boy's got more debt than Carter's got liver pills. Someday I may just haul off and sell it, be done with it." Mr. Lunsford handed the pen to Dreamy and watched her scrawl circles across the advertisements. He glanced into his empty coffee mug.

"Mr. Lunsford, if you want I could clean out Darrell's bedroom, box up all that stuff. But not unless you're ready."

"You'd do that for me, honey?"

"I want to do it for you. You've been good to my sister and this baby. Let me return the favor."

"Between you and Darlene, this place'll look like a palace soon. What will I do with the extra room?"

"We could fix up a playroom for Dreamy."

"Do that. I'll give you some money for some dolls and such. Buy some pictures and a set of those little girl curtains."

"It'll make a fine playroom, Mr. Lunsford. Dreamy might not be so interested in rummaging through your things if she's got a place of her own to play in."

"Darlene can bring her grandbaby over too. This'll make this gal-baby happy, I believe. You want a doll, little girl?"

Dreamy clapped. Then she crawled out of his lap and latched on to me while mouthing *doll*. I believe she understood.

Eden peered around the door, her face flushed. "I'm taking a ride with Carl, and he's going to take me home afterwards, Katrina. Will you watch Dreamy until I get back?"

"I thought you were supposed to take her in for vaccinations today, Eden."

"Please, you do it? She nearly pulls my clothes off when I take her."

"Eden, I think you should take her."

"Please, just this once?" I could almost see Carl effervescing in her eyes. "He's a real cowboy, Katrina." The door closed. Carl revved the engine. It backfired, which probably pleased Eden.

Mr. Lunsford and I listened until the sound of the engine became a far-off hum and then was gone. He put aside the yellow pages, lifted a cotton shirt from a basket of clean laundry, and slipped it on. As he buttoned the shirt he said, "Carl's not a good one for commitments."

"Eden doesn't listen to me, Mr. Lunsford. She gets things in her head and, well, I can't ever get anywhere with her. Wish I could."

"Shame. She's got a pretty child here to take care of."

"I should go now. Thank you for the coffee and dessert. Tomorrow's Saturday. I'll be back to clean out the room."

"Let me give you money for the dolls."

"I'll get it tomorrow. Can't do much until we make room, anyway. Dreamy, say 'bye-bye' to Pappy."

She gave him a kiss and squeezed his neck.

"Katrina, I got three bedrooms in this place. I'm thinkin', why don't we just leave Darrell's things as is for a while. You fix up the spare for Dreamy. How would that be?"

"Whatever you say, Mr. Lunsford."

"I sound like a silly fool, I reckon, hangin' on to Darrell's things."

"Not at all."

He followed me to the door and then opened it for us. "You're a fine young woman, Katrina. And don't you worry your head about your sister. You got your own life to live. I'll see this baby gets taken care of."

"See you tomorrow." I held Dreamy close all the way to the car.

CHAPTER 11

*S*ixteen sparkling trophies sat on a table on the school gymnasium floor during the senior awards day. No pithy copier certificates for our class. The table cover, purple satin, flaunted our high school mascot in gold sequined appliqué—a garish mockingbird with a menacing bill and a purple *M* emblazoned across the chest. Our principal, Mrs. Nedreddy, dressed herself in a fastidious fashion—even more so than usual.

"To the senior class of nineteen hundred and seventy-six, I wish to commend you all," she said, "for exemplifying the highest standards of any class that I can remember for many years. Today's tokens of esteem are simply our recognition of those qualities that reflect your achievements and effort in making Mockingbird Valley High the best 4A school in five counties."

My classmates cheered. Caught up in the revelry, I felt a certain mix of glee and melancholy. Each presented award subtly surprised me, leaving me sidelined and wondering when and how the line had formed to apply for achievements. I wondered if those students had been told of those awards years ago on the sly, with the rest of us poor underachieving souls left out in the rain. *Give me any old token of your esteem, Mrs. Nedreddy. But do give one to me.*

Beth sat to my left. Jenny sat perched on the right and slipped M&M's to us both.

"Where's Jane, Beth?" It surprised me to see them separated.

"She's mad at me."

"Jane's always mad at someone," said Jenny. She dabbed at her eyes. Plagued with allergies, dark circles under her eyes gave her a fatigued appearance.

"Give me another M&M," I said.

"I told her she shouldn't get her hopes up about the Randolph Award for Musical Excellence," Beth said. Culpability marked her life. I could see guilt wash through her—the way she raked her fingers through her hair and stared into the doorway of the incident instead of looking at me. "She's miffed."

"Her voice is the best in the high school chorus," I said as I rummaged around inside the brown bag for chocolate strays, those little damaged M&M's.

"It's her GPA. She won't study. She just tries to fly by on talent."

"I didn't even know about the award," I said. "Mrs. Curry always ignored me in the chorus. I should have never dropped art class. May as well say it. All those trophies have left me in the dust."

"Where have we been all these years, Katrina? Did your momma tell you about this stuff?" Jenny curled the candy bag into a megaphone shape and shouted into it whenever Mrs. Nedreddy roused the crowd.

"My mother? She just wants me married off to some guy who goes to tractor pulls every weekend."

That did it. Our goal each day was to see how often we could make Beth laugh. Her odd laugh started as a low intermittent chuckle then spilled out in a tinny hyena clatter. That sent Jenny and me over the edge until our classmates in front of us shamed us with their imperious stares.

"Breathe, Beth," I said. "In your nose and out your mouth."

After she stopped laughing, Beth said, "Katrina, I remember when you always made the grades."

"It got away from me somehow."

"I see Sol Houston," said Jenny. "What happened to your date?"

I stopped smiling. "You're grieving me, Jenny."

"Boys are just animals by nature. If it were me, I'd walk right up to Sol Houston and tell it to him straight." Jenny kept her eyes to the right and planted on Sol. "The fact that he never called back puts him down on my list with the swine."

"Just don't look at him, Jenny. Turn your eyes."

Mrs. Nedreddy announced the winner of the music award, a lanky, scholarly boy who played the trumpet and took first chair at All-State. Several rows up, we heard enough of a clamor and a murmur of complaint to make us turn and stare. Jane loped up the stairs, and we did not see her again until graduation.

"Tell me how I look." Eden wore a plum cotton western shirt, with a sort of cape collar on the back that flapped when she jogged down the steps to the hall. She teased her hair on top, and it looked darker, nearly black, as though she had put a rinse to it.

"I'll just call you Dale from now on."

"Should I wear the hat, or is it too much?"

"How you going to fit it over all that hair?"

"I don't know why you can't just say somethin' nice every now and then instead of inspectin' me all the time for flaws."

"You look nice," I said.

"Good. You goin' with us to the rodeo tonight?"

"Do I have to?" I rearranged the pink and blue plastic combs on the dresser. Momma bought combs by the bag. Convinced the nation's supply had dwindled, she bought more.

"I need you to come, to hold Dreamy if she gets to fussing and eating too much cotton candy. Please help me with her." She stood in front of my mirror with her arms extended and her gaze fixed on her own face.

"Just leave her at home. I'll stay with her."

"No. I want Carl to get used to having her around."

"Eden, rushing Carl's not the thing to do. I told you what Mr. Lunsford said about him."

"Carl's nothing like Darrell, Katrina."

"Right. He has blue eyes instead of hazel. He drives a Mustang instead of a Chevy, and he doesn't mind clutter."

"You noticed too."

"Eden, Carl is like Darrell in every way. Maybe it's like that in the Lunsford gene pool or one of those anomalies that hits families every other generation, so it missed Mr. Lunsford but landed on Darrell and Carl. You can't see it now, but you'll wake up one morning and you'll have let a louse infiltrate your life, and he'll have your checkbook and be eating all your groceries." I looked her up and down. "Where did you get all this stuff?"

"Hold this boot while I put it on. These Ropers are slide-ons, and my ankles are swollen today."

"No way would Daddy would pay for all this, Eden. He won't let Momma buy socks."

"Carl's got a credit card. That's how it is when you date a twenty-year-old. You ought to date an older fellow, Katrina. Then you'd see what I mean. It's as different as night and day." The way Eden lit up as she puttered about the bathroom sink and dug through the lipsticks in my makeup bag sent a foreign pulse all through our home. I found her tossing her old T-shirts into a brown grocery bag and hanging up western outfits that Carl had paid for with plastic expectations. The girl I knew as Eden disappeared from sight and forced her identity to become shadow to another.

Dreamy tottered past her mother and planted herself between my legs.

"I'm having her ears pierced," said Eden. "She needs something done to fix her up. I like those little earrings they make for babies now. I bet Carl will pay for it, if I ask him sweet."

"She won't sit still for you in the car, Eden. Dreamy's not going to let you hold her down and poke holes in her little ears."

The phone rang. Eden tried to leap down the hall but missed two steps and fell face first onto the rust carpet. She lay on the floor with her Ropers pressed against the wall before she swore, picked herself up, and ran for the phone. I heard her saying mostly "uh-huh" to the caller until she finally hung up and then tromped back up the hall to rap on my bedroom door. "Katrina, open up."

"It's open." Dreamy had crawled onto my bed and fallen asleep with her pudgy arms curled around one of my dolls. "Don't wake her, Eden."

"It's not time for her nap," said Eden. "If she sleeps this early, I'll not get her down for the afternoon."

"You let her stay up too late watching the late show last night. That's why she's tired. Why did you knock?"

"Carl says not to bring Dreamy tonight. He thinks the rodeo dust is bad for babies. It's so sweet of him to think of her like that." She rubbed her hipbone, apparently noticing for the first time that it smarted from the fall.

I teased my hair around the crown.

"Everything has changed, so would you mind?" Eden stood over the threshold glancing down at the floor and then leaning back to stare down the hallway.

"You like my hair?" I lifted it with a hair pick until daylight shone through.

"It's kind of tangled like a rat's nest."

"You never say kind things to me, Eden," I said and melodramatically held my hand against my brow.

"I could get Carl's cousin Esther to watch Dreamy."

"Who is Esther?"

"Oh, you know Esther. She's the single girl with five kids and a touch of retardation," she said. "Her momma's threatening to have her fixed."

"I see."

"I don't know where people get off calling her retarded, myself. I met her one night at Momma Lou's in Morrilton, and we had us a good time. I didn't see nothin' wrong with her. Besides, Esther likes kids and you don't have to be all there to keep an eye out for them."

"I'll keep Dreamy with me. Tonight's the last night of the county peach festival. I'll take her to that. Leave her stroller by the kitchen door." I took sections of my hair and combed out the tangles.

The phone rang again. "That's Carl. You've decided, then? Don't look at me so odd. I'll tell him the good news."


The county festivals ushered in a zestful joy to the valley as desperately needed for morale as rain and parades and state elections. Peach season marshaled in an annual food festival into nearby Johnson County as well as a beauty pageant where girls vied for the title of Miss Alberta Peach. The year of my grandmother's death, a cousin on my daddy's side once swept all the points for the crown—an event that set off jealous bells throughout the entire clan. When her momma called excited and gushing about the title and the scholarship money, Daddy waggled his head and said, "Katrina could never do something like that."

The drive to the county seat of Clarksville cleared the morning webs and offered a quiet moment to teach Dreamy new words. Her chatter enlivened me and helped to ease the troubled worries batted around my mind in regard to Eden. Eden's concept of language was buried in the mucky rudiment and vulgarity handed down by generations of Hurleys who preserved their ignorance beneath a hard shell of self-absorbed apathy. Teaching words to Eden's offspring offered the most supreme sense of satisfaction, as Dreamy took hold of each new word like an anchor. Eden had denied herself the luxury of knowledge in exchange for whatever means floated her boat as near the easy bank as possible. Therefore, she didn't teach Dreamy, but instead allowed her to prattle nonsense, spitting out her little vowels and consonants like aimless marbles.

Dreamy loved the downtown bustle, the Clarksville farmers, and the locals who hawked their wares beneath canvas tents while they poured endless pitchers of sweet tea. We sampled the peach cobblers, the turnovers, and the funnel cakes. Every baked or fried pastry not stuffed with peaches was suffocated with sugar-infused peach topping. A man wearing a giant felt peach costume had just scared the living daylights out of Dreamy when a voice penetrated her screams.

"Katrina Hurley?"

I wanted to keep walking, to not admit that I recognized Sol Houston's voice.

"I don't blame you for not answering, if you'd rather not."

I made a quick decision and turned. "Hello, Sol. This is my niece, Dreamy."

"Lots of curls. She looks like her father."

"Her momma's got curls too, but she straightens them out."

Sol held a bushel of peaches the same way he had held his mother's purse in the emergency room. Forced servitude. "My mother buys these every year. I'm taking them out to the station wagon. I'll be free after that, though."

"Have a good time," I said. I turned and walked away. I imagined his eyes lingering on me, studying my back because that was all that was left of me to study. A breeze wafted through the avenue and stirred the festival dust into a ghostlike twister, enough to make everyone turn and look. So I turned and looked and found Sol gone.

*God forgive me, I hate him, and please keep him away from me.*

"Katrina?"

"Sol? I thought you had gone." He had returned, still holding the bushel of peaches. "Meet me at the merry-go-round. I've still got extra tickets my little brothers didn't use, and we can give your niece a ride."

"Okay." He sauntered away and my gaze followed him, dumb girl that I was.

Eden stood in line at the rodeo gate and stubbed out her cigarette on a fence post. Carl had left no ticket for her as he had promised, so she stood counting out her money. Daddy had handed her a wad of ones when he dropped her off. He always had cash on the ready like that because of his hoarding habit, but seldom parted with it. Called it mad money in case Carl made her mad and she needed to come home in a cab. But she did not mind using it for a ticket—a ticket to watch Carl ride the Brahman bull and make the girls swoon, while all along he only had eyes for Eden Hurley.

The air had a raw, sweaty smell, but Eden liked it and felt at home around the cowboys. Too bad for Katrina that she wanted no part of it and did not try to understand men like Carl, or she could pick one out for herself and feel like a queen. Just like Eden.

Her eyes lifted and she saw the moon sharing the sky with the sun; one lone star was embedded in a perfect, deep blue sky that was trying to pull the curtain down on the day. She bought her ticket and sat alone amidst the spectators on the bleachers and wished that she had made Katrina come so that isolation would not sit so close to her.

The rodeo queen sat atop her palomino in the center of the arena, while the little boys on ponies paraded round in circles and round the barrels and round the queen, little worker bees born to serve on their daddies' farms. Never wanting more than the valley could provide. Yet life on the farm was its own kind of monarchy, one that Eden envied, because she really only observed instead of participated. Hurleys were not rodeo queens or even rulers of their own places. They accepted their station along with the other spectators.

Eden lit another cigarette. The cowboys entered and the spectators lifted a chorus of shouts and applause. Katrina called them men who lived to personify the past, mere players conjuring up the games lonely chaps once played in the desert. That riled Eden for some reason. She perched on the edge of her seat and saw one of the bull riders, recognized him because Carl introduced him to her once when they went dancing at José's. But no Carl.

The rodeo queen made the loop and waved at everyone on Eden's side of the stands. The floodlights danced on her rhinestone-encircled hat, while dust rose up around her; the particles turned blue in the fluorescent lights and enfolded her like the petals of a flower in Momma's garden. Eden hated her and watched all the girls smiling back at her from the onlookers' gallery and wondered if they hid their jealousy while all their men friends gaped at the queen.

She felt uneasy. Katrina would be bathing Dreamy about now. She would make her coo and laugh. Dreamy acted differently around her Aunt Katrina. It irritated Eden. She looked around the arena again. *Where is Carl?*

If she could have mustered any smarts at all, she might be sitting in the stands a free bird instead of always having the weight of this child marring up her romances. Yet Eden awoke in the night to run to the kid's bed and feel her breath against her fingertips. Dreamy's cries shot up her spine so that she moved heaven and earth to make her happy again. Dreamy never noticed any of it. She wondered if most kids were so unappreciative of how their mommas worked so hard to make them happy. If only she could make herself happy.

*Carl.* It was Carl that summed up all she needed to fill the vacuum inside of her—the vacuum that threatened to send her over the edge like Aunt Velda.

"Miss, I think that man down there is trying to get your attention."

Eden awoke from her float down the dreamy river. "Are you talking to me?" she asked the woman in front of her. The woman pointed and then adjusted a silk posy hair comb.

Eden searched the bleachers and then made eye contact with Carl. He stood down on the grass in front of a group of children who swung their boots back and forth, little impatient pendulums. "Carl!" She waved at him, but he did not return her smile, only nodded in a sideways fashion. He strode out of sight as though he had her on a leash and knew she would follow.

Eden followed. She caught sight of his plaid shirt and tried to catch up to him as he meandered through men perched on the iron railings with numbers pinned to their shirts. Carl stood next to the tailgate of a truck, opening his beer from a red cooler.

"You had me worried, Carl," she said.

"Eden, do me a favor and don't talk."

"Your voice sounds funny."

"Did you hear what I said, girl?"

Ray Cornelius, Carl's riding buddy, stood two feet away, with his sinewy arms parked akimbo on his bony hips, his gaze on the ground. Eden and he had become friends, so she approached him and said, "Ray, tell me what's wrong with Carl. You know, don't you? I can tell by the look on your face."

"Carl's not riding tonight." Ray never looked up.

"But it's such a perfect night and, look, I done bought my ticket. Go on in and get your number, baby. You'll do fine." Eden returned to Carl's side and tried to comfort him, as though he left his nerve somewhere along the roadside.

Carl hurled his beer against the side of the truck and glared at Ray and the men, who fell silent and stared at him.

Ray tried to take Eden aside and put some distance between her and Carl. "You'd best go on back inside and watch the rodeo. Carl's not himself."

"I want to be with him. He just needs to talk to someone, and I'll help make it better."

"Let me call you a cab, Eden. Give him some time," Ray said.

"Eden's coming with me." Carl grabbed her arm.

"Carl, you're hurting me! Let go."

Carl dragged her to the cab of his pickup, leaving her by the passenger door. "Get in. We don't need them."

"Eden, he's drunk. The rodeo boss wouldn't let him ride in such a state." Ray sounded softer, like he was coaxing a kitten from a burning building.

"Carl, is that true?"

"I said get in, Eden. You goin' with me or not?" He climbed into the driver's seat.

"I can't let you leave like this, Carl," said Ray. "Let me call you a cab." He tried to wrestle the keys from Carl's grasp but got belted in the process.

"You go off and kill yourself, then! But I'm not letting this girl leave with you. I happen to know she's a minor." Ray swore and wiped the blood from his lip.

Carl gunned the engine.

"I can't let him leave all alone, Ray." Eden climbed into the cab. The pickup careened across the grassy field with the pickup hatch flapping up and down and the bumper scraping the ground, while Eden stared back at the onlookers, vague forms fading behind them. Her stomach roiled. She borrowed one of Katrina's confident stares, then turned away from them all. But no one could see that in the dark anyway.

CHAPTER 12

$S$ol and I sipped coffee beneath a dogwood tree, a nice old tree with roots firmly set and blossoms packed thick as the silk petals on an old woman's bonnet. Sol had bought the drinks from a man who sold coffee, tea, and lemonade, along with some beaded necklaces and antique buttons that had nothing to do with the beverage menu. But that only added to the quaint flea-market feel of the booths in the quadrant that sold homemade apparel. The southern pecan blend tasted pleasant with my usual cream and four packets of sugar. Not boiled down with a hint of tar like Momma's tin-pot brew.

Details such as what he wore the day of the peach festival or what I wore made a home in my mind, painted with vivid clarity. Sol donned his usual faded jeans and wore a sweater, royal blue and oversize—but big in a pleasing manner. My red cotton sweater that I slipped over my head when the mornings were cool became its usual afternoon burden. I walked around in my "Jesus Is Lord" T-shirt with the sweater tied at my waist, above my faded jeans and worn Keds, sans socks. While Sol had fetched the coffee, I purchased a rag doll at one of the craft booths and carried it in a tote on my shoulder, a handy place in which to drop other nonessential binge buys as we meandered around the little festival shacks and tents.

Sol cut grass for his uncle. That accounted for the deeper hue of olive in his complexion. His features were well defined and balanced out nicely with his blue cotton shirt and sweater. Everything on Sol balanced out nicely, for that matter.

Dreamy curled her arms over her head and fell asleep in her large blue stroller. She was fast to realize that Sol carried all the merry-go-round tickets in his blue jeans pocket, so as the carousel had wound down, she mimicked the riding motion and said to Sol, "More ride, more ride." Sol laughed, and I was encouraged to see that her knack for figuring things out had emerged early.

"Have you settled on a school yet?" Sol locked the paper cup between his knees and wrapped his arms loosely around his calves in the same relaxed manner of men that camp in front of Saturday afternoon football games. It looked pleasing on him.

"I heard about Cirrus Bible College in Springfield, Missouri. So I applied for admission. But I haven't heard back from them yet."

"Why Bible school?"

"I'll go just about anywhere as long as it's out of here." I said it so often it had become my litany. "Los Angeles, New York…I'd even go overseas."

"You must really hate it here."

"I used to think so. But since Dreamy came along, I think leaving will be harder now."

"But she's not your child."

"She seems to think she is. Momma refused to help Eden much with Dreamy except for buying her a few odds and ends. I can understand the sense of it—in *not* helping her, I mean. But Eden's always been so needy herself. Hand her a job and she'll find a way to foul it up or just not do it at all."

"There are special programs. I don't mean anything by that—just that some kids need remedial help."

"Don't I know? Once a woman calling herself a representative of the Head Start program came calling. I don't know who called her, but Momma felt it awfully intrusive that she would show up un-announced and warn her how she ought to do what was right for Eden. Momma blessed her out and sent her running out to the car as fast as her little stiletto heels could carry her. I found Momma slumped in her chair, staring at the floor as though she knew that she should have listened to the woman. But she's proud."

Sol set aside his coffee and stretched out on the grass with his arms stretched above his head like Dreamy's. "I like hearing you talk. I like your voice."

"No one's ever said that before." I stared at my hands, the ragged cuticle line and the traces of ink around my fingertips. I had started a new ink-and-watercolor project. Girls like me never sprang for mani-cures.

"What do most people say that they like about you, Katrina?"

"Mostly they talk about my legs, which is odd to me. They're so long and thin."

Sol lifted his head and glanced at my legs. He nodded in a sort of jockish approval and then lay back down again.

"Are they right?"

"Who?"

"*They.* About my legs."

"I like your legs. But you have more things about you that deserve a compliment."

"Such as?"

"You're kind. And you're pretty, but you don't know it."

"Wait. Let me find a pencil."

I made him laugh. "Are you going to school next year, Sol?"

"Yes, but at the same time I have to work with my father. Dad has this idea about handing the brokerage over to me. My mother would do cartwheels if I went to Cirrus." He said it with a tone that hinted of sour disapproval.

"It would be worth it just to see your mother do cartwheels. Why do all the moms have such a liking for Bible school?"

"You would have to understand the mothers at our church. They're all bent on shipping their sons off to become preachers and their daughters off to marry them."

"Why?"

"Maybe they think it will guarantee their ticket into heaven."

"If you don't mind me saying so, I've watched some of the kids, and they wouldn't do Bible school no good at all, Sol. No offense to any of them, and not like I'm so perfect and all. I'm not."

"Maybe the mothers believe it will make us all be good." Sol tossed pebbles at the lowest-hanging limbs, but I couldn't tell if he was tossing it at all those mothers instead.

"Sister Bickle says that Bible school can't save you and you'd best be on your knees and reading the Bible if you want to know God better."

"Good old Sister Bickle. So does she approve of your going?"

"I think she's really happy about it. I like her. She always makes me mull things over, which is good. I tend to leap into matters and then figure it out as I go." I pulled the doll out of the bag and examined its face. It was a rag doll with blond braids and a checkered dress. I should have bought the dark-haired country doll with the yarn wound up in ringlets—something more in keeping with Dreamy's features. The more I thought about it, the more I realized that I had not bought the doll for Dreamy at all.

"I've thought of going to Sumner Hill," said Sol. "There's always Sumner. I'm certain I can manage that by the fall."

"But then you wouldn't need a dorm room. The fun of college is staying in a dorm and meeting new people."

"You seem to know what you want."

"Maybe I just know what I don't want, Sol. That's about as close as I've gotten. I wish God would just write it out in the dirt—*Katrina, go to Africa.*" Dreamy shifted, then laughed in her sleep. I tucked her blanket around her. "I was going to return this doll, maybe swap it for another. But I think I'll keep her and set her on my bed in the dorm."

"When are you leaving?"

"August. I'd like to drive up sooner and find a job, maybe at the campus bookstore. I love books. Do you read?"

"Isaac Asimov."

"Science fiction. He's really the best. No one can top him in the genre."

"Do you know about everything, Katrina?"

"I'm talking too much again." It was my truest flaw, and one I could not rein in. Three squirrels sprinted around our tree and clamped on to the trunk without stirring the dead leaf deposits from winter or making a sound. I wanted to be like the squirrels, a quiet girl who never offended a soul and seldom offered her opinion without prompting. With that kind of finesse, I would never rile Momma or Daddy. The furry rodents scuttled up into the dense new spring foliage.

"What's your father like? I haven't seen him at church. Only met him that one time at your house."

"Daddy doesn't go to church. He hates that I go, but he doesn't try to stop me. He tried to talk me out of it once and said I had turned fanatical. But he doesn't say much anymore. Daddy lives in a different place than me."

"Your folks are separated?"

"No, I don't mean separated. I suppose that sounds confusing. Daddy's world is different from everyone else's." I stopped short of saying that we found him out in the yard only yesterday, ogling the sky and wearing nothing but his boxers. He talked to no one in particular but had a stem-winding argument with the wind.

Two boys stopped on the sidewalk and stared at us. If Sol noticed, he gave no inkling of it. I recognized them from school, basketball players that ran with freshmen from Sumner.

"Your father hates church."

"Hates church people is a more apt description. Daddy hates everyone, though—especially those with different skin. He's a bigot, dyed in the wool."

"Still fighting the Civil War."

"Once I caught a ride home from school with a friend. You don't know Beth, I guess. But we gave a lift to a black friend who sits with us in Spanish. Her name is Lonnie, and she tells the best jokes and picked up Spanish must faster than I did, so she helped me after school sometimes. But we passed the courthouse and Beth saw my daddy standing out on the corner yammering at one of those men who hang out around the café. Beth had to stop at the light, and when she saw my daddy looking toward us she yelled, "Duck, Lonnie! Katrina's dad is a bigot, and he'll kill us all if he sees us together!"

"He's that bad?"

"I felt so awful when Lonnie ducked. I wished that she had waved at Daddy out the window. Better yet, I'm the one who should have waved. But I'll never stop praying for Daddy. Jesus can save a bigot same as he can a harlot or a politician."

"Your dad's not really violent, is he?" A horn sounded with a loud, peremptory blare. The festival closed down at six o'clock to allow the grounds crew to do their cleanup before the town dance. The sun faded behind the hills and left pink and blue streaks across the horizon, chalky remnants from heaven. I could hear the fiddlers warming up, plucking out notes in the same manner as crickets along the lakeshore.

I untied the sweater sleeves and slid the neck opening over my head. "Guess what, Sol? Your coffee cup is empty. Why don't I get us a refill and you can take it home with you?"

"You're a good friend, Katrina."

"I like hearing that, Sol." I told myself it was true.

I fell asleep rehashing the afternoon and scolding myself for allowing my imagination to chase off after itself, unexpurgated and taking hikes down invisible rabbit trails. I could almost smell the dogwood again if I closed my eyes. The unfettered mirth of the valley's families and the soft, natural interplay that had transpired between Sol and me trickled over my soul, humming a tune of happier days. The valley looked greener and gentler when Sol was in it.

I could not walk into the park or hike down the creek bank without speculating about whether or not Sol had been there, or trying to remember if our lives had crossed when we were children. I wondered how I could have gone so long without sensing his soul nearby—this boy who called me his good friend. It was simple to understand why I had passed over so many friendships when my spirit waited for just the right one.

I was rapt, content for a while to be Sol's friend, and it was a sweet thought that lulled me to sleep until the morning roused us with the startling news.

Eden had not come home.

Whatever rain had been held back for the festival attendees now drenched in a merciless deluge the soft hollows of the fields and the town streets on Sunday morning. The sky grew dark like night, and deep clouds swept a crescendo of thunder from hill to hill, answered by arcs of stark blinding lightning that rattled the wood-framed windows—a Wagnerian morning song that clashed with quiet Sundays.

Momma stared through the glass of the front door, both petrified by storms and riled by Eden's disappearance.

"Daddy, should we call the police?" I asked.

My father looked at me with a dazed expression.

"Eden doesn't have an address book or anything, so I don't know how to reach her friends." I sat cross-legged on the telephone bench and thumbed through the thin-as-sliced-cheese town directory in hopes that Eden's familiar scrawling might reveal a friend or two.

"She went off to the rodeo with that Carl feller, and he seemed so nice and all," said Momma. "A mite better lookin' than some of the men she's drug in here lately."

"Carl is full of trouble just like his cousin Darrell," I said.

The phone rang. Daddy nodded at me. "You answer it, Katrina, and tell us who it is. I hope it's not the morgue."

I answered and heard Mr. Lunsford's voice, a bit shaky. He asked if Eden had come home, and when I told him no, he seemed worried, as though he suspected it all along.

"It's Mr. Lunsford," I said to Daddy. "He says that Eden left the rodeo with Carl last night. Carl was drinking and was thrown out by the rodeo boss, he says. His rodeo buddy called to ask if he had heard from Carl. No, Mr. Lunsford, we haven't heard from Carl, either. But please call us right away if you hear from either of them." We both hung up to keep the phone lines freed up.

Dreamy scooted across the floor in her footy pajamas. She held an old yellow blanket against her face and climbed into my lap. She was rather blithe about the whole matter and spent most of her time turning the TV knob off and on. That made Momma nervous as rain on a hot roof. The Dixie Echoes were singing "I'll Fly Away, O Glory," so when Dreamy flicked them off and on, it made their bass singer sound like he was repeating himself after a big supper. It messed up the anointing altogether. "Dreamy, let Aunt Kateen fix you some Tony the Tiger," I said, to rescue her from Momma's nervous anxiety.

"Reckon Katrina's right, Ho? Should we call the law?" said Momma.

Daddy stared at the floor and ran his thumbs up and down beneath his undershirt straps.

"Katrina, you get dressed and drive around and see if you spot Carl's pickup parked somewhere." Momma was grasping at straws.

"Why don't I dress myself and Dreamy for church instead? Eden's bound to call sooner or later. If we drive around all day, we'll not find them—not unless they want to be found."

"Just listen to our daughter, Donelle. Go ahead, Katrina, and abandon your family," Daddy said. "Just go on off to that place with all the religious nuts and leave us here to worry."

"Daddy, I'll stay, but it won't remedy anything."

"You better believe you're staying. You go change out your night-clothes into some sensible things. We might need you."

It was futile to argue with him when his insides were wrung out and left to harden in a twisted state. Besides knowing that I was trapped in a losing proposition, I realized that Hurleys turned stone cold to get their own way. Leaping over the art of persuasion or reasoning altogether, they aimed for the jugular instead of the heart. I might as well have been arguing with the wind.


Pushed away by a warm gulf stream, the rain receded once it exhausted its spring vengeance on the valley, lifting the riverbanks near to spilling over. Small leaves had sprouted all over the large elm in the front yard, allowing sparse beads of dusky light to dapple the ground with pleasant evening shade just before sunset. The branches, heavy with water and sagging like old sweaty men over their plows, dribbled slow droplets to the ground. The Canterbury bells emitted a faint aroma beaten out of the petals by the rain, a cross between honeysuckle and daffodil, while the mounds of portulaca closed up for the evening, ordinary and barbwirelike in appearance. In spite of the number of times Momma took a shovel to the blazing red canna last year, the broad leaves had divided and made several more plants near the corner of the pop-bottle porch and mulch pile, where Momma dumped vegetables from the supper dishes.

I said a prayer for Eden in hopes that she had sense to stay out of the rain and keep her wits about her in the company of a youth as cunning as Carl.

Daddy inspected the potato mounds for erosion while Momma counted pop bottles, placed them one by one into cola cartons, and carted them to the Pontiac for future redemption. Hers, not Daddy's.

A patrol car wheeled into the driveway, twirling its light even though Daddy told me to tell them emphatically no lights or sirens. But the cops in the valley were excitable and never passed up a chance to flash the single patrol light that sat like a cherry eye—a Cyclops, rusted from disuse—although they had had the sense to turn off the siren. I watched the deputy sheriff flip out a writing pad. He was tall with wide shoulders. The rest of him withered from the chest down, making him look like a long toy balloon, expanded and then left to deflate in the sun.

The officer approached Daddy on the knoll beneath the peach tree. Daddy said very little, mostly answering the officer with a shake of his head or a nod. Momma stood, her shoulders drawn up and her small hands clasped in front of her, saying things to the patrolman that did not help. But it appeared to ease the anxiety to let her spill out the woes of rearing a hardheaded child.

Dreamy and I moved out onto the porch so that she could eat strawberries without dribbling juice all over Momma's freshly waxed floor. I heard the officer tell Daddy that Carl could be arrested for abducting a minor. When he talked about the penalty for crossing the state line with Eden, Momma stepped back, floored to realize that they could be that far away. I found a photo of Eden, although she would not like it—her hair was cropped shorter and flat on the top, without a hint of teasing.

The neighbors had all moved out onto their porches, sipping iced tea with their lawn chairs aimed in our direction. Daddy turned his back on them.

A silent knell fell upon Erie Street once the policeman had filed his report and driven away. The neighbors, too intimidated to approach Hobart or Donelle Hurley, kept to themselves and gossiped about the troublesome Hurley girl before they gathered their dime-store pitchers and Mason jars to amble inside their two-bedroom rental chambers and camp in front of *60 Minutes* with a beer and the satisfaction that bad news knocked on the doorpost of every family.

I could not sleep. Dreamy slept next to me, although she would have agreeably slept in any bed. But I needed the comfort of her close by, the rhythm of her breathing, and the sighs she made in the night.

The fact that I had not attended church either in the morning or on this night left me feeling sulky. But I laid that thought to rest with a prayer and the realization that my family needed me near them, if only to speak peace when they spoke strife. If I had an ounce of selfish desire dwelling in me, I asked the Lord to flush it from me and make me as close to him as possible. I often imagined my prayers for Eden flying off to heaven and then spiraling back down to the valley, answered. But before it could land in her lap, she swatted it away, sensing it as the breath of God coming too near her heart and compelling her to surrender. I pressed my face into my pillow and fired off yet another plea for God to call to my sister again, in hopes that her batting average would be off on this night.

CHAPTER 13

*M*osquito weather descended on our green valley, some said with insects large enough to kill cattle, but exaggerations tended to flourish in the spring. I believe that when God created Mockingbird Valley, he could not allow it to be too perfect, too close to heaven. So he opened the gate and allowed in mosquitoes and stray dogs. Oh, and Hurleys.

We were hit with finals week at Mockingbird High, but tolerated it, knowing final exams were the last onslaught of stones thrown at us before we walked the line draped in our paper-thin ten-dollar robes of purple and gold.

Momma ceased her vigil around the phone by midmorning on Monday when the state police called to say no accidents involving a pickup were called in. That satisfied my mother enough to build up a good steam of fury and one she intended to lob at Eden the moment she traipsed through the door.

On Friday, before all this came down, I had collected all my brushes, canvases, and linseed oil into a satchel and carried them home. So on Monday at noon, I lingered on the school steps with only a couple of books to cart home and a prayer that I might steal a glimpse at Sol Houston and he would return my gaze and realize we had the summer ahead to get more acquainted.

The class of '76 milled around the school's front landing to taste what was, before they experienced what was to be. It was our last day of invincibility: the patriots whose prom sported an American flag motif and enough class spirit to light up the District of Columbia, New York City, and other places that did not acknowledge our existence. Beth met up with me and bummed a ride home. As we walked, we promised to stay in touch over the summer—like I heard at least three hundred and fifty-six times from others before I reached the Chevy.

It surprised me little that not one old buddy of Eden's approached to ask her whereabouts or inquire about her child. Eden had joined the rank and file of Hurleys who passed through life without leaving notches on trees or memoirs on hearts.

"Have you seen Sol?" Beth dropped her voice. She scanned the lapping ocean of faces, my self-appointed lookout.

"Sol has to find me, Beth. I can't spend eternity standing on the curb, passively waiting while Sol throws me an occasional crumb."

"So go and find him."

"I'm leaving in August. What's the point?"

"Maybe he'll follow you."

"He's going to Sumner Hill."

"When did he tell you that?"

"Saturday."

"And you were going to tell me this…"

"I've not had the time."

"You had a date with him, and you didn't tell me?"

"It wasn't a date."

"Where were you?"

"At the peach festival."

"You went together to the peach festival. Where was I?"

"No, not together. We just sort of bumped into each other. I looked up and there he was. We had coffee. We talked."

"Did he pay for the coffee?"

"I believe so. Yes, he did."

"That's a date."

"It wasn't like that. He called me his 'good friend.'"

"Katrina, I'm your good friend. When's the last time I bought you coffee?"

"Sol is an odd bird, Beth. He's not someone you can put your finger on and say 'this is Sol and this is what he's like.' I don't know where I stand with him. He doesn't call me, and then I look up and there we are, conversing, as though it was planned. But it's never planned, and I need a little planning in my life."

"He's fickle." Beth's mouth curved at one side. She looked pathetically wistful.

"Maybe he is."

"Perfect for you."

A cheerleader tried to pass between Beth and me. I gave her a look that said "the party's over," and she walked around us. I believe cheerleaders all have their wake-up call about the real world right around graduation time. It's hard to stay top dog if all you have on your résumé is "can do splits all the way to the gymnasium floor."

"I don't know if Sol wants to work for his dad."

"See. He's trying to tell you something."

"But he doesn't tell me anything. He must have problems. Maybe perfectly interesting problems, but he keeps it all under lock and key. So if he wants to leave Mockingbird Valley, he hasn't clued me in on it."

Beth kept rolling my words around in her head in an effort to shape that little meaningless interlude with Sol into something hopeful because she did not possess a life of her own. But I had thought over the afternoon a thousand times myself—it meant nothing to Sol. We stood around with a stack of those little name cards that seniors give one another and everyone throws away. "I want to go home," I said.

"I've never heard you say that."

"My sister, you know."

"Katrina, I'm sorry. I wasn't thinking straight. You must be worried sick."

"If Eden's home by now, first I'll hug her. Then I'll put a pillow over her face and do her in." We made it to the end of the walk.

"What will come of Eden? She reminds me of one of those girls down at the Burger and Shake drive-in who start out thinking they'll just earn some extra spending money while they're young. Then the next thing you know they've grown old, flipping burgers."

"Eden's never held down a job more than two weeks before the boss figures out she can't count back change and that she cusses out the customers who don't agree with her. She'd do well to flip burgers into old age. Actually, I'd feel relieved if she did."

Two juniors, pock-faced males, asked us to sign their yearbooks. Beth and I meandered through the senior mélange, two little pits that had somehow made our way into the marmalade. Beth stopped to swap cards again. I tossed my bag and the books into the Chevy to unburden myself. The heat hit me in the face from inside the car, so I opened the doors to cool off the sticky vinyl seats. That's when I heard the roar of Sol's motorcycle. "Katrina. You're hard to find." Sol held a biker helmet under one arm with his graduation robe folded over the other.

"You've been looking for me?"

He allowed himself the faintest smile, but it was unreadable.

"I'm glad you found me. Have a good day," I said.

"Have you ever ridden?" he asked. A second helmet was strapped to his bike. It occurred to me that perhaps he had thought in advance about a matter or two.

"I've never ridden. Momma thinks motorcycles are death traps." My attempt to cast him a blasé look fell into wrack and ruin. "But she says that about airplanes, too, and people fly every day."

Sol left the bike in neutral and carried his robe toward me. He hung it on the clothing hook inside my Chevy. He never glanced up when he adjusted his helmet, but straddled the motorcycle, gunned the engine, then sat with one arm outstretched while he waggled the other helmet at me.

I remembered the reasons why I should not go with him, one being that I promised to take Beth home. But when I glanced up, she waved good-bye through the dingy glass of the Chevy and mouthed that she would wait for me.

The helmet strap confused me and bungled my hopes for a little biker savoir-faire. Sol adjusted the strap, slid it over my hair, and then snapped it next to my chin. But my gauzy white blouse still lacked the biker chic of Sol's leathers. I straddled the seat and found a comfortable place between the sissy bar and his back, but then realized that I had a decision to make about handholds.

"You better hold on!" I could scarcely hear his voice above the din.

I liked the roaring sound, the buzzing against my calves. Best of all, I liked holding on to Sol and noticing things about him that I had never noticed before.

Momma's kitchen contained an unsettling silence, except for the row of canned beets that pinged on the open window sill. The door stood open, a common occurrence in the valley even if the household mistress was away at the grocer's. I glanced around the kitchen and felt as though the walls wanted to tell me things, but I could not understand because of my hurry to find my own way and understand without the aid of my past or the acknowledgement of my roots.

I ran to Eden's room and found her closet ransacked, as though Momma took her belongings, stuffed them into grocery bags, and carted them off to the Goodwill to be resold to other girls like Eden who had no money, no sense of worth, and no plan of escape.

The rear screen door screeched as though it were being opened slowly. I do not remember lurching down the hallway, but suddenly I stopped at the threshold, looking out at my mother. She toted a carton of milk and could not hide the flash of guilt in her pupils no more than I could hide my own anger. Little bubbles of resentment boiled over inside of me.

"Eden's clothes… They're gone, Momma. You know about this?"

"I didn't take them, if that's what you mean." She hefted the milk up over the porch landing and set it on the floor just inside the door, then turned methodically to gather up a sack of flour. The phone rang and sent a jolt through me, while Momma muttered about a headache and how she needed to see the dentist. Dreamy toddled up the stairs waving her arms for balance, the tail on her grandmother's kite. But I did not notice until later the new pair of cowboy boots she wore.

The operator asked if I would accept a collect call from Eden Hurley. I muttered a "yes," knowing how Momma felt about collect calls. I wanted to talk to Eden first. "Eden, we've been so worried. Are you all right, and has Carl gotten you into trouble?"

"Momma hasn't said a word about me and Carl?"

"What's Eden talking about?" I cupped my hand over the receiver, but Momma walked past and disappeared into her bedroom.

"I guess I should expect as much." Eden spoke in such rapid syllables that it was difficult to detect whether she was buoyant or disturbed. "She gave me and Carl the worst cussin' and said we could never come back. But I think she's changed her mind about all that. I'm just tellin' you why I had to call collect and all. Momma wouldn't give me no money, not that I would stoop to ask. But I could tell she was in no mood."

"Eden, you're not making sense, and you have me sick to death with worry."

"Just listen to what I have to say, then you'll see how it will all turn out." I could hear her blowing smoke away from the receiver. "Carl was all down in the mouth because he let himself drink too much and, well, that doesn't set well with those rodeo people at all."

"I wouldn't think so."

"I felt so sorry for him, sorrier than I've ever felt about any man, and I just had to help him, so we stayed together all night. But it's not what you think. Carl's a real gentleman. We made beds in his truck out of blankets and spent all night up on Twinkle Land countin' the stars and watchin' kids shoot off bottle rockets on the other side of the river."

"Of all places."

"You're not listenin', now listen. Lo and behold, Carl got to feelin' better about things the next mornin', and I said he should just march back and tell that rodeo boss man that he made a mistake and ask for another chance. He got his rodeo privileges back, Katrina, and I helped him do it."

"Eden, you could have called."

"Then Carl told me that I was the missin' piece in life's puzzle and that until now nothin' made sense and he, well, we're gettin' married. Can you believe I'm sayin' it? We spent all day yesterday plannin' the wedding, and I bought this dress all lacy white with sil-ver conchas. Kind of a western angel. That's what Carl says I look like, anyway."

I could hear Carl in the background. "Momma won't go for that, Eden."

"She signed the papers herself, what with me bein' a minor, although it was in a sort of 'good riddance' way and said we had to leave and not come back. That part makes me sad. But she'll change her mind, don't you think?"

I pulled the phone receiver away and yelled up the hall. "Momma, you didn't sign for Eden to marry Carl. Did you?" I could still hear Eden's voice squeaking out of the receiver.

"Katrina, can't I have some peace around here without being nagged at?" she shouted down the hallway.

"You told her she could marry?"

"Let her reap the same pain she's given me all these years."

Eden rattled on, breathlessly oblivious. "We found this brochure about a little mountain church called Thorncrown Chapel up in Eureka Springs and just listen: 'Considered the wedding cap-a-tul of the Midwest, Eureka Springs offers,' and then they go on about all the different places to get married, but the best one is Thorncrown and it's all glassed in and settin' in a mountainside. I wish you could come."

"You don't want any of us to come? No bridesmaids or rice or anything?"

"Momma said because of your finals and all, we'd have to go without all of you."

"She did? Can't you wait a little while longer?"

"Carl's got to get back on the circuit this weekend, and we'll be travelin' all over the country. This is such a kick, ain't it, Katrina? Me, married."

"What about school?"

"I don't need school anymore. Carl will take care of me."

"You have a daughter. How does he feel about caring for a toddler? I can't see Carl loving on a baby."

"He says he could get used to it. We'll be back tomorrow to get Dreamy. Not until nightfall, though. Will you get all her things together?"

"You can't haul Dreamy all over the country in a pickup. You can't even drive her across town, Eden. Why don't you come home and just give this more time?"

"I believe it's easier to talk to Momma right now. Put her on."

I left the receiver on the telephone stand. "Momma, you can't let her take Dreamy."

"This ain't your affair, Katrina."

"She can't take care of herself, let alone a husband and certainly not Dreamy."

"Dreamy is Eden's kid. Let her take care of her for a change." Momma disappeared, carting a load of wet laundry out to the clothesline as though the clothes dryer was tainted—her list of modern stigmata to be avoided had grown. *Airplanes, motorcycles, blow-dryers, pierced earrings, clothes dryers...*

"Eden, Momma can't talk right now."

"She'll come around."

"Please come home."

"Oh, and I forgot all about this one thing. When we come home, Mr. Lunsford's got those two extra bedrooms, and Carl's going to see if he'll let us stay every now and then when we're home. Dreamy will actually have her own room, that one you dolled up so nice. When we're home, that is. Doesn't that sound like God, Katrina? How is it you always say it—like he had a hand in all of this? Katrina? Are you there?"

I slept little that night, standing up in my bed to gaze out of the window to see if the sun might delay the day or offer a reprieve from the course of catastrophe our lives had taken. Dreamy collapsed in her mother's bed, still clad in her Sylvester the Cat romper and too young to believe anything except that life spins sweetly without interruption. Compulsion dragged me across the hall to watch her sleep.

The odds for seeing her again in this blissful condition of "all is well" were against her. The moonlight blanketed her, a celestial rug woven with little girl dreams and eyelash kisses and romps in the clouds. How I yearned to see it whisk her away in hiding from the big bad cowboy with the cheap haircut who gave boots without socks to little girls. With some willful effort, I eventually turned away from Dreamy, tears streaming down my face. I swallowed hard as I climbed into bed and managed to fall asleep, but then awaken with only enough time to just make it to my last final exam.

I attempted to banish the memory of Eden's phone call, but it trailed after me, pursued me until I pulled into the drive once more and found Dreamy twirling Salome's chain at her feet.

She babbled out a few syllables, enough to let me know that Salome had gotten off her leash. I walked Dreamy around the house and garage looking for signs of the mother dog, but even her feeding dish was missing from the stone slab near the foundation's crawl space.

"Aunt Kateen, Salome go bye-bye." Dreamy grasped my finger and tugged while she gestured toward the driveway. Momma's cooked cabbage spread a sour aroma, one that spilled out of the kitchen and violated every nose in the neighborhood. "Let's tell Granny we're going to Al's, Dreamy. I'll pack your things when we get back. Maybe Salome will haul herself back from her cavorting around the neighborhood by then."

"Salome's not comin' back," Momma said, but she positioned herself close enough to the screen door so that I could hear without making eye contact.

"She'll come back when it's dinnertime," I said.

"I gave her away. A peddler came through and sharpened some knives for me. He took a likin' to Salome; said he had a little grandson that would play with her."

"You gave away my dog?"

"She was trouble to me."

"I paid for her food!"

"She was always growlin' and barkin' at nonsense."

"But she was mine! And Dreamy's! We loved her! She was no bother to you. I took her for her walks and fed her, and she was never neglected. Salome's probably scared to death wondering where she is right now."

"She's better off."

"You didn't ask me, Momma. Don't I account for at least a percentage of the opinions around here? First you sign away your youngest daughter to some drifter. Then you allow two adolescent rejects from the Ponderosa to cart away your only grandchild. Here's what you should do—run an ad in the *Courier* and auction off Daddy and me. Then won't your world be just keen as a peach, Momma? If you wanted to be alone, you should have been a spinster librarian! Why include all of us in your misery?"

"Don't you yell at me, Katrina, or I'll box your ears!"

"I'm leaving, Momma. And you get on the phone and you find Salome. I'll go fetch her back myself." My voice choked and I felt queasy.

"I told you it was a peddler, Katrina. I paid the man cash for the knife sharpenin', so how am I goin' to find him? He bartered me a deal and a good one—Salome for a new skillet. I'm not givin' it back, Katrina, for some mangy old dog I'll be left here in my old age to worry over."

I found useful things to keep me busy after taking Dreamy to Al's, an avoidance tactic marshaled in a pinch to help me steer clear of Momma for the remainder of the day. I first picked out some of Dreamy's better outfits, but then thought better of it. Roadside Laundromats notoriously reduced knit toddler wear to doll clothes, aside from Eden's inability to sort colors. Dreamy removed her clothing from the duffel bag, made a game of it, believing all along that she was going for a weeknight slumber party at Pappy Lunsford's. Then she curled her legs over her head into a pose a contortionist would envy—to enable herself to kiss the pink blisters rubbed on her feet by the cowboy boots.

She allowed me to massage Corn Huskers Lotion all over her feet and then pull a pair of white socks over them. "I'll have to tell your mother to make you wear socks with these toe traps." We played cat's cradle until sunset.

Daddy made his way up the hall to tell us that Eden and Carl had arrived. I held Dreamy against me, and we watched the sun drop, a penny in an empty gumball machine.

CHAPTER 14

*E*den and Carl never set a boot in Thorncrown Chapel. Somewhere between Berryville and Green Forest, Carl's credit card found its limit, forcing the two of them to elope in the home of some justice of the peace calling himself "Sam, Sam, the Marrying Man." Eden downplayed the entire subject of the wedding by passing it all off as "not so important, just as long as we're married," as though she were above all of the other females in the valley who rehearsed wedding vows from age six. She enumerated the ceremony in a farcical manner as she shuffled through a stack of Polaroid snapshots, all captured on the spot by the official's wife, who ran back and forth between the piano and camera to accommodate the happy lovers.

Carl made certain that she and Dreamy returned for my Saturday graduation commencement, while Eden apologized all over herself for neglecting to buy a gift. But it took no genius to ascertain her financial status. She herself had graduated—from being the sad Hurley child with not a thought in her head to the pubescent bride who cried "poor mouth"—plunking into her new station with verve and a mountain of cowboy debt.

"Katrina, you look so differ'nt in your graduation robe." Eden said, but did not really look at me. Dreamy pulled away from her and tottered toward me.

"I brought my camera. Eden, you get a picture of me with Momma and Daddy. Then Carl can take one of you and me."

"Dreamy, let go of your Aunt Kateen!" Eden scolded her.

"Here, let me have the baby," said Momma.

She tried to take Dreamy's hand, but she jerked away. "Hold me, Aunt Kateen!"

"It's okay if Dreamy's in the picture, Eden. I want her in it, anyway," I said.

Every photo was a shot of me standing next to Eden, or myself between Momma and Daddy with two chubby hands curled around my knees, indicating the child that had her face buried in my robe behind me.

"Well, I guess we've got to go and…" Eden stopped to glance at Carl as though she now took all her cues from him. "Carl's got a rodeo tonight in Danville. Guess we're goin' to be livin' on the road from now on."

"Bye, Eden. Carl," Daddy said. "Donelle, I'll bring the car around." Daddy plodded toward the parking lot.

I hugged Eden. "You take care. Now get on out of here before you make me cry."

"Bye-bye, Mommy." Dreamy curled her hand inside mine.

"You're going with your momma now, Baby Girl. Going to go and see the ponies and cowboys." I led her to Eden.

"No! Don't want to go." Dreamy hid behind me.

"You stop it right now, kid!" Eden's voice grew terse.

"What if Aunt Kateen carries you to Carl's truck? Would you like that?" I asked.

Dreamy held her arms up to me. I lifted her onto my hip and

followed Eden to Carl's pickup. We all stared at the pavement while Dreamy fastened on to me, burying her face in my chest. We did not engage in small talk, but instead allowed the awkward silence to bully us. Finally Carl said, "Dreamy, go to your momma. Time to go." He walked toward the passenger side of the cab and unlocked the door.

"Let's go," said Eden. She reached for Dreamy again.

Dreamy shrieked until several passersby paused to look.

I pulled her fingers free from my gown. Eden yanked her inside the cab and slammed the door. She stuffed Dreamy into her car seat without strapping her in, then reached into her vinyl purse for her pack of Pall Malls.

The truck roared off, out of the parking lot. Dreamy lifted her head and wailed, her watery eyes accusing me of abandonment. She did not understand that she was not mine to abandon. I sat in my car and cried, brooding over how a little child should be allowed to select the momma that wanted her. Not the other way around.

Beth arranged an all-nighter at her folks' home the evening of graduation, a simple affair, but her mother promised no shortage of eats, with endless platters of popcorn shrimp, pizza rolls, and a concoction of punch made with pineapple juice and 7UP. I drove home from the college coliseum, where we had been officially released from high school, to change into my blue jeans and gather a bag of clothes and toiletries, along with another roll of film.

Firm yellow pears had ripened on the two trees near the Dutch iris beds. For good measure, I picked three golden ones tinged with a ruby blush encircling the round pear belly and stuffed them into a bag to give to Beth's mother, who appreciated the bounty of our gardens more than any friend. Two knee prints dented the soft mulch near the floral border of ageratum. I pondered over whether Momma had stopped to pray or spray for aphids. Most likely it was the latter.

I sensed a quiet, somewhat monastery-like peace that had settled upon the house, even though Dreamy's absence proffered a raw void.

A wide envelope lay in a crumple of blue sheets on my bed, inked with a postal imprint from Springfield, Missouri, and fluttering slightly from a breeze that lilted through the open window. I kissed it once then tore it open, noticing the Cirrus Bible College secretary who sealed it had sprayed herself with Chantilly Lace, or else Momma had allowed Ms. Perkins next door to bring in the mail. (She held everything close to her bosom.) The letter inside was of a congratulatory nature, acknowledging my acceptance for the fall semester. A smaller manila envelope contained more papers for me to fill out and inquired about my housing needs and other such goings-on that would have delighted any wild child from the sticks.

I smelled the warm, ushering winds of summer, as tempting as anything chocolate, an enticement to make my final bows in the valley and never return again until I had discovered that elusive sweet bubbly dream called life. I felt giddy. My collection of where-I-might-one-day-go periodicals had grown into two eleven-inch tall stacks of magazines sporting pictures of all the needy population groups of the world. Little children surfed atop trains and slept in vermin-contaminated alleys in Rio de Janeiro, no momma to fuss after them for not wearing their shoes. How difficult could it be to speak Portuguese?

I shouted down the hall for Momma, stuck my head into her bedroom and then Daddy's.

"She ran to the store, Katrina. Needed to get her some eggs, I reckon." Daddy nested in the kitchen alcove. He still wore the same gray polyester trousers that Momma insisted he wear to my graduation. Both he and Momma slipped quietly into and out of the coliseum that afternoon, grateful to be finished with child rearing and even more relieved to be free from the graduation mob.

"My acceptance letter, Daddy—it's here. Want to read it?"

"Acceptance to what? Sumner Hill? You applied to Sumner, didn't you, Katrina?"

"Bible school. Missouri, Daddy." I gave him a maternal pat. "You forgot."

"*Bible school.*" He might have said, "bah, humbug" in the same breath. His tone embodied the corrosive nature harbored by years of finely tuned scorn.

"Just go on and read it," I said.

The alcove suddenly felt smaller, quieter, and alien as he finally read.

"You've ruined everything!" His hand trembled.

"What did I ruin, Daddy?"

"All your grant money—to this *preacher* school—it's not even a real college!"

"It is or it couldn't accept grant money. See, it says right there on the letterhead."

"You've thrown it all away!" He came to his feet, lunged at me.

"Daddy, stop! You're scaring me."

"No kid a mine's goin' off to—Bible school! What will you do when you git out? You tell me that."

"Help people."

He mocked me. During the Depression, no one offered him aid, so why should he contribute one daughter to the needy?

"Folks ought to help themselves!" he shot out. "Nobody helped us when we was kids and close to starvation."

But from what Momma divulged to me, their families could not deliver themselves during the Depression nor would they ask for help. It is far more simple to slowly waste away in your pride than to lift up your head and cry out like the wounded fallen in battle, "Don't step on me. I'm alive and have need of you." At least among the civilized, that is true.

"Listen to me, Daddy, I've told you for months about this college. Have you heard anything I've said at all?"

He tried to shove me, but I sidestepped him.

"Don't you pull away."

"Daddy, you're acting crazy—like some hill jack."

"I'll teach you." Deep lines furrowed around his brows. His voice grew coarse, more grave and then more threatening. He used his softest backhand—that's what he told Momma, at least—and put me on the floor.

Momma drove back from the store and heard the commotion just as her feet hit the gravel, although neither of us heard her sidling up the steps, what with me trying to dodge Daddy's fire—and Daddy set on shaping my will to fit his. A farmer selling eggs and produce along Highway 64 had sidetracked her in her walk across the A & P parking lot. So she walked up the steps, hauling a large old sack full of eggs. She peeked in in time to see me on the floor and watch Daddy shove me down. He wouldn't allow me to come to my feet.

"Have you sent that place any money?" Daddy squawked.

"Nothing at all. Just signed the registration papers is all."

"Where's my matches?" He slapped all around his shirt pocket.

"You left them on the kitchen table, next to your pack of Salems. Want me to fetch your cigarettes? Needin' a cigarette, Daddy?"

He was heaving and still glared at me in a bulldogged, oblique manner. "I'm burnin' this trash." The letter crumpled inside his grip, forming jagged star creases from the center out.

"Let me keep the letter, Daddy." Twin tears raced down my face. My palms tingled from slapping the linoleum. I eased toward him. It took me many years to rise above the little-girls-need-their-daddy's-acceptance syndrome. Perhaps that is why so many girls I knew intermingled sadness with their triumphs. They did not desire success—simply approval.

The match lit on the first strike against the chrome frame that held the green Formica together at every joint.

"Give it to me, Daddy! What right have you to take it, let alone burn it?"

Momma dropped the sack.

The letter caught fire at the corner before he dropped it into the sink. Then a broom came down on Daddy's head, thwacked him from behind. It was Momma.

"Donelle, have you lost your mind?" She didn't hit him with a deliberate force, so as to knock him forward or catch him off balance. I never knew of a single time when one raised a hand to the other. We got whippings often enough, but they never hit one another. So the thwacking riled him.

"Put out that fire, Hobart, or I'll call the law," Momma said.

Daddy tried to wrench the broom from her hands, but she held firm.

"Take your hands off, Donelle. You'll hurt yourself." Daddy turned ashen, almost to the point of appearing peaked, such as when he had the influenza.

"First you let go, then I will," Momma said.

It seemed the best opportunity to reach around them both and flip the faucet handle and douse the letter. "Both of you, just stop quarreling."

"You're a good one to be talkin', Katrina." Her gaze traveled the expanse of the floor where she saw the sack of farmer's eggs dumped next to the stove. Runny yolk dripped out of the shells, the sticky remnant of our war.

I shook the water off the scorched letter. The flame had traveled dead up the center, the remaining white edges scarcely legible or coming close to resembling anything I could keep for a memento.

"What is that, anyway?" Momma pulled away the broom, but kept it close by.

"An acceptance letter to Bible school," I said.

"That girl came in here to provoke me, Donelle." Daddy said to Momma.

"I showed you the letter and that's that."

"I thought you were just goin' on about all that, anyway, Katrina," Momma said and then took on a reasoning tone. "Tell your daddy how you were just explorin', like girls do these days. It don't mean nothin', Ho, that letter. Tell him, Katrina."

"Why is it nobody listens around here or pays any heed to me? Is it a shame for me to want to try and make a difference in the world?"

"People like that aren't real, Katrina." Momma carried a roll of paper towels to the egg spill. "You done dreamed all that up. How many people we know who go off and save the world?"

"I can't save the world, Momma, and I'd be a pitiful one to believe I could."

"She's throwin' away her whole life, Donelle."

"Let her talk, Ho."

"Don't you ever see those children on TV with the drawn-looking faces and their bellies swollen and, well, know you've either got to switch the channel or do something about it?"

"Girl, they just want your money," said Momma. The gook had spread, resisting her cleanup altogether.

"Moneygrubbers," said Daddy.

"I know certain people want to milk Americans, but I'm not drawn to those kind." My voice contained the residue of our earlier emotional bout. "It's the faces of those kids that look worse off than any of those families down by the creek who sponge off the welfare. That keeps me up at nights, you know. You expect me to know exactly where I'm going with all this, but nobody knows at this age. It's kind of like I sense some candle burning in another room, and I just want to go to it."

"That church has ruined her." Daddy lifted himself from the counter.

"Go ahead and be difficult; blame the church, Daddy."

"Ever since we came out of hard times, Katrina, I always said my kids would have it better, go off to college. Somethin' I never did," Daddy seemed to come back from insanity's brink. "Eden never would have finished high school, let alone attempted college. You're all I've got. I can't bear thinking one of mine is wasting her life on religious nuts." His voice broke.

"Katrina, you've upset your Daddy for the last time. Go on back to your room."

"This is all gone crazy, Momma. None of this was supposed to happen. I thought you'd be happy for me."

"Go on," she said. "I'll get this mess cleaned up myself."

The weight of the moment anchored me, acted as a sort of sedative or a wash for my brain that twisted my insides into some sort of obsequious ooze. "What do you want me to say, Daddy—that I'll go to Sumner? I'll be a schoolteacher?"

"I'm sayin' this—save yourself first, Katrina, before you go off tryin' to save the world."

"I'll do it, Daddy. Just calm yourself. I'll be a teacher if that will make you happy."

"See, Ho, I told you right—girls just explore," Momma said, elated to find the end of the spilled eggs.

"You're a good girl, Katrina. I always knew that about you." He gave me a small smile. Daddy was himself again.

"Look, will you look at those pears! You can make the most elegant dessert with a poached pear. Katrina, you bring me the best gifts out of all Beth's friends. For that matter, none of her friends are high on gift giving, now that I think about it. But, oh, who cares? What good times you girls will have tonight!" Mrs. Hoover had decorated her house with paper graduation caps and diminutive scrolls she had rolled up herself and tied with purple satin ribbons.

Her husband had some engineering job out at the lock and dam—a job that imparted her with a nice, large house on the lake and massive quantities of furnishings with which to fill it.

She had collected graduation caps at the coliseum, those thrown illegally into the air even under the threat of losing a diploma. She donned one with the gold tassel hanging down in front, even though Beth begged her numerous times over to remove it. One of the kids cranked the music just to see Mrs. Hoover shake her tassel.

Mrs. Hoover was the only mother I knew who towered over six feet tall in her bare feet, yet measured in a paltry four inches shorter than her husband. She maneuvered through life scarcely making a wake, inventing pleasant devices out of disagreeable situations. Mr. Hoover occasionally flew out of state on business. Beth and her brother always knew their patriarch's absence inevitably gifted them with a week-long slumber party in their parents' massive king-sized bed at night, although Beth's father never understood the lack of long faces in his absence. It seemed odd to me that they would find so much joy in the matter until Beth later told me her father was a bit rigid. His absence generated a party.

Mrs. Hoover had taught Beth to sew, to watercolor, and to look for the good inside every person. She cared little for trips to the mall, her only frivolous appurtenance being shoes. Beth said she had towers of them, and come to think of it, I never saw her wear the same pair twice.

"Katrina, it's about time you got here," said Beth. "Your daddy keep you late digging potatoes?" Beth stood amid several boys who had arrived early enough to seriously deplete the supply of cheese dip. About twenty or more seniors moved from huddle to huddle, conversing and occasionally releasing a whoop of relief, grateful for their liberation.

" 'Course not," said Mrs. Hoover. "It's far too early for potatoes, isn't it, Katrina? I believe I'll leave all you young people with the food. Beth, you need anything, I'll be in my room. Don't forget about the slaw. I've made three bowls of it."

"Thank you for all the care you've taken, Mrs. Hoover," I said.

"Somehow the word spread about this little shindig." Beth dropped her tone, eschewing the cap placed on her head by her mother. "We may have sixty kids here tonight, all the ones who don't drink, I imagine. Maybe even someone you know. Some person in particular."

"Should I put these pears in the crisper?" I asked. "Your mother left them out."

"Tell me you don't care if Sol shows, and see if I buy it. If I didn't know better, Katrina, I'd say you got some kind of blues all over you, girl. Now you know you can't come to one of my mother's parties all glum faced."

"Sol didn't bother to look me up today at graduation. Tells me something. He makes me feel like I'm walking out on a wire every time I spend any time with him at all. But in spite of what you believe, I really don't have him on my mind at all."

"Think of that big family and what with him bein' the oldest. He probably got hit up with every aunt from here to Toad Suck Ferry giving him graduation ties and other stuff he'll not use." Beth cut up more cheese for the dip.

"Who told him about the party?"

"Hoover? Houston? I sat right in front of him in the *H* rows."

"I know. I'm a Hurley."

"Sol smiled at you. I saw him."

"Now tell me, what does that mean exactly? It's odd little things like that—Sol catching my eye in the hall, smiling at me in the graduation line—that make me feel strung along. I'm some bass that he's got on a line, but he can't decide if he's going to keep me or throw me back."

"Have you ever made any of this known to Sol?"

"Let me have that knife before you cut yourself. You open that can of chili tomatoes while I cube. No, I haven't had a chance. Try hollering out something meaningful over the roar of a motorcycle engine. Besides all that, our chats are always…pleasant."

"Do you use a whole can of this stuff?"

"Just a half. You could strip cars with it, if you had a mind to. More people are out there ringing your doorbell. I hope your mother has extra canapés."

"Jenny, be a sweetie will you, and get the door?" Beth used her arm to dab her eye. "Is this supposed to make your eyes burn?"

"Katrina? Phone." Mrs. Hoover emerged, having forgotten she had donned a pair of furry Snoopy slippers.

Beth stared at her mother's feet. "Now that's a fashion statement."

"It's so noisy, Katrina. Take it out on the deck, right through that door," said Mrs. Hoover. "On a little rattan stand. Oh, and be careful of that cactus garden. I need to move those plants before someone hauls off and gouges themself."

"All right, Beth, now you just stir the chili tomatoes into the cheese and microwave it." I scraped the cheese cubes into the bowl.

"I'll do it, Beth. You go join your friends. What's wrong with these shoes? Oh, would you look!" I heard Mrs. Hoover tittering even after I closed the door to the deck.

The sun was gone but left a pale sprinkling of color on a horizon the color of cinnamon. The endless firmament appeared to float on the lake, little rivulets of celestial spice, and all of it just a mirror. I answered the phone and could at once hear Eden sniffing, emitting little clouded heaving coughs that gave way to the fact that she had been crying. "What happened?"

"Carl, he, everthang's just goin' too fast, and when he's drinkin'—"

"Take it easy, Eden. Just tell what happened, one thing at a time."

"Momma told me you were at your graduation party, and I hated like all get out to call. Anyone I know? I'll bet you're just havin' the best time."

"Never mind all that. Are you all right? Dreamy?"

"Asleep. How she sleeps through all the racket, I'll never know. Carl had a bad night at the rodeo tonight. He didn't break anything but almost got his head stomped, and he went off afterwards, left me and Dreamy alone in this—I guess you'd call it a fleabag sort of motel. It's called the Silver Nickel. They got this all-you-can-eat buffet, though, and me and Dreamy, we been eatin' good. Thank the Lord for a new credit card."

"Eden, why are you calling?"

"He come back to the room, and they's no tellin' how much he had to drink. But we got into the most awful brawl, and I told him maybe he couldn't handle the rodeo after all. Maybe it was time to settle down in the valley. Take over his uncle's shop. He took it real bad, like I was insultin' his manhood, and he struck me in the face. I can't take that business, so I struck him back. That's when he—he—"

"Did Carl hurt you, Eden?"

"He broke my arm. I just got back from the emergency room. If Momma hadn't helped me get that Medicaid, I don't know how we would have paid for it."

"I want you to tell me where you are right now. What town?"

"Jacksonville, you know—not too far from Little Rock."

"I'm on my way. I'll bring Daddy."

"No, no. And please don't tell Daddy or Momma. If Carl finds out I've called you, there's no tellin' what he'll do."

"I'm not afraid of Carl, Eden."

"He's gone to check out, says he's sorry and that he'll not ever touch me again. We're headed for Memphis. But I just felt so—I feel like I'm in the pits and hearin' you talk always makes me feel better. Painkillers are helpin' some too."

"Eden, please come home."

"I really love him, Katrina. He's not a bad daddy neither. I'll be fine. Once you get fixed up in that dorm in Missouri, maybe we'll come for a visit. We'll have us a good time, won't we? Let's go up to Branson and take in one of those fiddlin' shows."

"I can be in Jacksonville in an hour, Eden."

"I think I hear Carl. He's comin' back. I've already packed up our stuff into paper sacks. Carl says we're buyin' a suitcase at the Kmart tomorrow. That will be a relief. We're gettin' situated as a family as we go along. We'll be just fine. I love you, Katrina."

I saw a flash of history, a little girl running down the hallway of a hospital. She was in labor and telling me that she loved me.

"I love you too, Eden. I'm praying—"

*Click.* The phone line at the Silver Nickel went dead.

Before I could get down, vexed over Eden and Dreamy cavorting toward Memphis in cowboy hell, floodlights illumined all the grassy lawn from the Hoovers' home down to the dock. I could hear the sound of speakers, small sound boxes wired around the deck and awnings, pumping out the graduation anthem, a cacophony of reverb and excessive bass. It gave the lake cul-de-sac a surreal ambience. The procession of indigo caps and robes fluttering against the lake breeze startled me at first sight, as though robed knights had risen from their graves, cast upon some spiritual quest. The faces of the robed seniors looked stark and ghostlike in the twilight, somber at first appearance, until I ran to the deck's edge and found the mischief in their eyes.

"Katrina, where's your cap and gown?" asked Beth. She ran out from the kitchen, breathless, her mission ambiguous.

"It's…I left it in the car. What are we doing?"

"Hurry, run fetch your stuff. Put it on."

The Chevy was parked around the corner from the deck, enabling a swift reclamation of my graduation trappings. By the time I joined Beth and Jenny down by the shore, the seniors stood in slovenly procession all the way out to the dock, at least one hundred strong.

Twenty or more athletes had crashed the party. They stood like gladiators at the dock's end, their arms raised in triumph. One floodlight swiveled on its stand, then hit me full in the face. "Katrina, is that you?"

"Sol?"

"Let her pass, guys. Come down here—on the dock."

I felt myself break into a run, like a duck flushed from the reedy shoreline. I ran past the procession of faces until I saw the one I sought, the comely boy with the outstretched hand. "Sol!"

Together, we dived into the lake, followed by our comrades of the river valley, initiates of an unknown club representing our future. But the rapture we felt and the cup of bliss from which we supped washed all the trouble of tomorrow away. Our ignorance of mortality and the transient world that rushed like an unstoppable train would be faced on another day while tonight we swam, the valley underlings bathing with the heroes of Mockingbird Valley High, all watching our three-dollar violet caps float away on a moonlit bay.

It was paradise supreme, with a side of slaw.

CHAPTER 15

*I* held the class schedule in my hand. Sumner Hill College now owned me, a castigated slave tossed onto the embers of the Arkansas educational process.

Daddy could no more be accused of being more pleasant now than Americans were about the peace accords, but he was pleased to share the news of his daughter's teaching pursuits with the boys at the VFW. However, his tendency to have those little conversations with the small people who lived inside of him was on the rise.

"Are ye done?" Momma asked. She weeded the portulaca to make room for more mums.

"All done. I got all my classes. I had to take an art class. Art education, it's called."

"You'll be good at that," she said.

"Picked up my contact lenses today."

"They'll make you go blind," she said.

"Oh, Momma."

Daddy sat twenty feet from us. He rocked in an aluminum lawn chair. His lips moved slightly. Finally he moved his head and gave a wink as though he were telling someone his opinion of the matter.

"Stop it, Ho! Just stop it!" Momma threw down her trowel. "You keep talkin' to yourself like that, they'll send the boys with the white coats, they will."

Daddy looked surprised. Momma had never interrupted him before—never had she come between him and those people of his. He picked up his tea glass and took his meeting indoors.


Sol Houston commenced to seek me out. On Sunday evenings, instead of disappearing into the crowd, he milled about the church altars and waited for me to break free from the girls. But he always found me.

Most of what we discussed was trivial in nature. That led to Beth's discourse on the complexity of men, how often they hide behind their boyish idioms, and how adept they are at avoidance and meshing with their own feelings—this was found in immeasurable amounts even in the youngest of boys, she believed.

"Sol is mysterious, Beth," I said, keeping one eye out for him since the dismissal of the evening service.

"Now you're excusing him."

"His grandfather was Cherokee. That would account for his silent mannerisms, wouldn't it?"

"Sol's brother told me they were French ancestry. Was he lying?"

"Which brother?"

"Eddie."

"Probably. What's wrong with being Cherokee?"

"He's trying to talk me into a date, but I don't date underclassmen. Nothing's wrong with being Cherokee. Isn't your pastor here Cherokee?"

"Full-blooded."

"Doesn't look it. Not like that crying Indian on the 'Don't Litter

America' commercial. But your church always has that homogenized feel anyway."

"Iron Eyes Cody is dressed in full regalia, kind of an Indian metaphor. A minister can't get up in the pulpit wearing feathers and waving a tomahawk."

"I should go. I promised Mother I'd get in bed early. Class starts tomorrow. Summer's flown by. I've really missed you, but that little stint to France did me some good," Beth said and then shot Eddie Houston an instant stare. "Oh, I get it. He thought that being French would appeal to me. The boys at your church are such a hoot. Not so stoic, like the Baptist boys at my church. He is good-looking, though, just not as cute as his older brother… I'm glad you invited me here tonight. Did you get all the classes you wanted at Sumner?"

"I suppose so."

"Now that's a rah-rah sort of an answer, if ever I've heard one."

"I'm happy about it, sure. Don't expect me to dance a jig."

"You're certain you want to be a teacher?"

"What else is there?"

"Nursing, for me. I'm transferring to Florida next year. I suppose Sol is more interested in you now since he knows you're staying."

"Do you suppose that's right? I'd not thought of it like that."

"Makes perfect sense to me. If I didn't know better, I'd say you blew this whole Missouri business just so you could be near Sol."

Beth had a way of bringing the monkey around the mulberry bush in most situations, but in this instance, she was off by a long mile. "I had my reasons, but Sol was not one of them. People change their minds, Beth. It's not so uncommon. I'm not altogether certain I won't change my mind again."

"You don't suppose it's one of those Freudian faux pas do you, in which you shoot yourself in the foot just to make yourself miserable?"

"Beth, why would I purposefully hurt myself?"

"Because you don't believe you deserve to be happy."

"You're cheering me up."

"But you deserve happiness as much as the rest of us poor saps. When did you tell him, by the way? Sol, that is."

"I believe it was the night we all went swimming in our caps and gowns." I said it as though I had to dig far back into the archives of my memory. But I remembered it well.

"Did he kiss you that night, or was that a delicious rumor?"

"It wasn't that sort of kiss." I still remembered the faint aroma, that boy smell that emanated from him, even though doused by lake water. He was uncharacteristically jubilant, as though we had all landed on the moon or coined a historical dictum that would be quoted from every lip, though no one in our valley was ever quotable. I was about to say something really clever about us all being drowned by our own graduation robes when he reached out and clasped my face.

"Mouth or cheek?"

I swung back to the present. "Really only a sort of celebration kiss. A graduation kiss really."

"Katrina."

"Mouth. But platonic mouth." Sol had congratulated me in a manner that raised flags—but I told myself he was just being friendly. Later I chastened myself for wanting to believe otherwise.

"Oh, hush, he's coming this way." We had made it all the way out to the church aisle. Most of the older members had congregated outside on the landing, while a few singles gathered in broken circles down the aisles, their rambling chitchat broken intermittently by laughter. The organist had tucked her sheet music into the bench, while the sound technicians played a sort of church elevator music track. It kept the spirits up after a stirring service.

"Say, Katrina, you look good in your contacts."

"Thanks, Beth."

Sol had a clean smell. His blue shirt looked as if it had been taken right off the clothesline and placed directly onto the ironing board. His mother seemed like a woman who ironed all at once instead of waiting until morning to press out all the wrinkles. She even creased his sleeves. "Katrina, you sang in the choir tonight. I didn't know you could sing," said Sol.

I couldn't sing, except in my sensible stay-on-key approach that was better than most, but nothing like the girls who soared. "A little. I sing a little."

"Some of us are going to the Dixie Gal. I'd like it if you would go with me."

Everyone in the valley knew of the Dixie Gal restaurant. Famous for their house salad dressing, the Dixie Gal was a town gathering place on Sunday night among the local church crowd, as well as the truckers that passed through Interstate 40 on a habitual basis. While the old shops of the fifties were torn down to allow for newer commercial strips, the Dixie Gal remained a citadel of times olden in the valley.

"I should go," said Beth. "Good night, girl. I'll see you around campus."

"See you tomorrow," I said. "Sol, I have my car."

"We can come back for it later. If that's all right with you, Katrina."

"I'm not dressed to climb on that motorbike, Sol."

"I've got my car."

We walked to Sol's car, a little economy job that he had paid for by cutting grass and playing courier for the attorneys whose offices dotted the blocks that surrounded the courthouse. The sky had grown dusky but not fully dark, with a thumbnail moon that appeared to hook into the bell tower atop the church.

Sol's mother, Eva Houston, teetered past, almost leaning forward on her six-inch heels, a tall, stout woman who emitted a delicate air. "Where is everyone going tonight?" she asked.

"Dixie Gal, Mother."

"Your dad's tired. We're going home. Good night, all." She teetered away.

"I should leave my Bible in my car," I said. "I'll only be a minute." I could not remember how much cash I carried, but I didn't want to count it in front of Sol. If he ever called what we did a date, I could make a few sane assumptions. But in the event the bills were tallied and handed to me, I could cover it.

Two of his buddies stopped to yammer, but in spite of their athletes' status, he would not allow them to join us. His years on the high school track team had earned him favor with the athletes. I often saw him out early doing his stretches, his face dewy with youth, as the students filed from the buses across the rear of the high school lawn. He was just as comely tonight in the moonlight.

I heard the Toyota engine start, so I returned to his car and clambered into the front seat.

"You look different, Katrina."

"Got rid of those eyeglasses. I hated the things."

"You look good."

We passed the park where Eden and I once played. The streetlights infused it with enough light to betray its solitary vigil in the night. But parks are like that—only useful in the light of day.

"How's your little sister? Eden."

"Better, I believe. They've had a rocky start, but she is such a purist when it comes to love. Love conquers all, and all that, but Eden doesn't recognize when she's being mistreated."

"Do they still live here in the valley?"

"When they're home, they stay with Carl's uncle, but I think that gets to be tight quarters, what with Carl's impatient temperament. Mostly they live on the road."

"You sound concerned."

"If it weren't for little Dreamy, I could be a bit more cavalier, tell Eden to live her own life. It's the baby that worries me."

"We're here." Sol wheeled the Toyota into a small space around the back, from all appearances the last parking space on the lot. I reached for the door handle, but felt his eyes on me. He didn't say a word, but watched me step out. It could have been that the moon cast a sort of veil across my face and created one of those rare enchanting moments when a boy looks at a girl and for the first time really looks at her. But he was such the quiet type, I figured he probably just remembered that he left the lights on back home or some such business.

A crowd milled around the counter—a sort of glass aquarium filled with Tootsie Rolls and breath mints—while they waited for jukebox change. The only place I had ever noticed the same décor was in films that depicted the fifties era. I wouldn't have been surprised at all to see James Dean and Elvis jawing over a Ruby Dog and a glass of sweet iced tea, Ruby being the proprietor. Overstuffed red vinyl booths lined the walls, while café-style tables with chrome legs were scattered in tight, uneven rows—church people shifted them around to their own liking, anyway. I don't know that the main restaurant floor was all that massive, but the mirrored walls gave the room the feeling of being excessively large. Oil from the fried chicken vats somehow became airborne, and I always swore I left the place with grease in my lungs.

"Sol, Katrina, over here." A group of twenty-somethings sat in one of the larger booths that held up to twelve nimble and willing bodies at once.

Sol led me to their table and introduced me. "Some of you know

Katrina," he said. Three fellows and three young girls smiled up at me, all paired off—a sudden observable fact among the rank and file of the burgeoning young adults' group. One or two couples our age had been an item of sorts throughout their high school years, but it seemed that when the homecoming queen lost her beau to an out-of-state college, the deck was reshuffled, and a whole new hand had been dealt us in regard to available love interests. Suddenly the cogs were loosened. It slackened the rigid attitudes about who should be with whom. Maybe it had even changed something for Sol.

I knew most of them, anyway, but listened politely while the jukebox almost drowned out Sol's introduction with an Olivia Newton-John song about having never been mellow. "Melanie, Joe, Rodney, Charlotte, Rick, and Deirdre. Meet Katrina." Everyone scooted to one side to allow room for Sol and me.

I sat next to Charlotte, with Sol next to me. She was Sol's cousin on his daddy's side, a blond beauty, vivacious, with long lashes accented by a thin stream of eyeliner. The local boys feared rejection so badly that they never dared to ask her for a date. That's when Rodney, an Oklahoma transplant, swooped in, causing all the girls' heads to turn and all the guys to kick themselves for not making a move sooner. "Katrina, I have so been wanting to know you," said Charlotte. "Sol's been keeping you a secret."

"Nothing to tell, really, Charlotte," I said.

"You must wind your hair up in orange juice cans, what with it so straight and all. Mine's so curly it can hold straws in it. See?" She wedged a drinking straw into a springy strand. As luck would have it, it held the straw in place.

"Quite a gift," I said.

"You're dating just the most handsome boy in the valley, girl. If he wasn't my cousin, why I'd, I'd—"

"So, Deirdre," Sol interrupted Charlotte's rather sugary appraisal. "You still going off to Ouachita Baptist?"

"Rick, pass me that menu." Deirdre waited while Rick opened it in front of her. "No, and my father wants to kill me what with it being his alma mater and all. But I can't be expected to leave behind my main man here." Rick squeezed her hand and something inscrutable passed between them.

"It's romantic, Deirdre. You two are a pair, that's what I say," said Charlotte. "Name your first daughter after me." She tore open a package of Captain's Crackers. "Now what about you two, Sol and Katrina? You been dating awhile, and I see something there, kind of like in an intuitive way. My momma always says, 'Now that Charlotte, she's the girl with the intuition.' So you may as well fess up because I'll have it figured out before you know it, anyways."

"Katrina, you'll have to excuse my cousin here. She's a bit on the outspoken side." A tinge of blush appeared on each of Sol's cheeks.

"Now, Sol, don't you be avoiding the issue here, and the issue is this—are you two a steady-Eddie item or not?"

"Katrina and I have been getting to know one another for quite some time—"

"I can answer her, Sol." I wet my lips and stared down at the table. No words formed in my mind, even when I took a deep breath and assumed the most self-assured posture I could muster. "We're both mature people and know that whatever happens, that God will lead us." Fearing the lameness of it, I dared not look up.

"Well said, Katrina." Sol's hand reached over and gripped mine under the table.

"Sumner is having its first game Saturday night," said Charlotte. "Are you two going to cheer on the Wonder Boys?"

I chose to wait, observe what Sol might initiate.

A waitress appeared. "I'm Darlene. You all ready to order?"

Sol nodded.

"We got the blue plate tonight—meat loaf, mashed potaters with gravy, and green beans. Peach pie comes with that all for three dollars and ninety-eight cents." She scratched her chin with the eraser on her pencil.

"You're makin' us hungry, Darlene," said Rodney.

"I'll have the chef," said Deirdre. "House dressing."

"Same here," I said. "With sweet tea." The house chef salad was ordered all around the table.

"None of you wants the blue plate?"

We looked like little dogs waggling our heads in the back window of a car. Each Dixie Gal initiate had his own version of the various goings-on in the kitchen, but the best bet was to avoid anything that could be put through a meat grinder.

"Now where were we?" Charlotte's attention span retrenched itself. She dusted cracker crumbs from her arms.

"Maybe I ought to have ordered the blue plate," Rodney said.

"Go ahead, Rodney, as long as you're insured," said Sol.

"The Wonder Boy game—that's what we were talking about," said Charlotte.

"Charlotte, lay off." Sol pulled the basket of crackers away from her.

We all stopped and stared at him.

"You'll spoil your dinner," he said.

"Katrina and I are having a little talk. Aren't we, Katrina?" Charlotte opened the snap on her shiny pink purse and pulled out an ornamental hair comb with a silk rose attached to it. "Look at this, Katrina. Have you bought any hair combs yet?"

"No, I haven't."

"Every girl will be wearing one of these before Christmas. You wait and see if I'm right. I know fashion, and this little hair ornament is going to be big." She tucked it into her hair and then combed the strands of hair with her fingers.

"I see what you mean," I said. "You look lovely, Charlotte."

"Oh, and can you believe it? Shawls are back in. You know, like your grandmother drapes around her shoulders. It's kind of like when the hemlines were lowered again, all the old-fashioned accouterments returned. I like it, myself. I despise wondering how I am going to stand up with everything in place. Those miniskirts were such a bother that way."

Deirdre pulled up her knees, then wrapped her full printed skirt about them. "There's a mouse, sure as everything. Rodney, do something."

"Deirdre, honey, what do you expect me to do? Let the waitress tend to it." Rodney raked his fingers through his red hair. "You think they might have some of that meat loaf left still?"

"I won't be able to eat a blessed thing here," said Charlotte.

"Calm yourselves, ladies." Sol tapped a finger against the tabletop, sort of bit the side of his mouth, then eased slowly onto the booth's edge.

Charlotte handed Sol a cracker. "I can't even eat a cracker here now."

"I got four chefs here, house dressing." Darlene returned, balancing salad bowls proficiently on both arms.

"You've got a mouse, lady," said Charlotte.

Darlene glanced in an oblique manner without moving her head. "Who wants their salad first?"

"Can I change my order to the meat loaf?" said Rodney. "That salad's just not goin' to hold me, I'm afraid."

I took the first salad bowl from her hand and passed it around to Deirdre.

"I hope you all don't expect me to eat now," said Charlotte.

Darlene continued passing out the large oversize bowls as though engaged in another dimension.

"Is anybody listening to a thing I've said?" Charlotte asked.

"I'll get your tea refills and the rest of those salads." Darlene set the fourth bowl in front of me. "Meat loaf for you, sir. Comin' right up."

"She sure gives good service," said Rodney. "I, for one, am leavin' this woman a nice tip."

"Let me out of this booth," said Charlotte.

"Anybody mind if we pray?" asked Sol.

Charlotte seethed and shoved her house salad to the center of the table.

Sol walked me to my car under the large oak on the church parking lot. The air had taken on a chill, a sign that summer was fading. The rustle of autumn would soon uncloak the trees, leaving golden leaf trails along the highway easements. Arkansas was not so pretty in the naked season of our winters, so the hills in autumn lavished their natural beauty upon us, an apology for what was about to come.

"I hope you somehow managed to enjoy yourself, Katrina. My cousin, well, she's been spoiled by her mother."

"Tonight was wonderful, Sol."

"And you're so…I like your hair." His gaze started at the crown of my head, traveled down to my eyes. That's when I noticed his soft dimple. "I never know what I'm supposed to say. May I…" He stepped closer to me, actually stroked my hair with his fingers. "I want to kiss you, Katrina." He did not wait for my reply.

All I could do was manage a whisper. "Sol." He held me close, and I felt all at once so completely understanding of why things unseen had kept me here in the valley. When he kissed me I felt taken up, awakened from sleep, and told that my stint in a locked world was over. My time was served, and as Beth had pointed out, I deserved my happy moment. I prayed one prayer for myself—that God would grant an endless night, even though I no longer believed in a fairy-tale-wish-granting god, but someone greater.

"I'd better let you go," said Sol. "Or else I won't be able to."

I lifted myself onto my toes, a vulnerable soul in the arms of a spellbinder. We kissed again, briefly, and the bleakness of parting sent an ache through me, stillness and jubilance juxtaposed by an army of butterflies hammering against my insides.

"Careful with your steps. It's so dark out here." He opened my car door and, after watching me take my seat behind the wheel, kissed my forehead. I smelled the faint hint of cologne on his chest. "Oh, and about all that Saturday night business. Charlotte goes on a lot. She means well. Honest as the day is long, but she tends to put herself in other's affairs. Gets it from her mother. The deal is this: I have to go out of town. Otherwise, I would have already asked you to the game. I feel bad about it." He tried to smile at me.

"You don't have to feel bad. We'll make up for it another night."

"Good night, Katrina. I'll see you at school."

"That's right. Tomorrow."

He watched me pull away, followed me home, then disappeared in his gleaming Toyota. I could sleep knowing it was just a few hours until morning. Sumner had become a better place—and all in one night.

"Katrina, is that you?" Momma stood in the kitchen doorway, little pink curlers dangling around her ears and forehead.

"You didn't have to wait up," I said. "I had a date after church."

"One of your friends is callin' here. She's gone and woke me up for the second time. Talk to her and tell her not to call so late. Folks is tryin' to sleep."

I took the receiver, but held it next to me until Momma's feet padded from range. "This is Katrina."

"Girl, I know it's late, but this is Charlotte."

"Something's wrong. What's going on, Charlotte?"

"Sol called and I just felt so bad I couldn't let you go to bed without a call."

"Is he all right? Was he in an accident?"

"Mercy no, nothin' like that. He told me how rude it was of me to go on about Saturday night. Katrina, if I'd have known about Saturday, I wouldn't have rambled on. Please don't think poorly of me. I forgot about that girl he dates from Fort Smith. I wasn't trying to embarrass either of you. He told me how insensitive I was being to the both of you. I want to apologize, is all."

"He's dating a girl from Fort Smith? Saturday?"

"You mean to say you didn't know? Oh, Lord forgive me. I've gone and done it again. Katrina, I thought he told you about her. They've dated on and off all summer."

"Sol has a...girlfriend?"

She did not answer right away. "I thought you knew. What have I done?"

"Charlotte, it's not like Sol and I have made any commitments—"

"Promise me, Katrina, you'll let him tell you himself. That rotten fool should have explained things better to me and you as well. He really thinks the world of you, Katrina, and I'm certain as can be that he aims to tell you himself. This seems pretty deceptive, I realize, but he's got more character than you may think." I could hear the television in the background. "I'd best get myself to bed. Early class. You, too, I'll bet."

"As a matter of fact—"

"Good night, then. And don't let none of this trouble you. Sol's never been one to settle down with just one steady girl, so he's probably not serious with this one. But you've known him awhile. Probably already knew that anyway. Sorry to go on so." She breathed into the phone for a moment. "And I swear I'll not say a word to him about our talk. That way Sol will have time to bring it up to you in his own way. I just feel certain he'll do the right thing if you give him time."

"Good night, Charlotte." It was evident in her anxious tone that Charlotte meant well. But I had a headache, and that was reason enough to try and fall asleep.

Charlotte's words tumbled through my mind while I undressed. Then they rattled around my emotions until I felt weary enough to turn out the light and slip into bed. Love was so hard to determine. And if it blossomed into something that made young girls blush and young men perspire, well then, perhaps I had shook hands with the wrong end of it.

I do not recall which day that God created love. But Sister Bickle had told me more than once that he demonstrated it and gave man the ability to exercise it, which tells me that God's never-changing character embodies this ethereal nature called love. Always has. He owns it. He is love. And everything he touched left traces of it all over earth, an elixir that smelled good to girls and caused boys to lose their ever-loving minds. I figured that is what caused Sol to lose his when he had downright lied to me about Saturday.

It made me believe that if God had handed each person—say Adam and Eve, for starters—a little box and said, "Now, here's your portion of love. Don't spend it all in one place," man would have taken his box. But instead of handing it over to his mate, he would have poured it out all over his puny, quivering, naked body as he danced in paradise and shouted to Eve, "Look at me, I'm in love, I'm in love," while Eve just shook her head and said, "You certainly are, Adam. Have a good time without me."

But God allowed little potent traces of love to inhabit us in places where we could not extract it and use it for our own selfish purposes. We could only give it away. Therein lies the essence of heartache— the pain of what ensues thereafter.

And that is what robbed me of sleep.

CHAPTER 16

*T*he trick was to avoid Sol until I had a chance to force the pain from my eyes or at least face him with a genteel restraint. I schemed to avoid him, making each class by a hairsbreadth, only to split for the Chevy once the last class had dismissed. I threw my books onto the backseat. On the way home, I stopped by Burger Bob's to pick up one of those gallon-sized cups of cola with the crystallized crushed ice before I took the side road to Erie Lane.

All I could see for miles were moonstruck couples holding hands. Gray doves sat along the fence rows and the power lines, paired off, their eyes too small to see their fate.

"Anyone home?"

Momma had absorbed herself in *Dialing for Dollars,* her hand lazily swaying to the rhythm of the music while the show host selected a local name from the squirrel cage.

"They never pick anyone from Mockingbird Valley," she said. "I don't know if you've ever noticed that before, but it's rigged."

"I'll make us a scrambled-egg sandwich. You want bell peppers on yours?"

"This whole show is a gimmick so we'll stay tuned between *The Guiding Light* and *Days of Our Lives.*"

246   *Patricia Hickman*

I riffled through the vegetable crisper. "No bell pepper. How about red onion instead?"

"The peppers are put up in the deep freeze. You were up late last night, weren't you?"

"Had my mind on school. I like my English comp teacher. He's published."

"Something had you up. It was that phone call that upset you. What was the idea, callin' you so late? Somebody in trouble?"

"Pepper's in the meat tray, Momma."

"It's just as I said. They picked a woman from Little Rock. Probably tied in with that Hot Springs mob. *Have mercy!* She won the whole jackpot. I'd spend it on furniture, every dime, and not even tell your daddy." The entire time she spoke, she never lifted her gaze from the game show. Her emotions were so tied to her daily TV programs that her words mirrored the personalities she watched.

"Phone's ringing, Momma."

"I'll get it."

I sautéed the peppers before adding the egg mixture. The volume on the television was lowered probably several moments before I noticed it, having read Sol the riot act several times over in my head. His reply never surfaced in my one-act play, and that troubled me— that I knew so little about him before sharing those kisses.

"Everything all right, Momma?" I couldn't remember if she had said hello. "Can you hear me?" I scooped the cooked eggs onto two pieces of white bread. A fat tomato sat on the sill, ripening in the yellow rays of autumn. I considered sacrificing it. I loved nothing more than warm tomato slice with salt. But the stillness from the living room drew me, and I found Momma holding the telephone receiver to her ear with her right hand. The left hand trembled. She sat more silent than was her nature, with almost no trace of color in her face.

The caller's voice was an audible murmur, almost like a distant hornet in the quiet. Yet nothing was said that I could distinguish.

Momma's head made small dips, acknowledgments of what was being said, as though she were being instructed, but retaining no actual control over the flow of conversation. Just agreement. Laborious agreement, unseen by the caller.

"Thank you." She said it in a pithy tone, yet heavy as lead. Then she hung up.

I sensed the need to say nothing, to allow her to assimilate *whatever*. Her mother's health had disintegrated after my grandfather's death a year prior. She handled death poorly, but the news of Meemaw's cancer left her weakened.

She made unconscious circles around a hole in the chair arm, opened her mouth to speak twice, but only made frail moans.

"Can I do something, Momma? I'll bring you your sandwich. Tomato slice on the side, how about?"

"She said, that woman she said that your daddy is—"

"What woman? Something's wrong with Daddy?" It felt as though a vacuum had sucked all the oxygen from our living room. "Momma, you have to tell me."

"She wouldn't give her name. Only said that this floozy woman broke up her marriage, and she didn't want to see her do it all over again. Your daddy's over at the floozy's house right now. Katrina, he's seein' this woman."

"It's a crank call, surely."

"You should know some things, Katrina, now that you're all grown-up."

"I should have stayed on campus today." I pulled my hair back with both hands, my elbows making forward wingtips next to my ears.

"She gave me her name and said she's in the phone book."

"If she's lying, we'll know, then. I'll drive to this woman's house."
I felt afraid. "Why would someone say such a thing about Daddy?"

Momma broke into a thousand pieces, spilling stories about his
unfaithfulness.

"I know Daddy loses his temper, and we get all chafed with him.
But Momma, adultery?"

"Remember that divorcée, rented the house down the street I
always hated?"

"The one you said you were going to burn down?"

"He was with her."

"I was only, what, six? She was a bad mother. I'm glad no one
lives there now."

"She wasn't the last un neither."

"I'm going there myself."

She seemed oddly encouraged. Expectant. She handed me the
phone book and padded into the kitchen to finish the sandwiches.

As fiercely as I marched out to the Chevy for Momma's sake, I
felt my nerves curdle before I backed out of the drive. My throat was
raw, a tingling, dry burning. I choked on false courage. While at first
none of that hateful woman's story fit into any sort of sensible frame-
work, little pieces of reality flew to me from times past and became
whole. I saw it as one now—one big ugly mental image: I could
smell snow all at once. It wafted in from over my years, and it had
turned a sooty gray. Footprints in the snow, little girls being dropped
off on the front porches of strangers. I tried to breathe.

Patsy Cline sang "Crazy" on the radio. I did not remember turning to K-98, the golden oldies station.

It only took three minutes to find the street, then the house
number: seventy-six, seventy-eight, eighty. The house was dreadfully
apparent, painted yellow with haughty blue curtains. I don't know

what I expected to find, but it was no fable. Daddy had not driven far. The Pontiac looked tawdry in the driveway, a carriage for an old reprobate who thought family values was a steady government paycheck. All of my reflections disappeared into a soul blizzard.

I got out and sat on the woman's front porch, watching cars pass. It seemed as though I had sat on those boarded steps for eighteen years, waiting for my father to scoop me up, look at me with adoration, clean adoration. Not the kind he gave to those red-lipped Rubys, Minnies, and Bunnys. A picture materialized in my mind of a woman who stood at the door whispering to Daddy while Eden and I sat on an immaculate couch, each a docile mirror of the other. It had taken awhile to drive out to that rural home, be deposited into that woman's living room. Perhaps she was the mother of the girlfriend. I never knew, but she treated my sister and me with contempt, the kind of woman Momma would not have tolerated. She had a room filled with toys, Barbie dolls, and a small bin with a chalkboard and lots of little colored chalks that we could not touch. Her little granddaughter did not like her things touched. We could only sit on the couch and wait. I remember feeling intrusive, uncomfortable. Like I felt at this moment.

The squeak of hinges on a screen door groaned and then snapped as the door closed, but it was more of a far-off grating racket. It came from behind the yellow house. I recognized the stride—*step, step, cane, step, step, cane*—against the concrete. Daddy walked with his eyes to the ground, perhaps his thoughts moving ahead to the card game that waited at the spit and whittle. But he did not walk far before he noticed my car—the Chevy was parked right behind the Pontiac.

He looked at me, and when I lifted my eyes to meet his, I turned six years old again. I fully expected him to scold me, to take a switch to my backside and berate me for gazing upon what was supposed to be done in secret, what was supposed to be unspeakable. But he only looked away and turned invisible, as men like him are so apt to do. He walked to his car, never looking at me again. The Pontiac pulled forward, circled in the grass, and careened down the concrete drive. I watched him pull away, his face hidden by the brim of his black straw hat.

Brown elm leaves had scattered across the toe of my sneakers. I brushed them away, wishing that other dregs from the past could be as easily swept from my memory. The doorknob twisted and a woman appeared. She watched my father pull away, noticeably distressed when he did not return her farewell wave. "Who are you?" she asked.

"No one in particular."

"Is your car broken down? Can I call someone for you?"

I studied her intensely, trying to see something about her that was an improvement over my mother. I saw none, although it has come to me now that men do not chase women for their beauty. She had the appearance of a housewife, although her lipstick was smudged and her Clairol-dyed curls were tousled around the crown of her head.

"Are you lost, miss?"

"I once was lost, ma'am. But I know the way now. You have yourself a good day." I shambled back to the Chevy and drove away. I looked at my eyes in the rearview mirror. No trace of mascara on my lashes, just spidery black rivulets dried beneath my lower lashes. I thought of Momma seated sideways in her brown time-punctured Naugahyde, listening for the sound of tires on gravel, praying it was her older daughter with news that allayed her fears. Or knowing it was the man she could not trust. The leaves stopped falling, and all the gray doves had flown away. Even the martins had abandoned

Daddy's birdhouses. I sat in the car near the park until the sky turned a salt-and-pepper gray, the last tide of light before evening.

I told myself that every day could not be radiant.

Eden discovered that she hated sitting in a parked car with the windows down while Carl played Lord of the Lunch Menu. Instead of driving through a fast-food restaurant as he had done for the last several months, Carl drove past as many towns as possible, stopping only at small minimarts for food. He made Eden stay in the car with Dreamy while he gathered up pop-open cans of beans, potted meat, and twenty-five-cents-a-loaf sandwich bread. She could scarcely see Carl through the cigarette posters and the neon beer sign. He stood in line several feet from the door, glancing through the plate glass, but not looking at her so much as he looked past her, out toward the street. He had traded his tired demeanor for a look of desperation.

Dreamy had slept for an hour, weary of her own sporadic squeals when she spotted a herd of cattle or ponies. She shifted in her car seat, stretched her feet, and sat forward, noticing the truck had stopped. "I want a pop."

"You and me both, kid. Carl's getting us a bite to eat, but you need to lay off the pop and candy." One of her front incisors had colored, not exactly ruining her smile, but Katrina's tendency to throw one of her fits and call it neglect pushed Eden to mediate a treaty between Dreamy and sugary treats. It was a hard treaty to maintain, though. Sweets pacified her behavior during the long stretches between the rural counties of Tennessee.

A young blond woman paid out just ahead of Carl and sashayed through the exit door.

"Aunt Kateen! Take me home, take me home, Aunt Kateen!" Dreamy tossed aside her worn and naked Barbie. She strained at her child-safety belts.

"Simmer down; that ain't your Aunt Kateen. Besides, you know you wouldn't leave your momma and daddy now, ain't that right?"

"Want Aunt Kateen."

"You're stretchin' my patience, kid. Don't you like the ponies and such at the rodeos, and didn't Carl promise to build us our own ranch some day? We have to hang in there and be patient. Money doesn't just come to us. We have to go after it. Carl's doin' everything he can do to make a life for us."

Dreamy stared out the window and made little saliva bubbles on her lower lip. She reacted none at all when Carl ran through the door with an armful of canned meats and a half-gallon of milk.

"Eden, open that door," he said, with a cigarette clinging to his lower lip. Ashes scattered across his shirt yoke.

"All right, cranky face, what's your hurry?" She had to reach across Dreamy to flip the latch and shoved the door open with her toe. It infuriated her when he tossed the cans at her feet. "Haven't those hayseeds ever heard of a paper bag?"

"I had to do it, baby. Visa's no good."

"Carl, what are you babblin' about?"

"Best to strap yourself in, darlin', oh, and hide your face when we take off out of here." Carl jerked the gears, almost hit a beer delivery man, and caused the rear pickup tires to squawl out of the parking space.

"You'll kill us all, Carl Lunsford! You stop this truck right this instant and tell me what you're about!"

"Can't do that, baby. That shop attendant running out of those doors—that feller right there, see him—he'll be wantin' some money. And I'm a little shy of green right now." The man was shaking his fist at them as they turned onto the frontage road.

"You mean to say you *stole* those Vi-anny Sausages and that milk and that gawd-awful potted meat?"

"Man's got to feed his family, darlin'."

"They'll arrest you and me both! And for what—Vi-anny Sausages? I can explain to my grandchildren how I went to the penitentiary for fee-lay menyun but not pig innards!" Carl's erratic driving threw Eden against the door. "I can't keep goin' like this, Carl. If I get out of this alive, I'm goin' home."

Dreamy's eyes widened. She curled her fingers around the sides of the baby seat.

The traffic light at the interstate ramp turned red, but Carl drove through it and then veered onto the ramp. Eden watched the minimart attendant through the rear window. He looked like a stick man dashing for the inside of the store.

"I done told you; didn't I tell you last night? How I can't live without you, Eden? I did this for you, baby. Calm yourself. Besides, you can't run with a toddler and no money." Carl's truck careened onto the interstate, swerving around a beat-up red Pinto. "The kid's gotten used to me, like I'm her daddy and all. You leave me now, and it could damage her for life." Carl darted around an old codger pulling hay. He gave the old farmer a fright. "Anyways, they wouldn't arrest you. I'd tell them it was all my doin'."

"You think me and this baby gon' live on canned meat while you rust in some Tennessee jail?"

"You got to trust me, these hick towns don't have enough law to call spur of the moment. They do well to run their speed traps and all." He noticed a highway patrolman across the median headed west in the opposite lane. His boot eased off the gas pedal to placate the rattle of the pickup. "I'll win that money tonight bull ridin', and this won't ever happen again. It's a once-in-a-lifetime occurrence, kind of like when a banker shaves a little off the top to meet his mortgage.

You gon' have to let me manage these household matters, Eden. I know what I'm talkin' about."

"That cop's done turned on his lights, Carl."

"Probably chasin' a speeder." He glanced down at the speedometer.

"He's slowin' down, like he's about to make a turn."

"It'll take him awhile to take that ramp around. I'll have us in North Carolina, shake of a stick."

"He's cuttin' across the grass, right smack through the middle, Carl, and he's—why that cop's comin' after us, sure as everything."

"Eden, I told you to buckle your seat belt. We're goin' to have to find ourselves a new direction."

"You'll not outrun him. I have this bad feelin', like—I didn't want to say anything this mornin' back at the Friendly Griddle and Motel—but I woke up with it."

"Eden, you're goin' to have to stop your yappin'. I can't think straight!"

"You're busted, Carl! May as well pull over."

"Not yet, baby." He twisted the wheel, caused the pickup to bounce onto the next ramp.

Eden observed the sky behind the patrol car, a bright aster blue blanket, clear as a picnic day atop Mount Nebo. "I was goin' to fix us a nice picnic, and now all that's ruined. Just gone to the dogs, that's what."

◦◦◦

Momma and Daddy slept in their separate beds like always that night. I fell asleep listening to their silence. Way past the hour of midnight, sirens woke me. I slipped from the bed and peered out at the night sky, which blazed red from the fire. The old rent house was in flames. Several neighbors stood out on their front lawns, clad in their undershirts and tatty nightgowns.

*She didn't!* I crept down the hallway in nothing but an old T-shirt. Daddy's room was silent, with not even a warm cigarette butt glowing in the ashtray atop the nightstand next to his bed. In the fire's glow from the window, he looked like an old walrus washed ashore. I looked into Momma's room. She stirred, shifted beneath her covers, then kicked off her old house slippers onto the dilapidated rug beside her bed.

"Momma," I whispered.

She grew still, as I once did as a youngster when I wanted to convince her I had truly fallen asleep.

"The rent house, Momma, it's burning down."

"I'm asleep, Katrina. You go on back to your bed."

"You're *asleep?*"

She did not answer.

I watched the house burn until the sun came up. It was a small house, old and shoddy and full of bad memories. It turned to cinders within an hour or two. The *Courier* didn't so much as bother to report it.

When I asked Momma about it after school, she only said, "God has his ways. Who are we to question?"

The lot was cleared away within a few days. Whoever owned it never did sell it off like the other lots that went up for sell for a new gas station and a steakhouse. It was as though someone had cursed it. So between the new overpass and the steakhouse sat a little corner of the past, forgotten by everyone except my momma.

CHAPTER 17

*T*he Sumner Hill campus bookstore was the student hub. The hall that segued into a large café and grill was called the Commons. I took a cashier job in the bookstore. The job did not demand too awfully many hours. In the late afternoon, I stole several hours for study. It kept me away from home, where I was forced to inhere as a spectator to the tense charade that passed between Momma and Daddy. Between Meemaw's cancer and Daddy's transgressions, Momma's invectiveness spilled over into even the most ordinary parts of her life. I found her swearing at the soaps one day. That was reason enough to maintain my distance.

Saturday brought the sports fans into the bookstore, the mothers, fathers, and grandparents of the football players, cheerleaders, and band members that rummaged through the football placards, banners, and bumper stickers in order that they might show up at the game duly studded with team spirit for the Wonder Boys.

When the fans depleted the display of flags, I hiked around the counter to replenish the display, fluff up the satin green and gold ribbons tied to the silk mums, and pin more spirit ribbons to the felt board.

"Want to sell me some of those flags?" A Phi Lamb initiate walked up. Fraternities were new to the campus. I recognized him because he had dated a young woman from church. "How many you want?"

"However many it takes to keep you talking to me, Blondie."

"They're three for ten dollars."

"Just one, then. You're Katrina, aren't you?"

"You're Joe Geffen. You dated Heather Murray."

"Last year, that's right. Don't you stay at Jones?"

"I have a friend who lives in Jones Hall. You've probably seen me coming and going."

"I know it's kind of spur of the moment, but I'd love to take you to the game tonight. A bunch of us are going to a party afterwards, but you've probably already been asked."

"I'm already going with a friend, that's all. You may know Beth Hoover."

Sol strolled in wearing running shorts and a tank shirt. More of a T-shirt, actually, with the sleeves cut out. It was evident that he had been running. His face was slick with sweat, and the front of his hair was damp and pushed back from his forehead. He stood two aisles away counting out pencils, lending great importance to their selection. I figured he was acting aloof for the sole reason that he didn't expect to find me engaged in conversation with a Phi Lamb initiate. Avoiding him all week had been a chore, but I managed to keep my distance, never having returned his three phone calls. "But that could change, of course, Joe."

"Is that a yes?"

"Can't do the party scene, mind you. But if the game's still an option, I'm open to an early night."

"Where do you live?"

"I'll meet you at the stadium gate. Seven o'clock," I said.

Sol dumped the pencils onto the floor, fumbled to pick them up, irrevocably punting them beneath the floor stand.

"I'd rather pick you up, Katrina. But that's just me, I guess."

"I brought some clothes to change into from here. I thought meeting you might be more convenient."

"Let me pick you up here at the bookstore at five. I want to take you to dinner." Joe's persistence turned Sol's face a lovely crimson.

"Better make it five-fifteen. I'm locking up tonight."

Joe headed for the door with the Wonder Boy flag stuck into his back pocket.

"You'll want to pay for that," I said.

"See what you do to me, Katrina? Now I'm a shoplifter." He laid four dollars on the counter. "You can give me my change tonight."

I returned to the checkout stand, where three students waited with armloads of textbooks and parents' credit cards. A freshman girl had overheard my conversation with Joe. "You're going out with Joe Geffen?" she asked.

"Just to the game is all."

"Lucky."

"You want the workbook that goes with that course? It's required," I said.

"Thanks for telling me. Just keep ringing me up. I'll go get it." She disappeared in a flurry of auburn tendrils.

"While you're waiting for her, miss, mind answering a few questions for me?"

"Sol. How've you been?" I kept my eyes on the register, coding in the spiral notebooks for the female customer.

"Is your mother all there? I mean, I've left messages all week."

"Her mother's dying of cancer. She's not herself."

"I'm sorry; it never occurred to me. So you didn't get any of my messages?" He laid a handful of pencils on the counter.

"Sorry, two people are already ahead of you. I can't check those out just yet."

"Forget the pencils, Katrina," he said in a hushed tone, leaning toward me. "It's no secret that you and I, we haven't made any commitments. But it seemed to me we were headed toward something that could be a very good thing."

"You mean like a first date?"

"I can't ask if you're not there."

"You're absolutely right. We haven't made any sort of commitment. Miss, did you find that workbook?"

"It's here. What's my total?" The redhead dug through her handbag. She glanced up at Sol, who was invading her space.

"Are you really going out with that frat guy tonight?" Sol tipped forward with his hands against the counter, so close I could smell his sweat and see the dampness on his chest.

"Seventy-five dollars and forty-two cents," I said.

"Those aren't my pencils," said the girl.

"It's no problem. I didn't charge you for them."

"Joe Geffen hits on every freshman. He's known for that." Sol's sneakers squeaked against the waxed linoleum, the entire weight of himself pushing against the counter.

"I'm out of bags. I'll be right back." Sol followed me to the next counter.

"You do what you want, Katrina, but I'm telling you this guy's no good for you."

"Who is best for me, Sol?"

"Something's gotten you riled at me, I can see that."

"It would be best to talk later. But we're both busy tonight. So some other time?"

"Charlotte. She's said something."

"She's such a dear. I truly mean that."

"Tell me what she said."

"You know Charlotte better than I do. What could she say that would keep me awake at night and leave me feeling as if my body had been partially torn away?"

Every eye lifted from the student line.

He looked dumbstruck, embarrassed, as if caught in stealing. "I'm sorry. How can I make you understand the complication of it all? That other girl—she means nothing," he stammered. "Look, I'm open to suggestions, here. Help me out."

"Ah, here are the bags. Sorry I took so long, miss."

"Hey, buddy, you trying to cut in line?" The student behind the redhead grew testy.

"I'll only be a minute," said Sol. "Katrina, we have some issues here, and, well, you and I need to sit down and talk things out."

"Let's do get together soon," I said, my tone falsely sugarcoated. "But I wouldn't take too long. I won't be staying much longer."

"You're leaving."

"Possibly headed east. I had to take this little art class, see. All education majors take it—mostly we make maracas out of light bulbs, stuff like that. Here's your bag, miss. Thank you for shopping at the Sumner Bookstore." The redhead strode toward the exit, her calves turning out in anticipation of her next conquest. "He says—the art teacher—that I should pursue art. I've been thinking about it, how I ought to stop talking about my life as though it's all bits and pieces, as though all I need is some cosmic broom to just keep sweeping up what parts of me get scattered and trying to reshape what's left over. I am whole, Sol. Every part of me is who I am—I am a creative soul, a sister, a daughter, a woman of faith, and I am Katrina." I said it for myself as much as Sol. I said it to make it real. To make it come to life in my mind. "And I am leaving, Sol. I am. I'm really leaving."

"It's all settled, then, I guess."

"I guess it is."

"Are you really going out with Joe Geffen tonight?"

"I'm going," I said.

"Fine." Sol stalked toward the wide rectangular opening that led out to the Commons.

I could not allow myself to watch him flutter away from me.

"Carl, we can't stay holed up in this trailer forever." Eden propped open a window above the mattress where Dreamy slept.

"If I would have shown up at that Tennessee rodeo, it would have been crawlin' with cops, darlin'. Can't expect me to go to jail over some minimart job. My record's been clean until now. Let's just give the Tennessee state police time to forget about us. They got better things to do than to worry about a potted-meat thief. Not like I stole any money. I didn't pull a gun on that yahoo or nothin'."

"So you sayin' this farmer that gave you this job harvestin' apples, he didn't ask no questions?"

"He's short of help and saw we had a decency about us like ordinary folks. Likes the fact I got my own truck. I told him a job didn't work out for me in Charlotte, so he believed me. Just count it as a blessin', like your sister would say."

"You leave her out of this, Carl. She'd be ashamed to see us all hunkered down like some poor-white trash livin' hand-to-mouth in some trailer in North Carolina."

"Eden, I'm not goin' to leave us here. I'll be back on the circuit soon. We'll look back on this someday and split our sides laughin' about it."

"Ha-ha, Carl. Tell me another funny."

"Sittin' around here spittin' out your sarcasm will only make things worse than they are. You could do somethin' with the place, you know, like warsh the curtains and do womanly things to the place."

"You know I don't like fixin' up a place that ain't even my own to call home."

"If it helps to keep your mind off our troubles, then what's the harm? I found a bucket of paint down in that old barn. While I'm pickin' apples today you could paint the kitchen, make a pie crust, and have dinner ready when I get back. I left you a pail of apples out on the front steps. This little dream home is furnished with all the cookin' utilitaries you need. Grab you a parin' knife and go to town on those babies."

"How am I goin' to make a pie crust, if I never learned? Momma never taught me no kitchen skills."

"Here's the TV. Turn on one of those cookin' shows and just listen." Carl led her to a chair and pulled on the television knob. It came off in his hand. He replaced it and pounded the set a few times. "There she blows. Why that's a good picture on that set. Nothin' wrong with that little deal, is there?"

Eden stared into the set as he switched the channels and maneuvered the rabbit ears, twisting the antenna into a bow-tie shape.

"There's the Gallopin' Gourmet hisself. Why he'll have you whupped into the best cook, little gal."

"He's makin' flan, Carl. What on God's green earth is *flan?*"

"It's, why, some sort of puddin', but it's not *what* he's makin', don't you see? It's the finer points of cookin' I'm tryin' to show you. That's the deal. You'll just absorb it, see, and then next thing you know, you'll be dishin' up apple pies, fried chicken,"—he tapped the television screen—"and flan. Now watch the cookin' show then go through that sack of groceries and see what all you can come up with. They's a cookin' book, too."

"How'd you pay for groceries and a cookin' book?"

"That farmer, he advanced me some. Just to help us get by. He's a good ol' boy, that one."

"Are you for real sayin' we have genuine groceries? Did you buy Frosted Flakes? Milk? Eggs?"

"All of the above."

"Carl, don't you beat all. But I want you to be sure you work off what he gave us. No need to get in any hurry. It is kind of peaceable out in the country, and like you say, we need to lay low. We could make this farmin' business work for us."

"Don't get too attached, baby doll. I'll be itchin' to get back in the saddle soon as I can."

Eden kissed him good-bye, nuzzled her face against his neck. Carl stepped across the grassless path toward the orchard, and she watched him, tall, slender, full of vinegar as any man. A wind had picked up. It lifted a soft veil of dust around him, danced at his ankles, and caused him to look at the ground. He was one of those men born in the wrong place at the wrong time who belonged on the range chasing down stray calves, not hustling potted meat or picking apples to stay out of jail. Last night she had decided to leave him, scrawl a note on the back of a canned-good label, and stick it to his steering wheel. But he had made her feel secure again. She knew that Katrina would never understand the need for security. But it was something she coveted more than all of Katrina's lofty ideals wrapped up together.

She dug out a small knife that was wedged in the corner of a grimy kitchen drawer. She did not recall what a paring knife looked like, but it was similar to one Momma used to peel potatoes. She made a place for herself in the open door of the trailer and set to hacking the peels off apples. Katrina sometimes sat on the back porch paring vegetables for Momma and singing. Eden had never felt brazen enough to sing aloud. But with no one to hear, she thought that a song might charm the sting out of her troubles and swathe the musty air with normalcy. It was a song she heard her sister sing on occasion.

> *Jesus is tenderly calling you home*
> *Calling today, calling today,*
> *Why from the sunshine of love will you roam,*
> *Farther and farther away…*

I have always prized the mannish tang that lifts above the stadium bleachers, particles of expectation that rise from the field, climbing to the gleaming stadium lights, and as moisture turns to rain, male fervor falls glittering onto the players as they trample the sports ground.

The fact that we had to pull off our sweaters reminded us that summer had not left us completely. Still holding hands with autumn, summer pumped warm breezes through our hair, dovetailing green foliage with supple, dying gold and crimson leaves. It was the end of heat's tyranny, the promise of harvest, the trees full of the jewelry of apples and persimmon. The first game was our sweet farewell to summer, delicious watermelon summer, and salutations in full to all that was golden.

Varying groups of spectators had gathered like graded eggs upon the aluminum bleachers: The alumni sat cloistered in and near the glassed-in broadcasting booth, while the various fraternity brothers and sorority sisters mingled among themselves in matching sweat-shirts, their cheeks and some exposed trunks tattooed with fierce poster-painted Wonder Boys mascots. The ROTC students lolled casually, their faces painted green and gold entirely. I found a neutral zone and seated myself by Beth.

"So explain to me, will you, about this Phi Lamb fellow. You had a date, but now you don't. You have so many choices now, you're throwing away perfectly good men?"

"It was nothing. A stupid impulse on my part."

"Breaking it or making it?"

"Both, but especially agreeing to go out with someone who is so far removed from what I want. I want something less complicated than, say, Sol. But not so over the edge as Joe Geffen."

Beth waved at some girls who tripped over their own feet in an effort to join us. "Did you notice, are the concession lines long?"

"Eternally. You want popcorn? I'll get it," I said.

"Take a five. I'll spring for yours, too." Beth dug a bill out of the side pocket of her shoulder bag. "Here comes Cooter."

Cooter Ray Blevins loped into the end zone, a too-small helmet on his head and shoulder pads on the outside of his clothes. In a metropolis, Cooter would have been the man scarcely worth men-tioning, a vagabond more apt to wear a trench coat he dug up near the curb on trash day. But not so for Cooter Blevins. He was a respectable derelict. Small towns embrace their feeble-minded eccentrics as they do a mongrel pup clad in doll clothes and taught to dance on its hind legs.

The crowd cheered, all Cooter enthusiasts, whenever he took up his earnest stance beyond the goalposts. A child everlastingly ensnared in the body of a man, Cooter never missed a Wonder Boys' game and camped just beyond the goalposts for the lucid thrill of the

catch. He endeavored every Saturday night to intercept the scoring
pigskin after it catapulted through the uprights, a triumph as anticipated by the fans as those elusive goals— *"Two cheers for the home
team! Three cheers for Cooter Blevins!"* It would be his Pulitzer, when
he finally caught a ball.

A popcorn vendor tramped upward from out of the aluminum
depths, his purveyor tray loaded with popcorn, chocolate bars, and
watery, icy colas. I snagged two popcorns and two drinks for Beth
and me just in time for the kickoff. The Wonder Boys won the toss
and passed for a first down.

"I think you broke it off with Joe because you're holding out for
Sol."

"There's that shrink thing coming out in you again, Beth. Like
the same sock that never gets pulled from the dryer, you just keep
recycling the same old piece of blue lint."

"I'm trying to help. Don't be such a hind end, Katrina."

"Sol knows for certain now that it's not going to work for us."

"When did you see him again?"

"Today, for just a little while."

"I'm never around for the good stuff. *Second down! Go, Wonder
Boys!*"

"You're spilling your drink. My shoe, my shoe! Sol complicates
everything. We can't say that we've had anything going, nothing to
speak of as far as I can tell. So how do I break it off with someone
who never obligated himself?"

"But what if he was about to commit and you broke it off, but
then you realized later that you should have given it, him, more time?"

"I can't see someone who treats me like his sister."

"Does he treat you like his sister or his best friend? Big difference.
I think they're going for a touchdown. For real."

*"Best friend?"*

The fans lifted, one corporate cheering mob rooting for the gangly quarterback. Cooter Ray Blevins died twice waiting for the ball to lift—a faultless spiral thrown into the hands of the waiting tight end, who in turn ran, hips swiveling for an unspoiled touchdown. Cooter took his place between the uprights.

Beth stood, waving her arms, tossing popcorn, while I remained seated, holding our drink cups. I laughed while the fans settled back into the bleachers.

The broadcaster's voice squeaked through the cheap PA. *"The Wonder Boys' place-kicker Joel Wells lines up to attempt the extra point. There's the snap! The kick! And it's good!"*

The crowd roused from the bleachers with rowdy cheers and little victory dances in spilled illegal beer.

"Oh, did you see that? The ball hit Cooter right on his head!" Beth placed a hand on either side of her head.

"Then why are you laughing?" I asked.

"Poor guy, everyone's laughing. It bounced off his helmet and hit a car. Why would someone park a car near the end zone?"

*"Good news for the Wonder Boys, who seize the lead in the first quarter, but bad news for the owner of that Toyota parked in the end zone."*

The band pumped the victory song into the air as the spectators floated back down to their seats. I stood. I could see the Toyota now, the driver checking the top of his car and then sidling back inside alone.

"What are you doing, Katrina?"

"Watching Sol."

"Sol? He's here? What's he doing?"

"He's watching me. I should have sat with Joe."

"All right. Just so's I understand everything. Can you stop that hot dog man?"

CHAPTER 18

*I* actually fixed us a pie, Carl, out of them apples. It's not exactly what you call a blue-ribbon winner; somethin's not right about it, but I figure I'll get better with practice. Sort of kept comin' apart, but all I had to roll it out with was this old snuff glass. Kind of reminds me of one of Momma's patchwork quilts." She chuckled, tucked another powdery edge of crust under. She felt unsure of herself, as though she was uncertain of whether or not she had earned his approval. But she felt empowered when she mimicked Momma. "You lay your stuff on that chair and go warsh up now."

Carl stepped in one slow movement across the threshold as if all of the joints that fitted him together ached. Every part of his face looked as if it sagged, and he reminded Eden of one of those ancient island turtles. Calico turtles, she believed they were called, on Jack Coosto's *Wild Kingdom*.

"What's that you got under your arm? Is that a gun, Carl?"

"That Farmer Ledbetter, he's got too many deer out in his woods. They've taken to rummagin' around in his garden, and his wife wants them thinned out."

"Don't tell me you gon' shoot a little deer, Carl?"

"Don't give me none of that save-the-animals malarkey. We're about to eat steak tomorrow night, fresh deer steaks, and I don't want to hear any female whimperin' about Bambi."

"Tonight, I made somethin' and it's called—" She read the cookbook page once more. "Chicken à la king with oven fried potaters. Made it out of them chicken wings, but it'll still taste as good." She held up the unbaked pie. "And this."

"Somethin's smokin', Eden. You catch somethin' afire?"

"It's that old oven. Billows out in my face every time I open the door."

"Toss me a beer, baby doll. I need to unwind in front of the TV for a spell."

Eden retrieved a cold beer from the refrigerator. "I tried to put these cans of orange juice in the deep freeze, but none of it will go. I never seen one so frosted over, like, we only have about a can's worth of freezer space. So I just went ahead and made it up all at once in this old milk pitcher. But we're supposed to drink it soon, otherwise it goes bad."

Dreamy sat on the curling linoleum, playing toss-the-apple-peels.

"Just get somethin' on the table soon before I pass out. I've not been so tired in a while. You hear anything on the news? They talkin' about us?"

"I haven't watched the TV since the soaps went off."

"You ought to keep it on at all times. Let that be your job while I'm gone. We can't let nothin' slip up on us."

"We're in the middle of nowhere, Carl. I can't relax if I have to sit around ridin' shotgun for you, so let's just forget about the minimart and all. Let's sit ourselves down to the supper table like regular people. Let the rest of the world take care of itself." She pulled paper plates from a plastic wrapper and set three places at the foldout wall table, two beside each other so that she could hold Dreamy while she ate. "I managed to make a little ice, though, one tray. Got ice for the tea. I don't know why that seems like such a luxury now. Momma and Daddy got ice through the next century."

"Lower it, Eden. Can't hear the news. I don't need no tea. Just this beer."

She watched the back of his head tipped back against the recliner. That was all she could see besides the toes of his boots. It seemed he had all but nodded away when the news broke of the manhunt for an armed robber and his girlfriend accomplice. That's when a sketch of Carl's face flashed onto the screen. He came unglued soon thereafter.

Meemaw was slipping from us. That is all that Momma said to me before I dressed for class. She'd been failing for some time now, but never had Momma's use of the phrase "slippin' away" worked at me. So between art and physical science, I took the two-mile drive to St. Mary's.

Outside my grandmother's hospital room, I could pick out the voices of those confined to their beds as well as those who had dropped by for a visit. I sipped cafeteria coffee from a paper cup and listened to pain take up residence inside a once-hearty soul. It became clear to me that the fear of death was really the fear of leaving this place in little degrees of loss instead of all at once. One delirious old man quacked out a sharp, nasal sound repeatedly until a nurse disappeared into his room with a hypodermic. After that, I did not hear another peep out of him. Inside Meemaw's room, a young Korean nurse was checking her IV, wheeling it first to the head of her bed and then beside her, until she seemed satisfied with the tube that fed into Meemaw's right wrist. "Is she asleep?" I asked. "I'm her granddaughter, Katrina."

The nurse bent over Meemaw and shook her. "You granddaughter is here, missus."

Meemaw groaned, a nearly apologetic utterance, but did not open her eyes.

"Wake up! Time to see your granddaughter!" The Korean's aggressive manner unnerved me. If Meemaw did open her eyes, I imagined her asking me who in the blazes I thought I was, waking her from a restful sleep.

"Please don't shake her, miss. I'll just sit here with her for a while." The nurse picked up her clipboard and walked out of the room. Meemaw did not stir at all. She lay on her back with the sheet pulled over her chest. A sack rustled beneath my arm. I had purchased a small gift for her from the campus bookstore. I left it in the cold, hard chair next to her. Her Bible lay on the stand next to her bed, and I picked it up. A crocheted bookmark was stuck in between the crimped gold-edged pages. I opened it, struck by its musty smell, one she probably cherished. Someone stepped into the room. It was Edith. "Hello, Aunt Edith. She's sleeping."

"She's in a coma, Katrina."

"Momma didn't tell me. I'm sorry."

"Your momma took it hard. I believe she's denyin' all of this."

"She didn't tell me," I repeated.

Edith saw the Bible in my hands. "I been readin' her little bits every now and then. I saw her do it once for one of her friends who was dyin', so I just thought I'd do the same for her."

"Is Meemaw dying?"

"I believe she's ready to go. Told me who to have preach at her funeral."

"She talked to you about her own funeral?"

"Wants some yeller roses for her coffin. Momma always loved her roses."

"I didn't know that about her. Is that why Momma likes flowers so much—because of Meemaw?"

"Maybe so."

"I'm glad you came. I felt silly sitting here watching her breathe. She never really paid me much mind, though. I guess it's no different now."

"Momma cared about you, about all her grandchildren. After she found religion, she just changed—like she thought expressin' piety was above expressin' affection."

"She thought being cold to us would please God?"

"Now Katrina, I've never been good at sayin' things. Don't you know what I mean about your grandmother? She was doin' the best she knew how to do."

"I know." But I didn't.

"My momma never was one to be huggin' necks, passin' out kisses to all us kids. If she managed to get a hot pan of cornbread out to us by suppertime, well we knew she did it because she loved us."

"But how did you know, really know? I mean no disrespect, Aunt Edith. But some people do things because their forebears did it. You remember when Meemaw and Grandpa picked me up for church?" I glanced at her then, as if afraid that she might have awakened from her coma to hear me, and then lowered my tone. "She never made me feel like she was glad to see me, more like she was the high holy woman dragging the little heathen off to church. Almost as though she would stand in front of God one day and lay claim to my soul. Maybe it was just her obligation to bake you cornbread, to take care of you, because she brought you into the world."

"You think your momma feeds you out of obligation?"

I put down my coffee. It was cold and the sugar in it had taken over the flavor. "As you say, she does what she knows to do." I sighed. "I brought Meemaw this little devotion book. You want it?"

"Leave it with her Bible. I'll read to her from it."

Through the window I saw a few leaves had turned yellow. A few more had fallen to the ground, gold stars strewn upon the browning grass. I had thought of myself as the tree, starting from a seed, standing against the wind, weathering the rain and snow. But as I watched Meemaw, her face pale against white hospital linen, I realized I was only the leaf itself, living out my little season in life, then taking my bow, ready or not. Meemaw had tasted of faith, enough to make her conceited about it. I wanted what faith I had found to lift me above myself, to reach down into the darkest parts of me and root out the pieces that had grown bitter. I wanted more than just my ticket to heaven. God had set a fire inside of me, one that blazed enough to make me dissatisfied with sitting still while the rest of the world traipsed by in the dark. I was a far cry from being some bonfire for God. But I'd be switched before I'd paint imitation holiness all over myself in little faux letters that spelled out to all the heathen bystanders why I was better than them because I abided by some list of don'ts. I would not stand before God some wretched little forger.

"I look at Meemaw, and I realize that we don't have long on the earth, Aunt Edith."

"You're too young to be worryin' about such things, Katrina."

"Am I right?"

"Yes, you're right."

"Just wanted to hear you say it."

She smiled. "You got the mischief side of the family."

I rose, briefly touched Meemaw's hand, then turned to Aunt Edith. "I have to go."

"I know, child. You take care."

I could hear Aunt Edith reading a passage about the city that had no need of the sun or moon, for the glory of God gives it its light.

Meemaw would pass to that place on that night. And when she saw the purity of his love, I just knew she would finally get the gist of it all.

"Carl, you don't expect us to just leave behind all I've worked to make here. The pie's still bakin' in the oven. Let's just keep our heads and take it easy. Have a bite to eat—"

"I don't have time to argue! Now grab Dreamy's things, and let's go." While Eden rationalized about the good things they had experienced on the farm, Carl gathered the ammunition given to him by Ledbetter. Eden fumed. He scraped canned goods and cereal boxes back into the grocery bags in an unwieldy, robotlike mode and straddled Dreamy, who sat square in the middle of the floor with her apple peels. He frowned beneath a Farm-All cap while he huffed about the trailer.

"Can't we just please sit down and eat, Carl? Have a meal together and talk things out?"

"They think I robbed an armored truck, killed a security guard, and offed with a quarter of a mil, baby. These good ol' boys haven't had that much excitement since the last Christmas tree lighting in the town square. They'll shoot first, ask later. You expect me to sit around playin' John Boy while they pump me full of lead?"

"Let's just go down to the police precinct and explain thangs in a common sense kind of way—"

"Eden, get in the truck with the baby. It'd be faster just to not have you underfoot. I'll get the food."

"Oh, is that what I am now, *underfoot?* Well, that's a fine how-do-you-do after all I've put up with, draggin' me and 'is kid half-way across God's green earth, makin' us eat potted meat, drinkin' hot Coke from a can!"

Carl plucked three chicken wings from the dish and wrapped them in a napkin, his face pinched and sodden with irritation. He yanked the partially cooked pie from the cloudy oven and dumped it into a cardboard box. "Happy now? Out the door, my little love bug. Let's move!"

Eden sulked. The truck rolled away from the trailer across the pastures of folks who had carved happy lives for themselves, while Bonnie and Clyde passed into the sunset with a half-eaten dish of chicken à la king.

"I'm sorry about your grandmother, Katrina." Beth stopped by the art building on her way to chemistry. "Let's meet for lunch. Burger Bob's."

I nodded.

"What's that music?" she asked.

A cassette wheeled softly in a player next to me. "Some African children's choir. It moves me. Most of them are orphans. It's funny, but they help me when I paint."

"Kind of haunting. I sort of like it. See you at noon."

I ran my thumb across the bristles of the oil painter's brush. The horsehair splattered burnt-umber flecks across the mass of sienna and gray in the painting, an obelisk rising out of cool green lake water—turpentine, yellow ochre, cerulean blue, more umber. Every brush stroke felt like a prayer, but maybe that was due in part because Tom

Calypso's—"Dr. Calyps" to his students—airy studio felt like a chapel to me. Colored-glass hangings, shaped like small Madonnas, tinkled against the windows, all six windows that ran the length of the room stretching as high as the ceilings and down to the hardwood floor.

Fine art studies suited me, I decided, even if it meant that my easel and I were forced to suffer the shackles of the valley for four more months until I could transfer. *I could do it*—I repeated those four words until they sounded like an old bell in my head, tolling my last days in Death Valley. Fragile as I had felt, a new layer of crust formed, made of an obstinate resolve saying to me, "Attababy, Katrina. March, march, left, right, to the mountaintop, then hold your breath, spread your arms, wider, wider, and jump."

Momma cried all night, but I left her with a plate of fried eggs, sunny side up, Petit Jean bacon, crisped on both sides the way she liked, and biscuits. I reminded her that Meemaw struggled to break free of those intravenous manacles, that now she basked in heaven's pools with all her parts duly rejuvenated in one of those crystal watering holes where the angels play pitch, and she danced for the first time with Grandpa—possibly with a really sweet percussion section. I left her crying again in her eggs.

Sol had not shown his face, not called, or even narrowly acknowledged his ridiculous end-zone vigil. But that little fact did not taint my sleep as much as that moon-cursed rendezvous of ours, how I smelled him on my face that night when I went to sleep and I am almost positive that it brushed off on my pillow. It made me more than crazy.

A footstep nearby jerked me back to the present. "Katrina, if you don't want me here, just say so. I'll leave."

It was Sol.

Anyone could walk into the studio at any time. I acted as Dr.

Calyps's front person, directing that person down to his office or telling him or her where to buy the best gesso. But Sol's voice left me feeling rumpled, like I felt when someone walked into my bedroom impromptu and saw my bed unmade. "I can't talk, Sol. I have to work; it's tedious."

"Don't think I'm here to interrupt. I only wanted to say how sorry I am about your grandmother."

"Thank you. Who told you, by the way? Beth?"

"My father. He knows everything that goes on at church. Who dies, who gets married."

"My grandmother had her funny ways about her and all. But she's resting now in a better place. Momma's going to have a hard road, but she'll get by."

"Look at you. You're painting."

"It's lousy; you don't have to say anything."

"I wasn't going to say that it's lousy, Katrina. It looks something like, well, with the water and the large boulder—I'd say it's Long Pool. I just didn't know you were this good."

"How did you know it was Long Pool? You can already tell that about it?" The sun moved from its morning perch and streamed across the canvas, the watery image, and the girl swan-diving from the boulder top. "It's supposed to be impressionistic—linear, with a repeated design. A folk feeling, almost." I stepped away from it. "Or else I just don't have any earthly idea what to make of it."

"The large rock, the cove. I see it all in your painting. You know, I almost died at Long Pool."

I kept the sympathy from my eyes.

"A buddy of mine talked me into canoeing. I was ignorant of the flood stage it had reached. We hit a wall of water right as we careened around this point so placid, motionless like a mirror—then the wall. We flipped."

"Clearly this story has a happy ending."

"We, he and I, we gripped hands together over some rock." I imagined Sol doing Boy Scout maneuvers. "We both sat there for hours with that icy water rolling over us. The sun went down. We would have given up right about then, but that's when the helicopter came. It spotted us. A park ranger must have seen us stuck out on the rock just before sundown. Otherwise, we both would have been sucked away."

"Sounds like some bravery is tucked away in there."

"We were idiots."

"Warn me next time, then. I'll cover the painting with a cloth," I said.

"Don't do that. This painting is a side of you I didn't know about." It occurred to him, perhaps, that the conversation once again centered on him. But I gave him credit, since men seldom took notice. "That education stuff didn't work for you, I suppose."

I shook my head. "I was sitting in one of those teacher-type classes and I saw these girls, the ones who make certain they have the front chair in the classroom. The woman teaching child psych wore this sort of smock dress, little apples embroidered across the yoke, her hair bunned up like a geisha. Those girls worshiped her. I could see it in their faces. I knew I was the alien."

"A geisha?"

"Actually, yes, that's a pretty apt description. I wanted to get those little painted oriental sticks, walk up behind her, poke them in and say, 'There now, that makes it perfect.' I made a frame with my thumbs. Sol laughed and it arose inside of me, the misery of his approval. His eyes returned a meager coal of pain.

"Katrina, we could go and talk somewhere later today, if you like. I want to tell you some things, but not here." He gazed all around the studio. The room must have felt large to him, a milieu suitable for eavesdropping, or not boxed-in enough. Not as intimate to him as it felt to me.

While the sun moved across the wood floor, like light trickling through the spaces on a paper lantern, I turned once more to my canvas, filled in the cerulean across the water's surface, then in my mind's eye knew the distant shore must be spotted with yellow black-eyed Susans. And something red, a tincture of hibiscus red, but I didn't know what reds grew along the shore of Long Pool. I was afraid of falsely portraying nature. The best artists are such superior liars.

"We don't have to," he said.

"How about over by that window?" Two wooden foldout chairs faced one another in the morning sun.

Sol stood in that male pug-dog way of his, arms folded across his trunk, deliberating how he could next control the conversation.

"I have to clean out this brush, cover the palette with some plastic wrap. The mixes are perfect, and I want to save them." I twisted the brush handle within a fold of my plaid overshirt, my father's old shirt, actually, one Momma refused to mend for the gazillionth time. "Go ahead and take a seat. I'll be right there."

His sneaker tapped against the slick blond wood. I imagined he was deliberating what the damage control would be like if he just walked away. The fact that I cannot fathom the pressures of manhood has always been to my detriment.

"I have a class. I should go," he finally said.

He always made me feel as though I played lover's bingo against him, like I was a B-15 away from it all being right.

"Some other time, then." I completed my three-quarter stance and faced the palette table.

His shoes played ricochet with the wood, slow, deliberate, thumping and strumming against the chords of my soul. And then I felt his hands touching me, turning me around, and making me look at him, seeing myself in his eyes again, and all the while, me turning into a pillar of salt. His kiss was insufferably good. Sol walked me to a tree-shaded place where little concrete benches stood bolted into the ground. A smattering of students lolled on blankets or sat cross-legged on the benches. But we just stood beneath the trees, awkwardly holding one another, musing over the kiss we just had and how it might affect us for the rest of the day. Sol kept squeezing my hand, speaking quietly to me, while leaning to brush my face again with his lips.

One could sit square in the middle of the campus, absorb the solitariness of it, and feel at one with mechanisms greater than the valley. The architecture had such a classy, comely face about it, as though silent men with money sat behind massive oak doors, pumping capital into the place, ordering juniper borders and chrysanthemum promenades along the entrance while they waited to see if greatness ever shadowed its portals. I would miss that, I decided.

"I want to get this out, before I lose the nerve—that night, the night of the game. I didn't go to Fort Smith to see that girl."

"I know. I saw you in the end zone."

"You saw me?"

"Everyone saw you."

"I guess you think I'm a big idiot?"

"No. It was kind of sweet."

"I was scared."

"Scared?"

"Scared you'd be with that Phi Lamb lunkhead."

"Why didn't you join me, then, when you saw me without a date?"

"I don't know."

"What did you tell that Fort Smith girl?"

"She met me in town. We got in my car and I took her to the movies down at the Picwood. All she did the whole night was chatter about herself, so much so I thought I'd kill myself if she didn't shut up."

I smiled.

"After the movie, I told her I had other things to do, walked her to her car."

"She drove all that way. I'll bet it made her mad."

"Ooh, yeah. She peeled out of that parking lot. Anyway, I wanted to apologize…"

"Katrina, there you are." Dr. Calypso strolled across the lawn from the arts building. He looked like a walking mosaic, gauzy clay-colored shirt beaded up and down the yoke, sleeves catching the wind. His stomach led the way, the hem of his shirt flapping loosely above his belt. His bald head—he called it a rather wide part—reflected the sun like mottled headlight chrome.

"Dr. Calyps, this is Sol."

He ignored Sol. "Katrina, I wanted to bring this to you right away. These are, well…" He fumbled with a folder of what looked to be brochures and letterheads. "This one is really just a summer program. Good exposure to some fine artists up in Chautauqua. Arizona has a really well-developed arts department, as well as Southern Florida, but this one here… This school offers strictly nothing but, well, painting all day or talking about painting. Morning until night you're completely absorbed with art and artists. But you'd have to move to New York. The professors at the University of Arkansas are fine people too."

I must have look stunned or bereft of any intelligible thoughts.

"You *were* serious, weren't you? About transferring?" he asked.

"Let me see that one, the New York one." The architecture lured me, although I wouldn't have known Greek Renaissance from a neoteric cold potato at the time. "Would you look at that?"

"Look at what?" asked Dr. Calyps.

"When I think of New York, I think of dingy air, tatty, sort of soot-belching buildings. Just goes to show how little I know. See how pretty this place is?" I showed it to Sol, but never really glanced up to see whether or not he was looking at it. I was looking at it myself pretty hard.

"It was once a museum, but the museum moved, and the art school was established in its place. Lots of eclectic people, intensive. But no dorm to speak of."

"New York Studio School of Drawing, Painting, and Sculpture. Where would I live?"

"The Y, or you could sublet. They're not overly helpful with housing. But you'd have a lot of independence, what with it being in Greenwich Village and all. I don't want to steer you, though, or have you show up on my doorstep hating me for packing you off to those peculiar New Yorkers. You go through all these materials. Just let me know when you decide. You'll need references; we can help you with all that. And some slides of your work. How soon can you finish that flying woman painting?"

"Diving woman."

"Well either way, she's shaping up nicely. You need to tweak your composition; let me look at the early sketches. We'll do that tomorrow. But you have until November first to have your registration, references, and slides to them in order to start with the spring semester in January."

"This January?"

"If that's too much pressure, you could aim for the summer."

"I can manage. I owe you."

"You just get yourself accepted, Katrina."

I didn't watch him go. I was too absorbed in the brochure and thoughts of Greenwich Village. "Sol, I never knew a place like this existed. I knew I wanted to go; I just didn't know where."

He mostly sat without saying much, just reading over my shoulder.

I plunked my artist's satchel beneath the bench and sat with one sneaker curved around the concrete leg. "I wonder if they have students on some list, you know, for instance, ones who are in need of a roommate, or maybe they know a friend who'd let me stay with them. I'd hate to go just move in with someone I don't know. But I guess that's the chance I'd have to take."

I sat so close to him that my back took on the shape of his trunk, with my head in the curve of his neck. He continued gazing over my shoulder while I shuffled the brochures into an A list and B list sort of order. "You think they'll make fun of my accent? I never think much about it, but when my cousins visit from St. Louis, well, apparently, they say, anyway, it's pronounced."

Sol lifted the New York brochure from my hand, turned it over several times, then read the inside copy.

"Why do Yankees make fun of us, Sol? Is it because they really think we're all bigots still fighting, as you said, the Civil War? Or does it make them feel superior or somehow better than us to cast us into some rejection pile or censure us from the human race? I've tried to disconnect myself somehow from the South, working on my accent and telling people I was really born in California."

"Were you?"

"Yes. Only lived there four months. But the South...*dwells* in me. I still feel a sense of dignity when I stand in a patch of cotton. My mother's fingers used to bleed when she picked it as a girl. In that sense I find it's sacred. Should I be ashamed of that? Sol, where are you?"

"I don't know about Yankees or about New York or even Oklahoma, Katrina. You're the first person I've ever known to cut a trail out of here so fast."

"I don't mind asking you what you think, but I'm afraid to ask you what you want from me, that's the thing, as though you'll just stare a big gaping hole right through me and walk away in your wordless way."

He allowed my rambling avowal to stream through his consciousness for a moment or two. "I don't even know what I want from me."

"Sol, you're the only one I know who I've allowed to just wander in and out of the places where I am, letting you into a few of my private rooms, so to speak"—he laughed at that one—"and then you just sort of evaporate."

"Whenever I try to get close, you run away, Katrina, like I've spooked you. You remind me of some cat that's been out in the woods too long."

"I've been compared to a stray before."

"See, it's things like that, the way you make assumptions about what I'm trying to say that gets me—well, dang it, Katrina, sometimes you rile me."

"So I'm not a stray?"

"Mind if we get off the stray stuff? I've been trying to see you. I kiss you and then you run off. I don't wander away. You do. So we never actually make it to the earnest part of this deal, and that is so contrary to the way you...come across."

"Now this is a good starting point, Sol. You're not making any sense at all, but you're emoting. How about you tell me when you've actually attempted to, say, *date me*."

I could see that I had stumped him.

"How about this question: Do you want your daddy's brokerage?" I asked.

He held an elm leaf in his grasp, rubbed it between two fingers until it looked damp and then frayed. "I want to say all the things that will make you stay here—with me. But if you stay, you won't be Katrina."

"Staying here is no good for me, Sol."

"Somebody's wounded you. I'd like to wound them, give them an ounce of my medicine." He flicked the leaf.

"Maybe that's why I've been running. I'm no good for you, Sol. All of my family's problems are so convoluted." I thought of Daddy's rage and Momma's pain and Eden's troubles. I didn't want to be Katrina *Hurley* to Sol—just Katrina. I wanted to leave the taint of the Hurleys behind. I looked into his eyes and wondered how I could ever be worthy of him. But I was too proud to say so. "I wouldn't involve you if you begged."

"See? Now there's another example of how nothing gets past you. And no one, no matter what you say, makes it into a one of those private rooms, Katrina. You just keep telling yourself that you're doing it for me if it makes you feel better."

"I'm not all that protective of myself. Just of others."

"I suppose you think that puts you right up there with Joan of Arc."

"You're making fun of me."

"Tell me if you are really leaving, Katrina. I guess that sounds pretty foolish in light of what you're holding in your hand right now. But look at me and just tell me straight. You know… Let me into one of those rooms of yours."

I did look at him. But all he could do was try and kiss away my silly little tears.

I can be such an infant sometimes.

CHAPTER 19

*A*ll through autumn, Eden called home every few weeks, but she purposed to phone by midmorning while I was away at class or in the studio, either avoiding me or afraid that I might, as she put it, grill her about Dreamy. I always sensed when one of her phone calls had affected Momma, just as my mother could discern when the Mormon boys were about to impinge on our afternoon or that a member of her family had commenced to die. Either way she could be found holed up in her bedroom. Eden's calls left Momma coiled in front of her muted television set, nursing a fixated stare, a woman who was not allowed to romp in grandmother heaven nor to relish the longed-for sagacity and savvy of a well-brought-up son-in-law. But she had signed away her younger daughter as visibly as she might have relegated her to a Chinese work camp.

We eventually swore off that discussion altogether, just as we swore off talk of Daddy's discrepancies. It only threw more coals onto her churlish-disposition flames. But on matters regarding Dreamy, we had to connect, sometimes talking in circles as though we felt around in the dark for one another, and then touching and joining our only lifeline, little speculative discussions about what we would buy Lolita Dream for Christmas.

"If you're not going to listen in on *Guiding Light,* Momma, you may as well turn the whole thing off. No sense in wasting the electricity."

I milled through the refrigerator for the week-old Thanksgiving turkey, making wagers about the staleness of the cornbread dressing that had taken on the shape of a Rubbermaid bowl. "Could it be that my little sister called this morning?"

"She's not even tryin' to come home for Christmas. The only reason she asked to talk to your daddy, I imagine, is so she could finagle money out of him. But he's gone fishin' down by the dam, and I'll not even tell him she called. That'll fix her."

"Did she say this time where they are? I just can't figure out how they're making out, let alone taking proper care of Dreamy. It's gotten cold and Eden left all their warmer things here in her closet, like she's coming back for them."

"Said they was in Florida, but she's lyin'."

"How do you know?"

"That operator who said I had a collect call identified herself as bein' from Maryland. Now that's the complete opposite of Florida, ain't it? She's pulled some stunts, but this is the high queen of stunts, cartin' that baby around like it was a doll, an' her no more than just a girl herself."

"I wonder what's gone wrong with them? Do you suppose Carl's some ogre who won't let them have anything to do with us, kind of like he sees them as his possessions?"

"If she'd just bring that baby back home for Christmas, I'd be feelin' better about the matter."

"So you want Eden to come home?"

"'Course I do. You think I don't care, but I do."

"You might say so to Eden. It would do her good to hear it, Momma."

"If I do, she just takes advantage, is all." She stared into the TV for a moment.

"Maybe Mr. Lunsford knows something, but I can't imagine him not calling."

"I'm just sick over it. Maybe I won't put up a tree this year. It depresses me to know I can't play Santy Claus to my own granddaughter."

"I'll put up the tree."

My father made the same speech every Christmas, playing a cruel game with my mother, pitting himself against her and riling her for his own amusement. He did it to combat her obsession with buying us more than she had as a girl and would make pronouncements that we shouldn't celebrate Christmas and especially not worry with the bother of a tree. And, he always added, didn't my mother remember the Christmas she set fire to an overly brittle evergreen in a banana barrel and caught the grass on fire? It always made me remember how the fire chief had cursed at her for interrupting the bowl game.

When we finally did manage to haul Daddy out into the woods—he never paid serious green for one—Daddy would yield to Momma's pressure to chop down a nine footer that would never fit under our ceiling at home. Once home, she continued sending those silent little codes to my father that she didn't need him to do it. That was why she always ran around to the car trunk ahead of him, heaved it onto her back, and dragged it, limbs away, through the kitchen, her face solid crimson and eyes glinting in that gritty way that so distinguished her from other mothers. Of course, Daddy reversed all of her efforts, dragged the tree back out into the yard again since three feet of tree curled over against the ceiling.

First he had to shave away the trunk's thick, spiky undergrowth or else place the gifts in the center of the living room floor, which he would have done if we had not spouted dissent. Then there was the inevitable amputation of the tree's thorny top that always lent great importance to the care of an old treetop angel I had fashioned in ninth grade. After we had draped the poor topless tree with yards of those little silver cellophane icicles, paper chains, and blown-glass ornaments etched by the prior year's impatient New Year's Day packing up session, it looked more like vandalized landscaping. But it was all my mother's obsession that drove every bit of it—the two of us scouring the stores for icicles when all the rest of the world had moved on to garlands—and working endless hours screwing and unscrewing those old Christmas lights.

A more commercialized Christmas had made evergreens more available in the valley, with tree vendors peppering the highways, as well as a modern phenomenon called aluminum trees. People who bought the metallic freaks did tout the superiority of them. Momma would have none of that, though. So when Daddy came from his fishing excursion—perhaps he fished, but he never brought home a single catch—I explained that we should take her tree hunting and possibly that would help keep her mind off Eden. We packed Momma into the car and off we sailed. But Daddy, in his zeal to dispense with the drudgery of our tedious rite, hustled us into a thickly treed area, perhaps fifty acres or more of protected park land, not a stone's throw from a newly developed jogging trail.

As children we had never questioned our father's use of "out in the country." To us it had the same meaning as "out in the ocean" or "up in the sky." Out in the country, to us, meant that we had crossed over some divide, entered unclaimed, unfettered countryside—open season for anyone with a shovel or an ax. It somehow registered all at once with me as we careened down a paved park road that perhaps all of those flowering dogwood and fruit trees that shaded our little piece of heaven might fall within the bounds of, say, ill-gotten goods.

"I believe this is a state park, Daddy."

Both of them gawked straight ahead. Momma studied the little side roads, the small outbuilding that looked to be some sort of water-treatment facility. "No one out here but us."

"Let's go to a roadside stand. We could get one for five dollars," I said.

"Pull over, Ho. I like that pretty little evergreen, that one standing in the shade of that big pine." Momma's intrigue spilled over into her tone.

"This can't be right, I mean, what with it being in a park and all. They don't allow tree chopping in here, I would imagine," I said.

"This is gov'ment property. We pay taxes," said Momma.

Daddy pulled onto the grass. Momma slid out of her seat, wielding the ax. She sallied toward the tree, dragging Daddy along. After she pressed the ax into his hands, she said, "You ought to be able to have 'er down in a couple of whacks, Ho."

"Naw, Donelle, that's a sturdy trunk. It'll take some work. Step away, give me some swangin' room." He steadied himself on the cane, leaned in a sort of sideways swagger, then made short, vertical tapping swings into the trunk to shave away the feathery, uneven lower greenery.

"The fine for what you're about to do is a lot more than just buying a tree." I grew rigid. "I'm going back to the car."

"Katrina, take your Daddy's keys and open the trunk."

"That would make me an accomplice."

"Don't dawdle around. It's idiotic to let a perfectly good tree go to waste. No one's goin' to miss this little cedar." She made it sound as though she would provide the unfortunate orphan a good home.

"It's too tall, and it's *stealing*." Daddy's keys were pressed into my palm. I opened the trunk, although it pained me to do so.

He forced the prickly shaft forward then rearward to weaken the trunk at the point of assault. In a weary stance, he managed another couple of good swings, but they weren't hard enough for Momma. She stood two feet from him, her back humped out in a C shape, and her shoulders drawn up to her neck. The fact that she kept shaking her head in disgusted disapproval shot vexation clear through Daddy.

"Someone's coming," I said. They ignored me. Two miles distant, a park ranger sped down a hill, giving him the appearance of driving straight down from the sky. He disappeared down into the furrow of the road that undulated up and down, causing him to appear and then vanish, but also slowed his pursuit of us.

"Get to the car, Donelle." Daddy turned too fast and out moved his cane. The ax slipped from his fingers, but he managed to sidestep it.

"I'm not leavin', not without this tree. I'll have it down in two shakes." Momma seized the ax herself.

Daddy turned the car around while Momma kept thwacking and spitting out her dictums about being the only person alive to know how to finish a job. She jumped from one side of the tree to the other and then rearranged herself all over again.

"Law, Donelle, that ranger's almost here. Leave it. Get in the car." He allowed the Pontiac to lurch forward, as if he might leave her.

Momma yanked on the thready, sappish splinters that clung to the severed trunk in the way a child's loose tooth clings to the gum. Then her labors yielded to her conquest over nature. "You stop that car, Ho!" She ran with it, little fragrant branches pumping like some plump grass-skirted dancer who hid behind the adults-only curtain at the county fair. Momma was hidden too by the tree—the despot of her kingdom of "I"—tyrant, heroine, Christmas-tree thief.

Through the small crevice between the open trunk and the car, I saw limbs twirling, the trunk lifted, heaved, and dropped next to the tire jack and the spare without any consideration to the cedar. But at this stage, it was not about dragging home a superior tree. It was two dogs in a boneyard: a young neophyte of a ranger in need of initiating a crisp fine book—and my mother. She still had the better head start.

A Maryland emergency operator answered the call. "This is the operator," she said in her crisp Baltimore brogue. "May I help you?" She verified the number that matched up with a telephone booth in Silver Springs on Colesville Road.

"It's just that, oh, this is awful! My husband's bleeding, up in the motel…I can't tell if he's breathin' or not! Lady, do you hear a word of this?"

"Be calm, miss. Try to start at the beginning. First, your name, please."

"This is Eden, Eden Hurley. We had this fight, but it was his fault, you see he's been testy since he quit the rodeo circuit. Anyways, I don't hardly know how to explain. But Carl's shot. Right through the chest." She stopped to gather herself. "I never seen so much blood. Oh, please, God, don't let him die!"

"Is Carl your husband?"

"Yes, we married up in Arkansas. How I wish I was still there."

"Carl Hurley is the victim?"

"No, Lunsford. Did I say Hurley?"

"You did."

"It's not Hurley. He's Carl Lunsford and I'm his wife, Eden."

"What is the address, ma'am?"

"Dreamy, don't you eat that snow; it's all dirty! The address—I don't live here. See, we never have settled. That's why I'm calling from this pay phone. See, this little prissy clerk he wanted ten dollars to connect the phone. But Carl he won't pay. We're at this hotel with the green paint. It's called"—a pause ensued while she leaned away from the phone—"the Nite Light. Is that enough? Can you find us? We're in room twenty-two."

"I'll send out an ambulance and a police unit."

"Police? Do we have to involve them? Carl will be upset with me over this, what with the potted-meat mess back in Tennessee and all."

"I'm sorry, miss, I don't follow. Hello? Are you there?"

Eden left the phone hanging by its cord and floated across the icy snowbank grated into a heap by the five-at-dawn bulldozer, holding to Dreamy's hand, stopping to right her when she slipped. She ignored the smiling old man in blue coveralls who thought they were sisters out playing in the snow.

"But he was right on our tail, Momma, right up until the time we left the park. He had to have gotten our license plate," I said.

"Lean it more to the rear, toward the wall," Momma said. "That tree trunk is warped." Daddy tossed aside his hat.

"It was straight up from the ground, arrow straight," said Momma, mitigating in her usual manner. "Must be one of those freaks of nature, the tree forcing itself straight up from a crooked place in the ground. It's all a matter of gettin' that stand right. Ho, did you cut the tree straight off at the bottom?" The blame passed swiftly between them.

"I did." His tone started low, then curved upward, trailing with a bite. Daddy made the stand, as always, from weathered lumber that remained from the old garage project—two two-by-fours cut into two-foot strips, crossed and nailed in the center. He moved like a beaver, not aiming for a perfect interpretation of what a tree stand should finish out like. Just wanting the job over.

"I'll bring out the ornament boxes from the attic before I start the cider." I left them to quibble. "But if I see flashing lights out in the drive, don't expect me to cover for you."

I heard Momma snigger. "We outfoxed that little gen'l'man."

The attic had always belonged to me since my earliest kindling of memories. The crawlspace enjoined my mother's closet, a narrow length of clutter, dresses with enormous buttons and tight-toed shoes that packed and sculpted the female foot into an agonizing S shape. All of it dated back to the fifties, including the dress she wore when she married Daddy. But I never saw her wear any of it. Nor would she be shed of any of it as long as she could rattle off remembrances that had attached themselves to each belonging. Most women preserved an album. Momma held on to her old dresses.

I once set up several hideaways as a girl, one inside the closet, where I kept an upside-down cardboard box with my miniature tea setting. The other was in the attic, but I found early on that I could not invite Eden. The nimbleness needed to pad across the rafters without alerting Momma was a skill she never acquired, whereas I leaped plank to plank, deft and catlike, and so silent that Momma roved in and out of the house in search of me, but never finding me until I so desired.

Someone, probably my father at some earlier point, had nailed planks to the wall in the farthest, darkest corner of the closet, forming a ladder up to our attic. One year I left behind an Easter basket up there, near the air vent. The small, round yellow basket was filled with dyed and decorated eggs in a nest of pink diaphanous cellophane straw—the same company, no doubt, that manufactured the icicles. I returned later, it must have been much later, months later. A rat had hollowed out the eggs' insides, leaving nothing behind but blackened, partial shells. Even the worst desire to escape the misery on the lower floor could not get me back up into the attic for the longest time. It still tainted the place for me somewhat.

I sat on the frame of the crawlspace with my feet dangling down into a medley of summer blouses pushed to the rear. The loft appeared much smaller and had lost much of its magic. A broken doll stroller was folded in two. I could not recall if I had left it that way, but the entire room was no doubt frozen in time, dusted by particles at least as old as myself. I took a mental snapshot, a practice adopted since my acceptance letter had arrived from the New York Studio School of Drawing, Painting, and Sculpture.

The phone rang down in the living room. An ancient mischief arose, my old eavesdropping practice. I crawled on all fours, lifting my knees above the cable television wire. I even remembered when cable TV had infested our little bowl of primitive stew, along with the new color set. Eden and I used it as our excuse for torturing Momma with the reruns of *The Wizard of Oz* and *Oklahoma*. We would both say, "But Momma, we haven't seen it *in color.*"

I stopped directly over where I thought Momma stood. I listened to her. All the days that I had known her, she answered the phone in the same manner, her tone rankled with impatience. But it was funny to me now. I heard her utter her doctor's name, Doc Lingle. A lot of silence ensued, plus the squeak of her backside meshing with her pet chair. She thanked him as she thanked the stranger who had exposed my father's yellow house escapade—a quiver in her voice, with much of the life drained from it.

"Ho, where is Katrina? I need to talk to you both."

By sound, I traced my father's footsteps through the living room on into my mother's bedroom. He called out to me, but I could not utter a sound and felt trapped again, much like I did when Momma once searched the house for me. He returned to her, coaxed the news out of her.

"Donelle, what's wrong?"

"That was Doc Lingle, you know, about my biopsy and all."

*No, I did not know.*

"That lump in my breast, it's malignant, and, he says, it's quite large. He wants me to come in tomorrow for—he wants to do a mastectomy."

I did not hear much else. The loft was such a quiet place that I sat there for a good while, trying to become one with the dust. It was cowardly, I knew, not to run back down the attic ladder and go cry with Momma. But she had never tolerated a mutual cry, so I had to try and muster the best words, knowing we would have to express our fear without touching. And cry without crying.

CHAPTER 20

*T*he air had a frigid bite to it, as though it teased us with the possibility of snow, but white flakes seldom materialized in the valley, just as tornadoes never picked their way over the mountain peaks. I have heard rumors of places like Florida where the weather is at all times utterly obliging. In our valley, we could not will the sky to snow. Nor could we will bad days to pass us by.

Saturday had always been Daddy's usual stay-at-home day, one in which he spent puttering around the kitchen until the football games forestalled all other life as we knew it. But on that particular Saturday, we hovered around Momma, asking her more than once if she had packed her toothbrush, dallying around her walnut vanity to consider each thing she wanted, as though it made us feel sentimental, and digging through her underwear drawer until she ran us out onto the porch. Momma cobbled together old and new items—old like her Fred's Department store brassieres, new items like the pink nightgown she sent Daddy and me out shopping for the night before, as well as more hand lotion—she only had six bottles to her name—and a new toothbrush.

Daddy maneuvered the car through the small rear parking lot of St. Mary's, but found it packed sardine-full on a day typical for hospital visitation, especially from local clergymen who took one last swoop through the corridors before buckling down to the finite details of their Sunday morning sermons. He made for the side road. But the congregation near St. John's Catholic Church had sponged up all of those places to attend an early mass. The sunrise spread a spectacular marmalade across the eastern horizon. I agreed with the Catholics that it was a glorious day to pray.

All at once a pale blue Beetle pulled out, sputtering at the tailpipe, and we slid into its spot without delay, before the other drivers circling the hospital complex scuttled for the lone parking space. Daddy could be aggressive that way.

"Not that it's crossed your way of thinkin', I just feel I should settle the records here. I won't hear of you missin' class for any of this, Katrina," Momma said. "Your Daddy and I, we feel proud of your efforts to teach school and all. Some school's goin' to get themselves a fine girl for a teacher. That's what. I'll not be needin' no help, not of any kind."

I had not shared the news of my change of studies or my plans for transfer. It had become a private matter.

"Donelle, let me get your suitcase... Now you stop bein' so uppity about that luggage, like nobody's goin' to carry anything for you or do for you. Them speeches of yours will wear thin by this time tomorrow when you're laid up in that bed." Daddy covered the handle of her suitcase with his hand. She had placed it between them, her way of fortifying her little citadel of seclusion.

"You all don' want to fiddle around with me."

"Why, of course we want to help. Katrina wants to help too and you just goin' to have to let people lend a hand. Let family do odds and ends for you."

"I won't miss any classes, Momma." I finally had some grades to speak of, so why waste all of that? "But I'm finished around the noon hour. I'll tell my boss I need time off at the bookstore. He'll understand."

"Not none of you knows a lick about how I keep my house. Ho, you couldn't find a mop, let alone know how to use it. That'd be a purty sight—Hobart Hurley swabbin' a floor." She let out a weak little laugh, almost frilly.

"We may not do it just so, like you, Maw, but we can make do till you git back on you feet." Daddy walked on ahead of her.

I seldom saw them in situations where they walked together as a couple.

While Daddy checked her in and took care of the paperwork, Momma and I watched a morning show on a waiting-room TV.

"Momma, what made you go to Doc Lingle's in the first place? Was it Meemaw's breast cancer that did it?"

"No. It was somethin' silly I did out in the garden. I was out plantin' a few pansies around my mums and left that hoe right next to me. I found some cutworms in the soil and was about to run and fetch some Sevin Dust. But I stepped on that hoe and it hit me right here." She pointed above her right breast. "Made a place on me the size of an orange. That bruise never would heal up. That's when I went to Doc Lingle."

"Bruises become cancer?"

"No. But they can give it away, I reckon." She stared at the television screen. "I should have been checkin' myself better."

Daddy waited near two swinging doors. "I reckon they're ready for us, Donelle."

Momma's surgery lasted three hours. Doc Lingle called it a radical mastectomy, taking out more than just her breast, removing places that left her insufferably sore around her rib cage and right arm. She said later he must have carved out her soul to boot. Her face withered, her eyes scarcely opening enough to receive the light, so they peered out mutedly, frosty coals in the snow. We once owned a parakeet that had gotten free from its cage. It nibbled on some houseplant in the kitchen window sill that eventually snuffed out its life. The pet lay in its cage for several hours, its tiny chest barely heaving, if any at all, and its small eyes nothing but lifeless beads. Momma looked a lot like that dying bird.

She suddenly loathed her new pink nightgown, saying she had not thought in advance about losing the use of her arm and would I fetch her old button-up pajamas, thinly soft and faded at both the arm and knee joints. I left Daddy reading a magazine, propped in a breath-mint-green, plastic-backed chair next to her hospital bed. "I'll bring burgers, too," I told him. Before I drove away in Daddy's car, I saw that Aunt Pippa circled the lot. She ferried three other passengers, most likely family members out to see to my mother. It was a good time to make my escape.

The house reeked of bleach. The night before, Mother swabbed every piece of porcelain and chrome, even purifying the ceramic tile and baseboards, to kill germs, she said. But the chlorine smell only added to the impression of stark emptiness, even more sterile than her hospital room. As I had watched her, stooped over the bathroom floor, it occurred to me that perhaps she blamed the house for her cancer. If she doused it with chlorine cleanser, perhaps it stacked the odds in her favor that it would not return.

The idea came to me that I should ask Beth if I might sleep over one night. She lived closer to St. Mary's. If I stayed with her, it might possibly remove me from the gaping spate of negativity that settled over every piece of household furniture, even the brown Naugahyde rocker/recliner with the Donelle-shaped slump in the seat cushion.

The telephone rang right in my grasp, even before I lifted it, unnerving me. "Hello?"

"Mrs. Hurley?"

"No, *Miss* Hurley. I'm the daughter." It did strike me as odd that any person would try to phone Momma at home, void of concern for her surgery. Even hospital admissions got announced over KOMV, the voice of Mockingbird Valley. Hadn't she tuned in?

"I'm Ms. Barnes. Yolanda Barnes." To hear such a brisk voice, rapidly moving over syllables and with such a forced authority, took my breath. She rattled off a string of credentials that were completely inexplicable to me.

"Is there anything I can do for you?" I asked.

"We have a situation here. I'm phoning from Silver Spring, Maryland. I'm a social worker here for child services. Eden Lunsford—your sister, I assume—has been taken into custody and, I believe, as of this morning is being questioned for the attempted murder of her husband, Mr. Carl Lunsford. She's phoned you?"

I had known my sister long enough to suppress undue panic. "Custody?"

"Hasn't she phoned, Miss Hurley?"

"No, but we've been away. I don't think I'm following you, Mrs...."

"Yolanda Barnes. Your sister has gotten herself in trouble. Her husband, Carl, is in critical condition in ICU at the local hospital. Gunshot wound to the chest."

"That can't be. Eden, she, you don't know this about her, ma'am, but she couldn't hurt anything, let alone kill someone, especially her husband. Why would she shoot Carl?" I remembered her broken arm, but I kept that to myself.

"I'm calling because there is a child involved. That is my only purpose."

"My niece, you mean?"

"Little Lolita has been placed in a foster home, awaiting our track down of family members. This phone number was all that was provided by the defendant, your sister." A dog barked in the background, and from the sound of it, something quite large, such as a German shepherd. It was followed by an infant's cry. I wondered if she worked from home or if it were one of those busy offices cluttered with stacks of unfiled reports, foster mothers returning what did not work out for them, and the abandoned pets of foster children.

"Dreamy will be scared beyond imagining, ma'am. I don't think she answers to Lolita. Please tell whoever has her, she goes by Dreamy. And she's not a Lunsford. Carl, he's not her daddy."

I heard a silence as though she were writing everything down that I said, so I backed off of spilling out Eden's life story. "Please, I need to know, how can we get her back home? Do I fly there? I'll—see, my mother is having surgery. I'll have to come myself."

"What is your age?"

"Nineteen."

"What about your father? Is the child's grandfather able to care for her?"

I thought of Daddy, seated next to my mother in the hospital room, his lips moving, but not a syllable to be discerned, although he seemed cognizant most of the time. "Yes, he'll sign anything you need him to sign." That was completely true.

"What is your nearest airport?"

"Little Rock. There's only one airport to speak of, except near Fort Smith."

"We'll have to do this all through a collaboration of our Maryland office of Child Protective Services and the one in Little Rock."

"We don't live in Little Rock. Just the airport is there, that's what I meant. I don't suppose you've heard of Mockingbird Valley?"

I stopped along the hospital route to buy Daddy his burger and fries and, additionally, a sack of goodies—Doritos, hard candy, tangerine-colored marshmallows shaped like peanuts. I hated those tasteless confections and could not fathom the staying power of them. And banana moon pies. Momma hated all of it, so watching him nibble would be less of a temptation while she endured her liquid fast. But I would suggest that we eat the burgers in the snack and vending area, away from her. Then I would tell him about Eden.

Out in the hallway and inside Momma's semiprivate room were visitors from the family like Aunts Nola and Lillibelle and their docile husbands. Nola and Lillibelle were Daddy's sisters. They nattered mostly to one another. Momma treated guests with ill regard. To her they were a bother and nuisance. Aunt Pippa stood next to her daughter, Roxanne, who herself had gone off to school, but was home for the weekend. She now wore thick eyeglasses, amber frames with lenses wide and concave, like tea saucers. Pippa had her arms wrapped around herself, comfortable and peaceful, a satisfied Persian cat. Roxanne looked more as though her mother, whom she adored, had dragged her into a hospital room on an obligatory visit to watch an aging woman she scarcely knew suffer. If anyone had said, "boo," she would have bolted, possibly sprinted, all the way back to school.

Velda sat in a corner chair, her hair dyed a sickly red and coiled in tight springs all over her scalp, with jagged bits of hair splaying outward as though they had not made it completely around the roller. "There's our girl, Katrina." She never quite lanced the *a* on the end of my name. I almost thought I saw little puffs of smoke spew out through her teeth, and her words sounded more slurred than usual.

"Donelle, here's your oldest girl come back with your things. Now you can stop frettin' about that old drafty hospital gown. I'll bet you're happy now. Ain't you, Donelle? You're a good girl, Katrina." I wanted to pitch something at her, smite her with a tranquilizer, anything to keep her from saying my name. She kept placing two fingers against her lips, a signal that she craved a cigarette. I believe she must have needed money. I could tell because she always disguised her bitter hatred of all of us when her coffers had pulled up empty. "What's the deal on little Eden? Gawd love that little child." When she said "God," it slithered from her lips, meaningless. "Anyone heard from our little girl?" She gaped, expectant, but no one wanted to gladden her with a sour report.

She spread a pencil-drawn smile between the all-but-exposed bones of her cheeks, while each cheek mushroomed upward, looming dangerously at her eyes. She practiced her most earnest gaze, trained it on my father while she sat gripping the arm of her minion and sister, Ruby, who always looked hurt. On an outing, if the wrong person called, "dibs, next to the driver!" and it wasn't her, or if she was not formally invited into the family car at funerals (which was like watching an entire fraternity stuff itself into a phone booth, anyway), or not enough compliments were lavished over her about her covered dish at a family gathering, Ruby sulked. Her morose stare was more definably drawn than Velda's, as though the plate had been passed over her head too many times as a child and handed instead to her baby sister.

Uncle Hank stood with Daddy just inside Momma's door. He kept saying nice things about Momma.

Momma's nearest sister, Evelyn, would reserve her visit for later, so that they could talk freely without so many glib opinions floating about the foot of the bed. For that sole reason, I would later earmark that moment as the finest part of the day.

I handed Daddy the bag from Burger Bob's. "Lettuce, tomato, pickle, onion. You wanted mustard, but only on one side, right?"

"Thanks, Sis. I believe I'll take this out to that table in that sody pop room. Donelle, you be needin' anything?" he asked.

She brushed off his concern, not certain of how to return it. Her wrists and hands, limp and turned inward like partially opened shells, moved slightly, as if to gesture him from the room. "Nothin' for me." I was the only one who detected her secret desire to see the room cleared of Hurleys. I squelched a handful of hard candies from Daddy's sack and dropped them onto her tray for the sake of not knowing what else to do. "Excuse us," I said.

Daddy lumbered side to side, his usual approach for getting from here to there, but at a markedly slower pace and with no hint of tough bull terrier. I tried to imagine him as a boy and wondered how long ago he had lost his zest for waking up in the morning, or if he had ever actually sampled the tang of it: sweet orange-citrus dreams, pain of lemon defeat, sweet cherry victory. (You must climb for that one.) I had tried most of the flavors already, except the dark persimmon death, but understand it arrives posthumously. Haven't you met people who have told you they actually tasted of death? And you believed them?

I sat and watched him eat and killed time while waiting for the room to clear of chatty nurses' aides. We had long grown accustomed, both of us, to sitting in the same room with extended lulls of silence.

I touched his hand. It caused him to flinch. I wondered if he would withdraw from me completely, once I said what I had come to say. Maybe this, on top of Momma's health problems, would send him over the edge, never to return, like the man in *One Flew over the Cuckoo's Nest*. "Daddy, we have to make a phone call, you and I, once we're home. Eden has herself in some trouble, and I don't know the whole of it."

"I'm not getting her out of her messes anymore. Let this be her wake-up call. They wreck their truck or some such?"

"Carl's in the hospital. He was shot, and he's in a coma."

"What's that you say?"

"They're blaming Eden, but we need to listen to her side."

He rubbed his fingers aside his face. I believe I saw a tremor go all through him.

"They put Dreamy in some foster-care home. We have to get her home."

"Eden's what will be the cause of me dyin', when I go. Always said she'd kill me."

Roxanne ducked around the corner, her voice low, nearly inaudible. "Katrina, a friend of yours just walked in to see your mom. He asked about you, too. Sol?"

"Tell him, will you, to stay right there. I'll be in shortly. Thanks, Roxanne."

Her whole face looked taut and solemn. I wondered if she had overheard. She disappeared.

"Daddy, we can't tell Momma just yet. She's got to get herself through all this other."

"I can't hide nothin' from her. Never been no good at that, Katrina."

"I'll do it, then. I'm going to tell her that I talked to Eden, and she agreed that Dreamy should come and be with us for Christmas. That will make sense to her, Daddy. She wanted Dreamy home for Christmas. This will give her a reason to get well. I'll have her out shopping shy of two weeks."

"I'll go along, then. What about school?"

"School?" Somewhere between the time I spoke to that social worker from Maryland and now, I had forgotten to breathe, let alone think of classes. Dreamy had always fit into our lives. It only seemed natural to bring her home where she belonged. "I'll keep going to school like always, Daddy." I knew better than to mention the New York school.

"Your mother can't be expected to chase after little Dreamy. Doctor's not even given us the results of her surgery. Won't know until tomorrow. Times like these, they's hard, Katrina. But you're still a young girl. Got years to finish school."

"I only have one week left until semester break, finals and all that. Mostly I'm worried about Dreamy and her circumstances. I hadn't thought much beyond."

"This is goin' to sound cold, Katrina, but this is Eden's doin'. Not mine nor yours." Daddy stared down at his feet. He made no effort to let me down easily or make tender his words. "Her child will have to stay in foster care. I got your Momma to contend with now."

"No, I'll take care of Dreamy. I'll tell them we can take her in one week."

"That's the kind of woman you'll always be too. Your sister never followed in your footsteps much. Times like these pass, and then you look back and see you done what was right."

He bit into his burger and thoughtfully chewed. It came to me then that he hadn't disappeared into himself or started talking to unseen people. He had been in complete control.

I knew that his gentle coercion had won out over me again. And I had succumbed without him ever having landed a single blow.

"Dear God! You got to help me. I drove too far over the cliff, done pushed myself too hard, and, well, I feel like I'm in hell in case you don't know."

"Shut up! We're trying to sleep. Stupid hillbilly."

Eden faced the bars of her cell, white fingers gripping the iron. Her frail and vertical frame was close to collapse, so weary was she. But her greatest fear was to lie down next to those jail girls who already had their names written on their pillows. She pressed her forehead against her hands, opened her eyes. Nothing changed.

*Prayer changes things.* Katrina said it often. Had she ever lied? A sliver of window allowed only a shimmer of moonlight to pass through, pale, milky light, cold and stark against concrete—sweet as cream upon her pillow in the valley.

She closed her eyes to go there, standing straight up and sleeping, dreaming about the cradles of grass dipping, tossing two sisters in the jonquils; tadpoles squirming between toes and the unconstrained squeals rising from the creek. Girlish laughter as they slipped into their beds enjoined by the sound of her sister singing in the next room… *Calling today, calling today.* "Hey, you, don't you walk away, you cop, you! I haven't had my phone call," Eden said. "I know my rights, you people hear me? Listen to me, now. I just need to—" *Katrina, why aren't you home? Somebody's playin' tricks with me, with my mind, like mind control. Somebody's always home in Mockingbird Valley. They's always someone at the house, waitin' for me.*

"I want my little girl." Her head dropped back, arms aching to cleave to a child again, to sleep curled next to Carl, spoons. She ached to pray without need. Her voice was a ragged, cogent echo. *"Can someone hear me? Listen to me when I talk! I want—I need to talk to my sister. Anybody?"*

CHAPTER 21

*M*omma twisted satiny paper ribbon around the package top, taped it at the midpoint, and left a weakened little corkscrew of trimming drooped over the edge. The effects of either the chemo or the surgery had caused her face to swell. Her skin looked taut, even shiny, and to some extent younger. To look at her, absorbed in wrapping boxes and reminiscing about our family gene pool, one would not have guessed that she was dying. She had picked the wrapping paper out herself, red foil with kittens pouncing on glass ornaments.

"Now, I can't figure how Eden started with such light hair like you, then it turned so dark on her. Your daddy, he says when he was a young un, he was tow-headed as snow. But look at him now, hair black as the ace of spades. But Eden, she put that hair dye on, and don't it look so unnatural? I wish she wouldn't do that."

"We sure did spend the money today, Momma," I said.

She smiled at me. "Your daddy, he is one to hoard. Thinks he's gon' to save enough to wake up a millionaire someday. I told him he'd best fork some of that over. I'm buyin' Christmas presents for everyone. Even if they ain't here. Next thing you know, I won't be two shakes dead in the grave and he'll be out huntin' for another woman."

"Don't talk like that, Momma."

"I want to say my mind, Katrina. You just wait and see if I'm not right. He's kept me and you kids livin' on nothin' so he could save up and buy hisself a trashy new woman."

"Hand me another box, Momma." Above the sofa she had suspended a poster of kittens enclosed in a flimsy gold plastic frame. It pulled apart at the edges if one so much as straightened the picture by a hairsbreadth. As much as she had always hated our cats and the way they lolled in her flower beds on sunny afternoons, her sudden obsession with kittens baffled me. "If you had told me you wanted to redecorate," I said, "we could have spent some real money. I'd have taken you to Caitlyn's Frame and Décor shop."

"I *like* that picture." She lit up and her eyes were round. Her face had the appearance of a surprised twelve-year-old. "See, they's a bit of gold in the sofa, and it matches the tufts of yellow fur on the tabby kitten."

"I catch on. And the kitten wrapping paper?"

"It matches the framed art."

"Art?"

"To me it is."

"Ah. Well, if we don't hurry, your grandchild is going to climb out of the bed and ruin everything."

"She's still got her days and nights mixed up; she'll sleep another good hour. Law, her momma kept the awfulest hours. Her little belly's not right, neither."

Dreamy had had bouts of upset stomach every night for the week she had been home. The foster mother said that when she picked her up, it appeared she had been living on cow's milk in a baby bottle. She gave it to me along with some other personals. All of it looked dowdy and soiled. We tossed it all. Dreamy waved bye-bye to her beloved ba-ba.

I had gone after her myself. The social worker and the foster mom met me at Dulles Airport in the District of Columbia. Dreamy had formed an attachment to the woman, had clung to her for a few agonizing moments until realization struck. Then she bounded into my arms shouting, "Aunt Kateen! Aunt Kateen!"

I took her to see her mother, but Eden looked so haggard and weary, forced into a pathetic orange prison garb two sizes too big. Her pitiful ramblings made us both cry. Especially when I told her about Momma's cancer. Eden asked about Momma's surgery and understood why we could not tell her the truth. She seemed like she was grasping, desperate to tell me that she would never shoot anyone, especially Carl. I tried to ask her if he had hurt her again, but too many ears tuned in. When we left, I told Dreamy to kiss her momma and tell her bye-bye. She said, "I go, Aunt Kateen."

The necessity to catch the afternoon flight prevented a visit to Carl's bedside. But he never knew that we passed unannounced through Maryland, just like he never knew that Mr. Lunsford had flown all the way from Arkansas, looked into the hospital bed, and thought he saw Darrell all over again. He did not return a second time, to my knowledge.

"I can't ever do those ribbons like you, Katrina. How about I wrap, and you tie on the bow ribbons?"

"Hand me that box, then. What's inside?"

"You just never you mind, Nosy Nell."

"You wrapped my present right under my nose?"

"It's for me to know, and you to have to wait until Christmas." She panned the room as though she saw it for the first time, scrutinizing objects such as the brown chair. She ran her fingers across the braided rug that we had spent endless hours sewing together with needles and thread. "Did I hear you on the phone late last night?" she asked.

"You were supposed to be asleep."

"I don't hardly sleep anymore. This bandaged place is givin' me fits all the time. Has Doc Lingle said anything to you about it?"

"Just that you have to keep a clean dressing on it."

"Not anything else? He's not said if the cancer might come back?" I felt her gaze as she polarized me, ready to leap on any nuance in my tone or waver of my voice—anything that suggested that I said the opposite of what I knew to be true.

"Now, you don't sound like you're at all trying to catch the Christmas spirit." I fluffed the ribbon until I sensed that she had looked away.

"Who were you talkin' to?"

We concealed the truth about her diagnosis, although her pressing questions made me feel as guilty as the compunction over hiding Eden's murder charge. There was still the hope that Carl would live, that the charges would be dropped, anyway. I had taken the matter to the floor every night on my face, as I begged God for a shred of pity on Eden's behalf. "Can I talk with my sister if I want? I thought if I waited until later, we wouldn't disturb you."

"You talk to her more now, Katrina. Like the two of you are gettin' along. That's nice. I believe the violets need water."

I recalled how Eden had wept over the phone even more than the day I saw her in the Maryland jail. She faced a second charge, one really aimed at Carl, according to her, but her babbling about false charges, armed robbers, and potted meat destroyed the translation. The attorney assigned to her pro bono had given her a fifty-fifty chance for acquittal. She would wait in the Maryland jail without bail until March.

"It's about time Eden started appreciatin' family. Reckon she's recognizin' we all need each other?"

"I'll bet that's true," I said.

"It's true of me, I'll grant you."

"You got another box ready? Oh, cute. More kitten paper. You should be running out of that fairly soon."

"I need my family"—her voice broke—"all around me, I'll grant you that. Eden knows I'm sick, and this is how she treats me."

I folded the red ribbon in two, sliced it with the scissors, creating a double-pointed edge. It curled nicely.

"Sing to me, Katrina."

"I will."

"Somethin' festive."

" 'Joy to the World'?"

"That's a good un."

Sol came over more regularly, a bona fide gift-toting beau if ever I saw one. If we walked a lunch to the park, he carted Dreamy along, hefting her under one arm—his little Kewpie, he called her. He wasn't trying to climb onto my nerves, but I embraced the happy family persona less avidly than he, I suppose. The ache of being formerly separated from Dreamy swapped itself out with a battery of not-so-passionate feelings: fatigue, anxiety, the notion that my escape to New York had slipped down some trough, extinct.

Dreamy adopted Baby Peggy and nuzzled a bald spot right on the front of her doll scalp where stiff, dirty bangs once saluted. Poor tormented Peggy still had blue ink squiggled beneath one poked-out eye, little false lashes drawn on by Eden. I had saved all of my baby dolls, lined them up years ago around the left inside corner of my closet. I considered giving them to Dreamy. But as she sat on the picnic table, poking her finger into the doll's one good eye, I thought better of it.

"Your mother looked well today. Is she in remission?" he asked.

"Not remission, no. She's feeling better today. Her treatment a couple of days ago made her nauseous. I think she's relieved to be up and about. You want cheese and mayo on your ham sandwich?"

He lifted the plastic knife from my hand. "Don't be so domestic."

"I'll pour the drinks, then."

"I saw your professor, Dr. Kaleidoscope, or whatever is his name."

"Calypso."

"He said to tell you that the art school called. They found you a roommate."

I sighed. Dr. Calyps could not understand why I had to stick around to try and mend fences for my sister. But my staying had more far-reaching aspects—things bigger than fences. The wall of her entire life lay in ashes.

"Have you ever noticed he can't sibilate his *s*'s without whistling?"

"Men notice, but it doesn't bother any of us girls. He's such a brilliant teacher, we don't notice. He's too eccentric to grate on your nerves."

"Two perfect ham sandwiches. One half-sandwich for the kid."

"Paper plates, chips at twelve o'clock."

"Let us pray," he said. He cleared his throat and prayed, dramatizing what he thought to be an astute manner so as not to sound overly spiritual. I chalked it up to a guy thing. "Dear Lord, we thank thee for thy bounty…"

Dreamy and I slipped potato chips to one another underneath the table and giggled.

"…and for the gift of this most splendid day, the sunshine, the little birds"—he overheard the munching—"and bless that which is within us. Amen."

"Christ's name, amen."

"Amee," said Dreamy.

We finished our meal, rapt as we were by banners of sunlight across the cloudless blue. Dreamy allowed Sol to push her in the wooden swing. I lifted the seat before she climbed on and found the initials KH carved into it. Although my memory couldn't summon one detail about carving initials into that swing seat, some part of me must have drummed it up from the past. "Wonder how old I was when I did this?"

We took Dreamy to the old pedestrian bridge, but I would not allow her to climb down into the creek. "It's too dirty," I said, feeling like a hypocrite. Momma used to say the same thing to Eden and me five minutes before we disappeared beneath the creek bridge with our shoes sliding down the bank behind us.

"This creek runs all the way over to the other side of town," Sol said. "We skipped stones down off the banks all the time, almost every day. And once this mammoth tortoise came out of nowhere, as though he took a wrong turn in Ecuador. We could have ridden him."

"I wonder how they got here. I remember seeing them at least twice." I empathized with the beasts, seeing the way kids gathered on the bridge to stare at the oddities. Their helmet-shaped heads rose out of the morning mist and blinked at us like shrewd old men.

"Some of the meaner boys threw rocks at it. Killed it. They couldn't control it, I suppose, you know, like make it stay."

I had never known Sol to be so affected. He affected me, too.

"It was such a male domain. None of the girls would go down there, so we made a fort."

I mused over telling him about the girls who ruled this side of Galla Creek, who waded into mud up past their anklebones just to capture the most choice crawdads but left the turtles to their own devices. I refrained. Perhaps he had things that he kept from me too.

❦

While Sol said his good-nights to me at the door, Momma walked Dreamy to her bed. After I watched from the window as the Toyota pulled away, I crept down the hallway. Dreamy's high voice lifted above Momma's low one.

"Say night-night prayers, Granny," she said.

"Well, all right, then. How does Aunt Kateen do it?"

"Sits on her knees and talks to Jesus."

Momma crouched next to the bed where Eden once slept. "Dear Jesus…," she stammered, "bless Dreamy as she sleeps. Take care of her momma and that man she's with—Carl."

"Pray for Aunt Kateen," Dreamy said.

"And Aunt Kateen."

"And for Granny's boo-boo."

"My what?"

Dreamy pointed to the bandaged place hidden by Momma's blouse.

She bowed her head, and said, "You just take care of me as you see fit, now, Jesus, your lordship. I'm at peace and—" her voice broke.

"Don't cry, Granny." Dreamy stroked her hair while Momma sat with her face pressed against Eden's chenille bedspread.

"Oh, Momma…" I came in and knelt beside her. But Momma was still praying.

"If you just get that youngest of mine took care of, God, well then," she sniffed, "I can manage everthang else."

She sat quietly, finishing her prayer in silence, then padded back down the hall to her room.

Daddy loved attending auctions, loved watching the volley between auctioneer and bidder. Our county's auctions had none of the glitz of Sotheby's or Christie's and were nothing more than oversize flea markets wherein could be found a good herd of pigs in the morning or a complete boxed set of melamine dishes by night. When we were girls he seldom bought anything at auction, even stopped taking us, beleaguered by all of our nudging and arm wrenching.

But on Friday nights he tromped onto the porch bearing the oddest of baby dolls. Still in their boxes, they looked old, although not antique old. The flesh tones had dulled. Time had frozen their locks flat against them. I imagined them to be little dust collectors pushed to the rear of some general merchant's stockroom.

Momma fawned over the dolls, slid them immediately from their boxes, and set them up against the wall atop a three-legged table that he had also acquired at an auction. "Look at all my purty babies," she said. She mused over them. Laughed at them.

He spoke differently to her now, not so abrupt. "You like those, don't you, Donelle?" Moreover, he looked at her, which sounds run of the mill. But in that arena, he was not well practiced. She had taken on such a perfunctory idleness, though. She did not notice how he lingered over her. The determination to nurture her flower mania or her obsession to fill every inch of yard with daffodil bulbs was utterly gone. The longer she remained on painkillers, the more of herself she mislaid. Little bits of Donelle lay stuffed into cracks and crevices that were unreachable by anyone or by us.

Aunt Pippa noticed the crumbling away of my mother too. She dropped by that afternoon. When she addressed her, even she reverted to an almost rudimentary patois. She changed her tone, lilting over her name when she said it, and making over Momma in the same manner that she spilled accolades over Dreamy for no apparent reason.

"Now look at all those lovely children." Pippa picked up each doll and held it up for Momma to see. "Each one perfect and new."

I couldn't as readily allow that part of her to slip away in so natural a manner as Pippa. I snapped at Momma, in my own way trying to bring her back. But she only blinked, staring at me absently, a rabbit startled by a passing car. She had already purposed to float away from me. I felt at fault for not allowing her to follow her next appointed course.

We lived in that manner through Christmas and New Year's and watched her gravitate from cognizant moments to more childish prattling where she complained incessantly about the food or how she observed strange people barging into her room. People that weren't there, but nonetheless we had to satisfy her phobia. Daddy and I crawled around the floor and looked through her things in the closet as we shouted, "No one in here." Sometimes she fell into shrieking, and Daddy would stand over her, reassuring her that no one had come to take her away. She always looked at him suspiciously. Later she confessed to me her fear that he was a co-conspirator in the plot to steal her from us. Her doctor told me painkillers would cause hallucinations, but her people were not like Daddy's—a little argumentative and under his command. At times, she would shriek as though chased by the devil himself. Her frights brought Daddy back to us, as if he had to compensate for her mental distance, at least for a little while.

She also wanted to assure me that she had not had me out of wedlock and that if Aunt Velda or any person said anything to the contrary, they were to be ignored and taken for the liars we all knew them to be. So much of her day was spent obsessing over my legitimacy that I tried to dig out her old marriage license to clip it to my birth certificate as proof to those evil detractors. I couldn't find the license.

Several ladies from around the valley visited on a periodic basis, bringing us hot-dish casseroles, baked pies, cookies, and fresh-squeezed lemonade. One neighbor lived two doors down. She had lost her husband years ago to cancer. Her name was Amee Baldwin, a

thin woman with a full shock of hair, dyed yellow. Her habit of dropping off a vegetarian dish sent Momma off her course, rattling angry
accusations and swearing Daddy had put her up to it. And when
Amee spent too much time advising Daddy on how to feed Momma
one day, that sent my mother spiraling into her paranoia stew. After
Amee left, she shot up from her bed on the sofa.

"Throw out that dish, Katrina. That woman's out to pison me."
When she said "poison," it rhymed with "bison."

"Mrs. Baldwin's a thoughtful woman," I said. "Some people
don't think it's good to eat so much meat. It's her way of feeling useful to pass along her advice."

"Why a-course I'll eat meat, drink good healthy milk. Who does
she think she is, tellin' your daddy to put me on some *carrot* diet? She
wants him to starve me, and don't think I don't know why."

I knew from her tone what she meant. Daddy stood in the
kitchen, shaking his head.

"And did you see how she wore that bright red checkered dress
with her waist cinched?"

"Was it red? Hold it, I thought she wore slacks."

"Stood right in the middle of that floor and twirled for your
Daddy. Twirled and twirled. I thought I'd be sick to death of her
before she left."

"I missed the twirling," I said. "What was the twirling all about?"

"Why, kicking up her legs in front of your Daddy, that's what."

"So you saw Mrs. Baldwin twirling? Where was I?"

"In Missouri, like you've always been."

"And where was Daddy?"

"When?"

"During the twirling."

"Why, watchin' a-course. Why wouldn't he? He's a man, ain't he?"

The house became a collection bin for the most unnecessary

items but all of it clearly categorized: the numerous stacks of yellow tabloids—the *Sun,* the *Inquirer,* the *Observer*—none of them touching, as though one stack might be infected by the other; the collection of bargain auction dolls that peeped out at me, sort of sneering at me, jealous stepchildren; the collection of African violets. (The leaves had turned brown and lay curled over the pot edges in a lament, but it was only fitting that they follow in the steps of their mistress.) The book stacks became insurmountable: the small mass markets; every Agatha Christie in print; copies of romance novels she already owned, but because a friend had sacrificed ten cents apiece for them at a rummage sale, she wouldn't allow their removal; and the *TV Guide*s from months past. Momma acted as though their keeping was tantamount to our existence. Daddy brought her a collection of small knickknacks: little white plaster clowns wearing ruffled collars, all spotted with pink and blue polka dots—holding puppies, some of them, or kittens or balloons. They stood to themselves in a huddle atop the television in no particular arrangement, miniature heads tilted with pointed French hats and worth every bit of the buck and ten that was paid for the whole lot of them.

Little sentries had collected like that all over our house, all of them under her surly guardianship as though they each possessed some hidden celestial to keep guard but had shrouded themselves while they passed the time. And like gargoyles, they waited for some word from above so that, in unanimity, they could break open at once and carry her from the harrying nuisance of pain. From time to time, she gazed askance, turned her head as though she heard the flurry of their wings.

Chapter 22

*I* stayed in as close contact with Eden as the Maryland courts allowed. And Mr. Lunsford called more often than usual, telling us if the night nurse relayed to him that Carl's right big toe twitched, or if he mumbled in the night. I think he was as worried for Carl as I was for Eden.

Sol and I saw one another almost every day now, especially during Dreamy's nap, when he would drag me out of the house, but not against my will. Behind the new leafy foliage of the grape arbor, he held me until I lifted my face to him and then he took it from there. However long he had taken to come around to my way of thinking, he furrowed all new ground now, confessing little things like how relieved he was to look up that Saturday night in the bleachers at Sumner Stadium and find me sitting next to Beth. Or how it grieved him to see me give up my place at the New York art school. But also how selfishly glad it made him.

Dreamy had so encompassed every available moment of the day, I had not touched my easel in heaven only knows how long. Sol tempted me to return to my art by having me sketch his profile. It was a piece I could have done in my sleep as often as I had summoned his very fine image in my mind—firm jawbone with a whisper of a cleft, high cheeks that cradled blue eyes, lashes an adolescent girl would covet, and dark hair possessing a healthy sheen.

He and Dr. Calyps both conspired to see me back at Sumner's studio, stroking my visions onto a canvas. The two of them carted all of my materials back down to the studio from where I had stored them in Daddy's garage. Sol positioned my easel near the glass virgins and stowed all of my paints and brushes inside a drawer clearly marked with masking tape and marker. It read "Katrina's Wings." (It originally said "Katrina's Things," but Sol had marked over it.) One day, Dreamy found an errant tube at home and licked at the acrylic paint, calling it "ise keem." The carpet in that house is forever stained with a Kermit green, kidney-shaped splotch.

When Momma saw Sol's pencil portrait, she said, "Katrina, you ain't never done one of me. All I do is lay here. Do me one up, won't you?" Momma had not lost her hair and that pleased her to no end. But she rejected my idea when I suggested that we hire a hairdresser to come to the house to give her a nice wash, rinse, and curl before I finished the portrait. She believed that toying with her hair might weaken the roots. She had some peculiar idea about having her own hair for the Second Coming.

She talked about Jesus a lot. We had the best talks between us, her tucked beneath her sheets and me on an old chair near the window so that I could have more light. After lunch, I crawled up into her bed, as I once did when we shared a room. Girl talk became her favorite time of day. Her favorite diversion was telling on Daddy. Some of it shocked me until her doctor confided that most of it sprang out of her drug-induced dementia.

"And don't think you're kiddin' your old maw," she said one

night. "You and your daddy think you both wise, keepin' thangs from me, but I know."

I could think of a half-dozen things we were keeping from her. "Such as?" I penciled crisscrosses across the portrait to create a fine shade beneath her cheekbone, but nothing as dark as the circles beneath her eyes.

"Doc Lingle, he told me the truth about my cancer. You think I want to wake up dead and not know what hit me? I don't."

"We hoped it would help you fight it."

"Let me be the judge of how I fight things. The Lord, he knows when he wants to call me home. The two of you can't stand in his way."

"I thought I heard you praying last night, crying. Or was that a dream?"

"You didn't dream it. I ain't been the best of his flock, I reckon he knows that. But I've caught on to this surrender business. It wasn't so hard, like I thought."

"How do you feel about…"

"Dyin'? Peaceful, like all the dust can settle now." She smiled. "Dust. We all go back to that, don't we?"

"Anything else?"

"That baby done tolt me somethin' about her momma bein' locked up in jail. Now you goin' to tell me the rest, or do I rely on a child to tell me the truth?"

I could no longer postulate about the matter. "Carl was shot. He's in a coma, Momma. Eden must have spilled out too much over the phone when she called for the ambulance. They believe they have a recorded confession of her admitting to the crime."

"What?" There was a pause. "That girl has less sense than pea gravel, but I grant you she couldn't pull no trigger on no gun."

"Her trial is coming up. Two weeks. She's taken a sick headache."

"I know'd about the headache for some reason. Must have heard you whisperin' while I was laid up in here. But Eden's still my girl. How do I pray for her, less'n you give up a few of those details?"

"I'm glad you're praying, Momma."

"Why wouldn't I pray? I always talked to God. He just seems—closer now."

"What else, Momma?"

"I want you to go off to New York City, if that's what you want."

"You know?"

"I do."

"Does Daddy know?"

"No, and don't you tell him. Call him from someplace big, like the Statue of Liberty. Why he'll think you're up to somethin' so grandiose. Somethin' he can brag to the boys about down at the spit and whittle."

"How did you find out?"

"I found that letter one day when I was puttin' away some of your socks. Didn't have it too well hidden, did ya?"

"Doesn't matter, anyway. I can't leave. Maybe I'm not supposed to leave."

"Go and fetch that book, the one on the end." She tried to roll to one side, but finding it caused discomfort to her surgery wounds, she sunk back down and pressed her head into the pillow. "No, that's Agatha Christie. Fetch me the big thick one."

I pulled the clothbound book from her small bookcase. It was lodged between *Grimm's Fairy Tales* and *Betty Crocker*.

"I used to pore over this book," I said. "You ordered it from the Book-of-the-Month Club. I always thought it strange that you would order a book about illustrating."

"Open it. Or turn it upside down. Shake it."

Two papers fell out of it onto the floor. "My drawings. What was I, six?"

"About six. You didn't tear them all up before I managed to rescue a few."

"I thought you didn't care."

"When I was a girl, I had to walk to school out at Sunny Point. Back in those days all us kids had to sit under the same old schoolteacher, from the youngest all the way up through high school. His name was Herschel Caldwell. It wasn't no real education. Man was a pill, he was. He took the job because it beat the coal mines. Acted like he hated kids. I guess that's why I quit so early. What was the bother of it, I figured. But I had this special knack. When I finished up my arithmetic, I'd take the chalk and draw on my little board. I loved to draw, Katrina, just like you."

"You never told me that."

"One day, old Caldwell walked up behind me, saw my little pitcher, a nothin' sort of pitcher. Really and truly. But I liked it. He grabbed that measurin' stick of his, the one he used to whack the boys when they sassed him. In a blink, he grabbed my drawin' hand and beat it, called me evil. Said I was possessed of the devil." She shook her head. "It was him who was possessed. I keep apologizin' to God for bein' mad at religion all those years." A tear traveled across her cheek. "Herschel Caldwell, though, he wasn't the only one who made me afraid of God. My little hand, it was swollen by the time I got home." She stretched out her fingers and studied them as though the welts had raised themselves up again. "Poor old Momma, she wanted to do somethin' about it, but poor people—who listens? Those were days of sheer agnorance. Then Momma got religion down at a tent meetin'. Said she got the joy of the Lord. But I said she just got meaner. I had to ask forgiveness for that, too."

I curled my fingers between hers. I saw no need to interrupt.

"'Course your daddy, he had to quit college, so he never got his education neither. Went off to war, but not cause he wanted to fight the Koreans. His family, they needed that check to pay off the farm."

"When did Daddy go to college?" That surprised me.

"One semester, right after he graduated Mockingbird Valley High."

"What did he want to do?"

"Teach school."

Daddy took a hoe to every living thing, salvaging only the fruit trees and the grape arbor. I heard him talking to Momma about it one morning. They didn't know I heard them. Daddy said, "You're goin' to have to stop frettin' over your roses and thangs. I can't take care of them and you, too."

A frost warning was issued the evening before by the weather service. Momma took up the saddest lament. "It'll kill the tulips, Ho! Run out with blankets and cover the tulip beds. Drape sheets over the rose beds, too, or they'll all die." The strain of running outside in his sock feet to shelter the spring bloomers proved to be too much. And when he took a pair of shears to her roses to try and please her, she cried again. Whenever she stared through the window, it was agony to see her flowers tormented by two gardening neophytes. And when I tried my hand at it, Daddy waved his hands through the glass at me like I was a fool. I left the pruning shears on the kitchen table. "It's beyond me what you want," I said.

When Daddy tried to mow the lawn and yet avoid the Bermuda grass that had shot up around the borderless daffodils she had planted all through the lawn—refugees from her old toss-and-dig method—he said, "Your flowerin' days is over, Donelle. I can't do it anymore."

I picked the prettiest ones and made her a bouquet, although I held out hope he would change his mind. She lay with the sheets pulled up to her chin, staring at the vase of mixed flowers. "I was tired of the yard, anyway," she said.

I coaxed Daddy away from the far daffodil and iris borders that flanked Erie. In that way, I retained a grain of forgiveness for his onslaught against Momma's flowers. Besides, behind the thick rows of opaque greenery existed the best make-out spot. So my wishes far exceeded sentiment. Though I do believe that when Momma's crocuses lifted stout rows of yellow and purple hoods, they nodded in little waves of appreciation.

"It's too bad about your mother's flowers," Sol said.

"I'm taking it harder than she is."

"Could we—would you mind going out to the car?"

"I don't mind. I have to make that list for Easter dinner. You can help."

"I need to ask you something too."

I followed him around the house and down to the driveway. We sat in his car making Easter plans.

"I've never actually cooked an Easter ham," I said.

"My mother says she'll cook for all of you."

"Momma's too weak to move. Besides, she's never comfortable in someone else's home. I can do this, Sol. You have no faith."

"You just don't strike me as the little homemaker."

"Mashed potatoes, corn. We'll use brown-and-serve bread. Keep it simple."

"We should decorate eggs for Dreamy," he said.

"That I can do. Egg fashion extraordinaire." I scribbled all of it down on notebook paper.

"I'll bring my two youngest bratty brothers. Instant egg hunt. Then we'll have to go back to my mother's for the evening meal."

"We can do that. Get Dreamy out of Momma's hair for a while."

"I'm having déjà vu. You were going to ask me something, weren't you?"

Dreamy bolted from the house. "Aunt Kateen, come in! Papaw says!"

"What's wrong, Dreamy? Is Granny all right?"

"Momma, she's comin' home!"

"Katrina, can you believe it? I been falsely arrested, how do you like it? My lawyer, Bill, he says we could slap all kinds of lawsuits on Maryland." She breathed into the receiver. "But I told him that for now I just want to come home."

"You need to back up," I said. "What happened first?"

"Carl, he woke up. Just opened his eyes and asked for me. It surprised them real good when he told them how he was cleanin' his gun and it discharged on him. They questioned him overly too much, like they thought he was coverin' up for me, which would be kind of romantic in and of itself. But it just wasn't true. He's a different man, Katrina. But the best part of it is all the diggin' up done by Bill—we've become real good friends through all of this ordeal. I've reminded Carl several times he best keep his eye out for me and be sorrowful for all he's put me through. Else I could plant my attentions elsewhere."

"Bill was digging up—what?"

"Dirt. I mean, attorney dirt. He found out some shoddy police work let the real robbers get away. They fancied theyselves some high-time criminals. But the law surprised them this mornin' with a search warrant and some new bracelets—I don't understand Bill's point about the bracelets. But they found the loot and the little pistol that did their dirty work. We're free as little lovebirds, Carl and me. The State of Maryland, they done give us our airplane tickets, first class, and said we'd best get on our way. What a hoot! My first flight and first class all the way! They're puttin' us up in a hotel right in downtown D.C., right down the street from the president hisself. We're comin' home tomorrow mornin', Katrina! Dear Lord, here I am rattlin'! How is my baby?"

I put Dreamy on the phone.

Momma sat in her chair. She wiped her eyes. Daddy stared through the window behind the TV. Nothing had lifted off of him yet. He still looked caved in.

Sol held me and whispered things to me about New York. But he must have sensed the melancholy. We tuned our thoughts to other things instead. "I'll need to buy double the food for Sunday. Where's my list?" I ran out to the car and found that in the midst of our rush I had dropped the shopping list onto the floor. The pen was gone, but Sol always kept extras in the glove box. I scrounged through a few automobile documents. My hand fell on one small box. I took it inside. "Sol, what is this?"

He stared at me for the longest time, as though I had slapped him. Then he took the ring box from my hand and slipped it into the pocket of his Windbreaker. "Just a joke. It's an empty box. You ruined the joke, Katrina. Forget it."

"You bought me a ring."

"No ring. Vain imaginings on your part." He glanced at Daddy.

"Can I have the empty box?"

"It's my mother's box, the one she keeps her rings in."

"That's what you were going to ask me, when you said you wanted to ask me something, isn't it?"

"You're wrong."

"Where were you going to take me?"

He still had not looked at me. Finally he said, "Under the big oak out in the park."

"I'd rather it be at night on the sand bar."

"It's all a moot issue now."

"It has to be tonight. On the sand bar."

He kissed me. Smack dab in front of Daddy. Sol, the only boy I ever knew who possessed a fearless ilk in the presence of Hobart Hurley.


We found a quiet place on the sand, seated ourselves on a fallen tree washed smooth by the water and years. "It can't work, Katrina."

"You brought me all the way out here to tell me that? Why didn't you just tell me later over the phone? That way I wouldn't have to see your eyes. I can't take your eyes tonight, for some reason."

"I want you to go to New York. Take the summer session. What did you say about it—somethin' about going for seven weeks? See if you like it."

"And if I like it?"

"Then…then you stay, Katrina."

I never wanted any man to have this effect on me.

"I'm making you cry. I've never hated anyone as much as I hate me right at this instant."

"I'm just a little confused with myself, is all."

"You'll see one day that I'm right. I could never live with you as my wife, knowing that you lived with me full of regret."

"Sol's wife." I breathed it out through my tears. "I do like the sound of it."

"No. Katrina Hurley," he said, spreading his hands before him as if seeing it in lights, "she paints more than Easter eggs. Watch her fly."

"But that's just it, Sol. This valley never stopped me from doing what I'm supposed to do. I used it for an excuse, don't you see?"

"And now you're using me for an excuse. I want to be more than just an excuse to you."

"You are, Sol. Oh, you are so much more than an idle excuse." We sat near the water, hearing the clap it made against the wood and debris washed ashore. And as the lapping water weakened the splintered piles of drenched wood and carried them with nothing on their backs but the pale kiss of moonlight, I knew he ebbed from me. I grasped for the most perfect words so that I could tie them together and make a raft of optimism for our cause. But what came to mind was so frail, I felt I deserved nothing short of hanging for saying it. "You are my breath," I finally said.

"I can't keep you here, Katrina. I'll not be the one to extinguish your fire."

Momma would not linger for me, no matter how great my promises of grandchildren. Nothing could hold her back. I sat at her hospital bedside and arranged a vase of May flowers—old greenhouse imitations, she called them, because they paled in comparison to her yard bloomers. I took the ten o'clock watch and sent Eden home to bed.

"Sit close, so I can see your face."

I did as she asked, then I sang to her and stippled kisses all around her forehead and onto her cheek.

"Your daddy, now don't let him fool you. He's socked away a good little bit of money. Why else you think that aunt of yours is always sniffin' around? You girls take care of it now, you hear? But use a little of it for things he'd never let you use it for. See some place exotic, like those places in your magazines."

"Daddy won't be going anywhere soon, Momma."

"Don't ever settle, Katrina, like I've settled," she told me.

"You know I won't. But if I were to find someone, like Sol, well, to me, it wouldn't be like settling."

"No? His daddy expects him to stay and keep up the brokerage, don't he?"

"He does. Sol's good with math and other things that I can't fathom."

"What if you got him? How would that be, do you think?"

"Kind of like, if I reached up to pluck one of those stars. See them up there, kind of like they're stuck in the branches of that tree? Then I looked down all at once and found one sizzling right in my own hand—it would be like that."

"I'd reach if I was you, girl. Don't reckon your daddy ever thought that much of me. Has he ever said?"

I remember the way that Daddy looked at her after her cancer diagnosis, a kind of ache in his eyes. And on this night, he hovered near her, brought the flowers and placed them in a just-so fashion near her bed. "Yes, he's told me often."

"Yer such a bad liar, Katrina. But don't you ever be good at that."

"Daddy loves you, Momma. This is… I've never seen him have it so hard. If he could, I believe he would take your place right now."

"He'll have to wait his turn. I'm checkin' out of this blamed joint."

She sang then. It was a ditty with a singsong sort of tune. She had sung it just this morning, and it unnerved Daddy. He asked her to stop.

"I'm goin' to be with Jesus, I'm goin' to be with Jesus. You will find me at that river just beyond the portals fair. I won't see another sunrise, you'll not find me in the mornin', but you'll know that I'll be singin' with that angel band up there." She had written it herself. Or she heard it in the ether. All the best songs pass through there anyway, so it's tit for tat.

Momma's pain increased. I requested more morphine. "Sleep, Momma. When you see Jesus, now you run to him. You understand?"

She smiled at me, her eyes gauzy.

I turned my face. She had no need of seeing any further tears.

Aunt Evelyn had taken time off from her night job at the bank to be with her sister. She sat with me all night. I never felt I truly knew her until then. She told me stories about my mother that made us both laugh. "Why, your Momma wasn't no bigger'n a minute. But, law, how she'd come to blows with anyone who tried to hurt any of her brothers or sisters." She peered around me as though she feared Momma would hear. Moving closer to me, she lowered her voice. "Donelle was not the biological daughter of my father, although he treated her as his own."

I had figured it out long ago, but I liked hearing Evelyn tell it.

"Once the truth came out about your Momma's real daddy bein' someone else, it was whispered all through the family," said Evelyn. "She never shook the necessity to prove herself. Wardin' off bullies was her only tool, as though she could tackle all the bad guys, even the Depression, with her fists." Evelyn shared how she came to know the peace of her own faith. "It just took a little longer for some people like myself and your momma to grasp it all." I believe she meant the width of mercy. I realized Meemaw had done her share of sowing, even if it had the taint of legalism. We talked all night. It looked as though Momma would step into another day.

"I believe she's goin' to make it, Katrina. You know that scripture, don't you, about runnin' a race? Donelle, she's runnin' fast as she can go. They said she wouldn't live through the night. But look. There comes the sun." Evelyn shook her head. Both of us marveled.

Momma lifted up out of her bed and pointed upward. That is when she left us. Waltzed right out, with a thin crescent of sun just peeping over the rim.

Looking back, I don't believe Evelyn and I had ever hugged before that moment.

CHAPTER 23

*T*he Hurleys gathered in our living room, some of them at least. I had not visited with several of the cousins in over a decade.

Velda was already recanting her opinions of Momma to Daddy. She wanted to dispel any rumors that may have been spread by unscrupulous people and elucidated on her despicable run of luck. "Ho, you know I really loved Donelle, don't you? She had her ways about her, but no one messed with her, and that ought to make us all respect 'er for it. I'll bet she would love it if you helped me out from time to time. You know, toss me a little green to lighten my load."

"Aunt Velda," I whispered, "this is not the time." I sent her back into the living room with Ruby.

The kitchen table spilled over with food offerings from the neighbors and from the church members. I kept myself busy, swiping the table and the counter where Momma had once canned beets. I spread my fingers across the surface, closed my eyes and tried to imagine her bargaining with God over the years.

She had allowed parts of herself to open up to him, while she reserved the rest for her own way of thinking. How often I had fallen into the same pattern. I believe that God drew her to himself that way, in willing parts, perhaps even over a Formica altar that smelled of beet juice. I do not know if her simple thinking prevented her full surrender, or if it was the pain of her past that held her back for so long. I imagined her, lifting herself from the crush of cancer to throw herself wholly onto the cross. She never said exactly how it happened, or if she ever faced the secret places she denied ever existed as she hid behind the walls of our life. Eventually, the walls do speak.

"Knock, knock, anyone home?" Gertrude Bickle peered in through the screen door.

"Do come in, Sister Bickle," I said.

"Dear heart, how are you holding up through all of this?" She kissed me.

"Some days tolerable. Other days not."

After a glance toward my noisy, milling relatives, she said, "I came by to see your mother this week. She spoke of the Lord, Katrina. She made it, didn't she?"

"I have no doubt."

"Well, here's a chess pie. And something for you."

"You brought me a gift."

She handed me a painted bottle.

"You painted this yourself," I said.

"Hold it up to the light. The sun will shine through it," said Gertrude.

"This is the bottle from under our house. You didn't have to bring me anything."

"I paint one bottle for each of my girls—my little secret. I didn't want you to get away from us before I had a chance to give you yours."

"Get away?"

"I heard a rumor about you and New York. That maybe you might get your wish."

"I have my wish, Sister Bickle. Momma's with Jesus now."

"I do believe you've figured out a few things about yourself."

We hugged for a while.

"I'm going to head on over to the church, Katrina. You need anything?"

I shook my head.

"You call me if you do, now."

"I promise I will. Thank you for coming by. It means so much."

The baby blue limousine from Shrew's Funeral Service pulled up into our drive. I did not linger over how hostile it looked parked on our property. "Daddy, Aunt Velda, our carriage awaits. Eden, Dreamy's socks don't match. Oh, well, it doesn't matter."

Sister Bickle disappeared down the drive.

My aunts, Nola and Lillibelle, pushed their way through the mob and led their husbands out to ride in their own cars. The cousins followed. The sound of roaring tailpipes ensued. Velda hotfooted it for the limo, while Ruby held back, her eyes sullen caves.

"Katrina, your momma asked me to give this to you," Daddy said and handed me an envelope. "I don't know what it is. She made me swear on graves not to open it."

I waited for the house to clear. I imagined it was a good-bye letter. It wasn't anything of the sort. I pulled out an airplane ticket—Little Rock to New York. One way. Also inside was a wad of bills, all twenties. I didn't count them right then. She had attached a note to it that simply said "mad money."

I stepped out onto the pop-bottle porch. It chimed of distant county fair songs and hard-come-by goods. Sol drove up. I looked at Aunt Ruby. She had a look about her that said she had been pushed away too often. "Aunt Ruby?"

Velda's older sister would not look up at me. I walked past her and stood at the open door of the limo. Her feelings were not the most neglected part of our family. But I saw how Velda had rushed into the limousine to claim her place while Aunt Ruby waited out-side, expectant that she would once again be pushed outside the circle. "Aunt Velda, if I give you this twenty, will you make room for Ruby?"

"I'll do it, little Kat." She took the money and made her chubby grown son get out.

"Aunt Ruby, it would do us a great honor if you would join us in the family car," I said.

She climbed in. Daddy followed her, as well as Eden and Carl. Dreamy stood next to me.

"Daddy, it looks a little cramped. If you all don't mind, I'll take Dreamy. We can follow you in Sol's car."

"Go on, then, Sis. We'll see you there," Daddy said.

I seldom remember much about funerals. The vocalist is usually called in at the last minute. Overnight she learns some unfamiliar song about heaven only to stand in front of a sanctuary filled with unsmiling faces. To a singer, that equates to disapproval. It all goes downhill from that point on.

But what I remember about Momma's funeral is the rose. Not the large spray of Mr. Lincolns atop the casket. The one single rose.

"Who is that?" I heard Amee Baldwin whisper behind us.

"He's that former congressman," said her friend. "J. B. Holder-man. I didn't know the Hurleys knew the congressman."

"Lots of things you don't know about the Hurleys," said Amee.

He wore a dark pinstriped suit. He was alone and waited to be the last visitor to pass the casket before the family was asked to rise. He stood in front of Momma's open casket, bowed his head, then tucked a long-stemmed rose next to her. Eden speculated about it, still raw over the switchings she had gotten when Momma thought she had picked roses from her garden. But Evelyn told me later that no one ever knew the truth about her sister: Momma and J. B. Holderman, they were stepbrother and stepsister. He was Momma's only link to her real father, the man who refused to see her. They stopped meeting when the rumors spread about their alleged affair. Such was life in Mockingbird Valley.

Daddy never said a word about any of it. He never saw another woman again, either. That proved all of Momma's speculations to be false. His way of having the last say.

I do not believe daughters ever get over the deaths of their mothers. Sometimes when I'm out pulling weeds in my own garden, I feel her next to me. Her voice calls to me from within the sassy noise of starlings on the window sill. I smell her motherly bouquet in fresh laundry and garden manure and freshly tilled soil. I see her last spark of life in the faces of other women who have lost their way—but only for a moment. A breeze lifts the purple tendrils of a butterfly bush, and I see her reaching out to God.

That one always makes me cry.

On Thursday, Eden and I gathered up the dishes and washed them so that Daddy could deliver them each back to their rightful owner. It kept him busy and gave Eden and me a chance to talk. We sat out by Momma's iris bed. Dreamy played at our feet making daffodil crowns. She named the flowers, calling them "Aunt Kateen" and "Momma."

"Daddy never cries at funerals," Eden said. "There I was fallin' apart over Momma. He just sat there."

"He cried, Eden."

"When was that?"

"Right after Momma died. I sent Evelyn home and waited for

Daddy to come. I told him to stay home, that she was gone. But he wanted to come. So I waited."

"I wanted to come too, but he wouldn't let me." She peered down at the daffodils that Dreamy had stuck inside her curls. I knew why Daddy wouldn't let her come. He wanted to say good-bye to his lady in silence, and without a scene. When he walked into her room, I stepped out into the hall. "Never have I seen Daddy cry until I saw him stand over her bed, Eden. He fell over the footboard and said, 'Oh, my sweetheart. You are so sweet, my dear one.' He said things like that over and over."

"He called Momma his sweetheart, no kiddin'?"

"It was as though I wasn't in the room. He carried on like they were having a conversation. He told her how sorry he was."

"For her cancer?"

"He didn't say for what."

"Well, what else would he be sorry about? They had a good marriage. They was both religious and such."

Eden had managed to retain some of her innocence. I figured it best to leave things that way. For now, anyway. Perhaps she needed more time. Like Momma.

"Katrina, if you go away to New York, how will we make it? You been like a second momma to Dreamy. What if I mess up again?"

"I haven't said I'm going, Eden."

"Remember how scared I was the night Dreamy was born?"

"No more scared than I was."

"You were scared? Really?"

"It was bigger than me, Eden. I didn't know what to do."

"You did all the right things, that's what."

"Carl doesn't seem to mind living here with Daddy," I said. "And Mr. Lunsford's marrying that girl from the Courthouse Café. So when I told him what a help Carl could be to Daddy right now, he all but thanked me."

"I noticed that about him. I think Daddy likes havin' another man around to talk to."

"Here's what—if you mess up, Eden, you learn from it. Then you move on."

"It's the messin' up part that scares me. Daddy gets so mad."

"He messes up too, you know."

"You reckon he does?"

I nodded.


I invited Aunt Pippa to drop by and take home the remainder of desserts left behind in aluminum pie tins.

When she walked in, Eden was towel drying Dreamy's hair after her bath. I buttoned up her nightgown.

"Please take all that food, Aunt Pippa," I said. "Daddy wants it gone. Says he wants something not pressed into a casserole dish or a pie tin."

"Your Uncle Hank will gladly finish it off. Looks like you all have everything well in hand."

"I'm takin' Dreamy to bed. Say night-night to Aunt Pippa, Dreamy." Eden lifted her and held her in front of Pippa.

Dreamy kissed Pippa. She followed her mother up the hall. Carl worked late overhauling an engine. So Eden and Dreamy fell asleep in Eden's bed.

Pippa waited until they closed the door behind them. "Katrina, it's probably too soon to be saying any of this, but your mother wanted me to relay this to you."

"About New York?"

"She wanted that for you."

"I believe Momma told every person I know except Daddy. He still thinks I'm an education major."

"You aren't?"

"Please don't say anything."

"Is your daddy harsh, Katrina?"

"He can be harsh."

"I never could get your Uncle Hank to believe that about him. I wasn't much help, either."

"What would you have done? Adopted me?" I stacked the covered pies atop one another.

"The Hurleys are a strange lot. You fight one, you fight the whole lot of them."

"I guess every family has something odd about it."

"You can just sit those down in this paper sack. I'll take them home just like that." Pippa held out the bag. The brown paper shook around the rim from her trembling hands. "Oh, there go those old shaky hands again."

"Here, I'll fill the bag." I took it from her. "If you were me, would you go off to New York?"

"I'd go. Your family will always have problems. Sometime you just have to let people fly. See what happens."

Pippa looked surprised. She must have been mirroring my own expression. But she was right. I knew it.


Sol made me beg him to take me to the airport. All the way to Little Rock, we talked about other things, as was our custom, saving the worst part of the day for last. I held on to him at the gate and, as I did, realized I could not say good-bye. "I'm not going, Sol. Don't say I'm a wimp, either. I just can't leave you."

He watched me cry for just a few minutes. "You are such a cry-baby, Katrina Hurley." He kissed me and I ached inside.

"I mean it this time. I'm not getting on that airplane. New York will have to just get on without me."

"You promised your daddy a picture of the Statue of Liberty if he allowed Carl and Eden to live with him. Are you going to look him in the eye now and renege?"

I pressed my face against Sol's shoulder.

"They're calling your seat number, Katrina. Close your eyes and just walk." I felt his hand nudging me all the way up to the turnstile, then on past the flight attendant. He did not leave my side.

"What are you doing, Sol?"

"My father's brokerage, their franchise office is in New York. I told him that a summer there would do me good."

I looked at him squarely. He waited, stoic around the eyes, as though he'd been practicing his sober face in the mirror. "You're coming? How long have you known and left me to suffer?"

"Since the night that I neglected to ask you to marry me."

"The sand bar? Well this is rich, Sol. First, cast me off, then try and give me the rush!"

"Dad had to pull strings. It took some time. I didn't want to tell you because I didn't know for sure." He shrugged, but there was no guilt on his face. "Then I liked the idea of surprising you."

"I've a good mind to just not get on this plane. What will you do then?"

"Katrina, turn around, close your eyes, and walk—"

"Then we just fly."

"Something like that."

addy still hated Christmas. After Momma died, it was as though he'd been given his lease to forget about holidays and birthdays. But we still gathered in his living room every year, Eden and me, Sol and Carl, Lolita Dream. We unwrapped gifts while he complained of how he would just take his presents all back and keep the cash. But then his little people would come and engage him in talk of other things—and that would be the end of that.

Carl fixed up Daddy's garage so he could bring home work from Mr. Lunsford's shop, rebuild engines under a covered roof, and step out there for, I suppose, nothing more than whiffs of motor oil, which he had come to thrive on. In spite of his near-death experience, I never knew if he really did any earth-shattering about-faces, but he improved a good little deal. He quit taking his meanness out on Eden so much. I've learned to be satisfied in knowing that about him.

He and Eden and Dreamy and Daddy all live together at the house on Erie. Momma would love the flowers that Eden and I planted along her old portulaca bed, and I often wonder if she can see them from that heavenly paradise where she romps amid the flora Jesus prepared for her. I pray those angel boys let her do at least some of the planting because to her it was never toil. But if they let her dig

around long enough, they'll find themselves up to their noses in daffodils. She never did know when to quit. If Momma could listen in, I
would tell her about New York and how it's not ugly as we imagined,
once you get to know it

Sol has brought me back to Mockingbird Valley every summer.
He was hired on with that New York brokerage, even though his
daddy prayed for the day he'd come to his senses and take over
his perfectly good one in Arkansas. Looks like Mr. Houston got
his prayers answered. Sol let those city folks know he was grateful
for all they taught him, but the Houstons were going home. We've
taken a liking to the Big Apple but want to keep it on my list of good
places to visit. I've met people here who feel confined by the hostile
city life. I just tell them, it's not the place that keeps you down. It's
the wandering around in the dark for too long that will do you in.

Dreamy started school this fall. Eden complains that Lolita Dream
has days when she says she wants to run away from home. I've quit
doing that myself, now. But I will tell Dreamy about such things
when she is older. You can't run away from yourself.

I saw Sol watching me yesterday. I set up a chair and easel near
the iris border of our flat's rooftop garden and painted African children onto my canvas. Sol and I took our anniversary there this year
in Kampala, Uganda. I have almost a trunk full of photographs of
those pretty little African children.

I dreamed last night of those children running through an endless peach orchard. It seemed natural to me, their small feet running
through infinite groves of fruit trees and grape arbors in a place that
was a dead ringer for Mockingbird Valley. I do wish they all could
meet sometime. It would broaden their ideas about one another.

We will move back to the valley next week, so bits of yesterday are strewn all over our flat: baby dolls in a huddle, dog-eared paper-backs, little porcelain clowns left to wait upon a shelf like orphans. Over the mantel is a collection of photos: one of Sol and me dyeing Easter eggs, a snapshot of two little girls romping in their homemade frocks, and a picture of Daddy seated in his lawn chair. The camera captured a hollow look on his face, as though he stared beyond Erie Street into a time when boys worked like men, their stomachs empty.

I really should pack away the wedding dress for good. It will yellow in that front closet, and what good is a yellow bridal gown? Besides, I don't yet know if this is a girl I'm carrying, and if she is, if she'll even want my old wedding dress. Or all those old dolls. I'll not pass on things that she doesn't want. What would be the good of it? That dried rose I saved from Momma's casket won't make it halfway down the coast. I will scatter the petals out of the window and let the wind take them where it wills. In New York, no one can hear the whisper of a rose anyway, so it will tell no tales on me.

I keep finding little parts of myself that I've collected between New York and Arkansas, and when I do, I scribble it all down in a diary, hoping that when it is full, it will somehow make the most satisfying whole. But I know, in spite of my New York airs, that I am and always will be a daughter of the South. I could never escape my southern roots, even when I tried to flee their hold. Yet as deeply embedded as I am in Dixie, I do not believe she will rise again, in spite of those who still await the day.

But until I die, I will serve the One who did rise again. I will sing and march toward that eternal hope that leads homeward to a place that will never smell of abuse or strife or bigotry or hatred. Can they hear the song playing across my heartstrings? It is much sweeter than any anthem. Let it echo in their ears until it resurrects their weary souls, as it did for me. It is how I found my wings. It is how I began to fly.